BLOOD MONEY

Laura M. Rizio

DEDICATION:

To James Hamilton, my husband and
partner in all things.
Thank you

Chapter I

He had heard the litany before. It was not new. It was the plaintiff attorneys' lament. All around Philadelphia, small plaintiff's firms were biting the dust or taking the gas pipe. Carbon monoxide poisoning was not an unpopular way of ending it all for some solo practitioners who couldn't take it anymore.

He listened politely, but it was clear from his face that he wasn't truly interested. He shifted from foot to foot. The pavement was cold. It was Christmas week and he hadn't done any Christmas shopping. And he didn't have time to listen or empathize with the man facing him on the sidewalk. He was anxious to get back to the office to report that he had won an important motion on a huge products liability case—a tire blow-out that had killed three kids and left their mother paralyzed for life.

But Bobby Falcone just went on and on.

"Law schools are spitting them out by the thousands. There aren't enough cases to go around. Tort reform, auto insurance reforms, caps on jury awards; they put mountains in the way of getting decent money on a case. The fucking insurance companies pour salt on your wounds, too—like the appeal from the lousy five grand arbitration award I just won. Now I'm in the bucket for five grand, the money I have to pay the expert, the whore doctor who will testify for twenty minutes on video that my client has a bulging disc caused by the accident. The damn doctors are eating up what's left of any money we make, and they want it thirty days before the fucking video deposition. What kind of justice is this? The system is stacked against us, Nicky, and it ain't gettin' any better," he said, veins bulging in his neck and spittle flying everywhere as he failed to swallow between expletives.

Nick Ceratto nodded in agreement and stepped back, wanting to escape, embarrassed that they had become the object of attention of passing pedestrians. He hoped that Falcone would take the hint, but he didn't. He had an audience right there on the corner of Fifteenth and Market, in front of the towering, oversized sculpture of a clothespin. Not only did he have Nick's attention, but he had the attention of at least twenty-five pedestrians patiently waiting for a Septa bus in the biting December air.

"I'm not going to let them do this to me, Nicky," he said, waving his arms. "They're robbin' me of my livelihood. I've got three kids, a mortgage, a second mortgage, and tuition bills up the ass—not to mention my wife's fucking credit cards. The bitch won't get off her lazy ass, either."

"We gotta fight the good fight, my man," was all the politeness Nick had left. He gave Falcone a mock jab to the shoulder and turned to walk away.

But Falcone wasn't finished. He grabbed Nick by the shoulder.

"Look, you young, arrogant, little shit. You and your firm never fought the good fight. You got away with murder." His raised his voice, encouraging people to stop and look.

Nick dropped his briefcase and made a fist to deck Falcone, but his fist stopped before making contact. He wasn't about to make another mistake, a mistake that could cost him his career, the fruits of his hard work, and the friendship of his colleagues.

"Bobby, you're tired and angry. I don't blame you. Go home and take a rest. Everything will be OK in the morning."

Falcone sneered. "You shoulda hit me. Maybe I coulda made some fucking money from your hide instead," he laughed. "You think I'm nuts, don't you? But let me tell you something." He leaned toward Nick and in a low tone, almost a whisper, told him how the last five major cases had come into Nick's firm, and how they came to be: the malfunctioning heart monitor, the mis-filled prescription, the switched hospital cart, the exploding gas tank, and yes, Nick's own tire blowout case.

Nick shook loose from Falcone's grip. He had heard enough.

"You *are* nuts. I'm convinced you need a good shrink, Bobby. But first, you're gonna need a good lawyer."

"You'll see, Nicky," Bobby shouted. "You'll pay the price, too, unless you wise up. Get out while you can."

Nick crossed over Market Street and headed west. He could still hear Falcone ranting and raving as he crossed Sixteenth Street making his way toward his office building. It was clear to him that Falcone was crazy. Anyone could see it. But he was also dangerous. If he got to the right people with his lunatic theory, it would make things very uncomfortable for Nick and his firm. The last thing Maglio, Silvio and Levin needed was an investigation when these cases were due to go on the trial list. The cases that Bobby thought he knew about. These were major jury trials that would bring the firm millions. The distraction of an investigation would bring trial preparation to a standstill and give the defense, the insurance company attorneys, a bonanza. Plus the bad press would taint the minds of any jury. Even the most impartial minds would remember what they heard and saw on the news.

Nick knew there was nothing but insanity behind the diatribe. An investigation would prove nothing and lead nowhere, nowhere but to the ruination of his firm's reputation and the end of his job, the job he had fought so hard to get, the job any young associate would kill for.

His firm, Maglio, Silvio and Levin, litigated the largest cases in the city. More of them than any other firm in the city, or the surrounding counties for that matter. The cases were "bell ringers," as his mentor and boss, Joe Maglio, would say. They came to the firm because of the firm's reputation for winning the most cases and winning the most money. It was simple. When you're good, you don't have to advertise, especially when publicity is for free, thanks to the local newspapers and TV stations. People just know. After the funerals, when heads begin to clear, they think of vengeance and paybacks, big paybacks. And they think of Maglio, Silvio and Levin. When judges rule on motions and evidence presented at trial, and post-trial motions for a new trial or to throw out a jury verdict, they remember whose large contributions helped put them on the bench. And whose large contributions will keep them there at reelection time.

Maglio, Silvio and Levin did everything right. They shelled out at election time for favorite judges. They supported good causes: the homeless, victims of AIDS, cancer, or sexual abuse, and children's hospitals. And they made sure one of the partners was always shown in the papers handing his check to a grateful recipient.

You had to spend money to make money. The firm paid sizable amounts to political action committees to grease the right people in Harrisburg to stave off the insurance lobby that wanted to put an end to large jury awards. And if they had their way, there would be no awards to injured plaintiffs. The insurance industry wanted premiums, not payouts.

Marty Silvio and Harry Levin were masters at rainmaking. They worked at it night and day. And it was rumored that they would push their own mothers down an elevator shaft to sign up a premier case, preferably a class action where there were lots of plaintiffs suing the same defendant.

And then there was Joe Maglio who turned rain into blizzards—blizzards of dollars. The chief litigator could charm the pants off the most hostile juror and wrap all twelve around his little finger. And if the devil were on the stand, it was said that Joe could get him to make the sign of the cross. Joe was a natural and had honed his God-given talent to a fine edge, an edge Nick wanted for himself one day. And that's why he had to stop Falcone.

He pulled the heavy, glass door open and charged into the gray granite lobby of the Mark, a needle-shaped tower on the corner of Seventeenth and Market Streets. He didn't bother giving his usual wave to Gilbert, the security guard at the desk who knew every tenant by name. It was helpful, especially at Christmas. But Nick didn't acknowledge the "Good morning, Mr. Ceratto." He blew past Gilbert into an open elevator that took him to the thirty-seventh floor, the top of the building. He flew past Celia Lopez, the receptionist, not even bothering to check his messages, heading straight for Joe Maglio's office. But it was empty. He hit zero on the phone.

"Yes, Nick," Celia answered, indicating that she knew where he had been headed.

"Where's Joe?"

"How should I know? He never tells me, you know that."

"Did he come in today?"

"Nope. Unless he snuck in the back door," she chuckled. "Is something wrong?" Her tone had changed to one of concern.

"No, Celia, I just need to talk to him, that's all."

"Sounds like an emergency to me," she prodded, as usual, trying to squeeze as much information as possible out of him. Celia couldn't stand being outside the loop. "Catch your breath or something. Want me to dial his cell?"

"Sure." Nick tapped Joe's gold pen impatiently on the clean desktop. There was no point in his asking Shirley, Joe's secretary. Joe kept his own calendar and Shirley was useless—a gray-haired lady who smiled and brought Joe his coffee. She was nice enough, but still useless, one of Joe's charity cases, a fixture and nothing more. When Joe really needed something, he always relied on Grace Monahan, the firm's crackerjack paralegal, the one with a temper to match her flaming red hair. Nick continued to tap away. The phone clicked.

"Nope," she announced on the speaker, "Sorry, Nick. But can I help…?"

"No thanks." He hung up before she could cross question him.

Although he didn't relish it, he went straight to Marty Silvio's office. Nick had never had a great relationship with Silvio, or with Levin for that matter. Silvio's door was closed as usual Nick knocked lightly, feeling uneasy. There was no response. He knocked again, thinking maybe he should wait for Joe or talk to Silvio by phone. But no, the matter couldn't wait, and no, it wasn't something to discuss on the telephone. Seconds later he was standing face-to-face with the portly, slightly disheveled partner, the ever-present unlit cigar clenched in his teeth like a bulldog with a prized bone. Silvio pulled at his loosened tie and smoothed a stray strand of hair on his balding head. He ignored his un-tucked shirttail.

"Yes?" he asked sarcastically. "And to what do I owe the pleasure of this unannounced visit?"

Nick flushed as he caught a glimpse of Margo Griffin, the youngest associate, smoothing her skirt on the other side of the infamous brown leather sofa.

"Sorry, Marty, this is important. It can't wait."

Marty moved his large frame from the doorway and gave a nod to Margo. She passed Nick and disappeared down the hall.

Silvio took his seat behind a gargantuan desk that matched his frame, not to mention his belly. He struggled to prop his swollen feet on the desk and removed the wet cigar, fondling it tenderly between his thumb and forefinger, leaning back into his huge leather chair.

"Now let's hear what's so goddamned important."

It was nine p.m. and Bobby Falcone was still at his desk. He had gotten over his fury of the morning. He had taken two aspirin washed down with a large scotch, and had begun working on an appeal to the Superior Court on one of his many losses. He was tired. His anger and the scotch had taken their toll. His vision was becoming blurry, and he decided it was time to go home—home to nothing. His wife would be asleep and his kids on the phone. He heard a gentle tap on the door. He got up slowly and opened it.

"What are you doing here?" he said to the elderly gentleman outside the door. "It's late for cleaning, isn't it?"

The man smiled. His blue eyes matched his blue jumpsuit, which bore the name of the building, Four Adam Place.

"Need to empty your wastebasket, sir. I did all the others and dusted up. I'm just waiting on yours." He grinned apologetically. "Can't afford to miss an office. I'm new here and I need the job."

"Yeah. I don't know you. Where's Charlie?" Falcone turned away toward his papers and briefcase on the desk.

"Charlie's sick today. I'm just filling in. Don't worry, he'll be back." The elderly janitor began to slowly retrieve Falcon's oversized brass wastebasket.

"Hey, don't bother with that. You look like you're in worse shape than I am. I'll get it tomorrow," Falcone said, continuing to pack his papers.

The man smiled gratefully as Falcone bent to pick up a document which had fallen to the floor. He ignored Falcone's offer and picked up the brass can. In less than a second the plate glass window in Falcone's twentieth floor office shattered, and out went the trash, along with Bobby Falcone.

CHAPTER II

Nick read the headline in the *Inquirer* the next morning: "Lawyer Jumps Twenty Stories to Death." It was definitely a shocker. He had been ordered to file suit against Falcone for slander ASAP and to personally serve him with a copy of the complaint. It was Silvio's way of putting an end to the matter. But Falcone had put an end to it himself. It was better this way, Nick thought. He felt sorry for Bobby, but it was better for the firm. Who needed to spend two years litigating a defamation claim against a deadbeat? It was clear Falcone had nothing to back up what he had said. Nick felt sorry for Bobby's kids. Kids always suffered the most when their parents were nuts. He knew from personal experience.

He looked up from the paper and, from his penthouse condo in the Society Hill Towers, watched the sleet as it fell and coated the pavement below. He took a long, cautious sip of hot, cream-laced English Breakfast tea. He found the brew extremely comforting on cold winter mornings, especially when he had to work. He closed the paper and padded barefoot into his walk-in closet to face the first dilemma of the day: which suit to wear. The navy Armani, the black Versace, the chalk-stripe Polo? He chose the Armani. It fit him better. It hugged his tall, lean body like no other. The trousers fell just to the top of his black, mirror finished Italian shoes.

He wanted to make sure that he looked good—really good. Today was the firm's annual Christmas bash where he would be glad-handing Philadelphia's best, and worst, public figures. The firm didn't discriminate. As long as they made headlines, they were invited. The food and alcohol would flow nonstop from noon until seven p.m. And they would all come with appetites like gorillas: lawyers, doctors, judges, politicians, insurance claims managers. They came not just for the delectable tidbits, but also for deals, pledges, contributions, client referrals, and settlement offers. Inevitably several seven-figure cases were negotiated at the Christmas party. Joe would always manage to corner a battle-fatigued defense lawyer and badger him into making an offer he couldn't refuse.

Nick had learned how to shmooze the enemy and charm the pants off the ladies— lawyers, judges, it didn't matter. They had a weakness for his Mediterranean good looks. And he had a weakness for women in general. But he never took unfair advantage, and he never discussed the women he had been with. He didn't have to lie or promise, or "wine and dine" them. Women wanted him more than he wanted them and, cheap talk was for losers. Besides, his reputation for discretion only got him more women and the admiration of men unlike him. It was a matter of respect for the women he was with. He may not have loved them but he respected them and they knew it.

In forty minutes he was driving his red Boxster west on Spruce Street toward Broad. He checked his shave in the rearview mirror. It was clean. He looked good. He smoothed back his dark hair and guided the car into his reserved parking space in the garage under the Mark. Within a few minutes, he was on the thirty-seventh floor at his firm's double mahogany doors. He passed the glittering, twelve-foot Christmas tree in the marble floored foyer. The smell of the fresh pine garland wrapped with twinkling bee lights were all reminders of the season-to-be-merry—and not to worry about Falcone, or trials, or anything for that matter. The clatter of caterers echoed throughout the suite as they busily set out the firm's monogrammed china and glassware. Giorgio, the firm's head chef, checked the lobster remoulade and the platters of thinly sliced rare beef. The smells were delectable. Everything looked fine, except for Celia Lopez.

"Hey, why are you crying on this most festive occasion?" Nick asked jokingly as he stopped at her desk.

Celia dabbed as her eyes and shook her head.

"Come on. What's up? It can't be that bad."

"Did you read this?" She sniffled, trying her best to compose herself, and pointed to the headline in the *Legal Intelligencer* with her blazing red acrylic fingertips.

"Yeah. In this morning's paper. It's a shame, but he was really nuts. I guess the stress finally got to him. You know, all this friggin' fighting we have to do. It's not healthy…"

"What do you mean, nuts? He wasn't nuts."

"Hey, what do you care? You didn't know him, did you?"

She flushed.

"You did?" He leaned toward her. She dabbed her eyes again and nodded affirmatively.

"I went out with him a couple of times," she whispered, looking around to reassure herself that they were alone. "I'm ashamed. I knew he was married. But it was nothing, just drinks."

"Did he say anything to you about the firm?" Nick's voice had dropped.

She shook her head. "No—just that we had all the good cases, and wins." She looked over her shoulder apprehensively. "And that Silvio and Levin were thieving bastards."

"Is that it?"

"Yeah. Was he supposed to tell me more?"

Nick shook his head no and breathed a sigh of relief.

"Nick, why are you so concerned about what Bobby said?"

"I'm not." He hesitated a moment. "He was over the top when I last saw him. Babbling nonsense."

"What was it?" She stopped sniveling and looked squarely at Nick. "What nonsense?"

He smiled. "Just nonsense."

"Don't tell anyone, Nick. You know, about the drinks." She frowned. "I don't want…"

"I know, and I won't as long as you promise to cheer up. OK? Life goes on. Right?"

She nodded affirmatively.

"OK. Settled then." Nick slapped the marble countertop. "Any messages for me?"

"Nope. Nobody loves you. At least, last night nobody did." Deep dimples appeared as she smiled. Then the phones lit up. It was five past nine, and Celia had begun her daily routine, giving away as little information as possible and shielding her bosses from clients who wanted information, and answers.

The party began promptly at noon with Joe Maglio popping a bottle of Dom Perignon. He lifted the sparkling, crystal flute and made the usual speech thanking all the associates, paralegals, secretaries, and filing clerks for all their hard work making the firm a success. He wished everyone health, wealth, and happiness. He never underestimated the value of the lowest ranking employee. He always had a kind word—a word of encouragement, or a twenty dollar bill for anyone who needed it.

Joe had come a long way. Son of impoverished immigrants who had dreams for their son, he had fulfilled their dream. He had gotten a scholarship to the University of Pennsylvania Law School where he had graduated at the top of his class. But instead of following many of his classmates into large, conservative commercial firms where he would just push paper, he had gone to the Public Defenders Office where he got to try cases. There he learned to connect with a jury. Persuasion came naturally to him. He had gotten acquittals for many poor, innocent defendants, as well as some guilty ones. But then he became tired of being poor himself and set out to put his skill to work to his own advantage. And that he did.

Marty Silvio and Harry Levin met twenty years ago at Temple Law School. They were both in the bottom ten percent of their class, but most of the successful plaintiff's lawyers were not geniuses— just good businessmen and Slivio and Levin were just that. They were natural rainmakers, but neither could find their way to the courthouse. Neither had the guts or the talent to try cases. Both were used to settling cases with little or no effort. They often talked about themselves as "plaintiff's adjusters" rather than as lawyers. Their job was so easy. But as lawyers they were allowed to charge forty percent. Public adjusters had to be happy with ten.

But then came "insurance reform." Small fender-benders, the bread-and-butter cases, dried up. Anti-plaintiff ads appeared everywhere. Silvio and Levin had to either resign themselves to a greatly reduced lifestyle or fight back. They needed bigger cases. And they needed a star to try them. They needed products liability, medical malpractice, construction accident, explosion, and collapse cases. The bigger, the better. The more maiming or death— preferably preceded by several months of excruciating pain—the better.

And the star was Joe Maglio, supreme litigator, now known as the best criminal defense attorney in the commonwealth. It didn't matter that he didn't know much about civil cases. He already had the essential skills of advocacy. The medicine, the engineering, and the math were the province of his experts. It was his job to pull the information from them, simplify it, and play it back to the jury with his style. He always knew which two buttons to push—sympathy and prejudice.

Joe had never liked chasing cases. It was beneath him. That was somebody else's job. He loved turning cases into money—big money, money he won and spent with a vengeance to make up for all the years of self-denial. Instead of two five-year-old suits, he had fifty new ones. Instead of a three-room walk-up on Pine Street, he owned manor house in the blue blood suburb of Gladwyne with a horse barn and two thoroughbreds. Instead of a four-year-old Chevy, he drove a Mercedes SL 600. Instead of a mousy, middle-aged wife, he had Christy—a leggy Scandinavian fifteen years his junior who liked spending money more than he did. There was always more, even when balances were low. When Joe got an overdraft call from the bank, he simply tapped the partnership accounts. Bank balances bored him.

But balances were important to Harry Levin, a short, fuzzy-haired Jew who worried over everything. How many cases were coming in, how many they could have gotten but didn't, how many they must get to keep the engines of the firm running. Levin worried about money—the money Joe was spending so furiously.

He worried about being able to keep pace with Joe and Joe's *shiksa* wife who was worse than Joe. He was tired of Joe making it so difficult.

Marty Silvio, a balding, overweight, cocky, cigar-chewing egoist who never really got a good look at himself in a mirror, enjoyed manipulating everything, including the truth. He called it "creative responsiveness." He never worried. He was too busy being creative. For him worrying was a waste of time. You got what you wanted, when you wanted it if you simply did something about it—and most importantly if you paid for it. It was simple. But not every lawyer was as creative as Silvio at making rain. And only a select few knew his secret, his recipe for success. The tougher it got, the more creative Silvio got. Years went by, and the firm grew and became fatter and greedier. And that's when the trouble began.

Chapter III

At the front of the suite, the six-paneled double doors to the partners' conference room were tightly shut. The room was supposed to be soundproof, but the yelling had been audible for at least twenty minutes.

Celia Lopez was busy retrieving messages from the firm's voice mail system. She was worried. Although she couldn't make out the words, she could hear pushing and shoving and the crashing of expensive furniture. It sounded like a barroom brawl.

Celia nervously walked to the entrance of the conference room and stopped. Her three-inch spike heels dug into the plush oriental carpet. She waited apprehensively and listened. The Christmas party was over and the strong bodies were gone. What was she to do? It sounded as if the partners were killing each other. She thought she might knock, but she quickly reconsidered, holding her partly clenched fist away from the door.

Nick Ceratto had gone home with Grace Monahan.

Giorgio Santangelo, the chef, was on his way to Italy to visit his family for the Christmas holidays, and all the guests were long gone. It was nine thirty p.m. and Celia was alone—just her and the insanity in the "big room" as they all called it, and she was scared.

The commotion stopped briefly and then resumed as if those inside were aware that someone might be listening.

Celia could hear Harry Levin yelling something like "Call the cops!" and Marty Silvio spitting out four-letter expletives in rapid fire. She reconsidered knocking, but then she heard a loud scream. She dialed 911 instead.

Joe Maglio was coaxed out of the conference room by two large Philadelphia police officers who wouldn't take no for an answer and were impervious to his threats of being sued up the ass for false arrest and false imprisonment.

"Come on, buddy, let's go. Let's calm down before we have to take you in," said the enormous black cop. Joe unsuccessfully attempted to shake off his grip. He was tattered but looked the best of the three.

Levin was bleeding from the forehead. He blotted a large, open gash with a white silk pocket handkerchief that quickly filled with red.

Silvio's cheek was swelling and becoming darker by the second. His neck was severely bruised from Joe's grip. And the skin was opened above one eyebrow.

"Fuck you," snarled Joe as he looked back. His jacket hung in shreds. But all he bore was a superficial scratch across his right cheek. His clothes had taken most of the abuse as he had dodged and ducked out of the reach of his former partners. Although it had been two against one, Celia knew that Joe had gotten the best of them, and she was glad.

"You're out!" screamed Levin. "Expect the sheriff tomorrow, you crazy asshole." He spat three times. One of the gobs landed on Joe's chin. "And Merry Christmas."

"If I'm out, so are you, you greedy, thieving, cheap kike. If I go down so do you." Joe pulled an arm free from the police officer's grip. "I'll personally see to it."

"Get out, you motherfucker." Silvio threw a lifeless punch and missed completely.

"Come on, sir," the burly black officer huffed as he pushed Joe through the open door. "You guys can settle this in court."

"Yeah," said his partner, a six-foot, three-inch, fair-haired cop with broad shoulders and a large paunch. "You guys are lawyers, right? You're supposed to be better than the crumbs on the street. Work it out," he commanded in a shrill Fishtown accent. He held the other two partners off with an outstretched arm and closed the door to the suite with the other. "Come on, buddy. It ain't worth it. Believe me. You got the best of them, anyway."

"I know you," said the black cop as Joe smoothed back his tousled hair. "You're the lawyer who's always in the papers—suing the city and the cops and everybody else. Right?"

"Yeah, I am." Joe shook himself loose from the cop's grip aware that this was not an arrest but a routine call to break up a fight. He punched the down elevator button. "And you're gonna see a lot more of me in the papers, too, starting tomorrow."

Sleet fell in continuous sheets coating everything in frozen slush on contact. It was ten p.m., and traffic was mostly nonexistent due to travel advisories. The city was obediently quiet, wrapped in a blanket of ice and freezing rain. Traffic lights blinked eerily in the darkness—yellow then red then green. A few, lone snowflakes fell heavily and instantly melted as they hit Joe Maglio. He was rushing, coatless—pushing against the wind to get to the garage at the Bellevue Stratford Hotel where he kept his car. He was too angry to feel the cold.

Troy Stone, the night attendant, looked curiously at Joe. "You all right, Mr. M.?" He always called Joe "Mr. M." because he couldn't pronounce Joe's last name. It was too Italian. "Looks like you been in a fight."

Joe nodded, acknowledging the genuine concern of the chocolate-skinned man. "Yeah, but I won!" He gave Troy a thumbs up.

"That's all I wanna hear," said Troy smiling broadly. His sparkling white teeth were parted by a huge gap in the center. "You want me to call the police?"

"No," Joe quickly responded. "No need. I took care of it." Joe slapped the usual ten spot in Troy's palm after he opened the driver's side door for Joe.

"Thank you. And you be very, very careful," Troy warned. "It's real bad out there, Mr. M."

Joe slid into the driver's seat. "I'll try my best. You know me. I always do my best to stay alive."

Troy tipped his Phillies baseball cap, smiling and shaking his head as Joe started the engine and drove away in a cloud of carbon monoxide.

Joe reached in his breast pocket for his phone and punched in the number two. The call failed, and, preoccupied, he put the phone down.

He thought about partnering with Nick and somehow at the same time extricating himself from the mess he was in. He would take his files—his own cases. They were not the bulk of the firm's business, but most were high-profile cases referred to him by other lawyers. Lawyers who didn't have Joe's expertise, or the money to finance the litigation. There would be a fight, but so what? Lawyers always fought over money and cases. He would probably be in professional trouble. The mess he had brought on himself was bound to catch up with him. The books are the books and you can't hide skimming forever, even with accountants who give you a break and look the other way if you give them a plausible explanation. But maybe he could pull a few strings and dodge the Disciplinary Board. Although he had spent money that wasn't his, it always came back into the accounts. Payment of settlement funds to clients were always late—sometimes by three months, true—but the clients always got their share even though he had gotten his first. He would borrow from the proceeds from the most recent case he had won or settled in order to quiet those who complained the loudest. Once the client finally had a million in hand, it was a different story. Then it was, "Thank you, Mr. Maglio. You did a great job. You're the best. I'll recommend you to our relatives and friends—fellow union members." They practically knelt at his feet. And then they raced to the bank.

Money is a wonderful thing, he thought. *It changes everything. Warring nations become allies—enemies become friends— bad becomes good.* And Joe Maglio needed money. How else would he be able to pay for Woodmere, his ten-acre Gladwyne estate, his Arabian horses, and his wife Christy's designer wardrobe? Yes, the beautiful Christine Bergheim. The coltish Dane he had met in San Remo ten years ago—model, actress, great athlete, and an even better mother. Joe had never cheated on her—not even once. Why would he? She was his grand prize that he kept in absolute splendor in a gated estate. At first she had protested at some of the extravagances lavished on her by Joe—a four-carat Tiffany diamond, canary yellow and flanked by two blue white trilliants. But she got used to it and graciously accepted each succeeding gift. The Arabian horses were her favorite, though. She was truly thrilled with this gift, especially by its presentation—a double horse trailer decorated with huge red bows had pulled up the circular drive to the front doors. Christy had been blindfolded. She was then led to them, their reins placed in her hands by Joe.

How could he tell her that this was all about to end? Could he stave off the sheriff from executing on his home, his horses, his life? Would he go to prison? Could he file a feasible bankruptcy plan? Could he at least save his home?

The road was becoming almost impassable—now ice was forming on his windshield. The wipers strained to move the freezing lumps of slush. The car would occasionally slide, and Joe would tug lightly at the wheel to straighten it. He didn't know where he was. He drove slower, straining to read an exit sign. It was impossible. It was covered with snow. He strained to distinguish landmarks. Was this the Gladwyn exit? Joe pulled off the road to what he thought was the shoulder. In his rearview mirror he saw a state police car's flashing lights.

He picked up his phone and punched number two again.

"You've reached Nick Ceratto. I'm not able to come to the phone at the moment so leave your message and I'll try to get back to you sometime soon today—maybe tomorrow." Joe heard a female chuckle in the background and then the beep.

"Prick." Joe removed the phone from his left ear and threw it into the passenger seat.

Chapter IV

He wore the expressionless face of a state trooper. He practiced his routine, checked himself out, and was satisfied. He looked authentic. His uniform fit like a glove and his polished jackboots shone. Cars automatically slowed and their drivers looked the other way. His police car was perfectly painted. It carried the official Commonwealth seal on each door, and the plates were government issue but unregistered. It was amazing what you could do with the right contacts. And Rudi, as he was called, had the best that money could buy. He often thought how much fun it might be to borrow Air Force One for the night to do a job. It would be back the next day and no one would ever know. The uniform, the car, the police radio—all brand new and not yet assigned or registered. Friends in Harrisburg were important. And more importantly, they could be bought for the right price.

Rudi tilted the wide brim of his Mountie hat downward and carefully got out of the car and reached for the bell on the massive iron grates protecting *Woodmere*. He waited, brushing sleet from his jacket with a black-gloved hand. Nothing. He rang again. He knew that the security camera was trained on him, so he kept his head purposely in a lowered position, the brim of his hat shielding most of his features.

"Hello," an accented voice answered. It was female—rich and full with an air of concern about it.

"Ma'am, I'm Officer Henry with the state police." He held his identification up to the camera lens.

"Officer, is everything all right?" she asked in an alarmed tone. It had been a horrible night. The Christmas party had been over long ago. Joe hadn't called her. He wasn't home and undoubtedly he had been drinking. She quickly zoomed in on the officer's identification and zoomed out to view the immediate area. She recognized a state police vehicle. It looked authentic.

"Is it my husband? Is he hurt?" she asked the shadowed figure.

"There's been an accident, ma'am," he said in a stoic tone that indicated that he had repeated the same phrase a hundred times.

"Oh my God!" There was a pause and then a slight sob.

"May I come in, ma'am?" he asked politely.

Silence—he was about to repeat his request when he heard the lock click open. The heavy iron gates swung wide. He got back into the car and started slowly moving along the circular drive. He saw the gates automatically close behind him in his rearview mirror. He was in. *Step one complete.*

The mansion was brick—a three story expanse that seemed never ending. It had been built in 1890 in the Greek revival style and had once belonged to the Monroe family. Henry Monroe of coal, banking, and department stores had spared nothing in the construction of *Woodmere.* A row of white Ionic columns flanked the massive twelve-foot double doors and supported a portico that ran the length of the second floor. *Woodmere's* classical symmetry shimmered in the beams of the lawn lights.

But Rudi was not there to admire the mansion and paid it little attention. He slipped from the driver's seat. His boots crackled on the frozen Belgian block as he walked to the front door. He didn't have to ring. Christy opened the door and he stepped in. *Step two complete.*

"Evening, ma'am," he said politely, touching the brim of his hat, which glittered with droplets of melting ice. He wiped his feet deferentially on the oriental runner just inside the door.

Christy moved back toward the staircase which spiraled upward three stories to a glass dome. She took hold of one of the dark walnut handrails for support. The polished, white marble floor reflected her tall silhouette wrapped in long black velvet. Her robe was carefully tied at her narrow waist, and her silver-blond hair fell softly about her shoulders. Christy's expression was pained and her ice blue eyes shimmered with tears. But she would not cry. She fought to remain outwardly calm although her legs were shaking.

Rudi admired her poise and found her physically beautiful—in fact exquisite. *What a pity*, he thought.

"Can we sit for a minute, ma'am?" he asked. He sounded professional yet concerned— the perfect combination. He should have been an actor, he thought. No, he quickly changed his mind. This was more fun.

She wanted to avoid the news. Her instinct was to run, but instead she softly said, "Follow me," and led him toward the study.

He followed her closely through the hall guarded by massive Canton vases and bronze sculptures of nude male and female forms posed on marble pedestals.

A thousand books—old and new—looked down on him from the shelves covering the study walls. Her back was still turned.

"Are the children asleep?" he asked.

She swung around and faced him, her mouth agape and her eyes wide. Her expression had changed from apprehension to terror. "How do you know about the children?" she whispered.

What a shame, he thought as he pulled the slim 25-caliber automatic from inside his unbuttoned jacket and fired once. Only the spit of the silencer could be heard as Christy fell, a surprised expression locked into her features and a small hole in the center of her forehead oozing a steamy trickle of red onto the polished wood floor. *Step three complete.*

He had no remorse about the children. They were all the same to him—especially in their sleep. Joseph Junior and Melissa barely moved as he shot them each one in the back of the head. But Christy was different. She was a work of art. He was glad that his bullet hadn't shattered her beautiful face. Only a slight entrance wound and then out the other side. He had purposely planned it that way the moment he saw her. Joe Maglio had been a lucky man.

From the children's rooms he quickly moved back down to the study. He looked briefly about the bookcases, impressed by the authors: Homer, Virgil, Voltaire, Julius Caesar, Sartre, Marquis de Sade, St. Augustine, Dickens…

He located and moved to the security system set between two massive bookcases. It was now eleven thirty p.m. The screen for the front monitor showed the gate closed. The other three monitors— one showing the rear of the property and horse barns and the other two showing either side of the property— reassured him that no one was about. He popped out the tape that had been recording all that day, and put another in its place. The tape had been doctored so that it would appear to have been running without recording images or time. He knew about the system, about the placement of the cameras. Silvio had warned him. And he knew exactly what to do. *Step four complete..*

Five minutes later the front gates opened. Headlights shone down the drive and stopped behind the police car.

Rudi watched the monitor, waiting patiently while sitting on the brocade love seat beneath a first edition of *A Tale of Two Cities*, and slowly sipped a Remy Martin Louis XIII from a cut crystal balloon snifter. It was Baccarat. The Maglios had good taste, he thought as he tilted the snifter, watching the glints reflected from the facets of crystal.

CHAPTER V

Grace Monahan had left an hour ago. It was eleven a.m. Christmas Eve, and Nick had a vicious hangover. He had promised himself after his last bacchanalia that he wouldn't mix scotch with champagne ever again. Even if it was the best, it still hurt afterward. Two aspirin and four cups of black coffee later, he decided to return Joe's call. He played back the message. All he could hear was "Prick!" then a thud. He knew that Joe was pissed—really pissed, and he didn't look forward to hearing him yell and curse—something he heard frequently and was used to. He looked out his living room window thirty floors above. Society Hill, a miniature colonial village in the midst of urban Philadelphia, sparkled in the clear post-winter storm air. He looked down on Head House Square at the tiny cars moving busily on Second Street. He breathed deeply. Oxygen helped.

He dialed Joe's home. There was no answer. Maybe they were Christmas shopping, he thought. He had heard about Christy's penchant for shopping marathons. "And last-minute for her," Joe had said, "could turn into an entire day."

After the beep, "Yo, boss—sorry about last night. The only excuse I have is Grace." He paused and chuckled, "Enough said." Then he decided to try Joe's cell phone. A metallic voice told him to leave a message. He was relieved not to have to put his head in the lion's mouth. Joe had obviously turned his phone off.

A warm bath would be just the thing—this time without Grace. He ran the water in the marble Jacuzzi. He could still smell her perfume on his towels and thought about their night together. He hardened briefly and then sank into the quiet bliss that only a warm bath, or the womb, could supply.

The phone rang loudly, echoing across the black marble bathroom. Nick woke with a start. His watch said that it was one p.m. He shivered slightly from the now cool water as he reached for the wall phone. A few lingering Vitabath bubbles clung to the hair on his arm and crackled slightly as they exploded.

"Hello." He tried hard to sound as if he were alive.

"Nick?" Harry Levin did not quite recognize Nick's voice.

Nick closed his eyes, thanking God it wasn't Joe. "Yeah."

"This is Harry."

"Yeah, I know. How you doin'. Is everything OK?"

Nick wasn't used to being called at home by Levin. In fact, he had little contact with him at the office. There was a pause and a sigh. "No, Nick, I'm afraid not."

Nick rose in the tub, water dripping from him. Everything about him was shriveled— even his dick. "What's the matter?"

"There's been an incident at Joe's house…"

"What happened?' Nick's eyes opened wide. He stepped out of the tub grasping a towel that he wrapped around his waist while pressing the phone to his ear with an hunched shoulder.

"Nick…they're gone…" There was a pause and a purposeful sigh.

"What do you mean—gone?"

There was silence on the other end.

"Harry, what do you mean they're 'gone'?"

"I mean dead. All dead. Joe, Christy, the kids."

"What the fuck?" Nick felt like the wind had been knocked out of him. He tried to catch his breath. "Harry…how do you…know… who, who told you…" he stuttered, closing his eyes.

"I got a call from the state police and drove out right away."

"I'll be right there." Nick was already in the bedroom, pulling clothes from the walk-in closet.

"It's not necessary. The place is crawling with cops—state, local, crime lab people, the media—even CNN. The whole fucking world. You won't get through. Stay home, Nick. I'll call you in a little while."

"Like hell I will," Nick fired back. "Listen, Harry, I want to be there." He gulped as his throat tightened. "Joe was like my father. I have to be there. I'm leaving now."

Levin tried to speak, but Nick cut him off.

"I said now! Don't let them move him." Tears welled in his eyes. "I want to see him."

"OK, OK. Just get a hold of yourself and drive carefully. You hear? It's still bad on the roads."

"Yeah." Nick disconnected and let the sobs come.

Levin was right. The media and the cops *were* crawling around *Woodmere* like ants. Nick arrived to barricades, yellow tape, TV trucks, lights, ambulances, and hordes of people in and out of uniform. Neighbors, dogs, and yes, the miniskirted anchorwoman in a red suit with perfect makeup, looking wide-eyed into the camera. Her brightly painted mouth moved nonstop.

Nick tried to duck under the tape but was immediately stopped by a beefy, baton carrying, gun toting cop—one of Montgomery County's finest. The cop said nothing. He just blocked Nick with his body—legs apart, arms folded over his chest, and a scowl on his face.

Nick hated most cops, especially ones like this. He had run into this type before in his past. He would have liked to curse him out—hit him in the kneecap with a bat. Maybe in the balls. But his sense of reason overtook his temper. He had been taught well.

Joe always said, "With cops you talk real nice first. Then if they try to fuck with you, you get nasty. Use your mouth. Remember you're a lawyer now—not a punk. And always *smile*. It confuses them. They're not too smart."

"Officer, my name is Nick Cerrato. I'm one of the decedent's partners," he lied. "I may be able to assist the detectives inside."

The cop didn't move or change expression.

Nick started to lose it. He felt the blood mounting to his face. *Control, control, control,* he mentally commanded himself.

"Officer, is Mike Rosa inside? Or one of his assistants?" Nick knew the Montgomery County district attorney casually, but Rosa had been a good friend of Joe's. They had been classmates at Penn Law School. Rosa was a frequent guest at Maglio dinner parties, where Nick had met him. Nick and Rosa had instantly hit it off, both having been raised in South Philadelphia's Italian neighborhoods and both having risen above their blue collar roots.

"He called me and wanted me to come right away. Can you find him? Tell him I'm here?" Nick asked earnestly. *You motherfucker,* he thought.

At that moment Harry Levin walked out of the house with Rosa. As the two paused to talk in the doorway, the DA spotted Nick and gave him a nod and a wave to come on over.

The cop stepped aside and Nick ducked under the tape. The cameras started clicking away at what appeared a new development.

An anchorwoman chased after Nick. "Sir, sir—did you know the Maglios? Are you one of the attorneys in the firm? Do you have any information on the murder-suicide?" She pushed a mike close to his stubbled face.

"Murder-suicide?" Nick stopped short. He turned to the breathless woman in the red suit.

"That's what they're saying, sir. Do you have anything to add?"

"Yeah. Fuck you." He gave her the finger with both hands as he walked toward the front door. Sometimes your roots caught up with you.

The house looked as undisturbed and as elegant as ever—except for the bodies. The floral arrangements were fresh. Pink and yellow roses, Dutch iris, and baby's breath peeked out from cut crystal vases. Poinsettias lined the bottom of the stairs. A gigantic Christmas tree twinkled with bee lights and antique ornaments. Presents were elegantly wrapped and orchestrated in layers under the tree. The "Hallelujah Chorus" from Haydn's *Messiah* played softly through discretely hidden wall speakers. The setting was belied by the grisly scene in the study.

Nick stopped in the foyer and watched as the children's bodies were brought down from the bedrooms. Attendants from the coroner's office wearing white jackets and latex gloves carried the small, zippered black bags. Their feet wrapped in surgical booties, the attendants carefully trod down the thickly carpeted staircase. Nick's stomach churned. He swallowed hard. It was all he could do to prevent himself from heaving last night's champagne.

Mike Rosa pointed to the study at the rear of the house. The two men didn't speak as the DA led the way. Nick mustered all his strength and followed.

The bodies of Joe and Christy were in plain view just beyond the open door. Forensics were busy inside the dimly lit room dusting for fingerprints on the books, the mahogany paneling, the phone, the surveillance system, and scraping fibers from the carpet. Other members of the team were outlining the bodies with spray chalk on the Persian Herez carpet. Christy lay face up, wide-eyed, her mouth slightly open as if she were surprised and about to speak. The small dark hole in her forehead was crusted with dried blood, which had trickled onto her blond hair. Joe was facedown just in front of her. His head was turned to one side with his mouth twisted where it pressed heavily against the floor in a coagulated pool of blood. The bullet entrance wound was to his temple. His was a larger hole. Hair and bone were missing. It was definitely not as clean a job as Christy's. His eyes were squeezed shut as if in pain. His legs were splayed apart and his feet turned inward. A gun lay on the floor to the right of his body.

Rosa rubbed his hands together as always when he was tense. He paced for a few seconds between two Chippendale sofas while Nick looked on. His riding boots squeaked lightly with each step. He had been giving orders nonstop to county police and detectives—coordinating with the attorney general's office and the State Police while keeping the press at bay. *What a mess,* he thought. Just four hours ago he had been on the trail, riding his favorite horse.

"I'm sorry, Nick. I know how close you were to him." Rosa's voice was like sandpaper. It scratched and skipped over the unthinkable—murder, suicide—Joe had killed his family, the ones he loved most, and then himself. The evidence clearly pointed in that direction. The only question now was why.

Expressionless, Nick stared at the grisly scene. He wanted to pick Joe up from the floor and shake him. "Wake up, Joe! Wake up," was what he wanted to say. Instead he turned to Rosa.

"Nah, Mike. You can't possibly believe this. Not really." Nick's chin trembled as he gritted his perfectly white teeth. "This murder-suicide is crap. Joe would never hurt his family. You know that." His brown eyes fixed themselves defiantly on the DA. Rosa shifted uncomfortably.

"Look, Nick—the evidence is preliminary, but it looks pretty clear. Joe left a letter of apology on his computer. We're sending prints to the lab. There'll be autopsies, naturally, and ballistics will have a report. But it doesn't look like an outside job."

"I see," Nick retorted. "Guilt by computer. You're doing what you're supposed to do. You're being a cop—that's all. I understand." He paced. "The number one cop in the county— right? Well I want more than a note left on a computer. What else do you have? Where's the motive? He was a happy, successful guy. He had a beautiful wife, great kids, a storybook marriage."

"Nick, you're going to have to wake up." Rosa hesitated, almost apologetically. "There were a lot of problems." The DA's expression was intense.

Rosa's face was deeply lined from the outdoor work he loved: his garden, his horses, his dogs. He liked mucking out stalls better than dealing with dead bodies and the bereaved. He sometimes wondered what the hell he was doing in this job—first it was law school and then politics. Then the stress, all the crap and criticism that went along with the job. But then he remembered why. It was because of the slabs of cement which lined the South Philly streets where he had grown up. Where, if you were lucky, you might see some grass daring to peek from the cracks in the sidewalk. Where streets stunk with sewer gas and cooking odors. Where fire hydrants opened in summer to cool down melting asphalt and desperate kids.

"Joe had problems you don't know about. He was broke. He was losing everything. He was facing the forced sale of this house—a copy of the sheriff's sale notice was found this morning in the mail. He was facing prosecution, too…"

"For what?" Nick shouted, stepping back, defiantly.

Levin ran in from the open front door, his black hat tipped back, his black raincoat flapped behind him. He raised his hands excitedly. "Nick, Nick, keep your voice down. Have a little respect. Don't let them hear you."

Nick momentarily took his eyes off Rosa. He sensed that he had created a scene, that he had made a spectacle of himself. People were staring. This was not professional, this was not what Joe would have expected of him.

"Calm down, Nicky." Levin put a hand on Nick's shoulder. "It's all true. Here." He pulled a document from his inside coat pocket. "Here's a subpoena, it was served on us yesterday by the attorney general's office. We got the State on our ass." He handed the document to Nick and then nervously shoved it back in his pocket after Nick had read it.

It was like a dose of cold water. "I can't believe this. What the hell started all this? I thought the firm was solid, I thought Joe was solid." Nick saw his own future slipping away: his car, his condo, his career. Would he be painted with the same brush? Would he have to stand trial? Would he be disbarred—never get another job in a law office?

"It seems this has been going on for a long time, Nick. Joe was dipping into client funds—stealing from the escrow accounts to pay for his extravagances." Levin wiped perspiration from his forehead with a stained handkerchief. "It turns out that a couple of clients didn't want to wait until *he* felt like giving them their money. So they turned him in to the Disciplinary Committee— and the attorney general. And it just snowballed. Marty and I, of course, didn't know about this until just recently. He was hiding the mail. He got all the mail first. You know how he came in at seven a.m. And Celia would grab the mail if he wasn't in and save it for him."

"And you didn't know *any* of this? Aren't you partners? Didn't you review your accounts?" Nick's tone was one of total disbelief.

"*That* son of a bitch is on vacation,—took the red eye to Cairo" Levin said referring to Marty Silvio, "climbing the fuckin' pyramids probably. He manages—some how, some way to dodge shit." His eyes widened. "I'd like him to be here. With this crap. He'd shit himself." Levin tipped his hat back and wiped perspiration from his brow with his small pudgy hand. "We turned a blind eye. Life was good and things were going great. Joe was our star so we didn't rock the boat. Joe didn't want to hear it when we told him to stop dipping into the accounts."

Levin looked toward the district attorney. "Mike, what do we do now? You're a friend. Help us."

Rosa's eyes were pained as if he had just put down a favorite horse. One friend dead—his memory forever tarnished—others in trouble. And worse, he had to tear down Nick's god, his idol. Rosa was unable to help, and he knew it. The attorney general and the Disciplinary Board had their own agendas, and he wasn't about to mess with *them*. Right now he had to control the situation, protect the crime scene, avoid giving answers, and look as if he knew what the hell he was doing—all at the same time. He had stopped smoking fifteen years ago, but today he bummed a cigarette from one of the detectives, shoved it in his mouth, and continued giving orders.

CHAPTER VI

It was Monday morning, December 28. The doors to the suite were locked, and investigators from the AG's office were fending off staff, clients, the media, and the curious. The news had hit the streets four days ago, and the networks were still featuring the same story, *ad nauseam*. It seemed never ending. The headlines on the Christmas Eve edition of the newspaper screamed, "Prominent Philadelphia Lawyer Kills Wife, Kids, Self!" A subhead read, "Law Firm Under Investigation for Fraud and Misconduct." And it just went on.

This was the first day of business after the news broke and clients were beating down the doors wondering what had happened to their cases…and their money. Secretaries, paralegals, associate attorneys—all wanted to go to their desks, finish their work, collect their paychecks and their year-end bonuses—or collect their belongings if they were effectively out of a job. But the suite was sealed, and no one was allowed in except the AG's investigators. They were going through every piece of paper, carefully logging and boxing files for removal, downloading computer data, client lists, client distribution ledgers reflecting payment on settled cases, firm bills and accounts receivable, banking records, client addresses and phone numbers.

Only three staff members had been allowed inside: Shirley Moore, Joe's secretary; Celia Lopez; and Harry Levin.

Celia was essential to fielding the hundreds of calls. All telephone lines were lit and blinking. She had been picked up at six a.m. by the investigators and escorted to the office, ordered into the receptionist's chair, and closely monitored as she did her job. As a busybody and a trusted friend of Joe's, Celia knew everything that went on in the firm. The investigators had been told this by secretaries and associates whose calls and conferences she had interrupted or whose private meetings she had been caught eavesdropping on. Celia knew all the clients, their gripes, their cases. She knew the judges, their clerks, and the lawyers. She had become familiar with their personalities and their quirks as well as their plans—where they were going, where they were coming from. She was affable, and she encouraged callers to share personal information, which they were only too happy to do if they needed a sympathetic ear. Celia touched each and every person in or connected with the firm.

The problem was, she knew that she knew too much. And today she was scared. Scared of the investigators from the AG's office and scared of Silvio and Levin. She struggled to maintain her composure while every line on her board blinked for her attention.

"Yes, Mr. Kane. The firm is temporarily closed. No, not permanently—I said *temporarily*. I don't know how long sir. Yes, your case is still active. It's preserved. Yes another attorney will… can you hold please?

"Yes, Mr. Connley. Thank you for holding…I'll page Lieutenant Jones for you. I saw him a second ago…yes sir. Can you hold, my lines are…sir, I can't help…sir…" A click on the other end; Fred Connley, chief of the fraud unit, couldn't wait any longer. He was on his way over.

Celia dabbed her eyes, breathed deeply, and pulled her violet cable sweater down to her hips. She pressed another angrily flashing button with a recently sculpted, inch-long red fingernail.

"Yes, Your Honor. I'll try, Your Honor. Mr. Levin is with his attorney. But I'll interrupt him immediately. Thank you for holding, Your Honor.

"Mr. Levin, it's Judge Barnes. He wants to know who will be trying the Riley case next month. He wants to schedule a pretrial with the new attorney. Yes, Mr. Levin, Mr. Maglio was assigned that case. Yes sir." She paused a few seconds to listen to Levin's raving, then interrupted him. "I'll give the judge that message."

Celia knew better than to relay Levin's message: "Tell that fucking moron to shove his fucking trial schedule up his ass. Doesn't he read the papers?" And to tell him that Mr. Levin was busy with Christopher Henley, the best white-collar criminal defense lawyer in the fucking country and that the case would try when he was good and ready. And no, he wasn't talking to anybody, not the FBI, the President, or God, and certainly not to an idiot like Barnes!

Celia let the Judge's line flash. She took another deep breath and thought how she'd like to run back—run back in time to Puerto Rico. There she was poor, but happy, and it was safer there than where she was right now.

She took line twenty off hold. "Judge Barnes…yes, Your Honor, I'm so sorry. Mr. Levin is indisposed. He's in the restroom trying to compose himself. Yes sir, I'll do that, Your Honor. Mr. Silvio has cut his vacation short. He's on his way back from Cairo. I'll have Mr. Silvio call you the moment he arrives. I'll leave a message on his voice mail. Yes, I'll remind him of the Riley case and extend your sympathies concerning the Maglios…thank *you*, Your Honor."

She wasn't going to tell Harry Levin and Marty Silvio how Judge Barnes had chuckled when he talked about extending his sympathies.

Celia's line rang. She knew what it meant—it was her turn now. She picked up the receiver, and an unfamiliar voice directed her to the media room.

She put the phones on voice mail and walked slowly to the room used for video depositions. It had been Joe's favorite room: four TV monitors, four cameras, and four DVD players with surround sound—all the latest equipment—perfect for intimidating with all the right questions. And Joe had loved seeing himself on camera.

What a stupid, thankless job, she thought. Three layers of cops to go through before she could finally put on her coat and go home. She'd rather have her acrylic fingernails pulled off one by one than to have to answer questions. The AG's investigators were arrogant pricks, and she knew that even as smart as she was, she was likely to fall into a trap.

As she reached the glass door, Shirley Moore opened it and ran out in tears. They were all there, white shirtsleeves rolled up to the elbows. Eight of them ready for work—ready to pounce. *If worse comes to worst*, she thought, *I'll take the fifth.*

Chapter VII

Thirty thousand feet above the Atlantic, Nick Ceratto stared out of his first-class cabin window. He was on his third Dewar's on the rocks. Puffy clouds moved and stretched, changing shape beneath him. He thought about what it might be like to step out and walk on them—float on them like an angel. *Maybe when you're dead, you can do just that,* he thought. He chuckled to himself as he took a long sip. He was momentarily distracted by the flight attendant's shapely derriere as she leaned over to fix another passenger's pillow.

"Miss, can I have some water?" he asked, thinking it was best to appear sober when the plane landed.

He thought about Joe, Christy, and the kids in the same 737. Only they weren't traveling first-class. They were in the hold with the luggage. He wondered about death—if you knew and if you cared. One thing he was sure of, if Joe were alive he'd be happy now. He'd be happy that he was headed back to the place he loved, the village of San Lorenzo on the Amalfi coast, a walled, hillside-fortress town founded in the Middle Ages. It was named after St. Lawrence, the martyr who, as he was being roasted on a spit, told his executioners to turn him over since he was done on one side. Saint Lawrence had been loyal to his faith—unto the death. Loyalty was something the Lorenzanos, as the villagers called themselves, prided themselves on. They were fiercely devoted to family and friends. They had an unshakable code of honor—of ethics. These were people who knew how to live and how to love, as Joe would say. They were his people. San Lorenzo was the village of Joe's ancestors—of farmers and fishermen who squeezed every drop of life from each day.

Joe loved this tiny patch of earth on which he and Christy and the kids had spent a month each summer. Nick remembered how

Joe would joke about one day staying there and not returning to the States. *How prophetic*, Nick thought taking a long swig of Perrier to wash out some of the effects of the alcohol.

"Here's to you, Joe, and to the people of San Lorenzo," he said out loud as he held the fizzing glass up to the window.

"Sir, can I get you something?" the shapely blond attendant asked. "Did you call me? I wasn't sure if you called."

"No thanks. I don't need anything right now. I was just toasting my friends out there." He smiled boyishly, giving her a Maybe Your Phone Number? look.

She shook her head from side to side as if to say, *I'll just ignore that.*

The plane touched down three hours later. Nick had dozed off and the pretty blond gently woke him with a touch on his shoulder.

"Sir, we've landed. We're in Naples, sir."

"Yeah—yeah," Nick said, shaking his head to clear the fuzz. "What time is it?" He squinted, trying to focus on his watch.

"It's eleven p.m." She smiled and discretely handed him a note as she walked toward the cabin door to assist the deplaning passengers.

He unfolded the small sheet of paper. It read: *Sarah Jennings-212-875-0496, USA. Naples-Marriott, room 1020.*

The bodies had already been loaded into the hearses. There were three cars: one for Joe, one for Christy, and one for the two children. They slowly processed through Naples onto the *autostrada* toward San Lorenzo.

It was one thirty a.m. when they arrived at the stone church—a mini version of Santa Trinita in Florence with saints peering out from the cornice and capitals of the columns. Frescoes adorned the flat surfaces of the interior walls. Father Bernardino, a sixty-five-year-old Jesuit priest, waited patiently at the open chestnut doors. His cassock blew against his legs. The local undertaker, Ennio Correlli, an artist in his own right, stood next to the thin, aging priest. Correlli was a chubby, mustached man with a double chin and wild black eyebrows. He wore a black suit, and in his hand was a black fedora, which he waved to signal the hearses closer. "*Veni. Veni piu vecino.*" Come. Come closer. "*Attenzione con la cassa.*" Careful with the caskets.

It was a scene straight out of the movie *Rome: Open City*. Nick now fully understood Rossellini's genius. He was living it.

The hearses' headlights shone on the drivers as they lifted each casket carefully onto its wooden gurney which they then reverently wheeled into the church. Nick followed them down the candlelit nave to the area just in front of the altar. The men crossed themselves and left, leaving Nick, the priest, and the undertaker alone in the silence.

Father Bernardino kissed his *stola* and placed it around his neck. He began a prayer for the dead. He bowed his head and seemed to lose himself in the music of the language of the litany and the scent of burning candle wax until the "Requiescat in pace" at the end.

The priest removed his *stola*, kissed it, and folded it over his arm. He gave Correlli a nod.

"*Si, padre,*" he responded. He moved to the first casket. It as one of the two larger wooden boxes. He crossed himself as he unlocked the seal and slowly opened the lid.

Christy was wrapped in a white shroud, her face lovely but cold and bluish— the bullet hole still crisp between her eyes. Correlli spoke as he put his hands together. "*Che peccata. Che bella.*" What a shame. How beautiful.

Nick was sick. He was glad that he hadn't eaten anything. He would have lost it right there.

Father Bernardino pointed to the next box. Correlli obediently moved to it. It was Joe's. His face was black now and his features twisted in a near sneer. It was ghoulish. It was horrific. The body was beginning to smell.

Nick turned his head. "Christ," he whispered, "I can't do this anymore."

Then Father Bernardino moved to the smaller boxes and opened each one himself to reveal the kids.

Nick could stay no longer. He walked quickly toward the open doors. His way was lit by the hundreds of votive candles casting their flickering light on the frescoed saints crowded on the sixteenth-century walls. As he walked through the doorway toward the street, he could hear the priest reciting the last rites. He wept quietly, leaning against a bas relief of Saint John the Apostle carved on the door jamb.

"You should be happy." The voice came from the damp blackness.

Then he saw her face as she flicked her lighter and lit a cigarette. He was speechless for a moment as he studied her classic Italian features.

She drew in smoke and blew it out slowly. Almond eyes, full lips, thin delicate nose, and a full head of long, golden brown hair which fell loosely over her shoulders. She tossed it back and took another drag on the cigarette.

"You're crying. You shouldn't."

He quickly wiped his face, embarrassed by what he thought was an unmanly display of emotion.

Maria Elena Maglio didn't think him unmanly at all. She was touched by his obvious sensitivity and his dark good looks as she studied him, moving the flame of her lighter slowly up and down. She wondered how his two-day beard might feel good against her skin. It had been a while since she had felt such a face against hers. "I'm Joseph Maglio's cousin, Maria Elena."

She held out her hand. "I know you're Nick Ceratto. My cousin talked about you a lot. Come on. Come to my family's house. It's down the street. There—near the fountain." She pointed in the darkness toward the sound of trickling water where a stucco wall was barely visible in the moonlight. "Come on. Don't be shy."

Nick shook his head affirmatively. *What the hell,* he thought. *Why not?* If he was living in a nightmare, this could be the best part. He took her hand. It was warm and firm.

They walked toward the dimly lit house. Now he could see more of her. She was wearing a black leather trench coat tied tightly at the waist. Her collar was pulled up around her neck. She was almost as tall as he was. She drew on the cigarette then dropped it on the ground and stubbed it out with the toe of her black, knee-high boot. Her coat opened to reveal a creamy thigh.

There was a tense moment of silence as Nick fought to say something. He was normally never lost for words, but this was truly weird—abnormal.

"I'm sorry I'm such a mess. Such a baby. I should have been able to stay."

"And look into the coffins?" She laughed. "The priest is crazy. You'll see. But he's the only one we have. You shouldn't have had to see them. So terrible. Tomorrow night they'll all be beautiful when Ennio is finished with them. He's a master—the best."

"What difference does it make? They're dead. I brought them here for burial, not a party," Nick snapped as they reached the twelve-foot, open, arched doors. He followed her into a dark courtyard.

"That's right, they're dead. You're alive. You have to live and walk the earth and do what is right." She shook her thick hair. "What is right is to make the best of the situation. Dress these people up—give the village a good look at them—let everybody cry—and put them to rest in the family tomb. Then go back and find their killers." She took out another cigarette.

"Killers? You don't believe Joe killed himself and his family?"

"No. And neither do you."

"How do you know what I believe?" he answered.

"I know because you are here. You made the arrangements to send the bodies to the place he loved and the only place that would accept him. No one else would do this except someone who loved him and could not accept that Joseph Maglio is a murderer. You know my cousin was not a murderer. He loved everybody— especially his children. Look what he did for this village. He restored the church. Brought in irrigation for the farms. Bought new boats for the fishermen. No, my cousin did not do this." Her voice trembled with emotion. Her eyes were wide.

Nick couldn't help but be taken by her. She was a true Lorenzano, unshakable in her faith. He felt an instant kinship with her and a surge of relief that he was not the only one to believe in Joe's innocence. And who was this beautiful creature? Certainly not a simple villager. Her clothes were too sophisticated and expensive. She was poised, her English almost unaccented. And she was obviously well educated and sharp as hell.

"Please help me find my cousin's killer," Maria said putting her hand on Nick's chest. She turned her head away, trying to hide her face as silent sobs shook her.

Nick tenderly took hold of her shoulders, drawing her near. He lifted her chin and then looked deeply into her wet, golden eyes. "I want to help you," he said. "But how?"

Maria wiped her cheeks, tossing her cigarette to the ground. The embers burned briefly on the damp cobblestones and then fizzled out.

"I'll tell you inside," she said. She took Nick's hand and led him up a back staircase to a second floor entrance to the apartment. The room was large and high ceilinged—painted the lightest shade of blue. It was sparely furnished with only two silk brocade couches and an ancient monk's table in the center. Over it hung a huge, wrought-iron chandelier. Maria lit the wick in a long-handled candle lighter and touched the wick of each candle in the chandelier, lighting them all until the room glowed.

She put her arms around his neck and rubbed her damp face against his stubbled chin. "I've been wanting to do this since I saw you."

Nick closed his eyes, enjoying the feel of her smooth cheek. "Who are you, really? What do you want?"

She pressed her body close and then touched her full lips lightly to his. "I'll tell you later," she said.

What the hell, he thought. *This nightmare is getting better.*

The next morning it was raining and gray—almost dark, even at nine a.m. Nick and Maria had arrived together at the church. Mixed in with the prayers and clattering of rosary beads were whispers. Everyone knew where Nick had spent the night. There were stares and mutterings from the village women, and chuckles from the men. But Maria Elena didn't care, and neither did Father Bernardino.

"I'm sorry," Nick whispered. "I didn't mean to cause you grief."

"It's OK. Italians are realists." She smiled with her head down.

Although Nick was embarrassed, it was clear that she wasn't.

Four caskets lined the front of the altar. As predicted, Joe and the others looked as if they were sleeping. The children were dressed in white linen. They held handmade toy lambs as was the tradition in the village for those who had died before their time. The adults looked elegant— Joe in a black silk and wool suit and Christy in a light blue satin gown. Joe now looked at peace. His features were transformed. He had a slight smile on his now pink lips. There was no hole in Christy's forehead, and her long blond hair draped softly around her face and shoulders like an angel's.

They were beautiful. Too bad they weren't alive, Nick thought.

The small church was filled with mourners—figures in black packed the pews and aisles. Every Lorenzano was present to pay their last respects. The church bells Joe had donated mournfully tolled for this, his last visit. The women wept openly, clutching their hands together while the men hid their grief, shrugging their shoulders in acceptance.

It rained throughout the mass, and while the caskets were being carried by horse-drawn hearses to the Maglio family's tomb, their vigil lights burned for the capture of their killers.

Chapter VIII

Marty Silvio had slept late. He had a bad case of jet lag and needed to clear his head. He had left his wife, Celeste, in Tel Aviv where they had gone after getting the news of Joe Maglio's death. He and Celeste had planned to go to Israel after Cairo. She didn't want to cut their trip short. She wanted to see the Holy Land.

Just as well, he thought. He relished the time away from her. All she did was push, nag, shop, talk on the phone, and go to church. She didn't have an intellectual cell in her whole body. He conveniently overlooked his own boorishness when judging the shortcomings of others, especially Celeste. He didn't know why he had married her. She wasn't even a good lay anymore.

He put Celeste out of his mind as he turned over and reached for Margo Griffin, the twenty-nine-year-old associate with whom he had been sleeping for three years. Margo was a Villanova Law School graduate, a slender brunette with knockout legs that she wasn't loath to show. And her little black suits did just that. She lay on her stomach, close to him, her tight buttocks peeking out from under white silk sheets.

The phone rang, and her hand left his groin and went automatically to the phone.

"Oh shit!" Marty grabbed the receiver before her hand reached it. "Don't. It might be her." He put the phone to his ear and listened before he said anything.

"Hello?" a distantly recognizable voice echoed through the plastic. It was Harry Levin. Silvio grimaced and handed the phone to Margo, mouthing the caller's identity.

She took the phone while pulling the top sheet up to cover her nudity, as if Levin could see through the phone line.

"Mr. Levin…" She was always formal with him and Joe Maglio— a formality she didn't extend to men with whom she slept.

"Marty—I mean Mr. Silvio is still asleep, sir. I came over this morning to see if he had gotten home and was all right."

"Yeah, yeah, I'll bet," Levin said. "Let me talk to that bum."

"Shall I wake him, Mr. Levin?"

"Of course. What do you think this is—a hospitality call?" He held his hand over the mouthpiece and mumbled, "Stupid bitch."

Margo got out of bed and moved the phone over to Silvio.

"Marty," she whispered, "I'm sorry, he wants to talk to *you*."

"Yeah." Marty wiped his eyes with the silk sheet, a habit that his wife hated but that the women he slept with tolerated.

"Yeah?" Levin yelled. "Where the fuck are you? It's eleven a.m., and you're still in bed?"

Marty was awake now. "Listen— I just came halfway around the world to get back here—and you're screaming at me?" He put an unlit cigar in his mouth.

"OK, OK. Listen, we gotta do something about Lopez. So far she's held up pretty good, but they know she knows a lot and I'm afraid she's gonna crack."

"So what do you wanna do? Gag her—tie her up—send her back to Puerto Rico?'

Levin was silent for a few seconds.

"What then?"

"Tell Rudi to watch her."

"Watch her? Rudi doesn't watch—he moves, he acts. You know that, you stupid fuck." Silvio chomped on the end of his cigar.

Levin was silent. Then he sighed. "OK...not watch her."

"Then what?" Silvio liked this little game. He liked the idea of Levin coming up with solutions he had been thinking about for a long time. He motioned for Margo to come to him.

She flopped next to him, pulling her knees up to her chest and resting her head on them. She cooed to Marty and gently stroked his balls. He smiled and pushed her head between his legs.

"Then do her."

Celia Lopez pulled her car into an empty lot behind her row house on Butler Street. The lot was an abandoned parcel on which houses had once stood. The city had demolished them making way for weeds and empty bottles. The tires of her white Taurus crunched over broken glass and empty beer cans. It was ten p.m. and dark with few if any working street lights. It was eerie, but Celia had become used to it. Living in the drug center of Philadelphia was no picnic. But it was still her neighborhood where her friends and family lived. She had fixed up her house—taken it from a burned-out shell to a neat, clean, simply furnished residence. She owned it free and clear and she wasn't about to move. Her kids were savy about the neighborhood. They knew where their friends lived in case some creep was following them. Plus the doors were bolted and iron bars protected every window. No man could get in—that is, unless he was invited,

Tonight she thought that the lot was better than trying to find a parking space on the darkened street and possibly having to walk four or five blocks to her house. Besides it was cold and the wind was up.

She came to a stop, put the car in park, and reached into her purse, feeling for her house keys. Celia always took them out before leaving the safety of her car. She also carried a small flashlight, which she used to help her navigate the debris covered pavements. She didn't want to fall and cut herself; that's all she needed. There were used syringes all over the place. She opened the car door and shone the light on the ground as she stepped over the trash. She touched the button on her car keys, and the car doors automatically locked. Her heart was pounding as it always did when she left her car at night. She began to carefully walk through the litter towards her home. There it was. She could see it in the light of her flashlight.

The city had neglected this part of town for more years than she could remember, leaving it to the gangs and narcs to fight over. It had become a battleground. Suddenly Celia saw a long, dark object on the ground in front of her. She wasn't sure what it was. Could it be a dog? A large dead animal possibly? Celia shone the flashlight on it but still couldn't tell. She gave it a wide berth. She felt better when she was past it. Whatever it was, it would still be there in the morning, she thought.

The object moved as soon as she passed it. It rolled over and then sat up. Then it stood. It was a figure, dressed in black to match the night. The figure silently trotted up behind her. It grabbed her long hair and yanked her head back, and then slit her throat. Before she could scream, she was dead. It was clean and quick as usual. Celia was gone, and so was Rudi.

Detective Ralph Kirby of the Philadelphia Police Homicide Division had completed his routine questioning of neighbors along the block of Butler street where Celia Lopez had lived. Four other detectives had spread out over four blocks from Sixth to Tenth streets. They covered the small side streets adjacent to Butler, checking auto license plates and talking to shop owners, bartenders, and relatives of the victim. Her daughters, Carmen and Lily, were not able to answer questions about their mother or her whereabouts in the preceding twenty-four hours. Carmen, the older sibling, was purposely silent, and the younger, Lily, couldn't stop crying. All that Kirby and the others were able to ascertain was that Celia was a hardworking single mother who loved her two daughters, Carmen aged thirteen and Lily, nine.

Celia had no boyfriends. She kept to herself. She was clean and respectable, though not terribly religious. She only went to mass on Christmas and Easter. She was friendly, but not overly so, and she loved her job. She would often stay late or go in on a Saturday to return calls the attorneys did not care to make, or to help with extra typing when necessary. She had no criminal record. She voted. She had fifty thousand dollars in CDs in a safe-deposit box in the local branch of the Columbia National Savings Bank. The people who had known her felt particularly bad for the two girls—Celia had adored them and had enrolled them in a Catholic school. They took piano and ballet lessons. And Kirby wasn't able to answer the neighbors' inquiries. What were the girls going to do without their devoted mother? He shrugged his sagging shoulders. How would he know? What did other kids do whose parents were murdered?

There were no leads in the case—not yet, and maybe never. In a neighborhood where junkies roamed the streets, where drug dealing was routine and drug dependency was almost a residency requirement, people were not anxious to talk to the cops. This case was no different than any other where some poor son of a bitch was killed for the price of a fix. It was hit, kill, grab, and run. The motive was a quick buck. Celia's purse had been found five blocks away. Her wallet was found in a trash can in a different location, behind a convenience store. There was no cash—just a slip showing a two-hundred-dollar withdrawal from savings. That was a hell of a lot of money for some crackhead. Celia's credit cards were still in her wallet. This was unusual. This was no stupid, murdering thug. He'd left no trails to follow. Whoever it was, he had murdered her for cash and was smart enough not to steal her cards or her car. And that was the thing about the case which troubled Kirby. Usually in this neighborhood credit cards would be taken and quickly sold, often providing the only leads.

Kirby shook his gray head and put on his dime-store reading glasses. He pulled his coat collar up and began to review his notes. The time of death was estimated between ten and eleven p.m. The body was clean—no bruises or scrapes, nothing to indicate a struggle. The angle of the knife wound showed she had been attacked from behind; she had probably never seen her attacker. Her carotid artery was cleanly severed. With her esophagus severed, she had been unable to breathe or call out for help. She had died quickly. Thank God.

It was frustrating—another crime that was likely to remain unsolved, like so many others. And there he was, as usual, trying to do the impossible, trying to paint a face on a faceless murderer, trying to find a nugget in the ocean. Fat chance.

He clumsily slid into the seat of his black Mercury Marquis and picked up the handset of the police radio. It felt good to sit in the warmth of the car. His belt was too tight, and his feet hurt. His stomach hurt, and the Kevlar vest he was wearing made him feel heavier than usual. *How many more years of doing this?* he wondered. Perhaps he could stand it if he lost some weight, he thought, as he sank into the black vinyl.

"This is Kirby. Yeah, I'm parked on Butler near Eighth. It's a real picnic out here—a model neighborhood. That's right." He chuckled. "Dick, I need a tow truck right away. Yeah, it's going to the crime lab for a workup. Preliminary dusting just revealed the victim's prints. No leads—yeah, it sucks. We're just running in circles, as usual. I'm getting too old for this. No. No boyfriends. No jealous lovers."

He paused to hear the unsolicited theory of the young dispatcher: *Celia was a hooker, killed by her john.* What the fuck did Dick Harrison know? He was a fucking rookie: twenty-four years old, still wet behind the ears, just starting on the force, and just about good enough to do what he was told. So what if he had a certificate in criminal justice? Kirby had been on the force for twenty years, fifteen in homicide, and he was tired. He'd seen more dead bodies than a Viet Nam vet.

"The best shot we have right now is to make a lot of busts. These junkies will sing for a deal. There's plenty of crack houses out here—one on Eleventh. Yeah, tell the lieutenant I want to talk to him about this. Yeah, I'll be at the district in an hour."

Hooker! Kirby laughed, shaking his head as he lit a cigarette and threw the match into the overflowing ashtray. The burning match fell on the floor. He stamped it out with his foot as he jabbed the down button of the driver's side window. The car needed air. Even he thought it smelled foul.

Was there a possible connection between the Maglio deaths and this street murder? After all, she'd worked for Maglio's firm, and it had been less than a week since the Maglios were killed. *Ridiculous*, he thought as he took a deep breath of the city's stench. He laughed at himself and started the car's engine. *Getting as bad as Harrison*, he thought.

Chapter IX

Mike Rosa was on the phone expressing extreme displeasure to Philadelphia DA Muriel Gates about not being immediately informed about Celia Lopez's murder. He was hot under the collar, but controlled. She was a woman, and he respected women. It was part of his Catholic upbringing.

Gates knew she was being chastised although Rosa was choosing his words carefully. "I'm disappointed," not "I'm really pissed"; and "You neglected" instead of "You failed." She was not going to be treated like a child, nor was she going to be intimidated by a man. And she was certainly not going to *apologize* to Rosa or anyone else. This murder was hers. It was in her jurisdiction, over which she had complete control, control which she had rightfully earned. She was fifty-five years old—had been an assistant DA for twenty of those years—and chief of litigation for the last ten until she was elected district attorney. She had put hundreds of thugs, rapists, and murderers behind bars, and several on death row. They were all men. She knew all men were trouble, and she was not about to take crap from any man.

She was five feet, ten inches tall, weighed one hundred sixty-five pounds, was well muscled, and had a black belt in karate. She was also gay, not ashamed but not out of the closet.

"Look, Rosa. I don't have to explain anything to you. I don't have to give you any information. You run the murders in your county and I'll run the murders in mine. You do your job, I'll do mine," she said, nervously tapping a silver Tiffany pen on her desk.

"Muriel, I didn't call you to be abused." He wanted to say, "To be shit on," but he didn't. He was too much of a gentleman. "All I'm asking is that you keep me informed on the Lopez case."

"Why?" she fired back. "Do you think there's some tie-in with Maglio's death? His was a suicide—this one's a murder.

A drug-related hit. It's just a coincidence that they were from the same office and that they're both dead—that's all…"

Theresa White, Gates's secretary, brought in a cup of tea and a croissant. Gates waved her away. She was in no mood for breakfast.

Rosa interrupted. "Our investigation is continuing. This is a high-profile case…" He didn't have a chance to finish the sentence.

"Maglio's death was ruled a suicide by your own coroner. I respect Guy Wilkes as one of the best. Matching fingerprints on the weapon, all victim's shot by the same weapon, around the same time. Powder burns on Maglio's hand, a defective surveillance tape showing nothing."

"All true, Muriel, but just as a courtesy I'd like copies of all your reports. Joe was my friend…" Rosa was now having difficulty controlling his temper. At this point she was getting to him. He began clearing his throat and counting backwards from ten. He glanced at the framed picture of his wife Helen and his three boys on the credenza to his right. It was a technique that helped lower his blood pressure. "Please, Muriel. I'm asking as a matter of professional courtesy."

There was a momentary silence on the other end. Gates waved her secretary back to her and motioned to her to put the teapot on her desk. She liked it when men like Rosa said *please*. She laughed. "Rosa, you know how to play me. Just be nice to me, right?"

"As long as I'm not sitting opposite you in a courtroom, yes." He strained to be light, and chuckled.

She took a sip of tea after she had laced it with cream and two spoons of raw sugar. "I'll make you a deal," she said.

"What's that?"

"You send me all the gruesome details on the Maglios, and I'll send you what I have on Lopez."

"*And* any results on the fraud investigation of Joe's firm," Rosa quickly added.

"The attorney general's office is handling that."

"I know. But I'm sure that since it's a Philadelphia firm, you're going to get copies of any and all reports—right? I'm sure you have an interest in the outcome. The firm did make major contributions to your campaign. Didn't it?"

He had her and he knew it. He knew her well. Muriel Gates was not about to be outranked, outclassed, or outmaneuvered by any AG, white-collar-crime specialist. The crimes, if any, had been committed in her county upon the residents of her county, and she wanted to know everything pertaining to the investigation. She needed to monitor this investigation closely. After all, Maglio, Silvio and Levin's help had been instrumental in her winning the election.

He could hear the concession in her voice as she said, "I'll send you what I have, but I don't know why you're interested in this firm, or what happens to it or the Lopez case."

"Why are *you* interested in Joe Maglio's death?" he shot back.

She took a bite of the buttery croissant, letting crumbs fall on her desk. "Because," she said between chews, "it's an interesting case; murder, suicide, fraud, unethical dealing. It fascinates me." She swallowed. "I hear the bank is foreclosing on the estate. Everything to be sold."

"Yes. It's a beautiful place. And the horses are going, too. You interested?" He saw lights blinking on his phone and knew there were other urgencies like judges, cops, victims, their relatives, the press—he wished all of it would stop.

"Don't like horses, or grass," she quipped.

There was a knock on his door as he was saying good-bye. It was a relief to hang up the phone. *What a ball buster*, he thought. *She's perfect for the job.*

"Yeah," he called out, looking longingly at a pack of Marlboros sitting on the other side of his desk. He had stopped smoking three times in the two weeks since Joe Maglio's death, and had started three. Rosa got up and walked around the mission style table that he used as a desk, and reached for the pack again. His secretary opened the door and peeked in.

"Someone is here to see you, Mr. Rosa." She frowned at the red and white box in his hand.

"Does he have an appointment?"

"No sir, but he said you would want to see him."

"Who is it?"

It's Nicholas Ceratto, Mr. Maglio's associate. He said he's not leaving until he talks to you. I tried…"

"It's OK…OK." Rosa paused for a second. "I'll see him—but I need some coffee. Bring a whole damn pot—French roast. It's ten thirty and I haven't had a cup of coffee yet." He defiantly pulled a cigarette out of the pack and put it in his mouth. He was tired of women pushing him around, even if it was for his own good. As soon as she closed the door, he removed it and threw it into the waste can.

Wearing a black Versace suit and an unbuttoned antelope top coat, Nick Ceratto walked confidently into Mike Rosa's office. He was followed by Rosa's secretary, who was apparently attracted to him. Although she knew she could be his older sister, her cheeks flushed as she placed the glass squash pot on the coffee table for her boss.

Rosa nodded his thanks as she put two cups and two spoons on the table before leaving the room. He motioned to Nick to take a seat and gestured toward the coffee.

Nick held up a hand as he sat down. "No thanks, I don't touch the stuff. It's bad for me. It gives me the shakes."

Rosa took a long, careful swallow and sat slowly in his favorite, worn leather wing chair. "What can I do for you today, Nick?" he asked crossing his right foot casually over his left knee, exposing most of one of the Western riding boots he wore.

"I got back from the funeral last week…" Nick hesitated for a moment. "Joe's funeral. It was in Italy. You knew, didn't you?"

"Yes, I'm sorry I couldn't attend."

"It's OK. Nobody from the States was there—except me, of course."

Rosa looked down, slightly embarrassed. "I'm really sorry I couldn't go. I heard he was refused a Catholic burial here in the States."

Nick rose from his seat and walked toward the window, which was covered with heavy velvet drapes. He pulled one aside to look out. The view of Norristown was dreary and disappointing—a broken down, has-been town whose only claim to fame was a state mental hospital closed two decades ago. The wise had fled long ago, and the mentally troubled had wound up on the streets and on the steps of the courthouse, thanks to the fine work of the ACLU. No wonder the drapes were closed, he thought. He let the panel fall back in place.

"Yeah, the Church took his money for years and then they wouldn't bury him. Condemned him to hell. Can you imagine that! I'm glad I never gave them a dime." He walked back toward Mike Rosa and stopped. "But that's not what I'm here for. I'm here to ask you a favor."

Rosa put his cup down and looked squarely at the handsome young man. "What do you want, Nick?"

"I want you to help me find Joe's murderer."

Rosa smiled slightly. "You're a stubborn one. Nick, I told you that all the evidence—and you know what it is so I don't have to go through it again—it all points to murder-suicide."

"Suggests," Nick retorted. "Just suggests—and you know it," he said pointing at Rosa while pacing back and forth. "That's why you still have it as an 'open' case. Right?"

"All right, I do," Rosa admitted. "And I will as long as the fraud investigation is continuing."

"Why? Do you think there's some possible connection with Joe's death?"

"Not necessarily—and I don't have to explain my reasons to you, Nick."

"That's true. You don't. But in your heart you want to do the right thing by Joe. Don't you?"

"Look, you're emotional and not too rational right now. I can understand that…"

"Mike, don't you want to have the results of the attorney general's investigation?"

"Sure I do."

"Well so do I. Mike, maybe you *won't* get *all* the information. *The full story.* I can help you. Just help *me.* Keep the case open—that's all. And, most of all, give me your support."

Rosa shook his head. "Nick, how are you going to get any information? *They* have all the files, all the computer data, all the personnel files in that office—even yours. I have to rely on official records, records already in the hands of the attorney general."

Nick grinned at Rosa. He stood up and took off his coat and laid it on the sofa. "I'll show you how."

Rosa grinned back. "You have more balls than brains. But go ahead. Show me."

"Just wait two minutes. I'll be right back." Nick ran out the door and in two minutes was back with Maria Elena Maglio.

Her walk was purposely sexy. She glided gracefully into the room as if she were on a runway. She wore black leather jeans and an ivory silk blouse, partly unbuttoned to reveal the slightest cleavage. Her black leather coat was draped casually over her shoulders. She smiled.

Rosa tried not to stare. But he couldn't help it. His eyes were glued to her as they moved down her long, shimmering legs. He watched her as she moved to the cherry credenza where family photos were displayed. There were at least a dozen of them: Mike and his wife Clair in tennis whites, his sons Brian and Stephen, from diapers to Little League. But she ignored them.

"*Che belissimi,*" she said, picking up the photo of the twin white Arabians, Mike's other family—his pride and joy. "I adore horses." She pressed the photo to her breast. "You must let me ride one," she said turning toward Rosa.

Nick wanted to say, "Earth to Rosa," but instead he said, "This is Maria Elena Maglio, Joe's cousin."

The trance was instantly broken. "A great pleasure. Please sit." Rosa motioned to the sofa across from him and watched her carefully as she slid into the seat.

"Maria is a bank examiner for the Italian government," Nick explained. "She's on an assignment at the Banco di Roma in Philadelphia. She'll be working out of the main branch on Broad Street."

Rosa seemed delighted with the introduction, but it was clear from the expression on his face that he didn't quite see the connection between Nick's plea for help and this delightful creature who was thirty years his junior.

Maria sensed the confusion and broke the silence. "You see, Mr. Rosa…"

Rosa loved her accent. The slight upward lilt at the end of each sentence and the fullness of the vowels was music to his ears. It didn't matter what she said as long as she just kept talking.

"…I know my cousin didn't kill himself and his family. I know he *did* have a spending habit—perhaps out of control—but he wouldn't kill because of it. And I also know that his partners are thieving, conniving—what do you call them?—ah yes, crooks, as you say in America."

"How do you know this?" Rosa asked.

"My cousin told me. And he wanted me to help him. To expose them." Her eyes shone with the passion of her conviction.

"Could you prove this?" Rosa sat back into his chair and rested his head on the cracked brown leather.

"Yes. Remember I have access to all bank records—legitimately. I can look into all private accounts and see the transactions."

"So can the attorney general."

"But I can do traces of secret, foreign accounts—information even your own CIA would have trouble getting." She stood and walked confidently over to Rosa's desk, taking a Marlboro from the pack as if it were her own. She didn't ask him if she could smoke. She simply put a cigarette into her mouth and lit it with the silver art deco lighter Rosa kept on his desk. She took a long drag and blew the smoke out almost instantaneously, not quite inhaling it. She obviously smoked for effect, like many European women.

"What makes you think his partners had foreign bank accounts?" Rosa asked, struggling to concentrate.

"All wealthy thieves have secret accounts—especially Americans."

Rosa couldn't help admiring her brashness. "And what would the existence of such accounts prove?"

She shook her head, causing her dark hair to waft its scent toward him. "I can't tell you now. Not until I have the information. Then I will know why he was murdered. But I will need your help. Keep my cousin's case open. *Va bene?*"

Rosa smiled. "Why don't you go to the Philadelphia district attorney with your plan?"

Maria gave a crooked smile. "Because she's a woman. I have heard that she is a bitch...and she protects her political contributors." She let the smoke stream from her pursed lips again. "Also because my cousin was murdered in your *provence.*" She obviously meant county, but Rosa thought the mistake was charming.

He offered Maria a cup of coffee, which she refused. Pouring himself another cup, he asked, "You want me to help you link Marty Silvio and Harry Levin to Joe's murder? This is absurd. They depended on Joe for their financial success. He was the litigator who won the complex cases, who brought in the money, whose reputation brought in nothing but more money. So why would they want to kill the goose that laid the golden eggs?"

She dropped her eyes, drew on the cigarette, and blew smoke over Rosa's head. "I don't know yet. All I know is that Joe was worried about his partners activities. He didn't tell me everything, just that he might need my help soon. Now will you help me?"

How could he refuse? "What do you need, Maria?"

"I need your investigators' and detectives' cooperation, your coroner's report; and I need to know what you will do with any information that I turn over to you."

Rosa exchanged a glance with Nick. "As Nick has probably told you, the case is still open, pending the attorney general's report.

But I don't see why I can't receive information from you as long as it's obtained legally—and I mean legally." He emphasized the word *legally*. "With no hanky-panky, as we say here in America. The information leading to all evidence must be squeaky clean. Otherwise it will be thrown out —a waste of effort on your part and mine." He took a sip of his almost cold coffee. "Joe was my friend, but friend or no friend, I'm the district attorney here. Do you understand that? Both of you. And I will decide how this information and evidence will be handled."

Chapter X

A month to the day after the Christmas party, the firm was celebrating again. This time the occasion was its reopening for business. The new, brass door plate read *Silvio and Levin, P.C.* Maglio's name was conspicuously absent. The champagne flowed freely, and the same honored guests clinked glasses with the staff—happy that the biggest partying firm in Philadelphia was still alive and kicking.

Marty Silvio grinned widely as he raised his glass to the Waterford chandelier in the conference room. He chewed on his unlit cigar between statements to the press. It would make the front page in tomorrow's *Philadelphia Inquirer* and on the eleven o'clock news. "No Indictment" would be the paper's headline.

Soon the clients would be back in droves and the referrals would come pouring in. He couldn't wait to stick it to the competing law firms who had been ecstatic about the potential eradication of Maglio, Silvio and Levin, and the prospect of its clients and cases looking for new lawyers. *Fuck them,* he thought, as he gave Margo Griffin a hug. The cameras clicked away. He didn't care since his frigid wife only read church bulletins and couldn't give a flying fuck who he hugged—or slept with. As long as he kept her personal account flush and paid all her current charge card bills, Celeste was happy and left him to his own devices.

Margo slid from under Marty's arm to catch up with Giorgio Santangelo, who was frantically overseeing the hors d'oeuvres and calling for a server to refill the crostini trays. Now that Margo was in charge of the firm's social calendar, its parties and entertainment, she was in charge of Giorgio, too. She would make life miserable for him if her ignored her.

"Giorgio, we need more rock crab. It's going fast."

"I know. I'm holding more in the kitchen while the chef prepares a dill mayonnaise for it."

She licked her lips. "Take me back so I can sample some." She shook her long brown hair back over her shoulders and took a deep breath, straining the buttons of her herringbone jacket.

Margo's obvious come-on made him nervous. He gestured toward the mayor, who was about to propose a toast and made his escape.

"Get rid of those orchids," she angrily called after him. "They're dead."

"Putanna," he muttered as he nodded to her, making his way to the kitchen.

There was a hush over the filled room. Mayor Jack Filbert held out his glass, posing for the cameras.

"I'm sure you all know that Mr. Silvio and Mr. Levin have been cleared of any and all wrongdoing. Charges of unethical conduct or mishandling of client funds against them personally have been withdrawn. The attorney general has concluded that the firm's former partner was the only person to whom such conduct could be attributed. And I want to say, although I already know that you're fully aware of this, the firm of Silvio and Levin is by far one of the most talented law firms in Philadelphia. It has been a bulwark of legal accomplishment. It has been the common man's sword against the injustice of large companies and government. We all were always confidant that the attorney general wouldn't find any evidence of wrongdoing on the part of the firm's current leaders. I'm also told by Mr. Levin that the firm's professional liability carrier will stand by them and make any defrauded client whole—any client who was not fully compensated. No one will be deprived of any funds due them."

Harry Levin, sweating slightly, stepped out of the mayor's large shadow.

"I want to thank Mayor Filbert and all of you for your confidence in us, and my attorney, Christopher Henley, for his fine work and assistance to the attorney general in helping to determine where the responsibility actually lay."

Levin was sorry that Henley wasn't interested in the offer he had made him. If he would head the litigation division and take Maglio's place as their premier litigator, Levin would make him a partner. But Henley had flatly refused, saying that he preferred crooks to the injured. They were more honest and they paid up front. Further, he didn't want to share the limelight or the money, nor did he relish the civil justice system's four year backlog of cases; nor did he like the contingent fee system—getting paid only if you won. He wanted his money on the spot, win or lose. Plus he didn't know what land mines still lay out there ready to blow this firm to bits.

Staying in the background, as he had all evening, Nick Ceratto became physically ill listening to the self-serving speeches, and the overt disloyalty to his friend Joe. He wondered how they could tarnish the memory of one who had been nothing but good to them. One who had been directly responsible for their wealth and their elevated position in the legal community. He had almost walked out, but Maria Elena had tugged at his arm and coaxed him to stay.

No one at the party knew who she was. She was simply Nick's guest, and she wanted to keep it that way.

Giorgio saw that Nick wasn't drinking. He also saw the anger welling up in Nick. It was obvious to another Italian. He was angry, too. He sympathized because he, too, had to be silent. He walked over to Nick and handed him a single malt.

"Here, I think you need this," he said, speaking in a low tone so that only Nick and Elena could hear.

"Thank you, my friend." Nick raised the glass slightly in toast to the only other person loyal to Joe in the group.

"I would like one, too," Maria said.

As she took out a cigarette, Giorgio looked at her in surprise. This was a non-smoking suite. But he quickly lit it with the lighter that he always carried in his jacket pocket—and then he poured her a double.

"*Da quale parta d'Italia viene?*" he asked. From what part of Italy do you come?

"Sorrento," she lied as she drew on her cigarette and then took a long, slow sip of the strong, unwatered whiskey without wincing.

"Beautiful." His eyes lit up with pleasure as he began to reminisce about his last visit to Sorrento. He was familiar with the small coastal city.

"It's very close to…San Lorenzo," Maria quickly said. She leaned closer to Nick, shifting her hip slightly. The slit in the side of the clinging black cashmere dress opened just enough to reveal a leg to mid-thigh. "Yes. I heard about the unfortunate death of one of the partners," she said nonchalantly.

Giorgio didn't comment. His focus was on her leg.

All eyes were on them, including Levin's and Silvio's. Nick knew what they were thinking: *There's no smoking in this suite, and who the hell is this bitch?*

"Yo, Giorgio. You still up for the hockey game?" he asked trying to change the subject. "She won't go with me. She only likes soccer."

Maria shrugged. "I don't like the cold, and I hate watching barbarians beat each other with sticks. "*E vero?*" Isn't it true?

"Yes. But these barbarians are the same as ours. The difference is that they use sticks instead of kicks," laughed Giorgio.

Maria admired his sense of humor, and his good looks. She wondered briefly how he might be in bed but then dismissed the thought as quickly as it had come.

Grace Monahan watched from the reception desk forty feet away. She had become completely distracted from training Carmelita Delgado, Celia Lopez's replacement. Carmelita was aware of what was going on. She, too, was a woman. She was also smart, bilingual, and a night school law student. She wanted to move up in the ranks; out of the barrio and into a white middle class, professional neighborhood. She was losing patience with Grace.

"Grace," she said, "why don't you just go over there and tell her to go outside to smoke? This is a non-smoking building. Right?"

"Yes." Grace was surprised at the new employee's chutzpah.

"Then, when she goes outside, you follow her and smack her in the face. That's what we do where I come from." Carmelita laughed, trying to defuse the situation. She winked and then pulled her long, black hair through a barrette signaling that she was ready to get serious about the training session.

Silvio and Levin walked toward Nick, placing themselves directly in front of him. They purposely intruded into the conversation, which was simultaneously going on in English and Italian.

"So, Nick. Aren't you going to introduce us?" Marty Silvio asked as he inhaled the smoke from Maria's cigarette.

"Ah, Maria…this is Marty Silvio."

"A pleasure," she said, gripping his hand firmly after switching her cigarette to her left hand.

"And this is Harry Levin…"

Maria held out her hand, but Levin simply nodded. "You know you're not supposed to smoke in this building," he said.

"Oh, I'm sorry," she said. "Where can I put this out?" She wanted to snuff it out on his head.

Levin looked around but couldn't find anything that would serve as an ashtray.

"Oh, look—here." Maria picked up a small blue and white Canton bowl and stubbed her cigarette out in it. "See how useful beautiful antiques can be."

Levin instantly hated her. And she returned the feeling.

Silvio was already plotting how he was going to get her into bed. She, on the other hand, wondered how she could take advantage of him—without actually sleeping with the fat pig.

"Maria…do you have a last name?" Silvio asked in a patronizing tone.

"Nardo," Nick quickly responded for her.

"Yes, Nardo," she said. "I can speak for myself," she said coyly, sexily shifting her eyes to Nick and then back to Silvio.

Margo Griffin walked directly into the group. She wouldn't be ignored.

"Giorgio, why haven't you moved those dead orchids?"

"I'm sorry, Miss Griffin," he said. "They are not dead. I was going to…"

"They're dead and I want them out of here."

"Oh, can I have them?" Maria asked, remembering Joe's fondness for orchids and suspecting that they had been his.

Margo opened her mouth to say something, but nothing came out.

"I love orchids. I can revive them. Please, give them to me," Maria said smiling—happy that she had caught Margo in her own trap.

"Sure," Silvio said. He took the pots and moved them onto a table near Maria.

"Knock yourself out." Margo spun on one heel to quickly walk away. Then she stopped, turned, and signaled with a crooked index finger for Giorgio to come.

Putanna, he thought as he marched toward her.

The food was almost gone, and the trays looked bedraggled with limp lettuce and spatters of sauce. The suite was emptying quickly. Darkness was beginning to cover the windows, and the lights from surrounding buildings could be seen. Nick had finished his third single malt and was about to leave when Harry Levin called to him.

"Nick, can I see you? I need to talk to you about something." He looked toward Maria and, deliberately not using her name, said, "Young lady, you can go. We'll be awhile. No sense in your waiting. We can get you a taxi."

"No, no. I have plenty of time. I'll wait," she said, tapping her fingernails against one of the orchid pots.

"Sure?" Nick asked. "I'll give you my car keys."

"No, no I'll wait." She smiled at Levin, who turned and walked away followed by Nick.

She took a seat in the reception room, crossed her legs, and opened as copy of *Vogue*. Waiting was not easy for her. In fact, she was impatient, but she couldn't give that bastard Levin the pleasure of dismissing her. And she wondered what was so important that he needed Nick now.

As soon as the last guest had left, boxes containing the firm's files began to be brought up from the lobby below. There were hundreds of cartons being returned from the attorney general's office. The freight elevators had been ready and waiting—as well as fifty law students hired to receive the files.

Maria watched as the files were wheeled in on dollies. Enough of *Vogue* and *Cosmopolitan*. She had been waiting for over an hour. She decided to follow the cartons and the law students to the file rooms in the rear of the suite. Maybe she could learn something.

Chapter XI

It was ten p.m., and detective Ralph Kirby was busy typing with two fingers. Captain Lawrence wanted the 75-49s on the Celia Lopez case and had threatened to fire him if they weren't on his desk by eight a.m. Kirby knew it was an idle threat, but it was the captain's way of protecting his ass in case the DA got her balls twisted.

Kirby tiredly rubbed his head, forcing his gray hair to stand up on end. Seeing his reflection in the darkened window opposite him, he saw he that looked comical, but he didn't care. He yawned and stretched his arms out across his desk. He had been on his feet all day, combing the neighborhood for information on the Lopez murder. No one knew anything. Not even the junkies were interested—not even for a small bribe. No one had really known her and no one cared. She was just another victim murdered for cash—ten dollars or ten cents, it didn't matter. Desperate junkies took their chances, and sometimes they hit the jackpot. In Celia's case, the two hundred dollar withdrawal evidenced by the slip in her purse would be the jackpot for any one of the neighborhood crackheads.

His eyes were drawn to the coffee-stained blotter on his desktop. The stains were reminders of all the nights he had spent typing reports such as those before him, reports on the dead bodies and how they had died, what they wore and catalogues of their effects, property receipts, witness interviews, who had seen them last, and so on and so forth—but no suspects.

He thought he needed a replacement for the blotter. It would symbolize a new start. Perhaps it would make his job more bearable. He could have retired five years ago, but there were his grandchildren, ten-year-old Jason and eight-year-old Margaret. He almost had enough in their accounts to pay for the college tuition that his son should have been thinking about but hadn't, and never would.

What a waste, he thought. He had tried to raise Kevin to be a responsible, hardworking man. He had helped him to get a job with the city at the Department of Licenses and Inspections. But what did he do? Missed work, played the horses, and never saved a dime. He told himself: *Pretty soon, Ralph, pretty soon you'll retire and never have to sit at this broken-down desk, type on this ancient typewriter that skips whole words—or listen to Captain Lawrence whine about late reports, and how you'll be fired if you don't wise up.* Captain Lawrence didn't care about the victims—only the reports. Kirby cared about the victims, about solving their murders, about catching the perps. That was the difference between him and Lawrence, he thought. That was why he wasn't a captain like Lawrence. If a case needed more investigating and more cops to do the job, and if he were captain, there would be no problem. And he would have no problem standing up to the DA or the press. Even if it meant his job. That's why he wasn't now, and never would be, a captain.

Kirby put aside his resentment for a moment and turned his thoughts back to Celia Lopez and her children. All the items found in her safe-deposit box had been examined by Homicide, carefully catalogued, and turned over to a court appointed administrator who would oversee and distribute the assets of her estate, as well as pay her debts and her taxes. But there was one item that had not been checked or catalogued—a solid, oblong parcel, about seven-and-a-half inches long, four inches wide, and an inch thick in a sealed manila envelope. Kirby carefully opened it.

He was bleary-eyed with fatigue, but he was able to muster up enough energy to focus on the package. After all, you never knew what could be inside. He took out the contents—another sealed envelope with an address label on it: Nicholas Ceratto-210 Locust Street, #3850, Philadelphia, PA, 19106. He carefully peeled the self-adhesive flap open—and smiled. It was a video tape of *Raiders of the Lost Ark*. He turned it around and read the names of the actors. He had forgotten all except Harrison Ford. He had seen the film at least ten times since its release in 1981. He loved the movie and almost knew the script by heart. He thought of popping it into the VCR just in case there was something on the tape other than a movie. He toyed with the idea and went back and forth in his mind between yes and no. Finally he lifted his weary bones out of the rickety, wooden chair and walked into the conference room with its fading, pea green painted walls and chipped Formica topped conference table. It was clear that the homicide department didn't care much for decor, or sanitation either, for that matter. There were four half-empty Styrofoam cups on the table. It looked as if the coffee had been in them for a week. The liquid was so concentrated that it hardly moved when he picked a cup up. Disgusted, he tossed it into a half-filled plastic trash bucket, then popped the film into the VCR and hit PLAY.

Familiar sounds echoed against the peeling walls: the ominous music as Jones led his small band of Indian bearers through the steamy jungle, then the approach to the cave, then a scream…Kirby smiled again. So far it *was* only a film. He fast-forwarded it for a few seconds—still only *Raiders*. He punched STOP and then REWIND, wondering what the hell Lopez was doing with a video of *Raiders* in her safe-deposit box. Judging by the sleeve, it was an old copy. Did she possibly think it was valuable? Nah, he answered himself. There were thousands of these around. Oh well, it takes all kinds. Kirby smiled, shaking his head. He decided to personally deliver the package to Nick Ceratto. Maybe Ceratto knew something about the tape that made it safe-deposit box material.

Kirby lived in Fishtown, a working-class neighborhood mostly populated by the descendants of Irish immigrants. It was just north of Society Hill, where Nick's apartment was located. It was late, but Ceratto might still be up and about, and it wasn't far. In fact, it was on Kirby's way home. It was worth a try, at least.

Kirby parked in front of the Society Hill Towers. It was one of his favorite spots in the city. Three majestic buildings sitting high on a hill next to the Delaware River. He tried to imagine what the views must be from the apartments. He had never been inside one.

The buildings were the monumental creations of I.M. Pei, a student of Frank Lloyd Wright. They were perched on four-story concrete stilts, a honeycomb structure of concrete and glass. Nothing obstructed their dominant position or the view from inside. The entire city from the Delaware to the Schuylkill River could be seen from their windows. The towers loomed over the surrounding restored colonial homes. Nick lived in a three-bedroom penthouse on the thirty-eighth floor.

Kirby stepped out of his car. It was cold and quiet up on the hill. The fountain in the center of the cobblestone plaza had been turned off for the winter. The halyard on a flagpole clanged eerily, breaking the night silence as the wind drummed it against the metal.

A bird with outstretched wings, a seated woman and child, and a standing man—huge, rough sculpted piles of bronze—stared at Kirby and glistened under a coat of frost. He usually hated modern sculpture. It didn't look like what it was supposed to represent. But somehow he liked these pieces. They worked well against the backdrop of the concrete giants. He crossed the plaza, ignoring the figures, and quickly walked into the four-story lobby of the south tower. It was warm inside. The doorman politely tipped his hat.

"What apartment, sir?"

"Ah, I'm here to see Nick Ceratto."

"Thirty-eighth floor."

"Yep, that's it," Kirby responded rubbing his cold-reddened hands together.

"Who shall I say is here?"

"Ralph Kirby, Philadelphia police. I've got a package for him."

"I'll ring him for you, sir."

"Thanks." Kirby looked around, impressed. The sofas were leather, the carpets oriental, and the lighting soft. Hundreds of tiny lights twinkled in recesses in the four-story lobby ceiling. Not at all like Fishtown, thought Kirby. He hoped that his grandchildren would someday live in a place like this.

From the window of his penthouse study, Nick Ceratto watched as a tall sailing ship gracefully cut through the black water of the Delaware River. It would have been hardly visible at night except for its running lights, which shone brightly from the masts and the bulwarks. It moved slowly under full sail, aiming for the center of the Benjamin Franklin bridge, its highest point. The bridge was a blue ribbon of steel suspended from a huge inverted bow of cables spanning the river from Philadelphia to Camden. Spotlights from the cables beamed down on cars that steadily streamed across it. Every night was like a fireworks display, he thought. Nick had decided when he moved in two years ago that he would never leave this high perch for a home on the ground. Not even for one of the grand, eighteenth-century mansions like the Powell House or Keith-Physick House, which he could see below.

He poured himself a Glenfiddich. He had expensive tastes and was unwilling not to satisfy them most of the time. After all, he had earned it. He took a short sip, savoring the peaty flavor of the Highlands, and rubbed his tired eyes. He had just finished reviewing four boxes of pleadings and discovery materials in the case of Sean Riley, deceased. The formal case caption read: *Theresa Riley, Administratrix of the Estate of Sean Riley, deceased, versus Victor Manin, M.D. and City Memorial Hospital.* It was a case Harry Levin had assigned to him the night of the firm's reopening celebration. It had been Joe Maglio's case and was currently on the trial list. And the Honorable Joseph Barnes was not granting any more petitions to postpone the trial. He had already granted three continuances at Joe's request, which the defense had not contested.

As far as Barnes was concerned, the case had been hanging around far too long (four years), and the judge wanted it off his trial list, either settled or tried. It had to be resolved one way or another, to disappear. Otherwise, Judge Dominic Cortino, the administrative judge in charge of assigning cases to each trial judge, would be extremely disappointed. And that would hurt Barnes's bid for the Supreme Court of Pennsylvania, a job he had coveted for years. He was known as "Assembly Line Barnes," famous for moving cases through the system at any cost. He didn't want to be accused by his enemies (of which there were many) of favoring Joe Maglio and his firm with unusual tolerance. This was the oldest case on any judge's trial list and was also a high-profile case. The media had covered it extensively and was salivating for the trial. It involved the death of an often-publicized police captain, Sean Riley, known for his heroism, who had been shot in the leg in the line of duty. Captain Riley had suddenly died after routine surgery performed by another local celebrity, Doctor Victor Manin, a pillar of the community, who was at the forefront of medical research in surgical techniques. Dr. Manin sat on the boards of at least three major hospitals. He was a professor emeritus at Penn Medical School and had published dozens of articles in medical journals and hosted a myriad of charitable events to subsidize his work and the works of other deserving researchers in the field.

Manin had the misfortune of being in the hospital the night that Captain Riley was brought into the emergency room. The doctor was about to leave for an evening charity event, but he stayed to work on Riley's leg, which was bleeding badly from a severed femoral artery. Although the leg had been tourniqueted by the EMTs, Riley needed help fast, and Manin performed the emergency surgery. For him it was routine. He cleaned the area, sutured the artery, saw that it was not leaking, irrigated the wound, and personally closed the incision. He left Riley in the care of his surgical staff in whom he placed utmost faith.

But Captain Riley bled to death in the recovery room. One of the surgical nurses later claimed that the doctor had been in a hurry and hadn't sutured the artery properly.

Joe had filed several petitions to postpone the trial, and Nick couldn't figure out why. It was a slam dunk. Manin's medical malpractice carrier, Pro-Med, saw it the same way and had put two million dollars, the limits of their policy, on the table in exchange for the grieving Widow Riley's release. But Manin refused to settle—not even for one dollar. There was a clause in his policy requiring his approval to settle, which he had refused to give. He stood his ground even though he would be personally liable for any verdict over the policy. Any "excess" verdict would come out of his own pocket. Manin didn't seem to care, although there was a good chance that a jury would award a sum much greater than two million dollars. He was more concerned about the impact that a settlement would have on his reputation. To him a settlement was the same as admitting guilt. He wanted a jury verdict in his favor and nothing less.

It was all in Joe's pretrial memo, which Nick had been reading. He shook his head and picked up the thick document one more time. Joe was wordy, elegant in his writing style, but verbose to say the least. Nick knew that he could try the case. It was so well documented. And he wondered if Silvio and Levin knew what they were doing when they assigned him all Joe's cases, Joe's office, and his position as chief litigator with a full partnership. It was far too much for a young associate—even with his talent.

The telephone rang twice in quick sequence, signaling a call from the lobby. Nick carried his drink and the memo over to the table. He picked up the receiver.

"Yes," he answered.

"Mr. Ceratto, it's George."

"Yes, George."

"There's someone here to see you, sir."

"Send her up," Nick answered, thinking it was Maria Elena, whom he had planned to meet at his condo at eleven. When Nick had finally come out of Levin's office after the party, they had made plans for a midnight snack of fresh oysters, Beluga caviar, and Frascati. Nick had gotten all the ingredients at the Reading Terminal Market on the way home. The opened oysters were chilling in the refrigerator along with the chopped onion, capers, and hard-boiled egg for the caviar. Maria loved to eat late and then make love all night. Nick wasn't going to argue with that.

"Sir, it's a man."

"A man?"

"Yes, sir. It's a detective Ralph Kirby, and he says he has a package for you."

"Did you check his ID?"

"Yes sir. It appears to be in order…and the package is addressed to you."

"Tell him to leave it with you."

"I suggested that, sir, but he said that he would like to deliver it personally…and ask you a few questions."

"Damn cops! They're all pushy. Tell him to leave his card and I'll call him tomorrow." He heard mumbling on the other end of the phone, muffled, barely audible, voices.

"Sir, he says it's a package from someone at your office, addressed to you."

There was a pause as Nick tried to sort out the what the doorman had told him.

"OK. Let him in."

Kirby lightly tapped on the door of 3850 with the back of his hand. He ignored the brass lion's head knocker on the door. The dimly lit hall was quiet, and he didn't want to wake anyone. He stood for a few moments, waiting, remembering the halls of all the buildings he was used to waiting in. Some had been vermin infested with peeling paint and cracked plaster; some had been nice and clean. The nice, clean ones were pretty much the same no matter where you went, he thought. Like this hall. Although it was in a luxury building, it had ordinary looking vinyl-papered walls of a neutral color that wouldn't show dirt, and low wattage bulbs in the wall sconces that didn't use much electricity. The brightly lit lobbies, on the contrary, were like a woman's face, he thought, a lure, a promise, but once you were inside…

Nick finally opened the door. He checked Kirby's ID without saying a word, and then stepped back to let him into the foyer. Kirby stepped past Nick and walked into the living room. He wasn't shy about checking out the furnishings. He didn't have a great house himself. Fishtown, where he lived, was a modest neighborhood. It was kept alive by a few diehards like himself. But, Kirby, despite his origins, appreciated fine things. He had studied the homes of the wealthy, like the ones in Chestnut Hill and West Mount Airy on those rare occasions when he was assigned to a case where one aristocrat bumped off another. And he had promised himself a wonderful, oceanfront condo when he retired—with a few antiques sprinkled here and there. Maybe in Ocean City or Sea Isle City. He knew just how he would furnish it.

Kirby stepped back. He wasn't embarrassed to stare at the twelve-foot ceilings twinkling with tiny spider lights suspended on thin wires. He walked to the undraped windows showcasing the city below, and the view he had always imagined—and it didn't disappoint. He carefully walked over the intricately patterned reds, greens, and tans of the oriental carpets. His hand ran across the putty-colored leather sofas. And finally he went over to the crown jewels: Nick's collection of Warhol serigraphs, Marilyn with pursed blue lips and Mick Jagger with his signature wide open mouth. Kirby cocked his head and then turned to the Campbell soup can.

"Impressive." He nodded approvingly. He put on his glasses and looked at the signatures. "Originals, it looks like."

"Thanks. Now what can I do for you?" Nick was losing patience. He was never comfortable around cops, even ones who admired his taste. And moreover, he never felt the need to be accommodating.

"I have a package for you."

"From who?"

"Whom," Kirby corrected without making eye contact. He knew that Nick was a cocky young punk with a law degree. He had heard of him and was not the least bit impressed with him. Just with his apartment. He opened his twelve-year-old brown twill coat, the only coat he owned. It was frayed on the right cuff and had a sheen from too many pressings, but it was warm and serviceable and had ample pockets.

"OK. *Whom*?" Nick hated smart-ass cops, and this one in particular.

"From Celia Lopez." Kirby pulled the envelope containing the tape from his inside pocket.

"What?" Nick answered, stunned at hearing her name. He instinctively reached out for the package.

Kirby held it close. "Before I give it to you, will you answer a question for me—something which I don't understand, that's been bothering me?"

"Maybe. Ask me and I'll let you know if I can—or if I will." Nick reached for his drink on the glass coffee table.

'Do you know why Celia Lopez would have this in her safe-deposit box?" Kirby opened the envelope and showed Nick the tape, while keeping a firm grip on it.

"*Raiders of the Lost Ark*." Nick read the title aloud, paused, and reflected for a few minutes. "Yeah, I know why," he lied. "I collect old films, and I didn't have this one. She told me that she would make a copy for herself and give me the original. We used to talk about old movies all the time." He sipped the last of his single malt, put the glass back on the table, and held his hand out for the tape.

"But why wouldn't she just give it to you? Why would she keep it in a safe-deposit box?" Kirby continued to hold the tape, ignoring Nick's open hand.

"I don't know. Celia was a little weird. She thought some things were important that weren't. She'd make ten copies of ordinary correspondence, copy all the phone messages…she was paranoid… closed, if you know what I mean. She thought that since it was a first release…cassette…you know, original 1981…it had particular value. I told her it didn't, tapes lost quality with age. She wouldn't hear it. She said she'd will it to me when she died instead of giving it to me now. I don't know," he shook his head. "I guess she wanted to prove a point."

"I thought it was a little weird, too, so I watched some of it— you know—ran it for a while—then fast-forwarded it."

Nick's expression suddenly changed. Kirby noticed his smile had disappeared and his body had tensed. Body language. You couldn't hide it. It never failed, Kirby thought.

"And…?"

"And I found that it was just a *Raiders of the Lost Ark* tape. And you're right—the quality is poor." Kirby laughed. "Age has a way of knocking the hell out of things." He patted his stomach hanging over his worn, brown leather belt and handed Nick the tape.

"Thanks...if that's all, Detective Kirby...?" Nick moved toward the door hoping the old detective would take the hint.

But Kirby moved toward the coffee table and stopped to read the caption on the top of the pile of papers Nick had left on the glass top.

"Oh, Sean Riley. Are you trying that case?"

"Yes."

"Yeah, I knew Captain Riley. He was a good man. Shame, to die so young. He had a lot of life left in him. I know Dr. Manin, too. Always helped our injured when he could. You know, gave to the police and firemen's fund and all that...a true friend of the force."

"Yes. Well, good night, Detective." Nick opened the front door before Kirby had finished his sentence. He didn't see Maria Elena in Kirby's path, he was so intent on getting rid of him.

She smacked into Kirby in the doorway and practically ricocheted off his broad belly. Fortunately for her it was soft.

"Excuse me." The detective was visibly shaken—until he saw what it was he had collided with. Then he was visibly impressed. He smiled. "I'm sorry."

"Oh, pardon me. No. It's all my fault. I was so clumsy. I should have looked where I was going," she said coquettishly, tossing her dark hair back.

"Not as clumsy as I am. Sorry, miss." Kirby gestured gallantly with a hand toward the entrance as he stepped back to let Maria through. "Detective Ralph Kirby at your service, ma'am."

"Thank you." She stepped through the doorway past Kirby and then turned to him with an outstretched hand. "Maria Elena Maglio."

"Relative of Joseph Maglio?" Kirby asked, shaking her hand warmly.

"Yes, his cousin."

"Too bad. He was a great lawyer. A good man, too. I don't care what they say about him." Kirby paused, looking up. "What did Marc Antony say? 'The good is oft interred with the bones?' Not with me—I remember the good." He laughed, shaking his head, tipped his hat, and started on his way.

"Thank you," Maria said softly after him. "You are very kind."

Chapter XII

It was two twenty a.m. when Maria suddenly woke. She had been having a bad dream about being chased. She was running down a dark highway—car lights moving slowly behind her. They followed her, but they didn't pass her. She looked back but couldn't see the car or the driver, only an amorphous shape. She couldn't run off the macadam. She tried, but something kept pulling her back onto the same strip of road. Then she saw an intersection. She thought to run to the left or right as soon as she reached it. But she never got any closer no matter how fast she ran. Suddenly she was there at the intersection. But it wasn't a crossroad. It was a railroad track. Under it was water—dark, glistening syrup reflecting the lights of the car behind her. Suddenly a train appeared on the tracks, roaring toward her at top speed, its whistle blowing deafeningly, its headlights blinding her. She leaped into the darkness toward the water. And was falling, falling, falling. And then she awoke just before she hit the surface.

Maria was sweating. She knew she had been silently crying because her cheeks were wet, but she didn't wake Nick, who lay sound asleep beside her. She decided to get up. She would not try to go back to sleep, not after a dream like that. Her mouth was dry. She quickly walked, naked, into the kitchen and poured herself a glass of Pellegrino, and then walked into the living room and sat down on the leather sofa. She idly picked up the video cassette lying on the coffee table. She read the blurb on the box and decided she would watch it since she had never seen the film. Perhaps it would make her forget her dream. Besides, it sounded intriguing. Indiana Jones, assigned by the U.S. government to find the Ark of the Covenant before the dreaded Nazis did. How American. How like Nick, she thought. She had nothing better to do other than go back to that awful nightmare.

She put the tape in the VCR and hit PLAY. The low, suspenseful theme music came up gradually as the camera panned the jungle covered mountains of Central America. She lowered the volume, not wanting to wake Nick, and settled into the sofa, pulling the tan silk throw from the back of the couch over her nakedness and propping two overstuffed pillows behind her. She took a sip of the sparkling water and fixed her eyes on the screen. She didn't take them off for the next sixty-five minutes.

Suddenly the screen went blank and the sound went dead as the Nazis were tying Indiana Jones to a stake.

"*Merde! Que succedi?*" she muttered, annoyed at the interruption. Just as she was about to fast-forward with the remote, the screen lit again, but this time without the image of Harrison Ford. Instead, it was Joe Maglio. She stood, wrapping the throw tighter around her. She thought she must be dreaming again. Had she fallen asleep during the movie? No, she hadn't. She took a long drink of water and started pacing as she watched and listened as Joe spoke.

By five a.m. she had replayed Joe Maglio's portion at least four times, made fresh coffee, gotten a shower, and gotten dressed. Now it was time to wake Nick.

"Nick," she shook him lightly. He was unresponsive. "Nick." She shook him harder.

"What?" He yawned and tried to focus in the dark. "What time is it?" He rolled onto his back and gave her a distant stare.

"It's five o'clock."

"In the morning?" he asked, incredulous that she would be up so early. He looked at the blackness through his tall bedroom windows, which he never kept shaded. There was no need thirty-eight stories up.

"Get up now," she said. "You must see something."

"Maria, I'll see it when I get up," he said, pleading for two more hours' rest.

"No," she snapped. "Now!"

"What the hell is so important that I have to get up two hours ahead of the alarm? The answer is, nothing is that important." Nick rolled over grabbing his pillow.

"This," she said. She ran from the bedroom into the living room, cranked the volume on the VCR up to full, and hit play. Suddenly, Joe's voice boomed through the built-in surround-sound speakers. Before she had a chance to turn around, Nick was standing beside her without a stitch of clothing.

"What the fuck?"

CHAPTER XIII

The air was biting cold as Nick crossed Sixteenth Street toward Liberty Place, a blue-gray forty-story steel tower that matched the sky. He dodged the heavy morning traffic, walking between stopped cars jammed together as they slowly made their way to the parking garage under the massive tower. A few impatient drivers sounded their horns as if the noise would unlock the congestion.

Nick's heart pounded as he wheeled the heavy trial bags—two full leather cases, one on top of the other, through the mess. He saw his breath stream ahead of him as he pulled the bags up and over the curb in front of the entrance to the building. A strong sewer odor wafted past him. It was always there, at this exact point, in winter, spring, summer, and fall. It was the smell of the city. Something you had to forgive, or at least ignore if you were going to reap the city's rewards, money being one of them.

It was nine a.m. Tuesday morning, and Nick was on his way to take the deposition of Dr. Victor Manin. He was ready. He had prepared his hit list and was ready to fire away, to ask the doctor pointed questions under oath. Both the questions and answers would be recorded and made into a permanent record by a court reporter.

The case seemed like a no-brainer based on the evidence he had. The doctor's social obligation that evening, his haste, the operating room nurse who would reluctantly testify to that, as well as to the sloppy closure of the incision. But his instincts told him to watch out. He had seen Manin on CNN, talking about a new surgical technique that would save thousands of lives and spare patients weeks of pain. He had seen him both in front of the cameras and live, testifying for another doctor in a medical malpractice case. Manin had been clear, convincing, unwavering, polite, and extremely handsome. He had everything going for him—looks, image, sincerity, and poise. Much like Nick himself, the doctor would be formidable, despite the mountain of adverse evidence. As Joe used to say, "Don't count your chickens before they're hatched. And watch out for the saints. Don't let the jury feel sorry for them. Don't martyr them. Let them hang themselves. Always be polite and courteous, but deadly accurate with your questions—the ones you already know the answers to because there is only one answer. Always give them room to dig themselves in deeper when they try to evade the inevitable. And smile...always smile while you're questioning."

Nick was sweating by the time he reached the twenty-eighth floor offices where Asher, Smith, Brown and Finley, a preeminent medical malpractice defense firm, was located. The firm took up the entire floor—twenty thousand square feet of pure hell for the plaintiff's bar. Insurance defense was all the firm did, and they were damned good at it. Nick straightened his black cashmere topcoat, then checked his red-striped rep tie in the large, mirror-like brass plaque on the dark walnut door. He was satisfied with the way he looked. *Now let's see if I sound that good,* he thought.

A pretty blond sat at the serpentine rosewood reception desk. Her skin was white and smooth, with fine lines at the corners of her eyes and mouth. The lines deepened as her smile framed perfectly straight, pearly white teeth. Her hair was cut chin length and fell straight like golden fringe around her perfect features.

Pretty as a cameo, Nick thought admiring her refined WASP features.

"Good morning, sir," she said. Smile, smile—an obvious part of her job.

"Nick Ceratto." He handed her his card. "I'm here for a deposition."

"Yes, I know." Smile, smile. "I have your name here, sir. Just leave your coat with me and go straight down the short hall to conference room three. The court reporter is already setting up. I'll tell Mr. Asher that you're here." Smile, smile.

John Asher? he thought as he made his way to room three. It was supposed to be Mark Finley. Asher was much tougher. Nick remembered Joe and Asher going head to head in a cancer misdiagnosis case. Joe had actually been worried. Asher's so-called expert, Professor James Connelly, M.D. (a paid defense whore as Joe had called him), had sandbagged Joe by testifying that the plaintiff's form of cancer was so deadly and fast spreading that it didn't matter that the defendant had missed it. Even if the defendant doctor had diagnosed it six months earlier, when he should have, it wouldn't have made any difference in the outcome. The cancer had already metastasized. The plaintiff had suffered with malignant melanoma for two years and had to watch his body slowly rot away.

It had been the classic *So What?* defense. So what if the doctor didn't order a biopsy? The plaintiff was a dead man anyhow. So no harm done. Joe had objected and argued against admitting Asher's expert's damaging testimony since it hadn't been disclosed before the trial as the rules required.

After two days of briefing and oral argument in the judge's chambers—outside the hearing of the jury—Judge Josephine Hanks ruled in Joe's favor and sustained his objection. The damaging evidence was stricken, and the jury was instructed to ignore the professor's testimony. It could have killed the case. But the jury found in favor of Joe's client, the plaintiff's widow, in the amount of ten million dollars.

Watch your back. Those had been Joe's famous words about Asher. And no doubt the feeling was mutual as far as Asher was concerned. Now Nick wondered what Asher had in store for him. Whatever it was, he would be prepared to deal with it.

Asher stood just inside the conference room with his back to the glass door. Nick watched from the hall as the defense attorney rhythmically moved his hands giving last-minute instructions to his client, who stood facing him. Asher's words were inaudible but Nick knew the drill: "Don't volunteer any information. Don't answer a question you don't fully understand. Don't be afraid to say, 'I don't understand your question, Counselor.' And if you do understand but think the answer you'll have to give might be damaging, hesitate, so I can object and throw him off. You can weasel, you can waffle, but for Christ's sake, don't lie. Unless I tell you to. You'll know when."

Asher turned, opened the door, and let Nick into the brightly lit room—fully equipped with audio and video equipment. Pots of freshly brewed coffee and bottles of mineral water, cups monogrammed with the firm's logo, cream, and sugar were already laid out on the federal style sideboard at the far end of the room. Every professional courtesy and accommodation appeared to be available—except the truth.

Asher was tall and thin. His face was sharp featured and heavily lined from years on the tennis courts. He was dressed in a charcoal three-button suit, spread-collar shirt with a red and blue rep, silk tie, and black wing-tip shoes. He could have been a middle-aged model for Brooks Brothers. Instead he was a prick for the insurance companies, especially Pro-Med. His crystal blue eyes gleamed against his even tan—not too dark a tan, and definitely not peeling. His teeth were whiter than white as he smiled, stretching over the conference table to shake hands. Nick shook Asher's hand but didn't smile.

Asher always looked as though he had just returned from vacation, always poised, charming and relaxed, confident as ever. At least he appeared that way. His client, in contrast, looked tense and tired. Manin had bags and circles under his eyes. He apparently had not had much sleep in the past week. His dark brown eyes were dull, his brow was furrowed, and his skin looked pale. His handshake was clammy, Nick noted. The doctor's navy blue suit hung on his slightly stooped shoulders. He looked as though he had lost fifteen pounds and hadn't had the suit altered. Why bother? He would probably lose another fifteen before the trial was over. This was not the Doctor Victor Manin that Nick remembered. It was all too clear that he needed a haircut, a week's sleep, and a good meal. Although he looked bad, Nick knew that the doctor would evoke the jury's sympathy, and that was not good. That was Asher's only card, and so far he was playing it perfectly. He obviously had not told his client to clean up and dress up.

Nick would have to play his hand just as perfectly and plan his strategy accordingly. What strategy would he use, what script? What would erase the powerful emotion of sympathy that Manin would evoke? What would cancel out Asher's skillful portrayal of his client as the victim? The poor, bankrupt, downtrodden, unjustly accused doctor. Instead Nick had a dead cop—who *couldn't* be put on the stand, who *couldn't* testify.

The doctor would be primed. He would tell the jury, "I'm sorry. I did the best I could. But, I'm not God." It would be a perfect script.

In his mind, Nick heard Asher arguing that medicine is not an exact science, and that the good doctor did everything he possibly could to save Sean Riley's life. He even stayed at the hospital to perform the surgery when he could have as easily left for his social engagement. He cared for his patients as he would members of his own family. And he took a special interest in cops because they risked their lives every day for us. Because cops were heroes, and Doctor Manin respected them and appreciated their sacrifices— especially since Manin's father had been a cop. Sean Riley's death was an act of God. God wanted Sean, and God took him. Doctor Manin was not more powerful than God that night, and no mortal should expect him to be…

"Mr. Ceratto," the court reporter said, breaking Nick's reverie. "Shall I swear the witness in?"

"Yes, go ahead." Nick opened his notebook to his carefully prepared *hit list*: not a list of questions as one might suppose, but a carefully prepared list of facts—dates, times, actions, and reasons that he had to get the doctor to unequivocally admit to. Otherwise the doctor could give vague and ambiguous answers to open-ended questions. This was the only way that Nick could get the ammunition to effectively cross-examine the doctor at trial, and if possible destroy him on the stand.

"Doctor Manin, my name is Nick Ceratto, and I represent the Estate of Sean Riley. I'm going to ask you a series of questions about your involvement with Sean Riley on the night he died. Doctor, have you ever been deposed before? You're shaking your head, no. Then let me give you some instructions. If I ask you a question and you don't understand it, please tell me so I can rephrase in such a way that you will understand it. Is that clear? Second, if you answer my question, I will assume that you understood it and that your answer is full and complete. Finally…"

The phone rang. The ringer had been set on low so that it wouldn't startle anyone. It was only to be used to enlist the aid of a judge in settling a dispute between lawyers about the propriety of a question during a deposition or some other matter of great importance. Otherwise the staff had strict instructions to never interrupt a deposition.

Asher moved to the credenza and picked up the receiver after the first ring, holding up a hand to stop the proceeding. The court reporter instantly removed her hands from the small keyboard of her machine. Nick stopped mid-sentence and turned to hear what could be so important.

"Yes? Fine. I'll tell Mr. Ceratto. No, I have no objection. Just tell her to have a seat. There's a woman, a clerk of yours, who's here to sit in on the deposition."

Nick looked curiously at Asher but said nothing. *Clerk? What clerk*, he thought.

"She said her name is Maria Elena. She apologizes for being late. I certainly don't have an objection to her sitting in. I'm sure you'd accommodate one of our clerks in a similar situation," Asher smiled.

"Thank you," Nick responded, thinking, *What the fuck is she doing here?*

Maria Elena entered room three, accompanied by the receptionist. The difference between the two was glaring. Maria wore a navy pinstripe suit. The double-breasted jacket was cut low enough to reveal just the right amount of skin with a tad of cleavage. The hem of her skirt was just above the knee. She wore nude colored stockings and black leather pumps with a three-inch spike heel. She carried a black leather Prada briefcase. Her golden brown hair fell softly about her shoulders and slightly over her left eye. She wore thin, wire-rim glasses.

The receptionist wore a long, gray wool skirt, a white cotton blouse buttoned high at the neck, and flat shoes—black skimmers with grosgrain bows. She was pretty as a cameo alright– seated at her desk, but in full view, it was clear that she was stuck in the nineteen fifties, an image that fit perfectly with this firm. She smiled innocently, blushing slightly as she motioned Maria toward an empty seat next to Nick.

Asher rose to his feet, took Maria's hand, and smiled deeply, introducing himself before Nick had the opportunity. He held her hand a little longer than usual, the handshake continuing a few seconds after the introduction. Maria returned the smile and did not withdraw her hand. She liked his firm, warm grip; his smile; his tan.

"A pleasure," she said. "My name is Maria Elena." She purposely omitted her last name. "Thank you for allowing me to stay."

"What law school are you going to, Ms…?" He hesitated, wondering why his firm never received applicants such as this.

"Nardo. I went to the University of Rome," she answered without missing a beat. She lied well and was relaxed while doing it.

"Ah, that explains your charming accent. Well, if you need anything, please let me or a member of my staff know."

"Thank you, I will." She sat down in the tufted armchair and poured herself a glass of water from a carafe on the table. She crossed her legs and opened her briefcase, taking out a yellow legal pad and a Tiffany T-ball pen.

Nick watched her, trying to regain his train of thought, recall what his first question was to be, thinking that he just might put her on a plane and send her back to Italy the very first chance he got. She was a distraction, and that could be bad for him—as a matter of fact, deadly. "Where were we?" he asked the court reporter.

She pulled the folded tape from the box at the front of the stenotype machine and read from the strange mechanical shorthand symbols. "Second, if you answer my question, I will assume that you understood it and that your answer is full and complete."

Dr. Manin nodded in agreement and for the next seven hours maintained his innocence.

Chapter XIV

Mike Rosa felt like a new man. It was Saturday morning. The late January air, warmed by the sun, was cold but forgiving; and the scent of a beautiful day filled his nostrils as he was hurled rhythmically forward on the wintery trail on Khalil, his Arabian horse. His breath commingled and condensed in a haze with Khalil's. The powerful hooves pounded on the hard packed earth, echoing the staccato of another set of hooves close behind. A neigh of protest shrilled across the quiet, frozen woods as Maria Elena pulled back on the reins of Jamilia, Rosa's other white Arabian, slowing the horse to a trot. Mike was amazed at Maria's riding skills. She was strong, graceful, and fearless, just like her mount.

Both horses snorted loudly as they kept pace with each other, challenging their riders to keep them in check.

What could be more perfect, he thought, than to be away from the office, the telephone, the papers on his desk, the coroner's reports, and all the crap that went with his job. Instead he was riding next to this beautiful young woman. His wife and sons had gone to visit his in-laws in Naples, Florida, and he was left to fend for himself. *Too bad*, he thought, reveling in the moment of the day. Although he felt twinges of guilt remembering last night, it didn't spoil the joy he now felt. He hadn't made love like that in thirty years. And the thrill of knowing that he still had the stamina overwhelmed his sense of guilt—at least for the present. He knew himself too well, though. He knew that he'd suffer later for his pleasure. But later was later, and the present was too perfect to think about later.

It was ten a.m. They had been riding since eight. His ribs and his butt ached. He wasn't sure if it was from the horse or Maria.

"I'm hungry. How about we turn back?" he asked.

"I could go on forever," she said. Her thick brown hair billowed behind her in the wind.

"I'll bet you could," he laughed. His voice wavered with the movement of the horse as he stood in the stirrups to give his rear a rest.

"OK, but let's gallop back!" She pulled Jamilia's head around and quickly executed a turn in the opposite direction.

Rosa's turn was not as smooth, but he was glad to be going home to a warm shower. Both horses bolted forward and streaked toward the stables—white manes flying and hooves pounding like kettledrums.

Maria reached the barn first. She quickly whipped her right leg over the saddle and slid down the left side of the horse, laughing wildly at her victory and trying to catch her breath. She started to cough and choke. Rosa quickly dismounted and ran up to her, grabbing her from behind to attempt a Heimlich maneuver. But before he could apply any pressure, she turned in his arms and kissed him warmly on the lips.

"I'm all right," she said, impressed by his quick response and protectiveness.

"You scared me. I thought you were in trouble." He kissed her paternally on the head, holding her close. He was old enough to be her father, but he quickly dismissed the thought. "We smell of horse." He nuzzled her ear.

"You're right." She sniffed at her arm. "*Putzamo!* We stink. Let's wash, take showers."

"Together?" he asked. "I haven't taken a shower with a woman in over thirty years."

"*Cherto. Como no?* Certainly, why not? But first we have to take care of the horses." She tried to wriggle from his arms, but his grip was too strong. He led her into the barn and coaxed her onto the fresh stack of hay. He couldn't wait for a shower, and neither could she.

The warm water, the lather, and her hands had felt wonderful. Rosa lay across the canopied bed and was about to fall asleep when Maria shook him lightly.

"I have something I want you to see," she said authoritatively.

"What is it?" He was surprised at her tone.

"I have a film you have to see." She slid off the bed and walked over to the dresser, opened her purse, and took out the cassette.

"What film is it?" He sat up, holding out his hand. "Here, let me see it."

She dropped the cassette on the bed.

"*Raiders of the Lost Ark*?" he laughed. "I haven't seen this in at least…God knows how long."

"Probably twenty years ago. It was made in 1981." She took a cigarette from her bag and lit it.

"But why this film? Couldn't you have gotten us something a little more current?"

"This *is* current," she retorted, taking a long drag. She removed the cassette from the sleeve and put it in the VCR sitting in an armoire across from the bed. She carefully laid her cigarette on a saucer which had coffee rings from the night before. She pressed PLAY and then FAST FORWARD.

"What are you doing?" He laughed, amazed at her unpredictable behavior. He got up, the top sheet wrapped around his waist.

"You'll see." She stopped the film, reached for her cigarette, and hit PLAY.

A few seconds of Indiana Jones being tied to a stake…then a blank screen and silence for two seconds. The screen lit again, and there was Joe Maglio sitting at his desk in the study at his home. He was wearing casual clothes, a black turtleneck. He smiled into the camera, saying nothing. His hands were folded on the desktop. He cleared his throat.

Rosa walked toward the screen, mouth open.

"Nick, I asked Celia Lopez to give you this film if something happened to me. It's late, a little after midnight. Christy and the kids are asleep." He paused. "This is difficult for me." He laughed. "For the first time in my life, I'm at a loss for words. It's eerie, you know, talking from the grave. As I'm speaking I know that if you ever see this, I'll be a dead man…dead man talking." He shook his head and chuckled. Then his eyes became watery. "And I know it's got to be weird for you to be watching this, too. But it's very important that you listen to everything I have to say very carefully, and do what I tell you. I chose Celia because she's the only one in the firm that I trust with this tape. She's loyal, and you can count on her if you need her. She's never let me down, and she'll never betray you." He paused and cleared his throat.

"I never told you anything about the firm or myself that I was ashamed of—but I'm going to, now. I'm not good at confessions, so bear with me." He took a deep breath.

"Twenty years ago, I started this firm." He picked up a pen and started toying with it. "I knew I was a good trial lawyer but a terrible money manger. I didn't have the time to worry about money- or rainmaking. But I knew we needed both. Then Levin came along, and he could manage money. Boy, he could work miracles. He kept costs down, staved off creditors, and let the firm's coffers fill. And then came Silvio, always the supreme rainmaker, in with the unions. God knows what he gave them, but they always sent their business our way. Neither one of those fucks could try a case if their life depended on it. But back then we were a great team. We got along. We hired talent. Each one did what he did best. We started getting bigger verdicts, more cases, more important cases. The money started pouring in. We started taking bigger salaries—partnership draws—bigger houses, cars, you know. And I admit, I was the worst. The more I made, the more I spent. And Christy is no miser, as you know. My family started to demand more and more. The more they got, the more they wanted; and you know me—it was hard to say no. The bigger cases demanded heavy up-front costs to pay the experts witnesses. The explosion cases, the collapse cases, the defective tire cases—all those huge, open mouths to feed. And the politicians, judges. You know, Nick, if you don't want them against you, you got to feed them, too. It became a runaway train.

"I started robbing Peter to pay Paul. I took money from one account and put it another and then back in the original account. I took money from the escrow account to pay my mortgage.

The clients always got paid, but late instead of on time." He paused and picked up a glass with his left hand and took a drink.

Rosa hit the STOP button—"Son of a bitch."

"What are you doing? Let him finish." Maria stabbed out her cigarette and reached for the PLAY button.

"No." He pulled her hand away. "I want to rewind this last bit." He rewound the film and watched carefully as Joe picked up the glass. "Son of a bitch. He's left-handed."

Joe put the glass down and continued. "I always threw in a little extra, like interest on a loan—a thank you to the client for having patience. It worked out for a while. Silvio and Levin closed their eyes, I guess, and let me do my thing. Then we had a serious dry spell. Payments on cases we had won were delayed by appeals. Trials were being postponed and the bills kept coming in. We started fighting every day. They wanted me to stop spending money. Our line of credit was almost exhausted—a two million dollar line. I told them that the valve would open up the way it always has and we'd be flush again. We were owed millions. Cases *I* won.

"I was up against it. My mortgage was three months overdue. Foreclosure notices were coming fast. Celia hid the notices from everyone in the office but me—Christy had no idea what was going on because all the bills came to the office.

"I was between a rock and a hard place. We had checks coming in from two settled cases in about thirty days. Gross fees of about eight hundred thousand dollars were due then. But I couldn't wait thirty days because I was losing my home and I was too proud to tell Christy about the financial bind I was in.

"I wrote myself a check for twenty-five thousand from the client escrow account—enough to tide me until the settlement money arrived. The check overdrew the account, and the bank notified the Disciplinary Board. There were already two complaints against me, so the Board started an investigation. Silvio and Levin pointed to me as having control of the funds. When things got dry, those two bastards let me do all the finagling and check signing. I was the sacrificial lamb.

"I knew that I could resolve this with Don Harding, the head of the Board. I know Don personally, I would tell him I'd made a mistake, that my partners had nothing to do with my misconduct. I would pay back the twenty-five thousand, pay a fine, do some pro bono work, get a slap on the wrist. At the worst I might have to give up my license for a few months. But by then the money from the settled cases would be in the bank. The postponed cases would be ready to try and the cases on appeal would be breaking loose. We'd be flush again. But Silvio and Levin were ready to throw me to the wolves to save their own asses. They demanded my resignation."

He shook his head, looking down at the desk.

"I founded this fucking firm. I supported those fucks for twenty years, and they wanted to kick me out—see me disbarred so they could take all the cases and not pay me a dime on any of them. Cute—right? No license to practice. No right to collect a fee from a case—any case. Probably ten million dollars in outstanding fees, and I wouldn't have a legal right to one penny." His voice raised. "My money." He pounded his fist on the desk, then stared emptily into the camera lens and then paused.

"You see, I know they also stole money—the firm's money. But I don't know where they put it. I checked every bank to see if there was an account I could trace. But it was always a blind alley, a black hole into which they had siphoned money for twenty years." He paused and blinked. It was clear that he was distracted and struggling for control. Then he started again.

"Celia heard about the Board's investigation. There's no hiding anything from her. She was upset. She came to me. She has an incredible sense of justice, street justice. She swore that she would help me—and she has. And she collected information that will nail the coffin shut on Silvio and Levin, and send them away for a long time—a treasure trove. She's to give it to you after you see this tape. Remember, Nick, be careful. If they know you have this information, you'll be where I am now. Until you get out, you'll have to protect yourself. You'll have to pretend to be their friend. You'll have to be grateful for the crumbs they throw you, and flattered if they hand you any large cases—especially my cases. I don't want anything to happen to you. You're like a son to me. In fact, you *are* like me. You grew up in the streets, tough and smart. The best training a trial lawyer can have. And you're almost as good-looking." He laughed.

Then, almost schizoid, his brow furrowed. He became lost in thought, looking away from the camera for a moment as if in a dream. Then, just as suddenly, he focused on the camera and hunkered down like an animal ready to spring. He gritted his teeth and pointed his finger at the lens. "I want you to know that I'm going after the bastards. They're scum and I'm going to prove it with this." He held up a thin manila file. "Everything I need is right here, and they're going down. So far down, even the devil won't be able to find them. They're dead meat." He slapped the file down on the desk top and took another drink. "And *I'm* dead meat. So I've instructed Celia to deliver this to you if something happens to me. It will be in a sealed envelope. I'm not going to put your name on it in case it gets into the wrong hands. I want you to take it directly to the attorney general, Ron Fisk. And I mean directly. Don't show it to anyone but Fisk. He's smart. He's straight and he'll go right to the top with this information, undoubtedly the FBI. And heads will roll." Joe paused to take a deep breath and another sip of water. "Avoid Muriel Gates. This doesn't belong with the DA's office. If she gets her hands on this file, she'll just fuck it up. She's ambitious, vicious, and greedy. I know her like a book. I won't say anymore about her, only that I made a mistake helping to put her where she is—I must have been out of my mind. She's no friend. Before you hand this file over to Fisk, I want you to demand protection—from the feds, not the city cops.

"In case you're wondering why I haven't gone to Fisk with this myself, it's because I need more time. I don't have what I need yet, but I hope to have it before the Riley trial. I can't tell you more. If I don't make it, I don't want you caught up in this mess—out of loyalty to me. I don't want that to happen. It's my mess and I have to clean it up."

Joe smiled. Tapping the gold Waterman pen on the desk top, he looked down briefly, and then back up at the camera.

"It's also my redemption." His eyes moved from the camera to the digital readout on the VCR next to him. "As you gathered by now, I wanted this message buried in the film—kind of like the Ark itself—so I'm going to have to finish." He paused for a second, and then smiled. Nick, I know I haven't been the greatest role model, but I've always given my clients my best. I've never concocted evidence, paid for false testimony…" He pointed to the manila file on the desk. "Or killed for a case.

"I always looked for the truth in every case and fought hard for it—to prove what I believed to be right and just. My failing was my misplaced generosity, and overindulgence in just about everything. Call it pride, stupidity, mental illness. I don't know. But one thing I do know is that I don't want you victimized by the greed inherent in this profession. Because you're so like me, I fear for you. I fear that you will compromise your integrity and you'll suffer as I have. Or that you'll wind up dead like me. So get out." Joe wiped his hands together. "Clean your hands and get out. Become a farmer, a fisherman. Paint houses if you have to. But get out while you still have your honor, and your life."

He reached toward the off button on the video camera. There was a blue flash, and Joe Maglio was gone.

CHAPTER XV

It was two o'clock in the afternoon on a cold, gray day in January. Nick Ceratto had been preparing the Riley case for trial for two solid weeks, and he needed a break. He had gone through piles of medical records, depositions, medical experts' reports, autopsy reports and witness statements. As far as he was concerned, the case was still a slam dunk. He should have been ecstatic.

But he wasn't. He really didn't want to try this case. There was something wrong— something fishy about it. He couldn't get a handle on why he felt this way. The doctor was too good. The chances of him doing a lousy job were slim to none. He had hoped for a call from John Asher with a settlement offer, but none had come. And he figured that it was because Manin had remained steadfast in his refusal to settle.

Nick admired Manin. He saw in him what he had rarely seen in other defendants—especially in the medical profession—a dedicated physician with a humility and a true concern for others, a kindness and gentleness that made it difficult for him to go after Manin the way he should. Manin was a nice guy as well as a brilliant doctor, and defendants were not supposed to be that way, according to what he had been taught—according to Joe.

He knew that if he got an excess verdict, a verdict above the policy limits, the excess would have to come out of Manin's pocket. More than likely, it would destroy him. One more Good Samaritan down the tubes. Manin's wife, Nick had learned, had walked out on him because he had refused to settle, and the results could cramp her lifestyle. Manin was not the same. He was barely hanging on to his practice.

Enough, Nick thought. He wanted fresh air and a change of scene. He coaxed Maria away from the voluminous printout of the Maglio, Silvio and Levin bank account she had gotten from

Banco d'Italia on the pretext of doing a routine quarterly audit. She had been spending most of her time tracking credits, debits, and transfers from and to the firm's account for the past ten years. She balked but was able to be pried away, her stomach telling her that it was mealtime. She was starving. She hadn't eaten since noon yesterday, and it was noon again now—time for Sunday brunch.

They showered and dressed, barely speaking to each other as each thought and rethought about the trial, the bank accounts, the tape and the missing file, the deaths, and how nothing made any sense. Nothing tied together. Each event seemed a piece of an incomplete puzzle—each a mystery unto itself. Still lost in thought and not speaking, they hailed a taxi and headed for the Four Seasons Hotel.

Nick chose a table facing a large window looking out on the Benjamin Franklin Parkway. The Four Seasons had the best brunch in town, and even on a cold, gray Sunday the view was awesome. Traffic was minimal. A brownstone Victorian gothic cathedral loomed up on the other side of the Parkway. The view reminded Maria Elena of a winter scene in Paris. Large Sagamore trees, now skeletons, spread their powerful arms skyward as if to pull everything into their reach. To the left, the Parkway split to encircle a now dry fountain surrounded by bronze nudes covered with verdigris. They reclined on its edge, clutching struggling swans. Maria wondered, *Why swans?* Perhaps because of their grace, perhaps they represented something the viewer should know. She didn't know. They were just beautiful and that was enough. Their powerful bronze captors were composed and unfazed by everything around them, the traffic, the cold. They were eternal, like statues in Rome. They would never die. They were perfect, unlike herself.

Her eyes then moved to Nick. He hadn't shaved in two days, and she was worried. Although he was strikingly handsome with his five o'clock shadow, he looked tired. No, he *was* tired, she thought. She recognized the conflict in his eyes—conflict about whether he should try the case, withdraw from the case. Resign. She saw his eyes as he considered each option. Back and forth and then back again to the beginning.

He poured himself a third glass of chilled Pinot Grigio and stared at the razor-thin tuna carpaccio carefully arranged over baby greens on his plate. He wasn't hungry, and was feeling the wine.

"He didn't do it," she said.

"Who didn't do what?" knowing full well *who* and *what* she meant.

"Manin. He's innocent." She skewered a seared scallop.

"How do you know?" Nick played with his tuna, swirling it in the olive oil dressing.

"Eat. You're going to get sick," she said, avoiding the question. "Here." She lifted a scallop from her plate with her fork and put it to his mouth. "Open. You haven't eaten in two days."

Nick took the scallop and washed it down with a large swallow of wine. "I should have ordered the scallops. I don't know what I was thinking," he said smiling. "I hate raw fish."

"Here, take mine. I like raw tuna." Maria stood, leaning over the damask covered table, careful to avoid the burning candle and floral arrangement. She switched her plate with Nick's.

Nick knew he had no choice. She'd never accept no. So he ate the switched appetizer and actually felt better. "How *do* you know? You never answered my question."

"Know what?"

"Come on," he said. "You know what I mean. Don't play games."

"You play games, too. So why can't I?" She took a sip of her wine and blotted her full lips with her napkin.

"OK, you're right. Let's be straight with each other. I'm trying this case in less than two weeks, and you're telling me that you know Manin didn't malpractice. I've got to convince a jury that he *did*. So what do *you* know that I don't?"

"It's simple. I know because I feel it in here," she said, pointing to her heart. "And here," pointing to her head. "I know by his face that he's telling the truth. A liar doesn't have a face like his. He never took his eyes off you when you questioned him—no matter how you turned and twisted what he said. He always had the same answer.

"Is that all you have?" he mocked. "That the doctor looked honest and kind, and sounded truthful? Maria, do you know how many defendants should get Academy Awards when they lie on the witness stand?"

"He's not lying." She stood and pushed her chair back. "And you're going to lose. No jury is going to find him guilty."

"You *want* me to lose?" he asked rising from his chair, throwing his napkin down on the table.

Two waiters turned and stared as the couple argued. The conversation fascinated them and they couldn't help listening.

"No, I don't *want* you to lose. *Tu se matto.* You're crazy!" she yelled. "All I want is for you to find the truth—the truth about this case. This innocent is depending on you to be fair and honest."

"It's not my job to be fair and honest. It's my job to win," he yelled back, his jugular bulging from his neck. "What about Sean Riley? What about his wife? His kids? Who was fair and honest to them? It's my job to represent them to the best of my ability. They hired *me* to fight for them and to come home with the bacon."

"For you and your crooked partners, you mean." She slapped him across the face. "The ones who killed my cousin."

Nick turned away. His anger told him to choke the bitch, or at least give her a good back hand. Instead he threw his American Express card on the table and stormed out of the Fountain Room to the coat check area in the lobby.

She followed, throwing up her hands, yelling a string of obscenities. Too bad that no one understood what she said. She followed the headwaiter, who had chased Nick to the curb with his credit card. Nick put twenty dollars on the line of the charge slip for gratuities. The waiter scuttled away leaving Nick and Maria to continue their screaming match.

"You swore to uphold the law. The truth is first, isn't it?" Her eyes flashed. "Are you going into that courtroom just to crucify this innocent man—a doctor who cares about people? Isn't your job to find the truth? Isn't that winning?"

"No." Nick gritted his teeth. "*My job is to win for my clients.* Asher's job is to win for *his*." Nick pointed a finger directly at her.

She didn't budge an inch. "You didn't hear anything Joe Maglio said in that tape, did you? You don't care about anybody but yourself. You don't care about finding Joe's murderer, do you? You just want to make money for those bloodsucking thieves. That's all you care about—money is everything to you. I know this now. The tape meant nothing to you. You're doing nothing about it. That's why I went to Mike Rosa with it. Because he's a man—a man of honor and *he* cares about the truth."

"And you?" Nick snapped. "Does he care about you, too?"

"Yes, he does," she answered. "And he's going to help me—because you won't."

"Fuck you." He waved at a passing cab which immediately slid next to the curb. In a flash Nick opened the door and was in. The door slammed shut and he was gone. All before Maria could say, "He was great."

His study was dark except for one small light that illuminated the papers in front of him—reams of medical records.

The telephone rang loudly, startling Nick out of his trance. His gaze was fixed on the lengthy autopsy report he had stopped reading half an hour ago. He refused to pick up the phone.

"This is Nick Ceratto. Leave me a message."

"Mr. Ceratto, this is Ralph Kirby of homicide. Please call…"

Nick quickly changed his mind and snatched the receiver. "Yes…"

"Mr. Ceratto?"

"Yes."

"This is Ralph Kirby."

"Yes, I know. I heard you. What can I do for you?"

"Ah." Kirby paused, typically reaching for the appropriate words to phrase a request. "I wonder if you could help me. The chief wants me to wrap up the Lopez case. All the final reports are due this coming week. The DA, Muriel Gates, you know…"

"Yes, I know…"

"Well, she's got this thing about concluding this case. She wants all investigation suspended. She says we've got other murders to solve. She thinks this was an open-and-shut street murder, a drug-related case. And the perpetrator will show up sooner or later murdering someone else in the neighborhood—hopefully another doper…"

"And I still don't know what you want from me," Nick broke in impatiently.

"Well, I want to know if there's anything else you could tell me about Ms. Lopez that might be relevant to her case." He paused. "You know, before we close the case."

Nick thought for a moment, wondering what the detective might be up to. What could he tell him? Nothing, except about the tape and the file which Celia was supposed to have had. Maybe Kirby was playing cat-and-mouse with him. Maybe the old detective knew about the tape and was setting him up. He decided to play the same game.

"I don't believe there's anything I can tell you that you don't already know, Detective."

"I didn't think so. But," he chuckled. Nick could hear him drawing on his cigarette and inhaling the smoke. "I thought I'd try."

"Is that all…?"

"Ah," Kirby inhaled again. "One more thing…"

Nick sighed loudly, purposely, hoping Kirby would get the message that he was annoyed and at the end of his rope.

"Would you have happened to have found a key?"

"A key?"

"Yes, a small key, like a luggage key. It was in Ms. Lopez's safe-deposit box. It was on my desk with other contents of the box. Now it's gone I thought maybe I picked it up inadvertently with the film when I was bringing it to your apartment. Maybe it dropped out of my pocket when I took out the film."

"No, Detective. I haven't seen any key" Nick didn't like this. Kirby was asking too many questions, and Nick didn't believe in coincidence.

"Well, would you look for it? I'd really appreciate it."

"Detective Kirby. I would have come across it by now."

"Maybe so—but…"

"I'll look for it. OK?"

"Thank you, Mr. Ceratto. It was such a small key that it could be…"

"Good-bye, Detective."

"Ah—good-bye Mr. Ceratto." Kirby snuffed out the last inch of his cigarette, smiling. *The kid knows more*, he thought.

Nick was five minutes into Nurse Doletov's deposition when the phone rang again. He ignored the ringing and continued reading the deposition transcript:

> *Q: Were you present at the surgery of plaintiff's decedent, Sean Riley?*
>
> *A: Yes, I was.*
>
> *Q: And what was your position during that surgery?*
>
> *A: I was the chief operating room nurse.*
>
> *Q: And did you assist Dr. Manin throughout the course of the surgery?*
>
> *A: Yes, the entire procedure.*
>
> *Q: Including the closing of the incision?*
>
> *A: Yes, I was his assistant.*

"This is Nick Ceratto. Leave me a message."

"Nick, please pick up." Maria's voice was urgent. "I have something important to tell you." She paused, waiting. She sighed. "Nick, I know we had a fight. I'm sorry—sorry for doubting you… Please, please answer the phone."

He was torn between Maria and his pride. His pride won and he went back to Nurse Doletov's deposition:

> *Q: And did you go into the recovery room with the patient?*
>
> *A: Yes, that was the procedure we always followed.*
>
> *Q: And did you follow that procedure with Sean Riley?…*

The receiver was put down. Nick went for the Glenfiddich and poured himself a double.

Chapter XVI

The giant mahogany doors to the conference room were locked and the phones were put on DO NOT DISTURB. Harry Levin led the meeting. Marty Silvio sat at one end of the long table, shoeless feet propped up on the mirror like surface chewing on an unlit Cuban cigar. Levin paced as he spoke, occasionally glancing at his fuzzy image reflected in the table. Nick sat center and listened, as he was supposed to do.

"Tort reform is killing us. Just like it is every other plaintiff's firm in the city, the state…"

"Commonwealth," Nick corrected, still looking down at his notepad.

"OK. Commonwealth. State, fucking country. Whatever, it's killing us. That's what I'm concerned about. I'm concerned about *us*. Our cases have dropped in number. Every case we win is appealed these days. We have to wait for our money and at the same time keep this monster of a law firm alive, and everybody paid. Health insurance, 401ks. It's crazy. Expenses keep going up. As a matter of fact, they're out of control." Levin waved his arms wildly. "Juries are cheap as hell and getting cheaper by the year. Negative advertising is all over the place—TV and newspapers, never mind the billboards with pictures of plaintiffs behind bars," he sneered. "The insurance companies' message is sinking in. Every plaintiff is a phony. Every plaintiff's lawyer is a crook. While all along the insurance companies are the real robber barons. They make us look like Orphan Annie. Raising premiums, not paying claims, scaring the shit out of everyone."

Silvio rocked back in his red leather, swivel armchair. Taking the cigar out of his mouth momentarily, "We all know this, Harry. Even Nicky here , as young as he is, knows all this. Now what?"

"We have to fight fire with fire."

Levin pounded the table and quickly walked toward Nick. "If you're going to be a partner, you should know that you have a heavy burden to carry here. Not only winning cases, but also bringing them in. You have to have your finger on this business, on building it. You just can't take inventory for granted. It's not always going to be there. You'll have to think about creative ways of bringing in new clients, new contacts, new rainmaking talent. These political action committees and lobbyists aren't enough to keep us going. We increase contributions, grease politicians and judges, and what good does it do us? They take our money and fuck us anyhow."

Levin paused, looking at the ceiling. His hair stuck out at the sides from putting his glasses on and removing them. "I'll tell you." He paced some more and walked back to Nick. "It doesn't do us any good at all. So we have to go right to the horse's mouth. Find more runners and pay them."

"Those whores take more than twenty percent of our fees as it is," Silvio protested. "How can we pay them any more?"

Nick hadn't known the firm used runners. But he wasn't surprised, not after having watched the tape. Silvio and Levin now obviously thought him worthy of receiving the knowledge. Now that he was big time—just as Joe had predicted. Before seeing the tape, he had thought this firm was immune from the problems facing the plaintiff's bar. *How naive*, he thought, chuckling to himself. Joe had warned him about this, and now here it was.

"If we don't pay, we don't play," Levin continued, "Those bastards will just peddle the cases to another firm, that's all. So we cut expenses somewhere else and pay them more.

"Where are we supposed to cut expenses?" Silvio's words were barely intelligible since his lips were wrapped around the huge cigar.

"I guess we have to fire a few people," Nick joked, laughing at his own suggestion.

"That's right. We need to get rid of the fluff," agreed Levin enthusiastically. He folded his arms across his chest and nodded approvingly like a professor who had just gotten the answer he was looking for.

"Like who?" Suddenly Silvio became alert and interested.

"Like the translator we just hired. We can outsource all translations. There are plenty of companies out there that can provide us with court-certified translators for every language under the sun; Spanish, French, Nigerian…"

Nick wrote two names on his pad, tore off the page, and handed it to Levin. "Pro Trans is one and Global Life Speak is another. I'm surprised that you guys don't know about these firms. I see them at depositions and in court all the time."

"When was Harry last in court?" mocked Silvio.

"And when were you? When did you ever have a bell ringer of a verdict?" Levin shot back.

Silvio slid his feet off the table, put his cigar down, rose from his chair, and moved menacingly toward Levin. "At least I've tried a case, you fuzzy-headed Jew. You never fucking darkened the steps of City Hall."

Nick stood, reaching to pull Silvio from Levin if necessary. "This is no time to get personal. Let's have a civilized discussion and get on with business. I've got a case to try in ten days, and I need to get back to work."

Silvio moved back to his chair, loosening his tie. His neck was red and his forehead wet. "Sounds like Maglio. Must have rubbed off," he said, spitting a piece of cigar into the ashtray. "So who else goes?"

They decided each would prepare a list of five employees—all the most junior and none of them women, Hispanics, or black, since they were protected under federal employment laws—Title VII. The last thing Silvio and Levin, soon to be Levin, Silvio and Ceratto, wanted was the EEOC on its back.

Giorgio Santangelo was first on Silvio's list. He hated the way Margo looked at him. He knew lust when he saw it, and he didn't need the greaser as competition. Nick protested, saying that the firm needed him not only for catering its parties,but also because he had quite a following. Giorgio was a fixture with the judges and politicians. He added class and refinement to the firm. And if he was fired, he'd go to the enemy; one of the defense firms, and the loyalties of certain powerful people might go with him. Like the Honorable Josephine Hanks and Joseph Barnes, not to mention the mayor, Jack Filbert.

Levin was quick to agree. Silvio was outnumbered and sank deeper into his chair with his cigar, fantasizing about sending the bastard back to Italy, preferably in a box. Nick sat quietly listening to Levin carry on.

"Your share of the draw depends on the percentage of cases you bring in. Don't think you're a prima donna because you try big cases and win some of them." Levin pointed to Nick who understood the reference to Joe, although Joe's name was never mentioned in this context. "You have to make contacts, develop your sources—instead of spending all your spare time with that Italian girl, whatever her name is…"

"Maria Elena." Nick sank down in his chair. How much more could he take without punching the asshole in the face? No wonder Joe had hated these bastards, he thought.

"Whatever," Levin said, ignoring her name, ignoring her humanity. "She bothers me, the way she hangs around here, in the library, in the file rooms. What the hell is she doing, anyway?"

Nick felt the blood rush to his temples. He would have liked to kill Levin. But he kept his cool. "I don't know how to answer that question, Harry. Except that she's curious. She's fascinated. And she likes the firm."

"Tell her to go down the street. There's a thousand law firms down the block."

Silvio chuckled. "Now he's picking on you, Nick. He's always picking on somebody. One day he's going to pick on the wrong guy, and wham!" Laughing, he smashed his hand on the table as though he were killing a bug. Then he abruptly stopped laughing and looked squarely at Levin. "I like her. She's kinda cute. She adds that cosmopolitan air, that charm, that…" he mocked, laughing again. He stopped. "Why're you so upset, Harry? She's not bothering anybody."

"She makes me nervous, the way she snoops around here. She walks around like she owns the place."

"Look," Nick said defensively, "I know I'm not a partner yet, but I *am* partnership material. I'll *be* a partner in a month…" He hesitated. "Hopefully—so can we cool it with Maria? She's only here for another month. She's a law student, an exchange student. She's studying at Temple, that's all. No big deal. Cut her some slack."

"Tell her to stay at Temple." Levin was dogged in his hate for her.

Nick had just about had it when there was a light tap on the conference room door. He rose and opened it. Mary O'Donald, one of the older secretaries—one who could get away with interrupting a partners' meeting—peeped into the room.

"I'm sorry to disturb you, Mr. Ceratto. But it's Ms. Nardo. She said it's urgent. She's called three times. I told her you were in an important meeting and couldn't be disturbed. But she said you'd be very upset if I didn't disturb you…should I tell her to call back?'

"No. That's fine, Mary. I'll take it in my office." It was a perfect excuse to escape, and he jumped at it. His nerves were shot, and his ability to control his temper was evaporating. He walked out without excusing himself.

He had moved into Joe Maglio's office. He had left Joe's memorabilia intact, just as it had been: the photo of Joe with President Clinton at a five thousand dollar a plate fundraiser, Joe with the Pope at St. Peter's Basilica, Joe with Frank Sinatra, the autographs, an engraving of Sir Thomas More, first editions of *Pride and Prejudice*, *Tom Jones*, and *Pickwick Papers*. It gave Nick a sense of continuity, a sense that Joe was still there, ready to help him, to protect him. Sometimes it felt eerie, but mostly it was comforting. Except when he thought about the tape. Then he felt guilty about doing nothing about Joe. But first things first. He had *Riley* to try, and that was in compartment number one. Joe was in compartment two, which he knew would require all his time and energy when he opened it.

"Hello."

"Oh, Nick. I'm so sorry about last weekend, I…"

"It's OK," he interrupted, coldly. "I was drunk."

"Nick, I need to see you. I have the information that we need," she said in a triumphant tone.

"Where are you?"

"I'm in Tel Aviv right now."

"Tel Aviv—what the hell are you doing there?"

"I was examining records, bank records at Bank Naomi. And I struck gold. Yes, gold, Nick," she laughed. "I'll tell you all about it when I see you tomorrow night. I land at Philadelphia International at 10:30 p.m."

"What airline?"

"El Al, flight 1006."

"I'll pick you up at the airport."

"No, no. I can take a taxi. It's easier for me. I won't have to worry about you waiting if the flight is delayed. You have to work on your trial."

He could hear her breathe, almost see her as he closed his eyes. He imagined how she must look and smell, with her hair blowing softly around her face, her smile, her luminous hazel eyes, her full breasts, her soft hips, long legs. He felt himself getting hard. She excited him like no other woman.

"I can't wait, Nick. I can't wait to tell you…"

"And I can't wait to see you , Maria. I'm sorry for my bad temper…"

"No, no, I deserved it. My temper was terrible—*is* terrible. I can't help it, it's a Maglio trait. We make a great pair, no?"

"We do make a great pair, yes," he sank back into the well-worn leather desk chair.

"I know," she laughed. "Make me dinner. I'm going to be very hungry when I arrive."

"How about veal with pepperoni and Marsala." He could feel his heart pounding. "We'll eat, drink wine, and make love."

"All night?"

"All night—and no fighting. Promise?"

"No fighting," she said. "*Ti amo.*"

He wanted to respond, but he hesitated a second. Before he could say "I love you, too," she said, *"Ciao,"* and hung up.

Levin punched the button under the edge of the conference table, silencing the bug on the phone in Joe Maglio's old office.

"Comes in handy, doesn't it? Aren't you glad I talked you into putting it in?"

"Yeah, I guess. But I really liked that girl. She had class." Silvio shook his head. "It's a fucking shame." He pulled his cell phone from his jacket pocket and dialed. He waited for the familiar voice to answer.

"What can I do for you today, Mr. Silvio?"

"I have another job for you."

Chapter XVII

It had been raining since six p.m. It was now ten o'clock at night, and the fog was dense. The air had warmed up to fifty degrees, a record for January thirtieth. He gnawed viciously on the steak and onion sandwich he had just purchased at Pat's Steaks. He blended in with the other inner city cab drivers talking with full mouths, standing outside Pat's eating steak sandwiches. The peppers he had plastered on the meat were hotter than he had expected. He choked and spit out a mouthful and disgustedly threw the rest of the still-wrapped sandwich into the trash barrel outside the corner establishment. The other drivers laughed. One of them pulled the uneaten portion from the barrel and gave it to the homeless man who hung out around the weirdly V-shaped outdoor diner.

Rudi jumped back into his cab and headed toward I-95. His headlights flooded the murkiness, but all he could really see was the steam rising from the road surface just in front of him. He cursed the lack of visibility. Arriving at Philadelphia International Airport at 10:20, he pulled into the cab stand at the Overseas terminal to wait for his passenger. He had checked with El Al and was told that flight 1005 was due to arrive on schedule. He had ten minutes to get rid of the cabs ahead of him and the ground transportation dispatcher. They would fuck up his plans if allowed to remain. He went directly into the airport and up the nearest escalator. Two minutes later he emerged, waving his arms, cursing, shouting that all international flights had been canceled until tomorrow morning due to the weather. The other drivers began leaving one by one for greener fields.

Rudi turned to the dispatcher, who had motioned him to move his cab. Speaking with a heavy Middle Eastern accent, "I need to stay, mister. I got to pick up a worker who's sick, she works upstairs. She's my sister…"

The dispatcher shook his head no, but Rudi immediately laid a twenty dollar bill on top of his desk. "Please, she's my sister and she's pregnant."

The dispatcher took the twenty and without a word strolled into the airport.

Rudi smiled, always amazed at his talent, as he reentered the cab. He checked his disguise in the rear view mirror. He looked the part—Middle Eastern, aquiline nose, dark complexion—dressed in neatly pressed khakis, jean jacket, and aviator glasses. He smiled approvingly. No Hollywood director or makeup artist could have done a better job. He thought of how he loved the challenge and artistry in his job. If he didn't like the real thing so much, he could have been an actor, and a good one at that. But he loved real death and real blood. He checked his watch. He had less than five minutes. He pulled his cab to the other side of the road, away from the sidewalk in front of the glass exit doors, and backed as far away as possible, still keeping a clear view through the lighted doors into the terminal. The lighting was yellow and eerie. It made his heart race. He was excited. He turned his headlights off so as not to attract the wrong passenger.

A man emerged from the yellow light, carrying a briefcase and pulling a black carryon. He spotted the cab through the fog and started toward it. Rudi leaned out of the open window and waved him away, but the man continued walking toward him. Rudi shook his head no and rolled up the window. But the would-be passenger began knocking on the closed window until he saw the driver slowly reach into his inside jacket pocket. Wisely, the man turned toward the safety of the terminal, where he could call another cab.

Rudi strained to see through the drifting fog and caught a glimpse of a shadowy figure of a woman with long hair, young, lean. She walked assertively through the glass doors. As she came closer, her image became clearer—it was her. He quickly compared her with the photo Silvio had sent by messenger. He readied himself, thanking his mother for telling him that he could be anything he wanted—this time a Middle Eastern cab driver with a three hundred thousand dollar fare—not bad for one night's work.

She saw the deserted cab stand. "*Merde*," she said.

Rudi turned on his taxi sign and flashed his headlights at her, and then waited. She waved at the cab, signaling him to come over to her as she slung her large, black tote bag over her shoulder. The cab didn't move.

"Taxi!" she yelled, "Taxi." she waved.

He flashed his headlights again, but didn't move.

"Taxi!" She stepped off the curb into the road. He switched his headlights to bright and started to move toward her. The lights blinded her as they came closer. She shielded her eyes with her free hand. She yelled at the faceless driver, "*Bruto!*" The engine revved loudly over the sound of her voice. Suddenly the blinding lights were on top of her. She had no time to escape, to scream. It was too late.

The thud of the cab striking her was music to Rudi's ears. The sight of her body catapulting over the hood of the cab was magnificent—a grand maneuver. No stunt man or woman could possibly fake this, he thought. This was the real thing. Maria smashed into the chain link fence on the other side of the road. It clanged loudly, and then bowed as her body slid to the ground.

Rudi pounded the steering wheel with clenched fists. "Yes, yes!" He quickly opened the door of the cab, leaped out, and ran to the crumpled, bleeding figure. He snatched the black tote bag and tossed it into his cab, humming Ravel's *Bolero* as he sped off into the fog toward I-95. He wished that he could have videotaped it—her face, beautifully wide-eyed and unsuspecting, like a deer caught in his headlights. And then—poof! like magic, she was gone. God, he loved his job!

Chapter XVIII

Nick nervously paced back and forth in his living room, watching the hands of the antique case clock. It had chimed eleven o'clock twenty minutes ago. He was worried. And he was pissed off at himself for not insisting on picking Maria up at the airport. He poured a glass of Chianti from a newly opened bottle of *Badia a Coltibuono* and took a swallow. He listened to the ticking of the old clock in the otherwise silent apartment.

Floured medallions of veal lay on a plate next to a sauté pan. Marsala sauce waited in a bowl next to the veal.

He had an apology speech ready. He had practiced it a dozen times. The glass dining table was set, the candles were lit, and the roses he had bought were already starting to wilt. Where *was* she, he asked himself. The plane had landed on time. He had already checked with the airport. Could there have been a car accident on the way to his apartment? He could barely make out the Benjamin Franklin bridge through the fog bank outside his penthouse window. He didn't like fog; it made him feel claustrophobic. It was like a heavy drape pulled across his mirror of the world. He fought the feeling. Then came another demon. The image of Madeline's dying body against the backdrop of all the machines that couldn't keep her alive. When the cancer had had its way with his mother, they had called him in to see her. He never forgot it, her shriveled body unresponsive to his pleas and his cries. He was ten years old then, and she was the only person on whom he could rely. His alcoholic father was useless. He beat them and stole their money for booze until one day Nick hit him with a baseball bat and sent him to the hospital with a skull fracture. The bastard didn't attend Madeline's funeral, and Nick didn't attend *his* when he was burned alive in a house fire on skid row.

Nick was still a kid, but he had gotten a reputation as a tough guy after putting his father in the hospital. The story had reached the ears of Vince DiCicco, head of the Philadelphia mob. Nick was alone and needed a family, and DiCicco needed a trustworthy bag boy to run cash between card games. Later, he was promoted to chauffeur and almost got himself killed a few times by a stray bullet. He would have been a dead man, or in jail, if it hadn't been for Joe Maglio.

The phone rang, jolting him out of his reverie.

"Hello"

"Mr. Ceratto?" asked a familiar sounding voice. "This is Detective Kirby. Remember me?"

"Yes, Detective."

"Sorry for the call this late. But I'm afraid I have bad news for you." Kirby was direct and brief. He extended his sympathies but did not stay on the line. He had work to do.

When the line went dead, Nick looked at the receiver in disbelief. Then he pulled the phone out of the jack and threw it against the window with all his strength, shattering the double-paned glass.

Chapter XIX

"A hit and run," Kirby said on the telephone. The ash from his most recent cigarette dropped onto his burnt, scarred desk. "That's all we've got right now, Captain. She had just come in on an El Al flight from Tel Aviv. Yeah. She just got off the plane. No luggage. Nothing checked on the plane. And no purse. Could have been stolen. She had her passport in her pocket. That's how we IDed her…Italian…yeah…I called her boyfriend, Nick Ceratto. I know him. I had met her at his apartment. Just a coincidence, I guess…Yeah, Nick Ceratto, from the same firm. They should be in the funeral business." Kirby chuckled slyly, drawing deeply. More ash fell into his lap. He ignored it.

"Some guy coming in on the same flight heard about it on the news and called the department…yeah…He'd seen a taxi across the road waiting in the dark that wouldn't pick him up. The driver reached in his coat pocket for something when the guy banged on the window, so he split. We were already out to talk to him. We got nothing—no make, no model, no license tag, not even the cab company. The dispatcher left because of the fog. He thought all flights had been canceled. Was seen at the airport bar. Real idiot, right? We're following up with that…I'll keep you posted, Captain." Kirby nodded his gray head, wondering where he got all the patience. "I'll get a report out right away, Cap. She has to be formally identified. Then the body can go straight to he medical examiner for an autopsy. But we'll have the report in a few hours… Yeah, the boyfriend, Ceratto's going to do it. I feel sorry for him. She's a mess. Car musta been flying when it slammed into her… Yeah, we're checking him out, too…no stone unturned, Captain. I'm meeting him at the morgue right now…Yeah, bye."

Kirby slowly raised himself from his desk chair. His arthritic knees protested the change in position. He buttoned his frayed shirt collar and pulled up his only tie. *More bodies,* he thought as he reached for his ancient coat. He put it on slowly, grimacing with the creaking of his aching bones.

Nick had been waiting for half an hour at 321 University Avenue, the medical examiner's headquarters. He sat alone on the scruffy steel and vinyl bench. He had been told that he had to wait for Detective Kirby before he would be permitted to see her. Nick was fuming inside. He got up and paced, hands in pockets. He turned on the male receptionist at the desk.

"Jesus Christ! I've been here a fucking half hour. I want to see her now!" he yelled, pointing a finger in the pale face of the man sitting at a scratched piece of metal furniture that vaguely resembled a desk.

"Sir, I have my orders. You'll have to wait. I'm sorry." The man went back to reading *The Daily News* and munching a Baby Ruth.

"I don't care if I have to pull every corpse out of every fucking drawer—I'll find her." Nick started to walk past the receptionist. Just then the heavy metal door opened with a loud bang.

"Mr. Ceratto," Kirby rushed in, breathless. "I'm so sorry you had to wait…"

"Yeah, I'm sure you are." Nick stood his ground menacingly as Kirby approached. The detective nodded at the receptionist and the young man pressed the buzzer, opening the automatic door into the morgue.

It was quiet and it was cold. The place had the stale smell of death. Nick knew it well. It was the arrested decomposition of human flesh without the masking smell of flowers.

They approached the viewing room and stood on one side of the glass wall.

"I want to warn you. She's a mess," Kirby said apologetically, hands tucked deeply into his pockets.

Nick remained silent, his heart pounding. He wanted to turn and run. He wanted to pretend that whatever was lying in there wasn't her. But he stayed, staring at the darkened glass. "Let's do it."

Kirby gave a signal and the lights were turned on. An attendant wearing a blue uniform and latex gloves wheeled a gurney up to the glass partition. He peeled back a black plastic sheet, uncovering Maria Elena to the collarbone.

Nick reeled. He turned his head. He'd seen death before. He'd seen mangled corpses, shot, stabbed, burned—but nothing like this. She was more than a mess. Her hair was a tangled mass of coagulated blood. Half her face had been torn off by the rough road surface. There were so many broken facial bones that there was hardly a nose or cheek. One eye was gone, and her jaw was so twisted it almost touched her left ear. He turned and vomited heavily on the white tile floor. He wiped his mouth with back of his hand. He screamed with a rage he had never known before.

Kirby waved the attendant away and the room went dark. He said nothing. He couldn't find any words.

"*They* did this," Nick's voice cracked. He was barely able to speak. "*They* knew what she had, and they fucking killed her for it. Squashed her like an insect." He turned and walked through the double doors past the man who was still chewing on his candy bar. Kirby quickly followed.

"Look, I know this is a bad time—a terrible time."

"Yes it is, Mr. Kirby. It sure is." Nick pulled his coat collar up and walked out of the building toward the parking lot.

"Mr. Ceratto, can you stop for a minute?" Kirby hobbled slightly from the pain in his arthritic knees. He couldn't keep up with the fast-walking younger man. "I'd like to talk to you, sir, just for a minute.

Nick turned to him, reaching into his coat pocket for the keys to his red Boxster. "I don't have time to talk," he snapped. "I have work to do." He squeezed the plastic tab on his key chain, and the car door locks clicked open.

"You're right, you know."

"Right about what?" snapped Nick, standing against the low sports car.

"About *them.*" Kirby took a cigarette out of the pack from the pocket in his threadbare coat. He lit it with one click from the cheap Bic lighter. His lined face was illuminated briefly by the flame, and Kirby's honesty became apparent to Nick in that one moment. He held the pack out to Nick, who took one and put it in his mouth. He drew on it heavily as Kirby lit it for him.

Kirby examined the face in the flame. It was young and determined, much like his when he was young. Kirby was not a believer in coincidence. He feared that the young trial lawyer might be next.

"So, now what?" Nick blew the smoke past Kirby's face.

"Don't know. It's all in the hands of Ms. Gates. Depends on what she wants to do."

"No. It's not. It's in my hands now. And I know what I have to do."

Chapter XX

Silvio refused to answer the phone. He had turned off the ringer so he wouldn't hear Celeste's whining, telling him to remember to lock the front door and feed the cat he had hated ever since she brought it home as a kitten, ten years ago. He had planned to poison it but decided against it after thinking about how she would complain about missing it, being lonely, how her life was meaningless. Celeste was on a retreat with her group, the Ladies of the Blessed Sacrament. They were praying for him in San Francisco, three thousand miles away, for one whole week. If he had believed in God, he would have thanked him.

Margo Griffin couldn't stand the ringing anymore. Silvio hadn't budged as he lay on the bed next to her. She grabbed the receiver, saying nothing as she lifted it to her ear in case it was the "holy one."

"Hello," a heavily accented male voice said. "Hello?"

"Yes?" She was careful to say nothing more.

"Is Mr. Silvio there?"

"Asleep," she answered curtly.

"Mrs. Silvio, I gather?"

Margo didn't respond.

"Sorry for disturbing you, but I must speak with Mr. Silvio. I'm calling from Tel Aviv."

"Hold."

Silvio lay with his back to her. Margo reluctantly shook his large, hairy shoulder. She knew how difficult he was to wake, and how pissed he could get when he was awakened.

"Marty, wake up. Marty."

"What?" he asked, giving her an elbow in the stomach as he flopped over.

"Ouch, you bastard," she said, holding her hand over the receiver. "Some asshole insists on speaking with you. He says he's calling from Tel Aviv."

Silvio bolted upright and grabbed the receiver. "Yes?"

"Mr. Silvio, I know this is very late your time and I'm sorry for the call. My name is Ari Miller. I'm with international accounts at the Bank Naomi. I must inform you, sir, that someone posing as a branch examiner obtained access to your account, the Midas Limited account in particular."

"How the hell did this happen?" Silvio went for the cold, damp cigar left from the night before.

"Well, sir, it was a woman, very beautiful. And she, well…" he stammered. "She used her charms to convince one of our managers to give her access to the account without consulting me first. She knew about the numbered Swiss accounts and their transfers to the Midas accounts. I'm sorry to say that she downloaded the account information onto a disc, so we were told."

"That's a disgrace!" Marty yelled. "What kind of security do you have there? That woman could be a thief—could pilfer our accounts—could be a terrorist, for Christ's sake."

"I know. I'm so sorry. We have fired the person responsible for the security breach and have assigned new account numbers and double security codes for Midas."

"I ought to move the account," Silvio yelled, reaching for the yellow disc on the night stand and kissing it.

"Please don't do that, sir. We guarantee nothing like this will ever happen again."

"I'll have to think about it and ask my partner what he wants to do…"

"Sir, one more thing; when we questioned the young man we fired, he told us she also printed out the material from the disc, and then made a phone call to Philadelphia. I don't know if that means anything?"

"Do you have the print-out?" snapped Marty.

"No, I'm afraid she took it with her."

"Fuck!" he said, spitting a piece of cigar into an empty glass. Rudi had only given him the disc, nothing more, and now he was worried. "Are you sure about the print-out? About the papers?"

"Yes. Why would the man mention the print-out if she only had a disc? He was with her all the time."

"Great. Just fucking great." Silvio's mind raced. What to do? What to do?

"Sorry…" Miller was about to go into another apologetic litany, but Silvio didn't let him.

"You're dead, Ari Miller. I'll see you're fired, too, you incompetent fuck!" and Silvio slammed down the receiver. He walked around the bed, balls-naked, to his jacket on the floor. He fumbled in the inside pocket for his cell phone and quickly accessed a number. Margo watched Silvio's anxiety build. She didn't know what was going on, and she knew better than to ask.

"Hello there, Mr. Silvio. What brings you to the phone so late, another job?"

Silvio heard classical music playing loudly in the background. "Could you turn that down? I need to talk to you."

"What's the matter? You don't like Bach? I could switch to Mozart." Rudi laughed loudly, enjoying the knowledge that he was annoying the piss out of Silvio.

"Listen, I don't have time to play games, you sadistic bastard. It's late. I'm tired. I know you don't sleep, so just turn that music the fuck down so we can talk."

The sound quickly died. "Good," Silvio said. "Now, you gave me a disc from the girl's bag, right?"

"That's right."

"You said that's all there was in it besides girl stuff, clothes, makeup?"

"Right. That was it. That's what you wanted, right?"

"I want the bag. Where is it?"

"I burned it."

"You sure you burned it?"

"Of course. I always burn evidence."

"I just got a call from a bank in Tel Aviv where she was before her *accident*. They told me she was carrying documents—papers as well as a compact disc. Now I need those papers." He grabbed a dry cigar from the box on his dresser and paced the floor.

"Look, there weren't any papers in that bag. She was only carrying the disk. I'm telling you," he laughed. He could sense Silvio's blood pressure rising, while he enjoyed his own detachment.

"Rudi, don't hold out on me and try any funny stuff."

"Hey, I wouldn't think of blackmailing you, if that's what you're thinking. You're a good customer," Rudi said patronizingly.

"If you're lying to me, you fuck, I'll kill you myself."

There was a menacing chuckle on the other end, and then the music became audible again. "Boss, don't ever threaten me—please. See, I like you and I wouldn't want to have to shove that cigar up your ass just before I break your neck." Rudi hung up and turned to the sweet young thing he had found on the street. He caressed her naked breasts and then bit her left nipple. Her screams drowned out the music. Oh, how he loved his job. *Thank you, Mama.*

Silvio could not sleep. He continued to pace, ignoring Margo's pleas for him to go back to bed. She watched. He paced. He finally sat on her side of the bed and put his arms around her.

"Ceratto's going to be on trial in less than a week. I want you on the case with him."

"Me?" she asked. "I don't know anything about the Riley case."

"You will," he said menacingly. "I want you to get real close to him in the next few days. I want to know everything he's doing, everything he's thinking. I want to know what's on his desk and what's in his desk. Everything."

"What are you looking for, Marty?"

"Documents. Bank transactions from an Israeli bank."

"Israeli bank?" Her nose wrinkled in curiosity.

"Look, I can't tell you everything now. Just look for bank records. There won't be a name on the account. And possibly an envelope with an Israeli postmark. In the wrong hands, those documents could kill us." He put his hand lustfully on her knee. "I want you to spend time in Ceratto's apartment. I want you to comfort him. Got it? He's just suffered a great loss."

"You and Harry are in trouble again, aren't you?" she asked.

Silvio lay back, resting his large frame against the twisted pillows.

She put her arms around his thick shoulders and pulled him close. "You know I'll do anything for you, Marty."

CHAPTER XXI

Mike Rosa had just finished a weeklong murder trial. It was just after the jury had come in with a death penalty verdict that he'd heard the news of Maria Elena's death. It hit him like a ton of bricks, but he grieved privately, wondering if it was his punishment, the one he had expected, the one his Catholic upbringing had taught him to expect. And then got back to work.

It became all too clear that all the deaths were connected, and all were murders. Rosa was reminded by the video Maria had played for him that Joe was left-handed, yet the powder burns were on his right hand. Celia Lopez was Joe's most trusted employee besides Ceratto, and she was dead. Maria Elena, Joe's cousin and vindicator, who had a tape providing a motive, speculative as it might be, for Silvio's and Levin's involvement in Joe's death, was dead herself.

Rosa ordered the Maglio case off the back burner and called his best investigators together: "Leave no stone unturned," he said. "I want hard evidence, and I don't care how much it costs or how long it takes."

Nick Ceratto had escorted Maria's body back to San Lorenzo and into the capable hands of Ennio Correlli, funeral director *par excellence*. Correlli threw up his hands after seeing her. He said for the first time in his life he could do nothing. "*Niente.*" She was irreparable. Like a sculpture hacked to pieces by a madman. So they wrapped her in linen and buried her with the rest of the Maglio clan in the family hillside tomb. At the funeral, Maria's parents spat on Nick, accusing him of being responsible for her death. He couldn't argue with them. He felt guilty, guilty as accused. He stayed at the tomb after everyone had left and prayed for her forgiveness and help. He stayed until the caretaker was about to lock the gates of the cemetery. Then he kissed her tomb and vowed to return when he had vindicated her and Joe. And when he had put Silvio and Levin on death row.

Nick's mission was now clear. There was no turning back even if it cost him everything—including his career—and maybe his life. Kirby could offer him no help. Gates wanted to bury the Lopez murder, and she sure as shit wasn't going to find any connection between it and Maria Elena's death. She wouldn't embarrass her department by conducting an investigation of Silvio and Levin, her political supporters and the firm to which she referred civil cases—cases brought by the victims of the criminals she prosecuted. But only the cases where there were deep pockets, like hotels where there was poor security resulting in rape, death, or both.

Seven hours after leaving San Lorenzo, Nick was back in Philadelphia. He had made a call to be picked up by some old friends. His friends were dressed in suits and long black coats. They were Vincent DiCicco's men, and they dressed to command respect.

Their greeting consisted of an exchange of looks only. Then the men started to walk along the brightly lit airport corridor without saying a word. The six-foot, five-inch Joey "Shoes" positioned himself in front of Nick with "Little Al" behind. Their heads turned to and fro as they walked with a quick pace. Their peripheral vision was excellent, a requirement of the job. Soon they were down the escalator to the ground level and out the double glass doors. A black Lincoln Town Car with tinted windows was waiting at the curb. As soon as the men were inside, it sped off, north on I-95 to the Penn's Landing exit and then north on Columbus Boulevard to the La Gondola, a restaurant on the Delaware river owned and operated by Vincenzo DiCicco, better known as Don DiCicco, capo di capi, boss of the Philadelphia crime family, prime suspect, sometimes arrested but never convicted. His businesses were all *legitimate*—at least the visible ones were. He paid taxes, gave to charities, voted—and was despised by Muriel Gates. He called her a frustrated lesbian and the press ate it up. She called him a murdering thug, and the press ate that up, too. Frequently their pictures were side-by-side on the front page of the Philadelphia Daily News.

Nick was escorted past the spotless kitchen to a back room, a wine cellar where DiCicco held court every day, and took his meals. There were no windows, just racks of fine wine, a huge Italian provincial desk, a couple of heavily carved red velvet chairs, and a prominent picture of the Sacred Heart of Jesus peering from between two old photos of his immigrant parents. Don DiCicco sat regally behind the desk, waving Joey Shoes and Little Al away. He was a large man in every respect. His face was heavily jowled. His black hair was slicked back, and his pencil-thin mustache was dyed to match. He was dressed in a starched white shirt, buttoned to the neck. He wore no tie. A tie got in the way of good food, he always said.

"It's a pleasure to see you, Mr. Ceratto. What can I do for you?" DiCicco folded his chubby fingers leaving room for his two-carat pinky ring.

"*Con tuto respeto,*" Nick started with the expected formality, "I need a favor."

Chapter XXII

"What the fuck are you doing in here?" Nick asked, shocked to find Margo Griffin sitting at his desk going through one of the twelve accordion case folders in the Riley case.

"Oh. Hi, Nick," she said nervously. "I was assigned to assist you—to sit as second chair at the trial," she said, her legs crossed and her skirt purposely hiked up. "Aren't you glad?"

"No, I'm *not* glad, and you're *not* going to assist me," he snapped closing the door behind him.

Still smiling, she moved her hands from the file and laid them on the desktop. "Nick, don't panic. Relax. Silvio wants me to help you finalize the exhibits, to make sure the subpoenas went out, to help with the witnesses, to help you prep them."

"That's a paralegal's job, not yours." He dropped his heavy trial bag and approached his desk. "I'd appreciate it if you'd get out of my chair. I don't want to be rude, Margo, but I don't need you."

Her smile quickly became a frown. "Excuse me," she snapped defensively. "You can't throw me off the case, you're not a partner, you're not ..."

Nick took Margo's arm and gently pulled her up out of his chair. He noticed that the center drawer of his desk was partly open. He was sure that she had been snooping. "Your boss is going to have to reassign you to some other case, not my cases, and certainly not the Riley case. This is my office, not yours, and I'd appreciate you're respecting my space. "

Margo smoothed her skirt as she stood. "I've spent two days reviewing documents in this case, and you *do* need help. You're going to need motions in limine to hold out damaging evidence. You know Asher's a prick. He's going to kill you with Sean Riley's past alcohol addiction. He's going to introduce past disciplinary actions against your dead guy to smear his character. Riley was suspended once for shoving a suspect down the stairs and breaking his leg."

Nick pointed his finger in her face. "You tell Silvio that I don't want or need you. And I don't want you in my office again."

She cast her eyes down at the floor. "Nick, I'm not trying to step on your toes. I heard about Maria and I'm sorry. I know you're grieving, and I just wanted to help, that's all. Marty felt you could use some help now."

"Tell Marty thanks, but I'd rather do it myself." He walked to the door and held it open.

"What do you have against me?" she said, moving closer. Her eyes welled up with forced tears. "You hate me, don't you?"

"No. I hate being spied on, having my work scrutinized while I'm away. My office broken into, my papers read and rearranged—" He pointed to the massive file and the documents scattered on his desk. "And being told by an associate that she's going to sit second chair on a trial that's about to start in a few days—that's what I hate."

Nick dialed Silvio's extension while Margo dabbed her eyes. He felt bad about making her cry, but he was furious at her, at Silvio, at the world.

"Yeah, Nick." Silvio saw Nick's extension flash on his phone screen.

"Marty, what's all this about Margo taking over my office and this file?"

"She's only going to help you," he laughed. "What's all the paranoia?"

"I don't *want* help. And I don't need it. Thanks, but no thanks."

"You *do* need it. You only have a few days to prepare, and there's a ton of it to do. You haven't outlined your case, your witness sequence, called your witnesses for prep. I don't see any trial book—you should have had it put together by now. I just see an empty binder marked 'Estate of Sean Riley'. There's nothing in it." He chewed on the end of his cigar, waiting for a response.

"Let me worry about what I have to do." Nick glared at Margo, who reached into her purse for a tissue, continuing to dab at her eyes.

"Ceratto," Silvio shouted, "this is a multimillion dollar case! You got a lot a work to do. Don't tell me not to worry about it. It's our money out there—over a hundred thousand out of pocket is riding on this case—with a potential three or four million dollar recovery."

"You think I don't know that?" Nick wanted to say, "You murdering fuck, I know what you're up to." Instead he insisted, "I just don't want anyone snooping around my desk while I'm away. She's in my face, telling me what to do, and I don't like it."

"She was doing what I told her to do—and if you don't like it…" There was a pause, and Harry Levin's voice could be heard telling Silvio to cool it. He had heard the shouting next door and had come to see what it was all about.

Nick stayed on the line as the two argued, and then it went dead. Margo left his office, still dabbing her eyes. He closed the door and put his phone on DO NOT DISTURB. Contrary to Margo's story, all the subpoenas *had* gone out except for one. He dialed Grace Monahan's extension. She had all the documents that Margo hadn't seen. Nick was grateful that he had listened to Grace's suggestion that she keep all trial preparation documents in *her* office.

"Grace, has Donna Price been served yet?"

Grace was still pissed at him for his liaison with another woman, even though that woman was dead. She answered coolly, "No. She's moved. We can't find her."

Nick ignored the tone. "It looks like she was an operating room nurse. She was there during Riley's surgery, right? It's important that we get to her. She should have been deposed. It's too late for that now, but at least we can send an investigator out to find out what she knows." Nick rubbed his forehead. This could be a bomb he didn't need. He couldn't believe that Joe hadn't tracked this witness more carefully. Joe was meticulous. Joe would surely have deposed her. She was on his witness list, but there was no deposition transcript in the file. In fact, she wasn't even subpoenaed. Maybe Asher had gotten to her? Maybe he was going to try to spring her on him without prior notice. "Grace. I don't want to hear 'can't find her.' I want her found!"

"We put an investigator on her over two months ago and came up with nothing. Mr. Maglio was concerned about it. He was frustrated about not finding her and wanted to postpone the trial. But Judge Barnes ruled against him. Look at the petition to postpone the trial. You'll see it all in there," she said defensively. "The judge ruled against us, so we have to go on without her." There was an audible sigh of frustration from Grace.

"Fuck."

"My sentiments exactly, Mr. Ceratto."

"You can dispense with the *Mr. Ceratto,* Grace." He wanted to keep his distance from her but couldn't stand feigned formality, nor her bitchiness.

He saw that Donna Price was also on Asher's pretrial witness list. Her address was the same as the one he had on his list. He dialed Asher's firm and asked for John Asher; who pleasantly told him that he had no further information on Donna Rice's whereabouts. And no, they were not going to spring her on him, and yes, they should file motions in limine on this issue just to be sure that the other wasn't lying.

Nick knew that the "great and wonderful" Judge Joseph Barnes would permit her to testify if she was found, even at the last minute. So he *had* to find her first. Something leading to her whereabouts had to be somewhere in the massive file. He rang the receptionist.

"Carmelita, please tell the two gentleman waiting for me to come to my office."

"Yes, Mr. Ceratto, I'll get them. They're out in the hall. They said they don't like sitting in lawyers' offices. It makes them nervous." she laughed. "What are their names, sir? They wouldn't give their names to me."

"Never mind, Carmelita. They don't like giving their names out. Just call them and tell them to come in."

"Yes, Mr. Ceratto."

In less than a minute Little Al and Joey Shoes were removing twelve file boxes from Nick's office. As they walked past Harry Levin's open door he yelled, "What the hell are you doing?" Harry chased the two men down the hall past the conference room into the reception area. "Stop! That's the firm's property. You can't take that. Stop before I call the police."

Two more men, similarly dressed in black trench coats, stood by the reception desk, waiting. Their faces were expressionless and they said nothing. They took the boxes from Little Al and Joey Shoes, loaded them on carts, and began wheeling them out the front door. All four men ignored Levin's threats. Little Al and Joey Shoes waited for Nick. They didn't have to wait long.

Silvio was running behind Nick, his face red and menacing. "Ceratto, you're off this case if you move those boxes one more inch." Nick kept walking. "OK. You're fucking fired." Silvio moved threateningly close as Nick stopped and turned to face him.

"Yeah. Tell that to His Honor, Joseph Barnes. See if you can get a competent trial attorney to try this case in twenty four hours or less. Or maybe tell him that Margo Griffin will be trying the case. She'd do a better job than you, you fuck."

Silvio threw his cigar on the floor and reached for Nick.

But Little Al smoothly stepped between them. "I wouldn't waste a good cigar like that," he said as he stooped to pick up the cigar. He straightened up and hit Silvio hard in the stomach, doubling him over, then pushed him onto the floor with his hand on his bald head.

"Call the police!" Levin yelled as he moved away from the fracas, afraid that he might be next.

Joey Shoes quickly moved behind the receptionist's desk and took the receiver from Carmelita before she could dial 911.

"I wouldn't do that, hon, if I were you," he said, glaring stonily at her.

She quickly put her hands down in her lap. She tried to smile at him, but her fear was all too apparent. Her legs were shaking.

Joey Shoes nodded. "That's right. Wise move, lady."

Nick and the four men were out the door and into a down elevator in a split second.

Chapter **XXIII**

Judge Joseph Barnes was adamant. He wanted everyone in his chambers: Nick Ceratto, Marty Silvio or Harry Levin, and John Asher. He wasn't about to make a procedural error in *this* case, or ruin his reputation as an administrative genius who got cases to settle or go to trial in record time. And he wasn't about to have a mistrial on his hands either.

He had gotten phone calls from Nick and Silvio and Levin. He had received an emergency petition from Nick to postpone the trial date; and from Silvio and Levin to not only postpone the trial but also to substitute a new attorney for Nick Ceratto as plaintiff's counsel. John Asher had followed with his own petition to postpone the trial to allow him to browbeat a settlement out of Manin. Judge Barnes now had three opposing parties to deal with besides presiding over the trial: Silvio and Levin versus Nick Ceratto, Nick Ceratto versus Silvio and Levin, and John Asher versus everybody. And all of them versus the Honorable Joseph Barnes. He wasn't going to have any of it. There would be a formal hearing on the petitions, on the record, in court.

All the attorneys showed up on time. Nick Ceratto sat on one side of the dingy courtroom, its magnificent Victorian paneling and ornate plaster work overlaid with generations of dirt, neglect, slovenly repairs, and botched modernizations. Marty Silvio and Harry Levin sat on the other side. John Asher preferred to stand. He didn't want to wrinkle his freshly pressed Ralph Lauren jacket. Besides, he knew what Barnes was going to say.

Preceded by his court reporter and tipstaff, Barnes strode briskly to the bench from the robing room. The red silk lining of his tailored black robe flashed momentarily with each stride. He sat down behind the bench with an authoritative air. The knot of his red silk tie peeked above the tiny gap at the top of his robe.

He was a regal sight. He reeked control as he took his seat behind the bench.

"Counsel, I've called you here today to rule on various petitions filed by each of you—Mr. Ceratto, Mr. Silvio, and Mr. Asher have all requested continuances." He paused, looking down at them over the top of his horn-rimmed half glasses. "I will not continue this trial to a later date. This case has been on my docket far too long. It was continued on two prior occasions at the request of Mr. Maglio. It is now a 'must try' and will move up on the trial list accordingly. You will be given twenty-four hours prior notice at which time you will be prepared to pick a jury and give your opening statements. You will all receive my signed order denying your petitions. As to the need for another settlement conference—Mr. Asher, if you cannot convince Dr. Manin of the prudence of agreeing to a fair settlement offer, no settlement master, and certainly not I, will be able to do so. Perhaps he will be more inclined to entertain settling this case after the plaintiff has put on his case. Therefore, gentlemen, we're back where we started. Please do not waste the Court's time with Petitions for Extraordinary Relief in the way of a postponement because none will be granted. I don't care what the reasons are. Even *death* won't do it. It appears that you will be getting a call from my secretary within a few days—and by that I mean less than a week—to begin this trial. This hearing is concluded."

The court reporter stopped tapping at the keys of her small, oblong machine, and the Honorable Joseph Barnes raised himself from his leather throne and left the bench without even a glance at anyone in the courtroom. He loved "putting it to" the wealthy and the arrogant. His power evened the balance. The money he had given up for the leather throne was worth it. He just needed a bigger throne, he thought.

Nick closed his briefcase and began to walk out of the courtroom. As he approached the double doors, Silvio ran to catch up, breathing heavily.

"Look, Nick, I'm sorry about the blowup. I was only trying to help, and then you got cocky with me."

Nick turned and gave him a straight stare. "You think an apology is going to coax me back to that office?"

Silvio looked down at his polished oxblood slip-ons. "Nick, come on. Be reasonable."

"I don't trust you fucks. I don't like you fucks. Everything you touch turns to shit or dies."

Silvio's conciliatory tone was gone. "Look, you little twerp, you need office support to try this case. What the fuck do you think you're doing? You gonna prep this trial at home with no secretaries, no paralegals? This is a big case."

"You don't have to remind me of my responsibility. Nor are you telling me how and where to prep this case."

"No? Well, it's the firm's case—not yours—and I'm assigning it to someone else. You're fucking fired!"

"No. *You're* fucking fired." Nick reached into his breast pocket and pulled out a sealed envelope. It was addressed to Silvio and Levin, and the name on the return address was Theresa Riley.

Silvio ripped it open after seeing who it was from, glanced at it, and threw it on the floor. The letter stated that the Rileys were discharging the firm of Silvio and Levin as their attorneys and requested that the firm cooperate in an orderly transfer of the documents to their new attorney, Nicholas Cerrato.

Nick pushed open the squealing door to courtroom 112. "That was only a copy," he said, smiling. "The original was sent certified, yesterday. I'm sure it's in this morning's mail. It must be on your desk by now."

He walked out into the dingy hall, his heels clicking on the brown and tan vinyl tiles covering the original Victorian mosaic floors. He was joined by two men who had been waiting for him at the elevator. Little Al hit the down button, and Joey Shoes brought up the rear as all three stepped into the elevator.

Nick knew Silvio, the prick, was right. But he wouldn't give him the satisfaction of admitting it. He'd been working on his opening statement—now he'd have to stop to prepare motions in limine, a device which would prevent Donna Price from testifying just in case Asher had found her and was going to spring her on him. He cursed Barnes and wished him cancer. His priorities were constantly shifting. He couldn't concentrate. The last three nights had been sleepless. He knew he needed help.

The phone rang. Nick checked the time. It was two a.m.

"Yes," he answered, staring at his fourth cup of black coffee which just wouldn't go down.

"Nick, it's Grace."

This was the last person he needed to call him at this hour— Grace Monahan, horny, no doubt.

"Sorry, Grace, I'm really tired now." He was sure she wanted to replay Christmas Eve, and he wasn't in the mood.

"No, I don't want to go to bed with you if that's what you're thinking. That's really all you care about, Nick. Isn't it?"

He didn't need a lecture. "No, Grace, that's not all I care about. That's why I've been awake the last four days and nights, working on this case—I'm alone on this and…"

"No, you're wrong. You're not alone. I'm going to help you."

"You can't," he snapped. He didn't mean to be curt, but he was so strung out, he couldn't help it. "You're working for my former employer, now my enemy. A firm I'm going to be litigating against, no doubt for the rest of my life, if I'm lucky enough to win this case. And if I'm lucky enough to be alive." Nick couldn't believe that he had blurted this out to her; the last thing he needed was to have her spread accusations about Silvio and Levin, even if they were true.

"I know. That's why I quit."

There was dead silence for a few seconds.

"You quit?"

"Yes," she whispered. Nick could detect a tremor in her voice.

"Why?"

"Because they are going to try to kill you. The same way they killed Joe and Celia and Maria Elena."

Nick was stunned. "How do you know this, Grace?" He was careful not to agree. She might be taping their conversation. At this point he was paranoid. He trusted no one.

"I went into Silvio's office the day you left to see him about cleaning out your desk. I wanted to pack your things and get them to you. He wasn't in, but I noticed the telephone extension light to your office was lit. I lifted the receiver and I heard them. Margo Griffin and Silvio were in your office. They were talking."

"How? Were they on the telephone?"

"No, that's just it. Your office was bugged. All Silvio had to do was hit your line to activate the bug and listen in. Everything you said could be heard in his office."

"Bugged?"

"Yes, I found it after they left when I went in to clean out your belongings. It was under your desk."

"What did they say?" His heart started pounding and he immediately became alert.

"Marty told her that you were going to be finished like the others—that your days were numbered. And he was going to make *her* a partner…" She paused.

"And…"

"And then they started making love. I could hear it. It was disgusting. I left his office. I still wanted to get your things so I asked Levin if it was all right. He said fine, after he checked your office for firm property. He said you were only entitled to your fucking coffee cup, your pictures, and your loose change because that's you would have when they got finished with you. So I have your stuff. I didn't want to come up without calling you. I'm worried about you, Nick."

"Thanks, Grace. But I don't think they're going to wipe me out literally, just figuratively. You were sweet to do this for me. I'll send someone for my things. Where are you now?"

Her voice trembled. She was on the verge of crying. "I know that you didn't want me to do this. I did it for you because I care and you're in trouble. I know you are."

"Don't worry about me—understand? Worry about you."

"Well, it's too late."

Nick was now really worried about her safety. Anyone affiliated with him was marked. They might just as well pick out their caskets.

"Jesus Christ, Grace. What the hell did you do this for?" he scolded.

"I can't be part of a firm that lies, cheats, steals, and murders— and I'm going to work for you."

"For *me?*" He was shocked. "Shit, Grace, I can't even pay you. I don't have a pot to piss in. Nothing except this condo, my car, and my clothes. Besides, if you're right, they're going to come after both of us now."

Her voice changed. She regained control and said authoritatively. "One—you don't have to pay me now. I know you need help and you're going to win this case, so you can pay me later. And two—I'm going to stay with you until this is over so I won't be alone and neither will you. Three, I have a gun. Four, I have savings and I can support us."

"Grace, where are you?"

"I'm downstairs in your lobby with a box of your junk. That's where I am. Can I please come in?"

She sounded tired and exasperated. And she needed a bed, he could tell. And he could certainly use the help. He hit the buzzer for the automatic door lock and let her in.

Shoes had been listening to the conversation. He had taken up residence in the living room, his bare feet propped up on the arm of the sofa. He had been watching *Casablanca* on the classic movie channel. *Just like a broad,* he thought. Pushing her way into a guy's life. Making herself indispensable and then shackling him with the old ball and chain. He hoped Nick knew better, but obviously he didn't. He wasn't like Bogie who knew how to leave 'em before things got too hot. "Here's looking at you, kid," was a line Nick wouldn't know how to use, or when to use it.

Then she came in. Shoes took a long look at the five-foot, eleven-inch, well-endowed redhead. Pure Rita Hayworth.

He decided that he wouldn't know when or how to use the famous line either.

Nick took the carton and quickly helped her out of her coat.

"This is Joe Scarpa," he said. "A friend of mine."

Shoes stood up, barefooted, and bowed from the waist. "Just call me 'Shoes', ma'am"

Grace looked down at his bare, size-fourteen feet and understood why. "Pleased to meet you, Shoes."

Nick led her to his study. It looked as if a bomb had hit it. Papers were everywhere.

"Oh my God." Grace pushed her hair back from her forehead.

"I know. It's a mess. You want a cup of coffee, a drink?"

"No. Not now. Tell me what you're working on." She moved toward the disassembled file.

"The opening." He gestured toward typed notes up on the computer.

"Here, let me put this back together for you so you don't go crazy looking for stuff. It looks as though you took a fit in here." She stooped to pick up papers scattered on the floor. "This is not good," she mumbled to herself, wondering how he was going to try this case. It was a disorganized mess, which she immediately began to organize.

Nick had fallen asleep at the computer. His head had fallen to one side, and Grace knew that he would have a neck from hell in the morning. She moved his trunk gently forward until his head and arms rested on the desk, and then slid a throw pillow under his head. She didn't want to wake him. She knew he would try to work instead of resting. And he'd be a basket case, more so than he was now.

Shoes snored loudly in the next room, half on and half off the sofa with his hand on his shoulder holster. His closely cropped black hair stood up on end, like porcupine quills.

Grace sorted the papers on the floor, filing them carefully, one by one, by date in the appropriate folders; all discovery in the discovery file, all correspondence in the correspondence file, all investigative reports in the…she stopped. She noticed a Post-it on the floor, folded over on itself. Obviously it had been attached to a document in the investigative file. She unfolded it and saw the name: Jane Welles R.N. with a phone number 626-527-0970. Under the number was scrawled, *Follow up ASAP*. It was written in Joe Maglio's unmistakable left-handed chicken scratch. His script had been so bizarre, it was easily identified. Besides, Grace had done enough work for Joe, had assisted him in putting enough trials together that she knew this was an important but overlooked piece of information.

She quickly looked in the Bell Atlantic white pages. Page 28 had a map of the United States showing the location of all the designated area codes. Page 29 listed all the area codes by state and city. Area code 626 was Pasadena, California. She checked her watch. It would be midnight in Pasadena. She decided to call anyway, even if she woke someone up. She dialed and listened as the phone rang, once, twice—six times. There was a click, and the answering machine came on. "You have reached Ms. Welles and Ms. Lamberti. Please leave a message." The beep sounded. Grace didn't want to leave a message. She didn't want to risk spooking Ms. Welles by telling her who she was and why she was calling. She knew she couldn't get away with pretending to be a telephone pollster, not at midnight in California, or trying to pump Welles for information—information that would possibly link her to Metropolitan Mercy and the Riley case.

As she started to put the receiver down, she heard, "Hello?" The voice was thick and low, as though the speaker had just been awakened.

"Ms. Welles?"

"Yes."

"I'm sorry to disturb you. But are you Jane Welles, Nurse Welles?"

There was a long pause. The voice seemed more alert. "Why do you want to know? I hope you're not trying to sell me anything at this hour."

"No, no. I'm really sorry to call you, but this is an emergency."

"Is there a problem? Are you from the hospital?" She cleared her throat. "You're not calling me to substitute? I had off tonight."

"I'm from Pasadena General," Grace lied, hoping there was such a hospital. Didn't all cities have a hospital whose name ended in *General?* "That's where you work, isn't it?" Grace prodded, praying that she, whoever she was, wouldn't hang up.

"No, I work at Saint Francis hospital. Can you please tell me what this is all about?" The voice sounded truly annoyed. Grace was afraid she'd lose her.

"You see, I'm trying to locate Donna Price. Your name was given to me by a friend of hers."

There was a long pause. "What friend?"

Grace held her breath. "Victor…Victor Manin."

There was an instantaneous disconnect.

Grace waited about five minutes, and as she expected Nick's phone rang. She picked it up in the middle of the first ring.

"Hello."

"Listen, I don't know who you are, but I don't know any Donna Price and I don't know any Doctor Victor Manin. I have your phone number on my caller ID. If you call me one more time I'm going to the phone company and the police!" Then there was a sharp click.

Grace danced around the study. She couldn't wait to tell Nick. She shook him awake. She had to. Even if she had to knock him out to put him back to sleep.

"What…" He lifted his head from the desk, his eyes blood-red slits.

"We found her." Grace planted a kiss on his cheek.

"Who?" he asked incoherently.

"Donna Price."

"Oh." His head plopped back down on the desk.

Grace was glad that she didn't have to knock him out after all. She dialed Jerry Fisher, an investigator with whom she had worked. She knew his number by heart.

"Jerry, it's Grace Monahan…. I know it's five in the morning," she sighed. "Look, don't bitch at me, hear? You're such a *yenta*." She had never liked his style, but he was good at what he did. "I have an important assignment and I need the answer yesterday. Got it?… OK, now listen. I need the address for the telephone number 626-527-0970. I want it by six a.m., today, no later. Call me back at 215-567-0713. Do not—and I mean—*do not* call me at the office. And send the bill to my home. I'm on a special assignment and the office doesn't want anything traceable to them. OK, Jerry?….Good. I love you."

Grace took a long breath as she hung up. She moved back to the floor and began assembling the file again, carefully looking at each and every document so as not to miss any other potential treasure.

She hadn't told Donna Price Victor Manin was a doctor.

Chapter XXIV

By eight a.m. all three were on a flight to Pasadena: Nick in the window seat, Grace in the center, and Joey Shoes on the aisle.

Nick stared out at the bright blue nothingness, trying to rid himself of the depression he felt—trying to dismiss thoughts of Maria Elena and the pain of never seeing her again. He was trying to focus on the missing witness and what she would say, if she would speak to him. How he could get her to testify, if what she had to say would be good for him. If she was damaging to his case, he would bury Donna Price, figuratively of course. He would destroy all notes, all recordings, anything used to track her, anything that would memorialize her testimony. It be against the rules of court to do so, but Asher would undoubtedly do the same in the same situation. Perhaps Asher was hiding her from him. He wouldn't put it past any defense lawyer. He certainly wouldn't put it past himself or any other plaintiff's lawyer.

Shoes quietly chewed his gum, his eyes tightly closed, thinking how helpless you were on a plane. You had no control, no matter how smart, how quick on your feet. If the fucking thing was going down, so were you. Body parts everywhere. The thought made him sick. He opened his eyes to relieve the mental picture. He felt the empty place in his jacket where he usually carried the 25-caliber Beretta. He'd had to leave it behind because of airport security. The gun had saved his life more than once. And now how was he supposed to protect this kid lawyer and the redheaded broad with nothing? He wondered why he was on the fucking plane at all. The kid gave him *acida*, and he couldn't wait until the trial was over. Ceratto had better win big, he thought, because DiCicco expected to be paid big—or the kid might wind up in the Delaware River. A job he wouldn't relish, since he was beginning to like the kid, even if he did get on his nerves.

Grace felt nauseous. Between the slow up-and-down movement of the plane on the air currents and Joey Shoes's cologne, she felt an urge to throw up which she was desperately fighting. She breathed deeply and concentrated on the new life inside her. So far God had been good to her, rewarded her obedient practice of the Catholic faith she had been brought up in: mass every Sunday and on holy days of obligation, confession once a month and no meat on Fridays during Lent. Except if you're pregnant, of course. She pulled a pack of saltines from her purse and slipped one into her mouth to calm her stomach.

The 757 touched down with a slight bounce. The reversed engines whirred loudly tugging back on the jet as it raced forward until it finally came to a halt. There was a brief silence and then the cacophony of seatbelts unlocking.

Shoes was the first out of his seat—terra firma. He would have kissed the ground, but he didn't want to lose his cool. Looking and staying cool was everything in his business, with the exception of staying alive.

He waited for Nick and Grace to exit their seats, shadowing them dutifully as they made their way to ground transportation. In a few minutes they were in the back seat of a black Chrysler. Shoes sat in front, mumbling unintelligibly to the driver. The driver mumbled back with grunts and groans and a few gestures, a language obviously all their own. Shoes reached under the seat to retrieve the Beretta—his old friend, shipped especially for him by air express. He kissed it and tucked inside his jacket where it belonged. He vowed he would never leave it behind again. Fuck airport security. He'd find a way.

The driver sped along the palm lined drive to the freeway. The air was warm and friendly. The sun shone brilliantly. Flowers, trees, and grass whizzed by, all the things that were missing from Philadelphia in February.

The driver was efficient and professional. He said nothing as he drove straight to 487 Jesse Street, the number given to him by his boss, who had received it from DiCicco.

No one said a word. There was tension in the air. They each knew what they had to do. In exactly one and a half hours they had to be on a return flight to Philadelphia. Nick nervously checked his watch. The driver pulled up to the curb and looked over at a white, stucco, U-shaped garden apartment complex. A twelve-foot black iron gate stood at the entrance, obviously locked for security reasons.

"This is it," he said as he put his flashers on. The rest was up to them.

Nick was the first out. "Wait here," he said to Shoes. Grace followed behind him, carrying a brown leather briefcase.

They reached the iron gate together and scanned the numbers on the directory.

"Here it is." Grace pointed to 327D. There were no names listed. "Shit, no names anywhere, not even on the mailboxes."

"Let's hope Jerry was right. Otherwise this trip was for nothing." Nick pushed the buzzer and waited thirty seconds. Pushed it again. Sixty seconds, and nothing.

Grace was nervous. She paced and then tugged at the gate. "Shit."

"Did you think it was unlocked?" Nick asked cockily.

"Don't mock me. I just did the natural thing. I tried." She shook the gate and leaned her face into it in despair. "Why didn't we think of this?" she said despondently.

"We did." Nick turned and motioned to the car. The front passenger door opened and Shoes immediately got out. Without a word, he reached into his pants pocket, took out a lock pick, and the gate swung open in a flash.

"Sometimes you have to use a little self-help," Nick said, boldly leading the way to the elevator which would take them to the third floor.

"This is illegal," Grace said. "You broke into this complex. You could be arrested—lose your license to practice."

"I know. But as I said, sometimes you have to do what you have to do—skirt the law, if necessary, fuck the law, if necessary. Sometimes justice demands it."

They were at the front door of 327D. Nick rang the doorbell, shifting from one foot to the other. Thirty seconds, sixty seconds—nothing. He knocked loudly. Nothing. He nodded to Shoes, who again practiced his craft.

Grace felt sick. She didn't like this at all. She didn't want to go to jail—not in her condition. She turned and started toward the elevator.

Nick quickly walked up behind her. "Come on, Grace, we came all this way. I thought you had balls."

She turned. "I do. But I can't do this—I'm not a burglar."

"Look," he took her by the shoulder, "we're not stealing anything. We're just going to wait inside for her and hope she'll be back. We'll apologize and then tell her that…that…" He stammered for a moment. "…that the gate was unlocked and…so was her front door."

"She'll never buy that." She shook her head. "You're being a stupid jerk."

"Who gives a fuck if she does or doesn't? Once we lay a subpoena on her and tell her that the law wants her back in Philadelphia, she's really not likely to call the cops, is she?"

Grace's eyes were brimming with tears. "Why did I ever get involved with this whole thing—with you?"

Nick put his arms around her and squeezed her tightly. "Because you love me, that's why."

Shoes was already inside, nosing around the neatly kept apartment. "This her?" he said as he sat down on the cream-colored leather sofa pointing to a photograph of two older people, a man and a woman flanking a young woman in a nurse's cap holding a diploma. Nick checked it against the photo he carried in his inside jacket pocket—the one he had taken from the Riley file. It wasn't Donna Price. It looked like her: blond, slim, petite features, dimples. But it clearly wasn't her.

His heart sank to his shoes. "This isn't Price," he said, shaking his head and flopping into a chair. He put his head in his hands, speaking to the floor, "I'm fucking nuts. You're right. Let's get out of here."

But Grace was already into the hall of the apartment. "There's two bedrooms here," she called as she raced into one of the bedrooms, looking wildly for something that would tell them that they had struck gold. She found toss pillows, an unmade bed, panties and a bra on the floor, a few stuffed animals. and a photo of a man in hospital greens with a stethoscope hanging from his neck. He was with the same woman as the older people in the living room photo. Definitely not Donna Price. It was obvious that this girl was a slob, hopefully not an operating room nurse. Grace tore into the next bedroom. It was pristine, neat as a pin. Everything was in its place, dried roses in a flower arrangement on the dresser, the only decoration. And no pictures. *Shit, shit*, she thought. She opened and ransacked each dresser drawer. Nothing but neatly folded clothing; sweaters, underwear, stockings, every item neatly stacked and color coordinated. Obviously anal. She went to the small desk next to the bed and opened the drawers. Again neatly arranged pens, paper clips, stamps, blank writing paper. Grace looked at the calendar opened on the desk. There was her work schedule—Monday through Thursday: two a.m. to ten a.m. Grace checked her watch. It was 10:20. Whoever she was, she was due home about now.

"Nick," she called. "Come here—hurry."

Nick slowly walked into the room, his jacket open, his tie pulled down. His hair was tousled from rubbing his head. "This whole thing sucks. Let's go—I don't need her."

"Nick, she's going to be here in a few minutes. Look." She pointed to the calendar on the desk. "Let's wait, let's…"

"What? You said you didn't want any part of this, you're not a criminal, and now you want to wait?"

"Yes." She looked at him defiantly. "I do. I have a plan."

"OK. Let's hear it."

"I'll go down and wait by the gate. When she comes in—she'll obviously have a nurse's uniform on—I'll call you on the cell phone." She copied the number from the bedside phone onto her hand. "I'll let you know if it's her before she gets on the elevator. If it's not, you can leave before she gets to the door. If it is her, you can wait." Grace looked wide-eyed at Nick, obviously proud of herself and waiting for his approval.

He shook his head, nixing the plan.

"What's wrong with it? It's perfect," she protested. "Hurry, she's going to be here in a few minutes. I know it. Nick!" she yelled. "Let's do it. We came all this way. Took this chance."

He rose from the bed, sighed, and quickly gave her a high five. "You're right. We came all this way. I'm just pissed I didn't think of it myself. Go on—get out of here."

Grace was gone before he finished the sentence. As soon as she walked through the door, she looked at her watch and started timing. Down the elevator and to the front gate was exactly one minute and twenty seconds.

She waited inside the courtyard, looking through the ornate Spanish ironwork to the street outside. She could see the black Chrysler. The driver sat motionless, staring ahead as if he were a crash dummy. Grace, on the other hand, was in motion, pacing, leaning, tapping her foot, and then pounding the gate. Nothing she did brought Donna Price any sooner. She looked at her watch. It had only been fifteen minutes since she left the apartment. It seemed an eternity. She had to go to the bathroom. She crossed her legs tightly for a minute and her bladder obeyed—thank heavens she had a good bladder, even pregnant.

After another five exasperating minutes, her cell phone rang. It was Nick.

"Anything?" he asked in a tense tone.

"No, Nick, nothing yet. But I'm about to pee myself."

"OK. We're coming down. We can't wait for her forever. We've got work to do."

"Don't—not yet. I'm coming up to go to the bathroom. Then if she doesn't show up in a few more minutes, we'll leave—OK?"

"You women with the bathroom. Does your whole life revolve around pissing and waiting to piss?" he said in an exasperated tone.

"Yes, a great deal of it. I don't have an extra long urethra like you, you prick," she retorted. She found Shoes standing on the third floor, hand in his coat pocket. This made Grace extremely nervous. "Can't you wait inside?" she asked.

"Somebody's gotta watch, lady, while you take a leak." He smiled while he chewed his gum intently.

Grace was just about to flush when she heard a shrill whistle—then a knock on the bathroom door.

"Grace, it's her. Let's move."

"Who?"

"Somebody. Shoes gave me a signal. Come on goddamn it, get the hell out of the bathroom."

She pulled the door open and ran to the elevator. It was waiting there for her on the third floor. It slowly moved down, two, one. Then the door opened and Grace stood face-to-face with her.

"Hi," the woman smiled. "Is this your floor?"

The face was identical to that in the color Xerox of the hospital ID badge that Grace had seen in the discovery materials in Philadelphia. Just a little older and a little more tired. But who wouldn't be, working through the night, caring for sick people? The same pure blue eyes, fine small nose, alabaster skin, blond hair pulled back in a barrette. And deep dimples. The dimples gave her away completely. They were like two bullet holes that appeared on command when she smiled. Even the slightest smile brought them on. "Dimples" was her nickname in the Metropolitan Hospital nursing school yearbook, which Grace had also seen in the discovery file, and which had led Maglio's investigator to her whereabouts.

"Hi," Grace responded breathlessly as she stepped out of the elevator, still holding the door back. "Yes. this is my floor. Sorry, I'm new in the complex."

"That's OK," the woman responded politely, pushing back a strand of hair which had fallen to her face. She walked into the elevator and pressed number three. The door closed.

Grace was immediately on the cell phone. She punched in the woman's phone number and the screen suddenly went blank. "Shit! Low battery." Grace wanted to cry. She hit SEND again and the phone rang. She looked up. She could see the woman stepping out of the elevator onto the open balcony that led to her apartment. She saw the woman turn toward her apartment.

Inside the apartment, Nick picked up the phone, but said nothing.

"It's her." Grace's heart was pounding. "Donna Price."

"OK," was all he said and then hung up.

Grace found herself on the third floor without even remembering the ride up. She saw the woman unlock the door and enter the apartment. The door closed just as Grace started to approach. She thought for a moment, gathered her courage, and knocked, wondering if they'd all wind up in the Pasadena jail.

"Yes," the woman answered through the partly open door held back by a chain lock.

"Oh, I'm sorry to bother you," Grace said. "I'm Grace Monahan and I just moved in today. My phone's not connected yet. And my cell phone's down. I have to make a quick call to the phone company. They were supposed to be here an hour ago." She looked at her watch. "I have to leave for work in an hour. I'd hate to be gone when they arrive."

The woman inspected her from head to toe as Grace assumed her most sugar sweet stance—shoulders slightly stooped, feet awkwardly turned in, and a smile that would melt the polar ice cap. She stared at Grace for a few seconds, saying nothing. Then she slid the chain lock off.

"Sure, come on in. I know what that's all about. I moved here three years ago and I still have problems with big monopolies coming out to do their job. Wait till you try to get your TV connected…"

Grace stepped in and closed the door behind her. "Thanks."

"The phone's over here. The woman pointed to the kitchen wall phone. "By the way, I'm Jane Welles." The woman held out her hand and Grace shook it firmly.

"Grace Monahan. You're a nurse, I see."

"Yes, I am. I guess you can tell from the high-fashion clothes I'm wearing." She laughed, looking down at her white, crepe-soled shoes.

Grace smiled as she removed her hand slowly, looking about to see if there was any evidence of the others in the apartment. "Very nice place you have here, Donna."

The woman's face suddenly froze. "What? What did you call me?"

"Donna. Isn't that your name? Donna? Donna Price?"

The nurse walked to the door. "Get out."

"Not before I leave this." Grace laid a witness subpoena on the entryway table.

"What the hell is that?" The woman snatched up the folded document.

"It's called a subpoena. You have to come to Philadelphia to testify in the trial of Sean Riley versus Dr. Victor Manin. It starts this Friday. Three days from today. Give this to your boss." Grace laid a copy of the subpoena down on the table. "Your airfare, wages, and hotel accommodations will be paid for by the plaintiff's attorney."

"That's me." Nick stepped into Jane's line of vision.

"Who…who are you—and what the hell are you doing in my apartment?" Jane's voice was rising as she grabbed her purse from the entryway table.

"I'm Nick Ceratto. I'm the attorney representing the Estate of Sean Riley, and you're Donna Price, the other operating room nurse, and I need to talk to you."

"I'm Jane Welles," she insisted. "And get out of here. You're breaking the law being in here without my consent. You just can't break into my apartment. Who the hell do you think you are?" She would have gone on, but Nick interrupted her diatribe.

"Yes." He removed the color copy of the ID badge from his pocket. "And so are you, breaking the law. That is, by impersonating another person, assuming someone else's identity, Ms. Price." He held the picture up for her to see.

"How did you get that?" she snapped.

"From hospital records provided in discovery. The defense has it, too. But…" he paused , noting how pale she had become—there wasn't a hint of color left in her face—"I presume we were the first to arrive, uninvited. Or were we?"

Jane began to shake uncontrollably. "I need my medication or I'm going to faint." She started rummaging in her purse, throwing the contents on the small table. She pulled out a container of pepper-mace and aimed squarely at Nick, a few inches from his face. "Get out," she snarled, her hand trembling. "Get out or you and your friend won't be able to see or breathe for twenty minutes."

Shoes soundlessly stepped out of the kitchen and pushed the barrel of the Beretta into the back of Jane's head. "Neither will you if I pull this trigger. And it'll be a lot more than twenty minutes."

Jane dropped the mace. Her shoulders sagged and she began to cry. "What do you want? Why are you here?" she wailed.

"I just want the truth. Just the truth, that's all," said Nick quietly. There was a note of sympathy in his voice. "I'm sorry we had to do this. But there are a lot of lives at stake, including yours, I'm sure you had a good reason for hiding out. I want to know why. And I want to know what went on in that operating room the day Mr. Riley died. I want to know everything."

"OK," Jane said defeat clearly in her voice . "You're right. I *am* Donna Price. But show me some ID." She wiped her eyes with her fingers trying hard to control the flow of tears. "If you're who you say you are, I'll talk to you. Only if I do, you have to promise to leave."

Grace handed her a tissue and led her to the leather couch.

Chapter XXV

It was coming through loud and clear. Marty Silvio and Harry Levin listened intently as Donna Price told her story in fits and starts between sobs. The bug, hidden in the ceiling above her head, picked up every word with amazing clarity. Neither she nor the others in the room with her knew that she was broadcasting live across the country.

"He was a police officer. Dr. Manin said he wanted to see Captain Riley through the surgery. He wanted to do it himself. Dr. Manin always took a special interest in cops. His father had been one. He said that he owed something to the people who protect us. He was going to perform the surgery himself, he said, even though he was on his way out of the hospital when Captain Riley was brought in. He told one of the nurses to call his wife and tell her that he had an emergency and she was to go on ahead without him. He'd meet her at the dinner party later. Then he told me to get scrubbed and get to the OR right away. Captain Riley was already in there. He'd lost a lot of blood, but his leg had been tourniqueted and the bleeding stopped. The wound was clean and his vitals were good. He was in good spirits, although a little groggy from morphine. But he was aware of us before the general anesthetic was given. He even smiled and said hi, and thanked us for helping him—for saving his life."

She stopped and asked for a glass of water and more tissues. Grace was quick to supply her with both and squeezed her hand for encouragement.

"The surgery went fine. It wasn't complex. The artery wasn't mangled. It was a clean cut. All we had to do was clamp it and suture it, which Dr. Manin did carefully, as usual. I watched. He's been doing this kind of surgery for years. I've seen artists like Manin as well as butchers, but I won't mention who. This op was as perfect as you could get. The wound was irrigated and Manin did the close himself. Captain Riley was sent to recovery in great shape. Everything—his vitals—perfect." She took a shuddering breath, and a quick sip of water. "I'm…I'm so afraid to go on…" Her hands shook as she clutched the glass.

Nick's enthusiasm for the case waned with each glowing reference to Dr. Manin. Dr. Manin's loyalty, Dr. Manin's selflessness, Dr. Manin's perfection. Shit, he thought, the last thing he needed was *her* on the stand. She was poison, death to the plaintiff's case. All she had to do was smile at the jury with her dimples and show a tear in her pretty blue eyes, and he was done—finished. She would hardly have to say a word. Nick knew how it worked with a jury. They either fell in love with you and believed every word out of your mouth, or they hated you—or, just as bad, dismissed you as boring.

He got up and started to roll his shirt sleeves down and then put on his jacket

"Nick, where are you going?" Grace asked.

"I really don't need to hear more." He picked up the subpoenas. "Forget this. Forget you were ever served. We're sorry to have bothered you."

"Sorry!" Donna sprang up, her expression instantly changed. She turned on Nick like a wild animal. "You break into my apartment. Scare me half to death. Jeopardize my life by forcing me to talk, and now you say sorry, forget about it? No." She shook her head violently. "No. You sit down," she commanded, pointing to the sofa, "and have the decency to let me finish. Because you don't know anything."

Nick, amazed at the change in her demeanor, began to worry how he could hide her from the defense. Asher would have a field day with her testimony. *Fuck*, he thought. She was right. It was the least he could do—listen to the truth for a change.

"OK, but make it short. We have a plane to catch." He looked at his watch.

She turned away from Nick and Grace and started to pace as she talked. "After the operation, Dr. Manin said he was going to change and go meet his wife, and would I please tell someone at the nurses' station to call her. I left the OR. I was behind him. Captain Riley had already been taken to recovery. I took off my mask and phoned Mrs. Manin's cell phone myself. I gave her the message and we joked for a few minutes about how unreliable Victor was. When it came to his home life, he always put his patients before family time and social life. I hung up and for some reason I decided to look in on Captain Riley before changing. I had planned to take a break in the nurse's lounge. I went into recovery and there he was, asleep and looking fine. Nurse Doletov, the other nurse on duty, was with him. Nobody else was in the room. I lifted the sheet up to check the op site." She turned quickly and stared directly at Nick. "He was bleeding badly. I yelled at Doletov to call Dr. Manin. I was going to call a code when she came at me. She dropped a pair of scissors and grabbed me. I saw blood on the scissors. I yelled at her to stop. She knocked me onto the floor and I saw her pull a syringe from her pocket. I knew it was meant to put me out, possibly permanently. I lay still for a second, and when she bent to give me the injection, I grabbed her foot and pulled it out from under her. She fell and the wind got knocked out of her. I ran to the nearest station for help— nobody was there—I called a code. No one responded. Somebody *should* have responded. And then Doletov came out of the room, yelling in Russian. And then *they* came at me—out of nowhere."

"Wait—who came at you?" Nick found her story hard to believe.

"I don't know who. They just started coming—two, maybe three men. I ran to an open elevator. Hit the down button. Two of the men came after me. I pushed a gurney into them—I thought I was trapped, but the gurney was heavy enough to knock the two of them off the elevator. As the doors started to close, the other one tried to hold the doors open and grab me with his other hand, so I bit it. He let go of the door, and the elevator went down. There was blood all over me and I had to spit out a piece of his skin.

My uniform was torn, and I just held it together and ran off the elevator on the first floor. I never went home. I knew they'd be waiting for me. I ran and walked four miles to my friend's house. She lived by the art museum. She gave me a credit card, some cash, and a change of clothes. Her name was Victoria Grant...Vicki, yes, Vicki...my friend, Vicki..." Donna's eyes had a faraway, glazed look.

"Was? Where is she now?" Grace asked gently.

"Dead. She was found murdered in her apartment the next day. I saw it in the papers. It was headlined in the *Daily News*. I saw at a newsstand in the airport just before I got a plane out of Philadelphia. It was supposed to be a rape-murder. They said the person was in her apartment waiting for her—like you were in mine." She half laughed and half sobbed, wiping her eyes. "I figured you would have killed me already if you were one of them. They said some things were stolen, like her purse, jewelry. But I knew better. Vicki didn't have any jewelry worth stealing. She was a simple person—a physical therapist just making ends meet. She tried to help me and she died. They killed her because they knew I told her what happened. They couldn't get to me because I caught a cab from her apartment to the airport and got the first plane out. I knew I had to cover my tracks, so I went to a MAC machine with the card Vicki had given me and drew out as much cash as I could. I used cash to pay for everything. I went to Chicago, transferred to Memphis, Seattle, and then L.A. I rented a car and drove to Pasadena. I got a new driver's license in L.A., ID, Social Security number, everything." She laughed. "It's amazing what you can do with cash. I bought Jane Welles, a thirty-two-year-old nurse, five feet seven inches, blond, blue eyes. And see, I even have her nursing diploma from Stanford University. Impressive, isn't it?" she laughed tearfully.

No one said a word when she stopped. Donna reached into her purse for a cigarette. After lighting it, she drew in the smoke without inhaling. She offered the pack. "Want one? Don't worry, these won't kill you. If they know you're here, you won't have time to get cancer." She paused. "So, Mr. Ceratto—what now?"

She exhaled. "Now that I've contaminated you with the information that's going to get us all killed—do you still want me to testify?"

"Yeah," he said. "Be at the Complex Litigation Center in Philadelphia at the Wanamaker Building on Friday at nine a.m." He held out his hand. "Gimme one of those." He took a cigarette from the offered pack, put it in his mouth, and then guided Donna's hand with the lit match as she held it to the tip.

Rudi had heard the match being struck and Nick drawing in on the cigarette as he watched the black sedan from his hotel room across the street. Everything had gone according to plan. He had been on a six a.m. flight out of Philadelphia, ahead of Ceratto by two hours. After locating the Jane Welles apartment, he had only needed twenty minutes to install the digital bug and transmitter that had transmitted everything said in Donna Price's apartment to the laptop in Rudi's hotel room. The laptop had, in turn, transmitted in real time over the Internet to the conference room computer at Silvio and Levin, P.C.

Rudi had been able to watch them carefully from the moment they had stepped out of the car and had broken into the gate and gone to the third floor apartment. He chuckled at the amateurish comings and goings of Nick, Grace, and the stupid hood. Probably couldn't shoot straight if his life depended on it, he thought. It was clear that they were all amateurs. His high-powered telescope picked up every movement made from the outside, and the bug picked up every sound from inside. His equipment was the best— state-of-the-art, the envy of spies the world over. They were the tools of his trade, expensive and worth every penny he paid to contacts who inventoried equipment for the CIA.

Silvio and Levin were ecstatic, high-fiving each other. This bitch had eluded them for two years, and now they had the break they had been waiting for. They had paid Jerry Fisher handsomely for the information he had given to Grace. Fisher had become suspicious when Grace had asked him to say nothing to anyone at the firm. Loyal to the source that always paid his inflated bills, he went to Silvio to find out what was going on. He was paid a hundred times the normal rate for this address and the phone number to match.

Rudi saw the elevator door open on the ground level as the threesome emerged. He typed a simple command into the laptop. The screen flickered for a second and then filled with a view of the interior of Donna Price's apartment, transmitted from the cigarette package sized box that he had taped under the coffee table when he had placed the bug in the overhead light. The lens, the size of a pin head and the thin fiber-optic filament connecting it to the transmitter was invisible as it lay under the lip of the table, but it showed a 180-degree view of the room. He watched, fascinated as he saw Donna close the door behind them.

Donna's nightmare had become a reality. She pulled the barrette from her hair and sat on the sofa, looking bewildered. She unlaced her white shoes, and then undressed down to her bra and panties. She lay on the sofa and closed her eyes. Her long, blond hair spread out loosely over the sofa arm. Her body was white and sinewy, a Nordic type, much like Christy Maglio's.

He found the type beautiful. It was pure. It was cold and distant. *Shame*, he thought. The cell phone rang. "Yeah," he said. "Good stuff, right? I know what you want, but I can't be two places at the same time. So who do you want me to do first?" He smiled as he received his orders. "Fine. Consider it done."

Chapter XXVI

Mike Rosa flipped his copy of the *Raiders* video cassette over on his desk as he talked to Muriel Gates on the telephone. It was tagged with an orange label marked "MAGLIO."

"I think we have to work together on this one, Muriel. Our suspicion right now is that Maglio was murdered. The powder burns were on his *right* hand. He was left-handed. No way could he handle a gun with his right hand. I had forgotten about it until recently, until I saw the videotape of him—yes, I was his friend. I also went to law school with him. We used to kid him about being a lefty. When he broke his left arm in a softball game and tried to write with his right hand, his classroom notes were illegible. Even *he* couldn't read them."

"Where's the connection with the Lopez murder?" she challenged. "I just don't see it, Mike. Just because she worked in the same office doesn't mean all the deaths are connected. Your guy and his family lived in a mansion in Gladwyne. My lady lived in a ghetto. Her purse was stolen and then emptied. I understand that none of the Maglio possessions were missing."

Gates eyed the pretty young woman sitting on the couch across from her desk. She was dressed in tight jeans and a pink angora cable-knit turtleneck. Gates couldn't wait to get her hands on all that soft material and what was under it.

"True. But we have a suspiciously blank video tape in the security system," Rosa quickly responded.

"But there was no burglary, right?"

"Right."

"Well that's enough for me. Case closed." She wanted the pretty woman.

"Muriel, you're going to look like shit if my investigation leads to a connection you're ignoring. The press will devour you. And

169

how will it look come campaign time? The Republicans will call you incompetent. Or better yet, they accuse you of conspiracy. You know how those law-and-order types can be, and how far they'll go.

"You threatening me, Rosa?" The DA frowned deeply and her voice dropped an octave. She wanted to pull him through the phone line and squeeze his neck until his eyes popped.

"No, Gates. I'm warning you. This case is a lot bigger than you think. And I'm asking for your help—as politely as I can. I want to work with you, not against you. I don't want to step on your toes. That's why I'm talking to you first and not the attorney general— not just yet. But I will if I have to, and you'll wind up looking like a smacked ass if I do."

Rosa knew that he had gotten her attention. She hadn't interrupted him, and then there was silence when he finished. Did she have nothing to say for the first time in the fifteen years he had known her? Was that possible? "Muriel, you still there?"

"Yes, I'm here." *Prick*, she thought. *He has me where he wants me.* Then she thought again. "Let me think about what you're asking."

"No, Muriel. What I'm *telling* you is that you have twenty-four hours to pick up the ball before I call the attorney general. I'd like to tell him you're cooperating on this case."

"I need to look at the file again."

"Files, Muriel. *Files.*"

"What do you mean—*files*?" She crumpled the Styrofoam cup she had been holding, wishing it were Rosa's neck that she was squeezing.

"Maria Elena Maglio is one you should look at."

"Who?"

"Muriel, aren't you aware that she was Joe's relative—his cousin to be exact. She's a Maglio. Her last name was Maglio. Doesn't that ring a bell with you?"

"The hit and run? The girl who was run over by a gypsy cab that fled the scene and couldn't be traced? You think that was intentional—that was a murder?"

"Yes, I do."

"Why? Because her last name was the same as Joe's?"

"No—because she knew too much, that's why. She came to the States to do her own investigation since we weren't interested, she said. Committing suicide and murdering one's own wife and kids is frowned on there, especially by the Catholic Church, and particularly within Italian families. It's a disgrace the family carries with it forever. She wanted his name cleared to protect their name and reputation."

"Mike, this is all too much, right now. You know—conspiracy around every corner, Italian culture mandates and their sense of justice. But I promise to pull the files if that'll make you happy"— she exaggerated the *s* in *files*—"and I'll get back to you tomorrow. Does that satisfy you?"

"Tomorrow morning, OK? Get your staff to do some work for a change." He thought that would get her blood pressure up and that she'd react in her normal, loud-mouthed, pushy fashion.

Instead, she chuckled. "By the way, Rosa, how did you know all this about the woman? Her mission, her purpose, and all that?"

"Because I met with her, personally. She came to me for help."

The DA laughed deeply. "I see. And on how many occasions did you meet with her?"

"None of your business," he snapped. Rosa was about to sign off and avoid Gates' verbal abuse. He had touched a nerve and knew she wanted to touch his.

"Did you fuck her, Mike?" she laughed.

"What the Christ are you asking, Muriel? If you're trying to piss me off, you are. What I do with my personal life is none of your goddamn business. Do I ask you which woman you're sleeping with?"

Rosa's blood boiled. He hated the bitch. Had she sensed his personal involvement? Had she picked up on his tone when he talked about Maria Elena? Had she read his mind? Had she had Maria followed? Was he just transparent, or did she actually know?

"Oh, touchy, touchy," she said mockingly and winking at the young woman. "Methinks the gentleman doth protest too much. Sorry, Rosa. I just had to give you some of your own medicine."

"I'll expect your call by nine a.m. tomorrow." Rosa hung up, wondering what the dyke had up her sleeve. And why would she have asked him that question? That is, unless she knew much more than he gave her credit for.

"He's going to stir up a lot of shit," Gates said, getting up from her desk and walking over to the couch.

"I know," Margo Griffin responded, kissing Muriel Gates' caressing hand as it swept across her pink angora sweater.

Chapter XXVII

It had been a terrible trip. The seat belt sign lit again, as it had throughout most of the miserable flight. But this time it signaled that the plane was finally going to land after circling JFK for an hour. There were mounds of snow piled up along the recently plowed runway, which was quickly becoming slick with fine snow mixed with ice. Nick Ceratto simply stared out of the window into the blackness, not really caring whether the fucking thing crashed. He was too tired and too strung out to worry about a simple thing like an air disaster. The Boeing 747 finally touched down and fought to stay on the runway as its brakes engaged, slowing the forward motion of the aircraft.

Shoes was joyous. A large smile crossed his face, pulling at his jaw—sore from his incessant gum chewing. He had been hesitant about boarding in California when it was announced that their flight out would be delayed at least three hours due to the weather along the East Coast. Four inches of snow had already fallen, and they were expecting six more along with high winds and temperatures in the single digits. Not a nice picture. But Shoes thought about home, the guys on the corner at Eighth and McKean, the Melrose Diner, his mother's meatballs, and how pissed DiCicco would be if he stayed behind and something happened to Ceratto. He would never get to eat another dish of penne with asparagus, a favorite that his mother made for him every Friday.

Grace thanked God for bringing her and her unborn child safely back to earth. She squeezed the rosary in her pocket, and when the plane rocked to a stop, she said a special prayer of thanks to Saint Christopher, patron saint of travelers. It wasn't that she was afraid of flying. It was flying in horrible weather that scared her.

The seat belts started to click open, but Nick, deep in thought, didn't budge until Grace gently nudged him. She was worried about him and how he would handle the dilemma he found himself in.

"Nick, let's go—we're here."

"Yeah, I know." What he wanted to say was, *Too bad.* He wished the plane had crashed. But it would be unfair for him to wish the same fate on others. After all, it was his problem, not theirs—winning a fraudulent case by concealing a murder, ruining an innocent doctor by suborning perjury, becoming a coconspirator in Sean Riley's murder, and turning his back on his oath to support and defend the law and protect the truth. Or, turning against his own innocent client, the widow Riley, and forcing a defense verdict by putting Donna Price on the stand.

Either way, he figured he was a dead man—disbarred, in prison, or physically dead—they were all the same. Any one of them meant the end to Nick, who had fought so hard to raise himself up from his unfortunate roots and into a noble profession. That is, unless he got to them first. He had to get to Silvio and Levin before they got to him. And that wouldn't be an easy task.

Grace moved out of her seat in front of Shoes, who was blocking the aisle, waiting for Nick. Two men behind him, clearly annoyed, cursed in Russian. Shoes was happy to be the source of their displeasure since all the Commie bastards had done for the past five-and-a-half hours was to talk in Russian. He turned and gave them a toothy grin as he slid his middle finger down the bridge of his nose while Nick stepped out in front of him.

The airport was empty. All flights had been canceled. The threesome quickly walked past the locked duty-free shops and empty newsstands. The moving walkway hummed under their feet, doubling their speed as they raced toward the exit hoping that their ride was waiting as planned, despite the weather. Grace had a hard time keeping up. She was exhausted and moving as fast as she could with Nick pulling her along. All she could think of was a warm bed and some saltines to ease her nausea.

Shoes stayed purposely a few feet behind, looking straight ahead, listening to footsteps as they hastened and quickly closed in behind them. He smelled trouble. It was a natural, God-given instinct. He knew what was coming, and so did Nick. Neither turned to face the Russians from the plane—that would have been a serious mistake. Instead Nick grabbed Grace's arm.

"Jump," he yelled, pulling her toward the low barrier separating the moving walkway from the rest of the corridor.

Grace hurled herself over the low steel wall, landing on her back, followed by Nick. Her purse flew from her arm and its contents scattered over the floor. She grabbed her bag as Nick yanked her up and into a dead run. Nick stumbled down the escalator, pulling Grace past the baggage claim. Neither looked back. The glass exit door slid open and the two charged into the snow, looking for any signs of life.

"Where's security?" she yelled, brushing the blowing snow from her eyes.

"How the fuck should I know? Just keep running." Nick held her hand and pulled her, sliding on the ice, unable to see in the blinding storm.

Grace held her side as she ran. "I can't do this anymore," she panted, slowing and stumbling.

"You have to, Grace—or you'll be dead. Come on. They're close. Keep up, Grace. Please."

Blurry figures, barely visible in the blowing snow, closed in behind them. Grace fell and lay in the snow. Nick tried to pull her up, using both hands, but he slid. He had no leverage. "You've got to help me, Grace. Come on. You're going to get us both killed."

Suddenly she thought of her baby and was on her feet, running, looking for anything, anyone, preferably headlights from a police car. Nick tried to catch his breath. He hung his head and coughed, looking back for an instant, trying to locate the enemy. Suddenly one figure, the one farthest behind, leaped onto the back of the other and the two fell, rolling in the snow. Clouds of white flew into the air as they struggled. "Come on," Grace yelled.

"Wait—one of them is Shoes," Nick said pointing.

"So what? Let's go!"

"We can't leave him—you go—go, go!" he yelled.

"No—not without you."

"I said get out of here." He spun Grace around toward the exit road. "Go. I'll catch up."

She instinctively hugged him. "I love you," she said and started to run in the knee-deep drifts. Her shoes were all but gone. Half-frozen, half-wet, they fell from her feet. She didn't bother to try to pick them up. She simply stumbled and clawed her way toward the ice-covered road, barely visible in the blinding storm. She headed toward the streetlights, hoping that was the direction in which she'd find help. *I'll never wish for snow again,* she thought as she tried to ignore her frozen, burning feet.

Nick strained to see what was happening in the fight behind them, but there was no movement. He was about three hundred yards from them. Both figures lay still in the snow. They were either badly injured or dead. He didn't know which. But he had to find out. He couldn't let Shoes freeze to death if he was still alive. Nick moved toward them, slowly and cautiously.

"Shoes!" he yelled. "Shoes, answer me."

There was nothing, just silence as the snowed drifted over the still forms. When he was finally within ten feet of them, he noticed a thin red line staining the white ground. He hesitated for a moment, wondering if he should approach, and then decided he had to.

One of the bodies moved, groaning. Nick saw it was Shoes. He slid as he tried to pull Shoes up from under his arms. But Shoes was in good enough shape to get to his feet by himself.

"You OK?" he asked breathlessly.

"Yeah." Shoes wiped the snow from his face. He had a small cut on his cheek but otherwise appeared intact. "Come on, let's get the fuck outta here."

"What about him?" Nick asked.

"Fuck him—the bastard's dead anyhow."

Shoes rolled the portly body over on its back, exposing the thin, bloody line around the man's throat where the nylon fishing line had cut through the flesh. "Can't carry metal in airports," he laughed. "Funny how this works just the same and nobody cares."

"What about the other guy?"

"Dead, too. What is this—twenty questions?" Shoes protested. "It's fuckin' cold out here. Let's move. Move!" Shoes started trotting ahead, pulling his coat collar up around his neck.

In the distance, headlights shone dimly through the relentless snow. Nick cautiously slowed his pace and squinted at the vehicle parked on the airport road. He shielded his eyes with his hand to get a better look.

"It's our pickup," shouted Shoes, who was at least twenty yards ahead. His voice was faint and muffled by the white blanket. He waved as he ran toward the car, passing Grace.

"How do you know?" she yelled. She stopped for a moment to catch her breath. She couldn't feel her feet any longer. Her light coat was frozen around her neck. She didn't think she could go much farther.

"Let's go." Nick tugged at her. "Let's go. Come on."

"How do you know?" she yelled, coughing while trudging forward as if on remote control. She wondered seriously if she could actually make it. *Dear God, please,* she thought.

"We don't. But we have no choice," Nick responded. "We'll freeze to death out here, slowly. Or we'll be shot and it'll be quick. Take your pick."

"Shot is better, I guess," she yelled back, stumbling and scraping her way through a drift.

The three moved on toward the headlights, which now began to flash. Bright, dim, bright, dim. The vehicle began to slowly move toward them, crushing the snow drifts under its huge wheels. From its wide, powerful shape, it was clear that it wasn't the black Chrysler that had brought them to the airport. And it certainly didn't look like it belonged to DiCicco's fleet either. Nick's heart raced with apprehension as the headlights came closer. The vehicle stopped. A dark figure descended from the driver's seat and quickly moved toward them.

Nick stopped, waiting to see what would happen before putting himself and Grace at the mercy of the figure. He held Grace protectively around the waist, her eyes closed against the blowing snow. She was going limp in his grip, and he knew that she couldn't take much more of the punishing cold. Shoes clawed ahead and then suddenly disappeared in a blowing drift. The dark figure moved quickly, and Nick watched as it located and then dragged Shoes into the vehicle. Nick stood frozen in the headlights, not knowing whether to run to or from the would-be rescuer or assassin. Then a voice rang out in the darkness.

"What the fuck are you waiting for? Santa Claus?"

The raucous and obscene voice was music to Nick's ears. He half dragged, half carried Grace to the waiting HumVee. The massive, dark figure, Billy Bonanno, better known as "Fatback," swiftly lifted Grace into the truck. He put the HumVee into gear and began plowing through the blizzard as though it was a flurry.

"You all right?" he asked. "I thought youse was never comin'. I waited out here for four-and-a-half hours in dis fuckin' tank." He reached into his inside coat pocket and pulled out the Beretta and handed it to Shoes.

Shivering, Shoes kissed it and shoved it into his coat pocket.

Chapter XXVIII

The phone rang loudly as Nick put the key into the lock of the door to his condo. He made his way in the dark to the first telephone he could reach and quickly picked up the receiver.

"Hello." His voice was hoarse and gravelly. His throat hurt, and he knew he was getting sick.

"Mr. Ceratto?"

"Yeah. Who's this?"

"This is Detective John Richie from the Pasadena Police Department."

Nick's heart raced for a moment, and then began to pound in his chest. He could hear it through the receiver which he held tightly to his ear. Had Price gone to the cops and charged them with breaking and entering?

"Yeah," he answered nonchalantly. "What can I do for you, Detective Richie?"

"Do you know a Ms. Jane Welles, a nurse?"

"Yes, I do."

"Maybe I should have said *did* you know Ms. Welles?"

"What do you mean—did?"

"Ms. Welles is dead."

"What?…But I just spoke with her about twelve hours ago."

"I know. That's why I'm calling you. Apparently you were one of the last people to see her alive. We found your subpoena in her purse along with your name and telephone number on it, et cetera, and instructions on her appearance in court, et cetera, and a copy of the affidavit of service, et cetera…"

"Will you please stop with the 'et ceteras'?" Nick yelled into the phone. He paused. "I'm sorry. I'm sorry. I had a terrible flight and I just got home."

"Yeah. That's OK. I know about the big storm out your way. You're lucky you got home at all."

"Yes, Detective Richie, you're right. You're so right." Nick shook his head. "Tell me, how did this happen? She was my star witness. I've got a case to try tomorrow, and I desperately needed her."

"I guessed that was the case, or you wouldn't have come all the way out here to serve her yourself."

"Can you tell me what happened to her?"

"I can tell you what we know."

Grace came up behind Nick and put her head on his shoulder, embracing him in the dark. It was warm and the dark comforted her now. She sensed something had gone wrong, and she knew it had to be with Donna Price.

"She was fatally stabbed in the parking lot behind the hospital. The coroner put her death at about eleven thirty p.m. our time. No weapon was found. Her body was a mess. Stab wounds in her neck, chest, arms, hands. Looks like she tried to fight off her attacker and lost. Her purse was found in the bushes behind her. Nurse's ID was intact, and so were the papers you served her with. But her wallet was missing. There was no cash or other valuables found on her. Oh, yeah. So was her watch. You could tell she wore one by the white mark on her wrist. Looks like robbery was the motive. But I wanted to call you to tell you that your witness is gonna be a no show. And to ask you if you know anything about her that would target her as a victim. Other than the first conclusion most cops jump to." He chuckled.

"Yeah, I know about the affinity cops have for conclusions, sometimes the wrong ones, or should I say most times? Well, Detective, I've got a long story to tell you. But I can't right now. I've got a case I've got to try tomorrow."

"You gonna try a case in a blizzard?"

"Judge Barnes doesn't care if there's an earthquake going on. This case will be tried, no matter what. "

"You Philadelphia lawyers are nuts, I swear," Richie laughed.

"Yeah, I'll call you later." Nick hung up and turned to Grace, smoothing her wet hair. "She's dead," he said.

"I thought so. I'm so sorry for all this…"

"For what?" he whispered, studying the silhouette of her fine-featured face in the dimness.

"For finding her, for almost getting us killed, for getting her killed. I should have just stayed out of this."

"Grace, you did what you had to do. You did what was right. Now I have to do what's right. He rubbed the top of her head and kissed her on the cheek, and then moved to the nearest light switch.

Grace screamed simultaneously with the click of the switch. Nick instantly turned and saw a large figure sitting in the overstuffed chair. The man stared intently, blinking from the glare of the sudden light. He fondled an AK47 equipped with a silencer.

"Don't have no heart attack on me. I'm wit' DiCicco," he said in a gravelly voice. "I'm Jake—'Jake the Shake.' Ever hear of me? They call me Shake because I'm the best shakedown artist in Philly—" he laughed—"maybe even in New York."

Nick stared incredulously at the man, his mouth agape, wondering what the fuck DiCicco was up to. He had never mentioned Jake. And Nick had never heard of him.

"I'm here to protect youse," he said apologetically. "I shoulda said somethin' when you opened the door, but the phone was ringin'. Sorry." He grinned and shook his head. "I'm really sorry."

Nick blew out the air stored in his lungs for a fast escape. "Why the hell did you have the lights out?"

"Cause *youse* had them out, and I didn't want nobody to know I was here. Capish?" The round, overweight man pulled himself out of the chair, puffing as though he had just run ten miles. His bald head was moist and glimmered as he walked under the recessed ceiling lights. His jowls shook as he plodded heavily toward the kitchen, carrying the awesome weapon with its muzzle pointed up.

"I'm hungry. I been here all day wit'out eatin' nothin'. You got anything to eat in here?" he said, peering into an almost empty refrigerator.

"Shoes went to get something at the Wawa. Hoagies I guess. I don't know." Nick pulled off his tie. "You know Shoes?"

"Yeah. You mean Scarpetta wit' dem big feet always getting in da way?" The man laughed.

"Help yourself to what's in there."

"I need a bed now," Grace said, heading straight for the bedroom. She disappeared into the darkened room and collapsed into an instant, deep sleep, damp clothes and all. In a few seconds she was comatose.

Jake plopped himself onto a kitchen stool, hips hanging over the sides of the seat. He had found some leftover pasta, which he was intently devouring. For him, this was simply an appetizer, pending whatever was coming from Wawa. Nick excused himself and headed for the shower.

The hot water felt good on his naked body. His muscles begin to relax. *If only life felt this good all the time*, he thought. A good meal, a great bottle of wine, sex, and a hot shower. He was easy to please. Forget the competition, the greed, the dark side of human nature. If only he could tell Judge Barnes to relax, get laid, and forget about the Supreme Court—forget about the Riley trial. If only *he* could forget about the Riley case. He decided he would request a meeting with Barnes, privately, at eight thirty in the morning. Nick knew that Barnes always showed up at eight or earlier to whip his courtroom into shape. He was obsessed with punctuality and time—a proper time for recess and a proper time for lunch and a proper time for breaks—the show *would* go on according to schedule. That meant that every court employee who had the misfortune to be appointed to Barnes's courtroom had to arrive at least half an hour early in order to inspect the courtroom, make sure all the chairs in the jury box were placed in a straight line, equally spaced apart. To make sure the bible was positioned so that it faced the witness to be sworn in. To make sure the sound system was set to the proper volume, not too loud, not too soft.

Barnes had the only courtroom in the city where his official court reporter was set up and sitting in her place, properly attired in a navy blue suit, ten minutes before Barnes made his entrance. His secretary, Mary, always made sure his robe was spotless and that his coffee was hot. Similarly, his bailiff had to be dressed in a starched white shirt, navy blue wool suit, and maroon tie with a scales of justice tie pin placed dead center.

Nick would have to convince the Nazi that the case should not go forward, that it was a fraud, a setup, and that the plaintiff didn't die as a result of negligence but as a result of premeditated murder. And he would have to do it without Donna Price. What chance did he stand? Little or none, he thought. But it was worth a try. Even if the judge thought it was just more legal shenanigans.

He turned toward the shower head. The water ran down his face and he closed his eyes tightly, relishing the feel of the light sting of the spray. Somehow a shower cleansed the mind as well as the body. He felt his strength and confidence returning. Things started to fall into perspective. He moved his head slightly to the right, away from the direct force of the water, and opened his eyes. For a second he thought he saw a figure in the mirror over the vanity. He rubbed the water from his eyes to see if they were playing tricks on him. They weren't. It was moving toward the shower. The figure stopped at the linen closet. Nick could see a dark object in the figure's hand. He recognized it as a gun with a silencer. He squinted, pretending not to see the figure. He knew that if he didn't move quickly, he'd be dead. He turned off the shower and opened the door.

The figure stepped back. Nick spotted him in the mirror as he grabbed for a towel. He started to dry himself while facing the shower, purposely keeping his back to the figure whose reflection he could now see on the chrome shower head. His heart raced and the blood pounded in his head. He could hear it whooshing through his brain as he scanned the reflected scene. Suddenly he turned and simultaneously ducked as the figure fired two shots—pop! pop! He lunged and tackled the would-be assassin, and the huge figure fell backward with a thud as his head hit the sharp edge of the marble Jacuzzi, spurting blood everywhere. The man's chest heaved once, and his eyes opened wide in a fixed stare. His skull was split open like a ripe watermelon.

Nick's instincts continued to rule. He crawled to the dropped gun, picked it up, stood, and shot the man between the eyes at close range. Maybe he was already dead and maybe not. He was taking no chances—and no prisoners—a lesson he had learned well on the streets. He dropped the gun, wrapped a towel around his waist, and ran into the bedroom, praying that Grace had not been harmed.

He saw her lying on the bed, still in her damp clothes. He walked quietly to her while he prayed to God. She was breathing. He pulled the blankets back. No blood. *Thank God*, he thought as he stroked her damp hair. She had been lucky that he was target number one. Maybe God hadn't abandoned him after all. He tried to think of a prayer of thanks, but he couldn't remember one.

He went into the living room, poured himself a double scotch, and was dialing 911 as Shoes arrived. Nick nodded toward the bathroom. Shoes took one look, checked the body still bleeding on the marble floor, shook his head, and walked back out to Nick, who had just finished reporting the killing.

"Where the fuck you come from?" Shoes yelled. "Nebraska? How could you let this guy get in here? This big hunk of salami ain't no Italian. He's a Russki-red Commie fuck. I *know* this guy." Shoes pulled Shakes's wallet from his jacket pocket and threw it, opened, on the floor. The driver's license showed the man's fat face, grinning broadly over the name Vladimir Cherobin.

Nick shook his head in disbelief. "I guess I've been away too long. You're right. What's the matter with my head?"

Shoes pointed his index finger at Nick. "You better come back and hang on the corner once in a while and get some fuckin' street smarts back in your brain—" pointing angrily at his own head—"or you'll be dead in a year. Capish?"

Nick ignored the absurd mandate but wondered how he could have been so naïve. How out of touch he had become! How easily manipulated. He never would have let this happen before his transformation. Trust a man he found sitting in the dark in his apartment? With a gun! What had he become? He had no answer.

Chapter XXIX

"Mr. Ceratto." Ralph Kirby touched the brim of his worn, half-frozen Kangol cap. Melting droplets of snow fell on the red Herez carpet. "May I sit down?"

"Please make this short, Detective. I've been traveling all night, I haven't had any sleep, and I have to start a trial tomorrow morning at eight o'clock—" Nick checked his watch—"just six hours from now."

"Sure, sure, I understand. You need your rest, and I know judges don't like waiting—especially for lawyers." Kirby chuckled. "But there's the simple matter of a dead man lying on your bathroom floor—that you shot." The detective paused, took off his hat, and shook the melting snow off onto the rare carpet.

"I gave the police a detailed statement. The man was in my apartment when I returned. He said that he was a bodyguard from the service I was using, and then he came after me when I was in the shower. I saw him, tackled him, grabbed his gun, and shot him."

"His head was smashed." Kirby put his hand to the back of his own head.

"Yeah. He must of hit his head on the way down."

"Ah—before or after you shot him?"

Nick looked squarely into the detective's wise, squinting eyes. "After."

"Of course, of course. You wouldn't shoot a helpless man, bleeding to death on the ground, would you?"

"No. That would be unreasonable force."

"Correct me if I'm wrong on the law." Kirby scratched his head. "But wouldn't that be *murder*?"

"Detective Kirby, are you accusing me of murdering this piece of shit, or are you just playing your usual games?"

Kirby laughed, shaking his head. "Of course not, Mr. Ceratto. Of course not. What makes you even begin to think I would do such a thing? I'm just trying to understand—to gather all the facts. I don't make such accusations—ever. That's the DA's job."

"Is that all then?" As Nick showed Kirby to the door, the black zippered bag containing the body was wheeled past them. The crime lab had finished with the photographs, prints, and samples and sealed the bathroom door with yellow tape.

"I hope you have another bathroom. I'd hate to see you go to court like this." Nick rubbed his hands across his chin. The stubble was as obvious as the bags under his eyes. "You'll need to look your best. Maybe I'll be there. What courtroom?" Kirby's eyes lit up. "Oh yes, the Sean Riley case. I know—Judge Barnes, right?"

"Yes. Good night, Detective."

"One more thing, please, Mr. Ceratto. I'm really sorry. The young lady, Ms. Monahan…?"

"She was asleep in the bedroom. She's still asleep. She's exhausted."

"Yes, yes, I know. I won't wake her now. But I'll need to talk to her. And to you, too. You'll have to come down to homicide as soon as you're out of court."

"I'll tell her." Nick waved his hand toward the open door. The coroner's men were in he hall with the body, waiting for a down elevator.

"Was there anyone else in your apartment?"

"No." Nick was quickly losing patience and irritably rubbed his upper lip.

"But wasn't there another person traveling with you, ah, from the protection service that you retained—a Mister…?"

"Scarpetta," Nick interrupted. "He had gone to get sandwiches when this happened."

"And…?"

"He wasn't here during the attack."

"But after?"

"He came back and left to see if he could find a cop on the street while I dialed for help."

"He didn't touch the body?"

"He may have. I don't know. I was busy dialing 911."

"Where is he now?"

"I don't know. Now, get out—please."

"I'm sorry. I know you're tired. I'll catch you tomorrow." Kirby clapped his damp hat onto his head. "Good luck tomorrow—oh, by the way…"

Nick sighed.

"Did you know that the Maglio and Lopez cases are active again?"

"No," Nick said flatly, covering his surprise.

"Yes, Gates and Mike Rosa—you know, the Montco DA—are working together on them. They think there might be something to them—a connection. You know, with that beautiful girl—what was her first name?"

"Maria Elena."

"Yeah. See, she was a cousin…"

"I know."

"Well, you're in luck. You were concerned about the investigation on this case—or the lack of interest." Kirby smiled and shifted his weight from one foot to the other. His knees were aching. "I'm proud to say I'm the man they've assigned to the Lopez and Maglio cases. Funny thing, I was cleaning out my desk—I'm about to retire soon, you know, and I thought I'd get a head start with going through all the junk—and what did I find?" Kirby put his hand in his pocket and pulled out a small key. "This."

"So. What's the significance?" Nick stared at the key with a perplexed look.

"Remember I asked you about a small key. You know, when I talked to you on the phone after the Lopez death. You know. After I met with you in this apartment? When I delivered the videotape. *Raiders?*"

"I guess," Nick said vaguely. "So what's the deal?"

"This was in her safe-deposit box along with the tape. I lost track of it in all the junk on my desk, and now I found it.

"Great. It was obviously important to her," Nick said, sarcastically.

"Bingo." Kirby laughed hoarsely. He tipped his hat as he turned to leave, reaching for the ever-present hard pack of Marlboros carefully tucked in his inside coat pocket. He waited until he was outside the door of Nick's condo before lighting up. Then he cupped the cigarette carefully in his right hand so as not to set off an ultra-sensitive smoke alarm. All this *No Smoking*, here, there, everywhere. It was unconstitutional, he thought as he entered the down elevator. Life, liberty, and the pursuit of happiness, wasn't that the guarantee? He shook his head as he walked into the cold outside and made his way to his salt-streaked car. He put the tired heap in gear and headed toward Graymont Street and his two-story row house, his cold dinner, and his sleeping wife.

Chapter XXX

Gusts of wind swept tiny, dry snowflakes across the frozen lawn. The leaded glass windows of the stone Tudor style Chestnut Hill home sparkled in the light of the wintry dawn. A limo driver paced nervously in the driveway, stamping his feet to keep warm as he waited for Judge Joseph Barnes. But the judge was taking his time. This was a big day—the opening of a high-profile trial where he would be prominently featured as the presiding trial judge. He carefully checked himself out in the long, antique mirror hanging over the entry hall table. He moved his face to and fro, checking his shave. It was clean. His skin was smooth and shiny. He patted his jowls with the back of his hand. He liked them. They made him look more distinguished, wiser and worthy of trust. He smoothed back his salt-and-pepper hair as he moved his head to the side to get a better view of the haircut he had recently gotten. It was fresh. It looked good, no stray hairs at the ears.

Next he donned a long, black, cashmere overcoat. It was almost as authoritative as his black robe. He adjusted his red silk tie so that it peeked ever so slightly out between the coat lapels. And then the last touch—the white silk scarf laid carefully around his neck so that the ends were absolutely even. He never tucked it inside his coat. He wanted the expensive, long, hand-knotted fringe to show.

Outside, the driver pulled up his collar against the cold. The blood seemed to leave his hands. He had rung the bell to alert the judge fifteen minutes ago. But he was made to wait outside until His Honor made his exit. He was not permitted to wait inside the limousine, which had to be kept running so that it would be just the right temperature for His Honor. Judge Barnes wanted his driver standing *outside,* ready to open the rear door for him when he decided that it was time. And it was not—at least not yet. He regretted accepting the assignment of being the driver for the peacock of the Court of Common Pleas. At first he had been pleased as hell with the patronage job. But then after a few weeks of being spoken down to, or not being spoken to at all, he came to hate the judge, and the job. But what good would it do? Wasting energy on hatred. It was too cold. He blew hard into his cupped, black leather gloves.

Finally, the dark oak door opened and His Honor stepped briskly out, avoiding eye contact with the underling.

The driver opened the nearest rear passenger door for the man he disliked, and could possibly hate, although it wasn't worth the effort. He didn't expect a thank-you, or a nod, or anything. And he didn't get it. Accepting his position, he simply closed the door, got into the driver's seat and put the limo into gear. The heavy car carefully made its way toward Kelly Drive, humming softly past other stately stone mansions built around the turn of the last century.

Barnes was proud of his neighborhood. It was still within the city limits, as a judge's home had to be by local law. The homes were large. Some were considered mansions by current standards—the palaces of nineteenth-century industrial tycoons. Some had been kept as single-family dwellings. Some had become schools for the children of the privileged. But the largest had been converted into small museums. He admired the ancient oaks and sycamores that he drove past each morning. He felt he had something in common with them—endurance, power, and timelessness. He was pleased with the high stone walls and ornate iron gates leading to meticulously maintained lawns. *Ah yes*, he thought, *this is living*. And when he was elected to Supreme Court, he'd move into one of the largest and the best—one with *ten* fireplaces. He liked fireplaces. They were traditional and enduring, like himself.

The limo phone rang softly. The driver picked it up on the first ring.

"Your Honor, it's your clerk, sir. He would like to speak with you."

Without responding to the driver, Judge Barnes continued his fix on his elegant surroundings as they quietly slid past his window.

He picked up the phone from the rear console, still staring out the window.

"Yes, Thomas. What is it?"

"Your Honor. It's Nick Ceratto. He's requesting an *ex parte* conference with you at eight a.m. He says it's urgent…"

"I don't care if it is urgent," Barnes interrupted coldly. "Didn't you tell him, Thomas, that I don't conduct *any* pretrial matters without the presence of *all* attorneys involved? In this case, John Asher?"

"I did, Your Honor. But he was insistent that I call you to make the request. He said that there's an ethical problem with the case and he's going to request leave to withdraw based on this serious problem."

"What? At this late date? Withdraw and postpone this case? Never! I won't allow it." Barnes's face reddened, something he hated. It represented a loss of control when control was critical. His career depended on this case—on his presiding over this case. He had groomed himself for it for three years. He was not about to hear something which might be so important that he would have to postpone the trial or, even worse, have to recuse himself.

"I agree, Your Honor. I agree. But shouldn't you meet with Ceratto to find out what he knows that you should be aware of before going public…?"

The U-word. His clerk hadn't used it, but Barnes was terrified of it. He prided himself on his purity of character and pristine professionalism, his ability to never be affiliated with anything or anyone that smacked in the least of impropriety…of *unethical conduct.* And in this case? Never. He had seen to it that the attorneys conducted themselves impeccably, that scheduling had been done fairly, giving each side ample time to conduct its investigation. It had to be the work of Joe Maglio, he thought. That lying, scheming wop. And now the other guinea was going public—and it was going to cost him his life's work. He wouldn't have it.

"Tell Ceratto to meet me in my chambers at eight sharp. And I want my court reporter present and ready. Call Mary. Tell her to be prepared to deal with this. And tell her to call John Asher. I want him waiting at my chambers while this meeting is going on. I want all staff on high alert and ready to go. Keep the jury happy. Get them doughnuts and coffee, comic books or something the simpletons understand. Ceratto's not going to do this to me!"

"And to his clients, sir," the clerk unwisely interjected.

"Fuck his clients. This is my trial and my courtroom and my reputation. Got that, Thomas?"

"Yes sir. Yes, Your Honor."

"Good." Barnes slammed the phone into its cradle. He had never taken his eyes from the window. His stare was as cold and icy as the half-frozen Schuylkill River, which had come into view as they turned onto Kelly Drive on their way toward the city's center and its impressive skyline.

Chapter XXXI

Cigarette smoke blew back into the detective's face as he exhaled into the wind. He flipped the butt from his open car window into the slush-covered street and moved his aching bones from the filthy vehicle he had been assigned. Finally out of the driver's seat, Ralph Kirby removed a few dangling threads from the sleeve of his frayed overcoat so that he could read his Timex. Eight o'clock. *Perfect*, he thought. He had fifteen or so minutes to talk to the Lopez girls before they went off to school. He rang the bell and waited on the freshly shoveled stoop. The exterior of the small, two-story, brick row house was immaculate. The trim was freshly painted. The brass doorknob was polished to a glimmer. A lighted statue of the Virgin Mary smiled kindly at him from the squeaky clean picture window. She was flanked by two small vases of plastic flowers. It was clear that the home was well kept and lovingly cared for by good, honest, hardworking people. It stood out like a jewel from the blight around it.

The detective rang the bell again, hoping for some relief from the relentless cold and wind. He squinted and pulled up his coat collar. He could feel a virus approaching, to which he would refuse to succumb as usual. Sometimes he won. Sometimes he didn't. But what was important to him was to keep fighting. As with this case, which he needed to wrap up before Gates put it in limbo again. He smelled a rat for sure and wanted to find it before it went underground again.

He felt for the small glassine envelope in his coat pocket. It was there, safely tucked away in the only pocket not opened at the seams from the wear and tear of carrying many small significant, and insignificant, pieces of evidence over the years. The coat, like he himself, was tired and needed a well-deserved rest. He finally heard the dead bolt disengage with a hard click. A sliver of space appeared at the edge of the door revealing part of a small face through the narrow opening protected by a chain lock. A brown eye framed by thick dark lashes appeared. Kirby bent down and put his face close to the door. He was hoping that his crouched position would minimize his largeness and make him more acceptable to the small person behind the partly opened door.

"Hello there," he smiled awkwardly. "My name is Detective Ralph Kirby."

The child said nothing. Her dark eye darted back and forth with caution as she surveyed the situation.

"I'd like to talk to you and your sister. Can I come in?"

Still no response.

Kirby desperately tried to think of something to say that would win her trust, but everything he thought of sounded as if it came from the mouth of a pederast: *Hello, little girl, I have something to show you.* But he did have something to show her. He decided to overcome his reluctance and just show it to her. "I have something that was your mother's." He reached hurriedly into his pocket, hoping that she wouldn't smash his nose between door and the frame, fumbling with the slippery flap of the envelope, and took the tiny, brass key between his thumb and forefinger. "See," he said, still feeling uncomfortable with the attempt to lure her to open the door.

Immediately the chain latch fell and the door swung open. Still crouching, Kirby found himself face-to-face with the second grader. The child stood under four feet tall. Her raven black hair was tightly pulled back into a pony tail and tied with a white ribbon. Her school uniform, a plaid jumper, was two sizes too large to allow for at least another two years of growth before another had to be bought. Either that, or it was a hand-me-down from her older sister. Although the hem almost reached to her ankles, she didn't appear to mind. It was clean and she was proud to wear it.

"Lily," a voice called angrily from behind her. Suddenly an older girl appeared, dressed in an identical uniform. She stepped protectively in front of the smaller child, obviously her sister.

"What do you want?" she asked in as husky and hostile a tone as she could muster. Her hand was on the door, ready to slam it shut in Kirby's face.

Kirby was quick to anticipate the girl's inevitable refusal to cooperate. And understanding it fully, he stood erect and gave her his most professional detective look. There was no conning this one, he thought. "I need to speak to you and your sister," he said. He pulled out his badge and flashed at the older girl. "I'm Detective Ralph Kirby."

"Can I see your badge again?" she said.

He opened the wallet and held it at her eye level. The girl studied it, looking back and forth between the ID and Kirby.

"You have another picture ID to match this—like a driver's license or passport, or something?"

Kirby laughed silently to himself. *The kid's savvy and got chutzpah.* He complied. *What's good for the goose is good for the gander,* he thought, as he waited while she compared photos and signatures.

"You look a lot younger in these pictures, mister," she said, suspiciously. "The job musta gotten to you. They say age kicks the shit outta ya."

"Yeah," he said, shaking his head.

"OK, step in." She allowed him only as far as the tiny, tiled vestibule. "What's this all about?"

"Do you have an adult who's in charge here?" he asked, patronizingly. This was proper procedure when questioning children, and he liked to go by the book, especially with kids.

"I'm an adult and I'm in charge," she said while pushing Lily back to allow Kirby room.

"No, I mean like a grandmother, an aunt, a neighbor, somebody in charge."

"*I'm* in charge," she insisted. "Can't you hear right?"

"But," he shook his head, "I can't…"

"What? You can't hear—or you can't talk to a kid?" She started moving forward to push him out the door. "OK, then you can leave."

"No. No, I can talk to you," he stammered. Outmaneuvered by a kid—*Damn!* he thought. "Ever think of being a detective?"

"Nope. I wanna be on the other side. I'm going for a law degree—criminal law. I wanna be a constitutional lawyer."

"You'd make a darn good one…ah…" he hesitated. "Your name?"–a standard question meant to break the ice.

"You gonna take out your pad and take notes?"

"No, I wasn't thinking of…"

"You better, mister," she warned, shaking her head. "A lotta bullshit's been going on around here."

"He wants to show us Mommy's key," Lily chimed in. "Mister, show her the key."

"Let's see it," the older girl commanded, holding out her hand.

"Unh, unh," Kirby shook his head. "I have to hold it. It's evidence. And I can't let it out of my possession—not even for a second." He guardedly opened his palm to reveal the tiny object.

"Turn it over," the older girl said, cocking her head, her hands authoritatively folded across her chest.

Kirby obeyed, carefully turning it over in his palm to reveal a gouge purposely cut in the head. "That's it. Yep. That's my mom's key. Now can I please have it?"

"No." Kirby quickly closed his hand. "It belongs to the district attorney and to the city of Philadelphia and to the courts. It's evidence."

"You know that Gates bitch that won't find my mother's killer."

Kirby reeled at the girl's language as well as her intuitiveness. "Why do say that?"

"I read the papers. I see people snooping around here. I hear people talking. I know what's going on. But nothing happens. Gates doesn't want anything to happen. She's covering for somebody. And what's another Latino corpse to her?"

"Well, *I* want to find your mother's killers before she closes the case and the guilty go unpunished." Kirby lowered his eyes realizing that he stood before a child with more intelligence than most adults he knew—a child who knew the truth.

The girl sensed his sincerity. "Why didn't you say that in the first place?" She held out her hand. "My name is Carmen, Carmen Lopez."

Chapter XXXII

Nick Ceratto sat in the hard wooden armchair behind the scarred walnut counsel table. His stomach was doing flips, but no one would know it. He was good at hiding anxiety and perfect at disguising fear. He knew that the best defense was an offense. He had learned this as a kid on the streets, and Joe Maglio had helped hone this natural talent to a perfect edge. He was dressed in his best imported trial uniform —a charcoal single-button Ralph Lauren suit that fit snugly around his muscular frame. His shave was fresh, his hair slicked back. His legs were crossed casually. His black Italian shoes glinted in the harsh lights of the poorly refurbished nineteenth-century courtroom. Air-conditioning units bulged from taped windows, and dappled brown stains surrounded the heating registers that had been carelessly gouged into the once impressive woodwork. Here, justice would be administered in the case of *The Estate of Sean Riley vs Victor Manin, M.D. et al*—here in the shabby courtroom of the Honorable Joseph Barnes.

Nick knew the nature of the contrary, power hungry beast which he would face. If he had requested a formal hearing on the record with a court reporter present, Barnes would have first conducted an informal meeting, off the record, and would have been forewarned and had time to think. If he requested a private meeting in the judge's chambers, he would get exactly what he wanted—a formal conference, on the record, which would put Barnes between a boulder and a mountain.

His assessment had been correct. Nick sat and watched and waited as Barnes struggled with the bomb Nick had put before him, trying to figure out which wire to cut first.

The courtroom was silent. The jury box was empty. The court reporter was ready with her fingers poised on the keys of her machine. John Asher waited anxiously outside the closed double doors guarded by security to prevent the intrusion of the ever-present, ever-pesky press. He wondered what the fuck Ceratto was doing in there alone with Judge Barnes. He felt assured that Barnes wouldn't hurt him. They were members of the same golf club and frequented the Union League, the exclusive Broad Street club—a bastion of male dominance since the Civil War. He would soon find out the purpose of this meeting, and then put his objection on the record as to its privacy. When you didn't know what to do, the motto of every lawyer was to do *something*, anything, rather than sit with your thumb up your ass.

Inside, Judge Barnes inwardly fumed. *I knew this little, fucking, corner-hanging, two-bit punk had something up his sleeve. How did I know that? Why did I put this mess on the record? I fell right into his hands,* he thought. He fidgeted on the bench. *Think, Barnes, think. Your life depends on it. And that little fucking machine between the bitch's legs is going to tell the world what you say.* His tortoiseshell half-glasses perched precariously on the bridge of his perfectly straight, WASP nose. They dared not slide. They served a purpose. He could look over the rims and smiling, strike terror and causing stomachs to churn. He recognized fear in the faces and in the body language of those before him, and he relished it. But this time he saw none of that in Nick Ceratto. This time when he looked down, he saw his own reflection in the polished wood of his bench. And he recognized fear in that reflection—his own.

"This morning, this court, with a court reporter present, conducted a *private* meeting with counsel for plaintiff, prior to jury selection, at the request of Nicholas Ceratto, attorney for the Estate of Sean Riley, in the matter of *The Estate of Sean Riley versus Dr. Victor Manin et al.* As the record shows, Mr. Ceratto has requested that this court postpone the trial pending investigation into alleged misconduct of his former partners, Martin Silvio and Harold Levin, in orchestrating the death of plaintiff's decedent, Sean Riley, in order to enable them to bring a and wrongful death case against Dr. Victor Manin, the surgeon who operated on Captain Riley prior to his demise. Mr. Ceratto has indicated that there is evidence that one of his own witnesses, Nurse Doletov, the operating room nurse who is to testify on behalf of the Riley family, intentionally caused Mr. Riley's death. Mr. Ceratto also indicates that his former partners, in some way, participated in the deaths of Joseph Maglio, a former partner of the firm, and of Celia Lopez, a receptionist in the firm, and of a woman named Maria Elena Maglio, a cousin of Joseph Maglio, in an effort to cover up their misdeeds. Mr. Ceratto, in essence, accuses his former employers of fraud and of conspiracy in the three deaths. He also accuses his own witness, Nurse Doletov, of perjury and murder. He also states that the witness he had intended to call to prove Nurse Doletov's involvement is now dead. This nurse, Donna Price, was also present during the surgery performed on Sean Riley and witnessed the murder and fled to California in fear of her life. Mr. Ceratto states that she was subpoenaed to testify and was mysteriously murdered just prior to her appearance here in court. Mr. Ceratto has no other proof other than himself and a paralegal, Ms. Grace Monahan, who heard Ms. Price describe the alleged murder. Mr. Ceratto has no further proof of the involvement of his former employers in any plot to murder anyone, only sheer speculation based on coincidence. This court finds Mr. Ceratto's accusations dangerous and defamatory. They should not be discussed outside this courtroom. Mr. Ceratto has indicated that his concern, and intentions, are to protect the integrity of our legal system and to protect the rights of all citizens including those of his opponent, the defendant, Dr. Victor Manin. He has requested that this court delay this trial until a full investigation into these allegations is conducted. He has requested not only an indefinite postponement, but also to be allowed to withdraw as plaintiff's counsel at this, the final hour, on the day of jury selection. Mr. Ceratto cites ethical considerations for his request.

"Based on what this court has heard today from Mr. Ceratto, this court has determined that this trial will *not* be postponed, that it will continue on schedule with jury selection to begin in one hour. That based on no evidence whatsoever, Mr. Ceratto's request is frivolous, foolhardy, and defamatory. It is the opinion of this court that Mr. Ceratto's conduct, if allowed to continue as requested, would breach the standards of ethical conduct required of a trial attorney to skillfully and zealously represent his client, in this case the Rileys. Mr. Ceratto would turn his back on his clients and prejudice their case with baseless allegations and dangerous speculation, something which this court cannot and will not allow.

"Therefore you will try this case, Mr. Ceratto. You will not offer, at any time, any evidence prejudicial to your clients' case. You will not turn this court into a media circus. You will not embarrass me or your former employers or yourself with scandalous and defamatory accusations. And lastly—you will do nothing to prejudice your clients' case. If you do, I will personally see that you never set foot inside another courtroom and that you will spend a long, long time regretting your actions—behind bars, if possible. This is a gag order, Mr. Ceratto. You will talk to no one about this—not to the press, not to Mr. Asher, not even to your own clients. Is that clear?"

Barnes's face was the color of his tie. He loosened his heavily starched collar with his index finger, moving his head back and forth as if to pry it away. His eyes flashed with rage. *How dare this little wop do this to me*, he thought.

Nick stood, smiled politely, nodded his head. "Very well, Your Honor. It's your call. I've given you the information. What happens with it now is Your Honor's responsibility. Now, I'm prepared to pick a jury...Judge."

Chapter XXXIII

Nick Ceratto studied them carefully as they shuffled through the jury box and into the scuffed wooden chairs they would call home until the trial was over. They were twelve, plain, ordinary folks, actually downright drab, the way they were supposed to be. Five men and seven women, bland and nameless people. For purposes of this case, they were perfect because they were nonthreatening to both sides, perfectly chosen by both Nick Ceratto and John Asher because of their neutrality. Those who had revealed any opinion on anything having to do with the justice system, cops, or doctors had been stricken. Nick had made sure there were no doctors or nurses, no one even remotely connected with medicine. And John Asher had struck all those in law enforcement, all city employees, as well as anyone who had a personal injury case: past, present, or anyone else who wished they had one.

The attorneys were left with solid citizens; blue collar, white collar, and the unemployed, who would hold the fates and futures of the litigants and their attorneys in their hands.

Nick had determined that there was nothing he could do at this point but try the case to win. He couldn't throw it—it would be too obvious, plus doing so would ensure his disbarment. He had made the record, he had put the decision in Barnes's hands. Now it was the judge's problem. Nick would close his eyes to justice, to what was right and what was true, and do his job as directed.

Judge Barnes started. His booming voice filled the courtroom with his obviously canned opening: instructions on the flag, the privilege of serving it not only on the field of battle but also in the jury box.

The idea of the courtroom being a battleground was not new, certainly not to the trial lawyers. Certainly they were more like gladiators than combatants on the field; and the jury, spectators

205

who would ultimately decide who would live and who would die. He blocked the judge's drivel out of his mind and focused on his client, the widow Riley, who sat quietly beside him clutching her Miraculous medal in her thin, veined hand. It was clear that she was scared to death. Her eyes were swollen and puffy from lack of sleep and crying. Her mostly gray hair was pulled into a tight bun. Her shapeless, black dress hung old and baggy from her hunched shoulders. She reminded Nick of a nun he once knew in grade school, but she looked far older. His sympathies surfaced as he deliberately put himself into a state to win. *She deserves something for her loss*, he thought, *regardless of who was responsible*. She was pathetic, he rationalized.

He gave her hand a quick squeeze of encouragement as Barnes carried on, warning the jury about the persistence of the press, and to resist the temptation to talk about the case. They were warned and re-warned against any communication with the outside or with each other. They were threatened with every sanction in the book, including fines and jail time if they failed in their duty. Judge Barnes paused for a moment, staring sternly at the jury.

"Do you understand your duties in this case? Do you accept the rule of silence regarding talking to any person about this case?"

The panel nodded, and mumbled their affirmation.

Juror number three, a wide-eyed schoolteacher, shook her curls as she moved her head up and down with approval. Most of the jurors were eager to begin and struck with the importance of the task ahead. Barnes made sure of that.

All except juror number one, who seemed angry at the world. Alonzo Hodge had just started a new job as a line chef at Dante's Downtown, and he was mighty pissed that he just might lose it because of jury duty. Not to mention the lost income. He had been told that he couldn't be fired for serving on a jury; but he knew better. They'd find some excuse, some legal loophole to fuck a black man. He sat erect, his arms folded tightly over his chest, his gaze intense. He said nothing, mumbled nothing. He didn't shake his head up and down with the rest of the jury. And he wasn't afraid of the honkey with the black robe sitting on the throne—no sir.

Nick zeroed in on Alonzo. He had coal black skin, sharp intelligent eyes, and a face unmarred by complacency. It was a face unlike the rest; it was not the face of a follower. He would be a tough one to get through to, he thought. But if he was successful, the jury was his. Nick accepted the challenge. He knew that juror number one would be guided by his own principles, whatever they were, and not by Barnes's, Asher's, or the widow Riley's. Nick liked that.

"Mr. Ceratto, you may open to the jury.," Judge Barnes proclaimed with the same fervor as an announcer at a stock car race: *Gentlemen, you may start your engines.*

"Thank you, Your Honor." Nick rose and slowly walked toward the jury. He rested a yellow legal pad on the narrow edge of the mahogany box and leaned against the partition to get as close to the them as possible, as if he were going to share a secret.

Suddenly the whoosh of a closing door broke the silence and the moment Nick had claimed as his own. All attention was diverted to the back of the room as a bailiff ushered in Silvio and Levin.

The sight of them was not a surprise to Nick, although he lost focus momentarily. Levin quietly followed Silvio as they took seats in the row just outside the bar of the court, and leaning over to Silvio, whispered into his ear, never taking his eyes off Nick. He somberly checked his watch and then shifted nervously in his seat as he checked the jury.

As Nick turned back toward the panel, the door whooshed open again. The bailiff's body blocked Nick's view momentarily, but then he turned aside and Nick watched as Shoes and Little Al each shook the bailiff's hand and then took seats directly behind Silvio and Levin.

Alonzo Hodge's eyes darted quickly back and forth from Nick to the spectators. It was as if he could read Nick's mind; that these two guys were not there to lend support, but to watch him carefully.

The room crackled with tension like an electric current arcing and then bouncing from one body to another.

"Mr. Ceratto, please begin your opening." Barnes glared over his half glasses at Nick, not appreciating the presence of the two thugs his bailiff had allowed in his courtroom. He would see about this during recess.

Nick turned back to the jury and smiled. He ignored Judge Barnes and spoke directly to them.

"Sorry—I was taken off stride by the unexpected presence of our guests." Some of the jury smiled, some shifted, some were deadpan and did nothing but wait patiently.

Nick paced to and fro for a few seconds, as if in thought, and then reached for his yellow pad. He tore off the first two pages and threw them into the trash bucket next to counsel table. Mrs. Riley stared at him, wondering what he was doing, what was going on as Nick unbuttoned his jacket and loosened his tie.

"Ladies and gentlemen of the jury." He paused and then chuckled. "I guess you've heard that a million times on TV. As a matter of fact, this kind of opening is old—isn't it? That prepared script is stale. It's boring, and you didn't come here to listen to the same old stuff. I'm not going to insult your intelligence either. So, I've dumped my opening statement in the can where it belongs."

Alonzo Hodges leaned forward, his brow creased with puzzlement. Bradley Jones, juror number ten, a mailman glad to be off his feet, opened his eyes for the first time since he had been seated.

"So, during our time together, I plan to be straight with you, to treat as you equals; as I would want to be treated if I was in your position. I won't blow smoke in your eyes. You're too intelligent for that. I won't talk over your heads, because I want you to understand what I'm saying to you. I promise to do this because I respect you for giving up part of your lives to be here—your families, your work, your hobbies, your paychecks in some instances…"

Damn straight, thought Alonzo, cocking his head and leaning back in his seat.

"I just ask one thing in return from you. I want you to respect me for being out here in this courtroom—in this ring fighting for justice. And no matter if you give me thumbs up or thumbs down, I will accept and respect your decision—along with Mrs. Riley." Nick walked toward her with his hand out, gesturing toward her along with Judge Barnes. Nick moved his hand up toward the bench and then pointed at the judge, annoying Barnes to no end. He had had enough of this insolent little punk and was about to take him down a peg or two.

John Asher sat upright and leaned forward, prepared to leap to his feet if necessary to object in case Nick overstepped the bounds in his opening by presenting objectionable evidence or making a closing argument, or whatever else he had up his sleeve.

Nick paraded back to the jury box. "I want you to know this before we begin. This is my bond, my word of honor. All I really care about in this case is justice. And that's all I want you to care about—what I want you to do—to do justice. Can I ask for your bond?"

All heads moved quickly up and down in agreement. Number three's blond curls shook with excitement as she ogled Nick with wide, limpid eyes.

All but Alonzo Hodge. It would not be cool for him to go along with the rest like some puppet, he thought. He held his head in a locked position, his face expressionless, his arms folded across his chest, and listened intently.

Nick looked squarely at Alonzo. Taking a grave chance, he asked, "May I have your bond, sir?"

The black man stared back, stonily. Seconds went by, and Nick, for the first time, doubted his instincts about Hodge. Nick's eyes fixed on the juror his as he waited.

The courtroom was unbearably silent. Nick wondered if he had misplaced his trust—if his gamble was a big mistake. Maybe he shouldn't have singled him out, forcing him to do what he obviously didn't want to do: go along with the rest. He watched as the jurors shifted in their seats waiting for juror number one's answer. All eyes, including the judge's, were on Alonzo Hodge.

Finally in his own good time, when he was ready to release the tension he had created, the black man's face broke into a wide grin as if to say: *Gotcha!* And with one nod, he coolly signaled his assent.

John Asher had risen to his feet to object to this bizarre tactic— this inappropriate opening statement. Simultaneously Judge Barnes was ready to jump down Nick Ceratto's throat and put the wop *and* the nigger juror in their respective places. But it was too late. Nick had gotten what he wanted. He had won the first round.

Chapter XXXIV

Grace Monahan rushed across Penn Square dodging the slush and the cars jockeying for position around the crowded four-lane circle that wound around City Hall. The cold wind pelted her coat against the fresh wounds on her legs, which she had gotten the night before at the airport. But she ignored the stinging and moved on. Her heart pounded as she made her way through the huge stone arch marked "South Broad Street" and into the courtyard of City Hall. The lions' heads peering down at her from the tops of the columns and the posed classical female figures carved in high relief in the thick, gray granite didn't make the smell of urine any more bearable. The cops had rounded up the homeless a month before, but they had left their indelible territorial mark inside the dark courtyard.

The message had been relayed to her by Little Al that Nick had begun the trial, that Barnes had forced him to try the case. She was pissed at Nick for not waking her. She wanted to be there with him when he made his pitch to Barnes to postpone the trial. But Nick had wanted her to rest, or so she was told by Little Al. But Grace didn't want to rest. She wanted to be there, to support Nick when Barnes pulled his usual No-Excuses-the-Case-Must-Go-On stunt. This would be no surprise to Grace. Everyone in the legal system knew Barnes. "No-break Barnes," "Bastard Barnes," "Prick on a Stick"; you name it. If it was unflattering, it was attached to his name. A man only a mother could love—and only a Republican mother at that.

Grace pushed her way through the press outside the courtroom: men and women in packs with still and video cameras, microphones, writing pads, tape recorders, waiting for any sign of movement, for any news.

"Are you involved in this case, miss?"

"Are you a witness? Will you be testifying?" asked a chubby TV news reporter dressed in a bright red suit.

Grace practically stomped on the middle-aged woman's foot who was blocking her path while shoving a microphone in her face. Grace towered over the short woman and pushed the mike down with the palm of her hand away from her face. "Move aside or you'll be testifying against me."

The reporter pulled the microphone back, getting Grace's clear message. Grace ignored the cacophony of sounds coming from the others as they rattled inquiries at her. She stepped into the room and focused on the bailiff, hearing only Nick's voice as he was finishing his opening statement.

"I'm Grace Monahan, Mr. Ceratto's assistant," she whispered firmly to the bailiff. "I'll be helping him throughout the trial."

"OK, miss. Let's see if I have your name on my list here." He held a clipboard at arm's length so his old, farsighted eyes could focus. "Take a seat up front behind counsel table," the silver-haired man whispered, motioning to the table where Mrs. Riley sat, dabbing at her eyes.

Grace walked slowly past Shoes and Little Al. Shoes silently chewed his gum while Little Al gave her a nod of recognition. She felt comfort in their presence, especially as she passed Silvio, who smirked at her. Harry Levin didn't look her way at all. He was concentrating on Nick and the jury's reaction to him. Two women in the rear of the box, Mrs. Claire Kimball, a supermarket clerk, and Ms. Anna Jones, a teacher's aide, dabbed at their eyes as Nick recited how Sean Riley had won the Silver Star in Viet Nam for single-handedly holding off an attack on a helicopter that was loading wounded soldiers. And how, just two weeks before his death, Officer Riley had received a distinguished service award from the City of Philadelphia for rushing into a burning building with a weakened floor to rescue two children before the fire department could get to the scene. It had been on a virtually abandoned block where he had been patrolling. He had seen smoke and two tiny heads peering out of a second story window. No one had even noticed the fire. The mother had left the toddlers unattended.

How his wife still set a place for him at dinner because she couldn't bear to think of him as gone forever. And how Doctor Manin, exhausted from performing two four-hour surgeries back to back just before Sean Riley was brought into the emergency room, should never have touched him.

"You will hear testimony, ladies and gentlemen, that the defendant, Victor Manin, was in a hurry to get to a social engagement, a black-tie party, and that he was in a hurry to put that tuxedo on. You will hear how Dr. Manin's eyes were so strained from the previous surgeries that he kept wiping them, and blinking and squinting as he operated on the decedent, Officer Riley. And you will hear how members of his staff asked him if he wished someone else to close. And, folks, there were other qualified surgeons on hand at the time. But Dr. Manin steadfastly refused this offer of help. You will hear testimony that one of the operating room nurses…"

Nick paused and looked hard and straight at Alonzo Hodge, staring into his coal black eyes as if to say: *Don't believe any of this bullshit. Justice demands that you keep your mind open and question everything you see and hear. Can't you see that I'm lying? Please see that this is a phony case, a set up.*

Silvio shifted nervously in his seat, fingering a fresh cigar in his jacket pocket. Levin frowned, rubbing his unkempt, fuzzy gray hair, badly in need of a cut.

Judge Barnes's hand was already on the gavel as he glanced first at Ceratto and then Asher, back and forth, back and forth, as if to say: *Asher, what's wrong with you? On your feet man. Object or this little punk is going to drop a bomb and kill us all.*

"…found Officer Riley bleeding to death and yelled for Dr. Manin, who was taking a shower in the physician's lounge before dressing in his tux, and how Doctor Manin refused to answer an emergency call because he was late for this social engagement.

How he showered and dressed and primped while Sean Riley's life was draining away."

Maureen Riley quietly sobbed, while fumbling desperately in her purse for tissues she couldn't see because her eyes were so clouded with tears. This was the way her beloved husband had died, needlessly died, alone with no one there to help him. And after he had helped so many.

"Mr. Ceratto," Judge Barnes leaned authoritatively over the bench. "Perhaps the plaintiff would like a short recess to compose herself?" His suggestion was more of a command.

Nick turned and looked quizzically at Mrs. Riley, hoping all the while she would say no.

And she did. She waved him on with quivering lips and a wet hankie.

"Judge, I think we can just move ahead."

Barnes hated being called "Judge." It was demeaning compared with "Your Honor."

"Mr. Ceratto, this court is nonetheless ordering a short recess in order to permit Mrs. Riley to compose herself. And during that time I want to see counsel in my chambers." *You little prick, he thought, this is* my *courtroom, not yours.*

CHAPTER XXXV

Marty Silvio's phone vibrated in his inside coat pocket, and he motioned to Harry that he was stepping out into the hall. Both men made their way through the members of the press, the tangle of cameras and microphones, and the myriad questions about what was happening inside. Silvio found a pre–World War II phone booth tucked darkly into a corner of the corridor that ran the length of the second floor of City Hall. The 1940s pay phone hadn't worked in years, but the booth was a good place to conduct business. If the booth could only talk! It would tell of the countless deals made with witnesses, city officials, criminal defendants, and hit men.

He flipped the cell phone open with one hand and took out a new cigar with the other, then licked it to give it a little moisture and taste. "Yeah?"

"Marty, we have a big problem…"

It was Margo's voice, and he knew she was scared from the tremolo in her voice. "What now?"

"There's a detective who is about to fuck up our lives."

"What detective? Who?"

"His name is Ralph Kirby and he's in Gates' office this second with papers." She paused to take a deep breath. "Lopez papers."

"What?"

"It seems that your deceased receptionist kept a list of cases that you set up—including the Riley case. You know, all those arranged death cases, tire blow-outs, heart monitors that didn't go off…"

"How the fuck could she do that—she wouldn't have known dick…"

"Yes, she would." He could hear Margo's voice shaking as she spoke. "She listened to conversations. Your private line wasn't very private, it seems."

"Her word against mine." Marty spit out the end of his Quay d'Orsay Imperiale.

"No, not really. There's a written statement from guess who?"

"Come on, don't play games with me."

"From Joe Maglio, who signed an affidavit that he suspected these cases were all setups of yours and Harry's."

"He's dead and he can't testify against us. Forget it. Don't worry. This is a bunch of shit."

"What about the two little girls, Marty? They can testify."

"What two little girls?"

The little girls who belonged to Celia Lopez, Marty. Her daughters."

"What the fuck do they know? What can they say?"

A lot, Marty." She exhaled hard into the receiver. "They heard their mother talk about this list, watched her prepare it and…"

"So what? You're a lawyer, aren't you?. Maybe they can authenticate the list, but not what's on it. It's fucking hearsay." He was screaming at this point. "Use your brain!" The more information he was given, the more hostile he became.

Harry Levin pried the closed door partly open to ask what was going on, only to have it slammed shut in his face. He hastily pulled back his fingers to protect them from being smashed in the door.

Margo persisted. "Marty, do you remember when Celia used to bring her daughters in during school holidays when she couldn't find a sitter?"

"OK. So…?" He closed his eyes. He could hardly take any more bad news, which he now believed Margo enjoyed giving him. "No, don't tell me."

"Yes, Marty. I'm telling you that they listened in on phone conversations that you had in several cases and they remember exactly what you said. Especially the Riley case where that nice policeman had to die so you could make money, lots of money… Marty, you're in big trouble.

He wanted to shoot the messenger. But first he needed to keep her quiet. The last thing he needed was for her to go running to the cops.

"Listen, Margo. Now's not the time to panic. Don't…"

"Marty, I don't want any part of this."

"Listen, cunt," he yelled. "You *are* part of this, remember?"

"I don't remember creating a med-mal case by killing the plaintiff, and then ordering a few more murders to cover it up. I wasn't involved in all the other special 'cases' of yours or Harry's other specially ordered 'plaintiffs.' From the looks of things on these documents, you could be classified as a serial killer."

"Margo, baby, calm down. I love you. Let's do what we have to do."

"What?" She was crying. "You've ruined my life."

Harry Levin banged on the door, his face twisted in anger. He had lost his patience. "What's happening?"

Marty ignored him. "Our lives are not ruined. After this trial, we'll be together permanently, baby. You have to help me this one last time, and I promise."

"What do you want me to do? This is a complete mess."

"I want you to get that file, the Lopez list. Make sure there's no copies. I'll take care of the rest."

"Right now Gates is skeptical. She thinks it's just bullshit that the kids came up with to prove their mother's murder was something more than a random street crime."

"Good, good. That's just what we want."

"How am I going to get the file? It's sitting on her desk."

"Margo, come on. I know how smart you are, baby. And I know how Gates feels about you. She's crazy about you. She's not going to let us go down the tubes—'cause if we go down, so does she. You know what she's afraid of. Use it. Use whatever you can, baby. OK?" Silvio paused, waiting. He could hear her breathing, thinking. He knew her well.

"I did it for you," she said. "My relationship with Gates was for you. You know that."

"I know. But see how it worked out? And you're gonna do this too, won't you…for us?" he snickered reflexively.

"Maybe…" Margo's voice had a sudden and distinctive change of tone, from frightened to defiant.

"What do you mean, maybe?"

"I want a piece of the Riley case."

"What's a piece?"

"A third. I want a third. I'm not putting myself out as bait for you without a cut, a big cut."

Silvio laughed, taking the cigar from his mouth. "That's why I love you, baby. OK, you're on." He flipped the cell phone shut. "Overreaching cunt," he said as he stepped out of the booth. "Who the fuck does she think she is? I'll give her a third," he laughed.

"What's going on? You were yelling." Levin followed close behind Silvio as he strode down the hall. "Tell me, for God's sake."

"You wanna hear, old man? I'll tell you." He pushed his cell phone in Harry's face. "First you do something for a change. Get your hands a little grimy." He punched a saved number on the cell phone and pushed it in Levin's face. "Tell him we need him right now."

Chapter XXXVI

Joseph Barnes had kept his robe on as he paced the floor of his chambers. He didn't like the smell of the case. And he didn't like Ceratto: he was ungentlemanly, unpredictable, and untrustworthy. He decided to focus his attention on John Asher.

"John, your client is bleeding and is going to hemorrhage to death in the next few days, just like his patient. Why won't he settle this case? Is he a madman?"

Asher sat back, casually crossing his legs, assuming a relaxed, confidant posture. But he was uneasy. "Your Honor, as you know, the insurance carrier wants to settle. They have expressed their interest right from the beginning. Mr. Ceratto knew this and agreed to accept the limits of the insurance coverage in this case, which as Your Honor knows is two million dollars. The hospital has already tendered its policy. This case should have settled. Mr. Ceratto knows this as well, and I'm assuming would accept the limits of insurance coverage to satisfy the Rileys' claim."

Judge Barnes turned to Nick, his glasses quivering on the bridge of his nose. "Well, Mr. Ceratto…"

"Judge, it's the defendant's prerogative, as you well know. His insurance policy gives him the option to settle or let it go to the jury. It's my understanding that he wishes the jury to decide his fate. It's out of my hands, Judge."

Barnes looked at Asher, his jowls quivering as his voice raised ten decibels. "You tell your client to settle this case. That's a jury from hell out there, and they're going to draw and quarter him, after they hang him." He sat down, folding his arms. He looked down at the document on his desk. "And after they dismember him, I'm going to disembowel him. I'm going to permit punitive damages in this case, which as you know, will at least triple any jury award. Your client will be spending the rest of his life sweeping floors at a welfare office."

"Your Honor." John Asher shook his head. "I've explained this to him at least twenty times. He remains steadfast. His position is that he is innocent. That he did no harm to Sean Riley, and he's willing to take his chance with the jury. He believes justice will prevail." Asher shrugged his shoulders. "What else can I do, Your Honor?"

"Is he mad?" Barnes face turned beet red. "There is no fucking justice, and you know that. There's only luck, and I see a *very* unlucky doctor out there."

Nick shrugged his shoulders. "You never know, Judge. Maybe he's right."

"Shut up." Barnes pointed a finger at Nick. "It's not your job to second-guess the jury."

"I do it all the time." Nick chuckled, crossing his arms and shaking his head. "This is why I go into that courtroom. That's the shot I take."

"Well, that's *my* courtroom you go into, and the shot you take is with my sufferance."

"Remove me from the case, then." Nick sat back, glaring.

Asher looked toward Nick, his eyebrows raised in surprise. "Is that what your *ex parte* meeting with His Honor was about— your wanting to withdraw from the case? I think I need to know why, don't you?"

"Ceratto, I ordered you to refrain from discussing this matter, and I remind you that…"

"Yes, Judge, I know. I'm under wraps." Nick looked at Asher, shaking his head. "Sorry."

John Asher stood. "Your Honor, with all due respect, I want to put my objection on the record that an *ex parte* meeting was conducted with Mr. Ceratto. And I was not only not permitted to be present, I was also not informed of what was said."

Nick smiled, looking squarely at the judge, watching him squirm, and enjoying every minute of it.

"Your objection is noted, Mr. Asher." Barnes picked up the phone and barked into it. "Mary, get me the court reporter. Mr. Asher wants to put an objection on the record. And tell the bailiff to bring in the defendant, Dr. Manin."

Chapter XXXVII

"Look, I love you, but you're asking the impossible. I can't just bury the Lopez file. What's in this list may be bullshit, but I have to investigate it. Now. We're talking very serious allegations. This list represents fraudulent cases, set-up accidents. Cases where people were intentionally injured, even murdered in order to present phony claims to insurance companies. They represent millions of dollars paid out on false claims. And allegedly one of them is on trial right now." Muriel Gates paced heavily between the wide, naked windows of her office. She occasionally looked below onto Arch Street, wishing she could just fly out and disappear into traffic. She needed a cigarette, but instead she gnawed on a plastic replica. She'd be damned if she'd start smoking again; not after six months of cold turkey and fifteen pounds of extra flab she didn't need.

"We're talking allegations of assault and battery and murder in order to produce lucrative cases. We're talking sending runners, ambulance chasers, to sign up grieving families after their loved ones were badly injured or killed. We're talking insurance fraud, bank fraud, mail fraud, gross violations of the Rules of Professional Conduct. The potential penalties here are life in prison, or possibly the death penalty, for several people we know. I can't walk away from this. I can't withhold this from the proper authorities: from the attorney general, from the U.S. attorney, or Mike Rosa. It's my head, too, remember. I clawed my way up to the top in this office, fighting every prick along the way."

"What? Are you kidding?" Margo interjected sarcastically, sitting back against the worn, brocade love seat. "You're the ultimate authority here. You're the district attorney. You make the decisions as to what to investigate and what to trash. A DA has ultimate discretion as to what to prosecute and what to drop. You're in command—aren't you, Muriel?

"Please," Margo said, lowering her voice to an almost inaudible level. "Do it for me, if not for the firm that put you in office. You see, if they go down, if Marty and Harry go to jail, it's going to make things very difficult for me. My life will be an open book, and…" She paused for a moment. "And so will yours."

Gates walked to her desk and picked up the tan manila folder, holding it up. "Withholding information contained in this thin little file could put me in prison for more years than I care to contemplate…and none of the inmates are going to be as pretty as you."

Margo sprang to her feet and started toward the door.

"Where the hell are you going?"

"I'm going to give the good news to Marty and Harry. They're at the Riley trial right now. You don't expect me not to warn them, do you? I think it's only fair. After all, I'm sure there's a lot they have to say. The media's already there in droves, waiting for any tidbit of information. Why not throw them a bone?" she cried, tears streaming down her pretty face.

Gates moved her ample frame in front of the door, blocking Margo's exit.

"I'm sorry." Margo stared innocently up into the DA's steel gray eyes, angry eyes the color of a stormy sea.

"I don't like being threatened. Nor do I like blackmail— especially when I'm the intended victim."

"Muriel, I'm just saying these guys won't go down without a fight."

"Look, Margo. If there's nothing to their story—if these arrogant little pissant kids just want to aggrandize their mother's death to make it more than just a street crime, we'll find out. *I'm* not going to go public with this right now."

Margo squared her shoulders in defiance. "But I am—about us—unless you destroy that file in front of me, right now."

"Griffin," the DA laughed nervously. "I don't understand why you're so protective of these assholes. Your career is not at stake here. They're your bosses; they are *not* your partners. You're a bright, attractive attorney. You can get a job anywhere. I'd even hire you," she said mockingly.

"No thanks. There's not enough money in the job. DAs make crappy money. You know that."

"So you love the money. What else do you do for it—besides practice law? It's no secret, Margo. You and Silvio, I don't talk about it, but I know all about it. Besides fucking him, what else have you done for money? Is that why you're so afraid of the Lopez file?" Gates' face was red with rage. No little cunt was going to ruin her. She had worked too hard and too long, and for too little money, to lose *her* job.

"None of your fucking business." Margo stepped closer to the door until she was flat up against the imposing figure. But Gates didn't budge. "Get out of my way." Margo's eyes were brimming with tears. She tossed her hair back and wiped her eyes with the back of her hand.

Gates knew she had to think, and think quickly. She could not allow Margo to leave, not now. She backed away, changing her expression from confrontational to compassionate. "Look, I'm sorry." She took the young woman's hand. "You just get to me, that's all. Don't leave. Let's sit down and calmly work through this. Let's talk about the alternatives and what we can do to make this all go away."

Margo lowered her eyes and smiled. "It's simple, Muriel. It really is. Just take those papers over to that little ol' shredder, right over there—" she pointed to the white machine that represented relief and tons of money coming her way—"and put them right through." She put her hand affectionately on the DA's shoulder. "No more evidence, no more problem."

"What about the two problems having breakfast at this very moment? We can't put them through the shredder, can we, Margo?"

"Kirby and the brats are easy," Margo purred. "They're already being taken care of. Trust me."

Chapter XXXVIII

"Eenie, meenie, miney, mo," he said out loud as he stared at the five photographs, which he held spread, fanlike, in his right hand. He was having the most difficult time deciding which he should do first. They had to be done close together in time, he knew that. But deciding which would be first, that was his problem. Usually it was one person, or possibly two in the same location. But this was different; two were in one location, three in another, although not very far apart. He had to find a way to move them together. This was a big job worth a hell of a lot of money, two hundred thousand a head, all in cash, half of which had already been wired to his Bahamian account. But all had to be done in less than an hour if he was going to receive the rest. Rudi couldn't afford to screw this up. None could get away alive. Death must be instantaneous. There must be no evidence which could lead to him, or his employers. He closed his eyes to meditate.

Recently he had begun feeling less confidant, less secure, less decisive. He worried about whether he was just losing it—losing his talent. He couldn't afford that, not now. He was too young to retire; only forty with an Alzheimer's stricken mother to support. He had put her in the best nursing home in the area, which he paid monthly in cash. He loved his mother. He loved his job. He loved seeing the look of surprise in his victims' eyes at the moment they knew that *he* was the last person they would ever see; hearing the last gasp of breath they would ever take as they all, each and every one of them, fought for the impossible: to regain the life they had already lost. Then the resignation and then calm. He felt honored to be present at these sacred moments.

He opened his eyes and suddenly it came to him. He had a plan. He went straight to work. He moved to the back seat of the silver Volvo he had "borrowed" from an unsuspecting visitor to the city who had left his car in the underground parking lot area of Penn Center Plaza. He reached into his large, black leather suit bag, which he always kept handy for occasions such as this. It was always with him when he knew he had a job to do. It contained getups for almost all occasions: wigs, makeup, glasses, a police uniform, executive wear, ties, white shirts, cufflinks, and work clothes: jeans, sweat shirts, work boots, an Eagles jacket, and a knit ski cap. He never knew what he needed to be. It was always determined by the job, and he needed to be ready to transform himself into what was necessary at a moment's notice, like a chameleon.

In thirty seconds he was dressed, using the back seat of the Volvo as a dressing room. The windows were tinted, so no pedestrians passing by had a clue what was going on. The metamorphosis was complete. Navy-blue blazer, rep stripe tie, white Polo button-down shirt, scuffed, well-worn wing-tips, and a camel hair coat, slightly worn but clean and pressed. He looked honest and hardworking, not slick, not like a model from *GQ*, although he could have been if he had wanted to. He had the angular good looks, but he never wanted to attract attention. He didn't want any questions asked. He wanted to meld into the quiet drabness of normal Philadelphia life, humdrum workers who passed each other on the streets with no attention given or gotten. He checked himself out in his handheld mirror. *Perfect*, he thought. Then he went through the zipper compartment inside the suit bag and quickly found what he needed: an ID that bore his photo, as did all the other phony identification cards in the bag. It was official; it read "Montgomery County District Attorney's Office" over the picture of his smiling face.

"Perfect," he said aloud. "It's good to have friends in high places." He chuckled to himself as he made his way to 1421 Arch Street, Executive Division.

Chapter XXXIX

You lose or win your case in your opening, John Asher silently repeated to himself, as he approached the jury.

"My name is John Asher," he said, smiling confidently. He was a dapper figure, dressed in the darkest gray pinstripe suit. His starched white shirt was the perfect background for the blazing tomato-red silk tie and matching handkerchief in the breast pocket of his suit jacket. His hair, graying at the temples, was perfectly cut and smoothed back. Not a strand was out of place. He was as cool as a cucumber, and in control of the situation. He carried no notes. He didn't need any. He had given this opening statement a hundred times before. He had it honed to perfection, eliminating all the unnecessary words and adding all the right ones. He knew which words to emphasize and which to gloss over casually. Corresponding hand gestures had been choreographed and fit neatly into the script.

Sometimes it worked, and sometimes it didn't. Romancing the jury was a crap shoot. Sometimes they fell in love with you, and sometimes they chewed you alive and spit you out all over the courtroom. It was hard to tell. But John Asher was hard to dislike and harder to distrust. This would be the challenge of his life, he thought. The case was a surefire loser and his client, a masochistic idiot. And Asher had been charged with doing the impossible.

"Friends—" he continued, walking with a slight swagger, back and forth in front of the box— "just because my client, Doctor Victor Manin, is here in front of you today, as the defendant, does *not* mean that he is guilty of negligence, in causing Sean Riley's death, or in contributing to it in any way. You have all heard the phrase 'innocent until proven guilty,' I'm sure. Well, that not only pertains to criminal cases and criminal defendants, but it also applies to civil cases such as this one. The judge," he looked and gestured in Barnes's direction, "Judge Joseph Barnes, will tell you this clearly in his instructions."

Barnes hated being used to bolster a point. He kept his head bent and scribbled on his pad so as to appear impartial and simply taking notes. He was actually drawing gallows with Doctor Manin as a stick-figure hanging man.

"Just remember there are two sides to each and every story. You know this from your own experience. So when you're listening to the witnesses in this case, I ask you to please keep an open mind. You swore a sacred oath when you were selected to serve, and I know, and so does Doctor Manin, that you will keep your oath. I ask that when you listen to the evidence that you remember that the Rileys have the burden of proving their case, that the evidence must favor them, must tip the scales in their direction." He held up an invisible scale with one hand while moving his other hand dramatically down, as if deeply depressing one side.

"And I'm going to ask that you consider my client Doctor Manin's track record, which you will hear about, as a doctor and a citizen—all that he has done in the name of goodwill, and all the care which he gave and still gives all his patients. Particularly the police.

"We will show that during Sean Riley's emergency surgery, everything went as well as it possibly could—not just well, but very well—like clockwork. We will present evidence that Officer Riley was doing fine and that Doctor Manin was so careful with this surgery that instead of leaving the closing of the incision to an assistant, as is often the case, Doctor Manin closed the wound himself, using fine, careful suturing. I ask you to remember that just because bad things happen doesn't mean that someone is at fault. Bad things happen in this life…and that's just the way life is sometimes."

Alonzo Hodge stared ahead, emotionless, arms crossed, not giving the white man the satisfaction of his attention. *Yeah, bad things happen all right—always to the little guy. Get real, man. Don't try to con me,* he thought.

"Acts of God are sometimes devastating, like floods and earthquake. Death happens, my friends…"

Nick shook his head. This was a closing argument if he had ever heard one. It was more a summation than a road map of where the defense was going. He could object to the entire opening. But no, this was all Asher had—bullshit and bravado. *Let Barnes make an ass of him by interrupting and telling him to get off Broadway and get back into the courtroom. Let Asher go on,* he thought. He was just tightening the noose around his client's neck. He could see this from Alonzo Hodge's body language. There was no sympathy in those eyes, only anger.

"We will prove to you that surgery is a risky business. Our expert will tell you that—" Asher turned away from the jury and walked toward Dr. Manin, and then quickly turned back to face the jury—"sometimes doctors can't do anything to prevent a tragedy. Sometimes it's not in their control, and we will show you that." Asher's steel blue eyes fixed themselves on juror number three, whom he had seen nodding her curly head. He walked toward the jury box and stood directly in front of her. *Ah, a sympathetic ear, an approving look. Gotcha,* he thought. Hopefully she would help turn the others. His eyes went to each and every juror except to juror number one. No one could get to him, so he decided to ignore Alonzo Hodge. He was poison to Asher's case and of no use to him. His tack was to butter the others up and have them gang up on Hodge. "Thank you," he said and then walked slowly to the defense table and to his seat next to Victor Manin, giving him a confident nod.

Patrick and Seamus Riley squirmed in their seats. They sat in the front row, just behind the railing which separated them from their mother and Nick Ceratto. They were twins, in their thirties, burly brutes, well over six feet tall with bellies on them that would rival an Eagles linebacker. It was clear from their girth that they had downed many a pitcher in their native Fishtown neighborhood— and that they knew how to handle themselves when things got rough.

Seamus leaned over to Patrick and whispered, "I'd like to beat the crap outta that fuckin' bastard. He's worse than the fuckin' murderer sittin' next to him. I'd like to rip that poker outta his ass right now and teach him a thing or two."

Patrick stared ahead and nodded in agreement.

Seamus continued, "Sometimes it's not in their control," he said, mocking Asher. "My ass. I'll have no control over the terrible things that happen to that cross-burnin', hymn-singin' faggot when I get my hands around his pale, scrawny neck…and squeeze until his fuckin' eyes pop outta his head." Seamus's face was beet red as he drew in his breath in preparation to continue his diatribe.

"Calm down," Patrick whispered. "The damned judge is looking right at us. We'll have our chance, Seamus, don't worry." He patted his brother's arm and with his other hand squeezed the rosary he kept in his jacket pocket. "We'll have our chance."

Chapter XL

Gloria Henley shook her white head adamantly. Her gold clip earrings jiggled with the movement, as she said no for the fifth time.

"I'm sorry Mr. Feinberg," she said, glancing over her half glasses at the ID which the man in front of her displayed in its worn, leather case. "Ms. Gates cannot see anyone without an appointment."

He smiled calmly, totally in control as always, looking down at the brass name plate on her desk. "Gloria. I'm sorry, *Ms. Henley*," he corrected himself. "I've come at the request of district attorney, Mike Rosa. You know him, don't you?"

"Yes, I do know *of* him. I've never met him, actually," she responded aloofly.

"OK. Excuse me again. Then you must understand that he and Ms. Gates have been in touch with each other and are collaborating in the investigation of several matters crossing county lines, like the Lopez-Maglio deaths…" He had his mouth open to start the next sentence, but she interrupted.

"Yes, I know, but…"

His turn to interrupt. "*No* and *but*, that's all you've been saying to me this morning, Gloria. All I'm asking you to do is call Ms. Gates, tell her I'm here with an important piece of evidence—a tape." He patted his inside coat pocket. "Which I'm sure she'll want to see."

"Why didn't Mr. Rosa call before sending you? Or why didn't *you* call?"

"He's a busy man, Gloria. And Mike Rosa didn't expect you to give me such a hard time. Plus I didn't want to waste time calling. Besides," he smiled his most charming smile. "I'd rather talk to you in person, Gloria. Phones are so impersonal."

"Why don't you leave the tape with me, Mr. Feinberg? I'll give it to Ms. Gates this morning. Or if you wish, you can wait until I can get an appointment for you." She opened her appointment calendar and smiled back defiantly.

"No, Gloria, I can't wait for an appointment. I need to see her *now*. And I'm sorry, but the tape stays with me." He lifted his hands apologetically. "Please tell her I'm here with something to deliver from Mike Rosa. That's the least you can do—for me and for yourself. You see, both of them will be mighty mad if I leave here with the tape."

Gloria sighed deeply, resigned to her defeat. Sparring with him was a waste of time, she could see that. She was now more interested in getting rid of him than winning a point.

"I don't normally do this, Mr. Feinberg. But I will interrupt her for you."

"Thank you, Gloria."

"Ms. Henley," she corrected, looking up at him sternly and gliding her glasses up the bridge of her nose with both hands

"*Ms. Henley*. Yes. Sorry."

"Have a seat."

"No, no thanks," he said. "Been sitting in traffic all morning." He moved from the desk and turned, casting his eyes around the office. He noted the position of the chairs, the coffee table, the magazine rack. He mentally mapped the area and planned a proper escape.

Her voice broke his concentration. "Mr. Feinberg?"

"Yes?"

"Ms. Gates will see you now, but just for a few minutes, mind you. That's all she can spare. You'll have to leave the tape with her."

"Fine," he said enthusiastically. "That's fine. Thank you." He paused and grinned disarmingly, turning on the obviously fake charm again. "Ms. Henley."

She opened the heavy oak door and Rudi confidently strode in, keeping his pasted-on smile intact.

He found Muriel Gates sitting at her desk, her black suit jacket straining across her ample chest. Her eyes were two dark slits which focused on Rudi as he made his way toward her desk.

He nodded a greeting at Margo Griffin who sat quietly on the white brocade love seat. *Pretty girl*, he thought as admired her long, slim legs crossed tightly under her short, navy blue, wool skirt. *Shame*, he thought. Then he focused back on Muriel Gates, who wore a grim expression, clearly annoyed at his intrusion.

"Mr. Feinberg, what do you have from Mike Rosa that's so important that it can't wait?" Gates asked, folding her hands on top of the file he had come for. It was marked in bold black ink: LOPEZ. *How easy*, he thought.

She cocked her head sarcastically, waiting for his reply.

"This." Rudi reached into his coat, pulled out the silenced automatic, and pulled the trigger.

Phutt, phutt. The sounds were barely audible. Gates slumped instantly with one perfect shot between her almost nonexistent eyes and one in the chest between the two large mounds that identified her as a female. Her head fell to the desk top with a hollow thud. A thin stream of blood trickled down into her lap and ran down her navy gabardine skirt to the patterned rug under her desk.

Without hesitating and before Muriel could utter a sound, he pivoted in a sharp, precise turn and then—*phutt, phutt.* The bullets slammed Margo back against the finely upholstered white sofa. Splotches of bright red marked the areas where her tissue had exploded onto it. Her throat was opened wide, and she futilely gasped for breath through her splintered larynx. She gurgled helplessly, looking wide-eyed at Rudi, who quickly put her out of her misery with one shot through her right eye. *Real shame*, he thought. He shrugged his shoulders as he tucked the gun back into his overcoat. Then he stood at attention and saluted the DA. He moved her head with a gloved hand and slid the file out from under her folded hands. It was smeared with blood. Rudi looked at in disgust and went immediately to the shredder. He slipped the folder and its contents into the tray and pushed the button. "Zap. No more file," he whispered to himself, chuckling. He carefully retrieved the shredded documents, crumpled them into a ball, and stuffed it into his pocket. "Big pockets come in handy," he continued, talking to himself. He hit the DND button on Gates' telephone before making his way out of the office and closing the door quietly behind him.

"See," he said, passing Gloria Henley on the way out. "That was easy, wasn't it, Gloria?"

She looked up at him, over the tops of her glasses. "Ms. Henley," she corrected without a smile.

"Sorry," he laughed, making his way to the door marked with a lit exit sign. "Ms. Henley," he said in an exaggerated, almost mocking tone. He was partway out of the door when he peeked his head back in. "Ah, Ms. Gates asked me to tell you that she'll be busy watching the tape for the next twenty minutes, and she doesn't want to be disturbed.

Gloria looked down at the small screen on her phone and saw the "Do Not Disturb" light on Muriel Gate's extension. She shook her head in affirmation. "Fine," she said without a smile. "Good day, Mr. Feinberg." It was clear from her tone that she would be happy to be rid of the pest.

"Glad to be of service." Rudi smiled and closed the door.

He took the stairs instead of the elevator. It was safer. In no time he was on the street, where he quickly disappeared into a crowd of pedestrians moving along Arch Street. He was a master at melding into the landscape, looking like any other citizen on his way somewhere to do something. For Rudi, he was on his way to business—his business. "Two down, three to go," he murmured as he walked along Arch street, briefly distracted by a hot dog vendor. "A hot dog would be perfect right now," he said to the small man. He laid a five on the slightly greasy counter of the vendor's cart, pointing to the catsup bottle. Before the little brown-skinned man could give him his change, Rudi was down the street with only one bite left of the oozing red wiener.

Chapter XLI

Ralph Kirby waited patiently for the call on his cell phone. He had laid it on the table in the McDonald's located at the corner of Broad and Arch, and was watching it as Carmen and Lily Lopez drank their third hot chocolate.

"Mister, can I have more fries?" Lily asked, wide-eyed.

"You just finished an extra large. How could you eat another fry?" he asked, taking a Marlboro out of a crumpled pack.

"Unh unh," Carmen warned, shaking her head. "Don't you know that smoking is bad for you?" She took another sip of the sweet brown liquid. "Besides, it's a terrible thing to do in front of kids."

"Yeah, I guess you're right." He put the smoke back into the pack and tucked the pack back into his inside jacket pocket. "I been smoking for so many years I just forgot."

"What? That it's bad for you or that it's bad to do in front of kids?" Carmen asked abruptly in an unsympathetic tone. A strand of her black hair fell over one eye, which she pushed back.

"Do I criticize you? Do I tell you that you have a smart mouth for a kid, and that you should comb your hair in the morning?" Kirby sat back, shaking his head in disapproval.

Carmen laughed. "You just did, Kirby. So you're fair game, right? Look, I just wanna remind you that you're killing yourself with that stuff, that's all. I'm trying to help you."

Lily laughed. "She says that all the time to me, mister." She scrunched up her little features and imitated her sister: "I'm just trying to help you."

"Look, kid. I been killing myself for years, more years than you can count. I'm old, I'm tired. So let me enjoy the rest of my life—whatever's left, OK?"

"OK." Carmen looked into her cup, grinning. "Suit yourself. But I'm not coming to your funeral."

It had been an hour, and Kirby couldn't stand waiting any longer, especially sitting with these brats. *Correction*, he thought, *one brat. The other, a nice little girl.* He felt sorry for Lily. Carmen he could definitely do without.

He picked up the phone and dialed Gates' office. The phone rang three times before Gloria Henley picked it up. "District Attorney Gates' office."

"Yeah, this is Ralph Kirby."

"Yes, Mr. Kirby, what can I do for you?"

"You can find out why I haven't received a call from Ms. Gates. I've been waiting here for an hour with these kids. She told me she wanted to see the file first and then talk to the girls."

"Mr. Kirby," Gloria interrupted, "I'm sorry, but her phone is on Do Not Disturb. I can't interrupt her. She was in with an assistant DA from Mike Rosa's office, you know, the DA from Montgomery County and…"

"Yeah, I know Mike Rosa. I've worked on cases with Montco detectives."

"Well there was an important tape—ah, something that Mr. Rosa wanted Ms. Gates to watch and get back to him on."

"For an hour? She's been watching for an hour?"

"Yes sir. I guess it's a long tape."

"Well, I gotta do something with these kids," he said, looking into Lily's large dark eyes.

"Don't send us back to school," she interrupted. Kirby put his finger to his lips to signal Lily to shut up.

"Well, you can bring them here if you wish. There's plenty of books here. Some children's books that we keep for children who visit."

"Children visit the DA?" Kirby responded in disbelief.

"Oh yes. Ms. Gates is fond of children and encourages employees to bring their children to visit on certain days. Schools are invited to see the workings of the criminal justice system, you know. To encourage career choices," she said earnestly.

"Great. I got one here who's a natural. Make a great prison warden," he said looking squarely at Carmen.

Gloria Henley chuckled. "Bring them here, Detective. I'll look after them."

"Let's go," he said, hitting the END button on his phone. His chair scraped the tile floor as he slowly got up. His bones ached, especially on cold, damp winter days like this one.

"To school?' asked Lily, obviously upset.

"No. To the DA's office. There's a nice lady there who's going to take care of you. I gotta get back to my desk. I got a lot of work to do."

"Before you retire?" Lily looked quizzically at him, her sweet voice pitched to the highest octave humanly possible. It made Kirby wince, like a long, slow scratch on a blackboard.

"Yeah, if I ever make it." He looked at Carmen, lit a cigarette, and blew out a long stream of smoke.

She fanned it away, annoyed, reaching for her coat. "We're getting on your nerves, huh?"

He nodded in affirmation. "My mother taught me to tell the truth," he groaned as he stood, taxing his aching bones, cigarette hanging from his mouth. "I do need a break from you kids. You're gonna wait in the DA's office until Ms. Gates can see us. And the nice lady at the reception desk is gonna give you some books to read.

"I hope they're dirty," Carmen laughed, pushing her chair away.

"Get outta here!" Kirby held back his own laughter, shooing them toward the door, as he clumsily lumbered behind.

He was way ahead of them. He had been standing in the cold looking into the two-story windows of McDonald's and he had lip-read every word Kirby had said. It was a skill for which he was eternally grateful. He was happy his father had been deaf and had taught him to sign and read lips. He could feel the old man's belt on his back if he made a mistake. He'd quickly learned to be accurate, and then there were no more beatings. But he'd nevertheless felt compelled to pay his teacher for the invaluable lessons he had learned. When he was fifteen, he stood silently behind his father, tapped him on the shoulder, and when he turned, pushed him down two flights of stairs. Instead of dying, the old man became a quadriplegic. He couldn't sign and he couldn't utter one sound since his larynx was crushed. He hung onto life by a breathing tube which Rudi was only too happy to toy with. He'd watched his father suffocate and signed to him the equivalent of "See you in hell, you fuck."

Rudi moved quickly. There were no sirens, no ambulances, and no police around, so it was clear that Gloria had not found the mess behind the closed door. She was a faithful and obedient servant, and he had gambled that she would continue to be so when he hit the Do Not Disturb button on the DA's phone.

He approached the building cautiously, looking for signs of trouble. The guard in the lobby gave him a nod of recognition, signaling that he could go on through. There was an open elevator waiting for him. The up arrow was lit and in a second he was on his way to Muriel Gates' floor again. Why was he returning? What would he tell her? He had to think fast. He opened the door and stood face-to-face with Gloria Henley. As expected she had been faithful to her boss.

She looked up from her computer screen, her glasses propped on the end of her nose. "Mr. Feinberg, you're back. I'm sorry, I can't…"

"Yes, I know. I don't want you to disturb Ms. Gates. You see, I lost my car keys. I looked all over, retraced my steps, and wound up back here." He feigned being out of breath, holding his chest. "Do you mind if I crawl around the floor here, looking for them?"

"No. Help yourself." She looked at the computer screen and began typing. The phone rang. She turned and picked it up on the first ring. "Ms. Gates office. Why, Mr. Rosa." She looked up over her glasses, smiling at Rudi.

Rudi turned red. He waved his arms at her, shaking his head to signal no. Gloria stared at him, surprised at his behavior. She paused, "Uh…"

He put his hands together as if he were praying and got down on one knee. Gloria chuckled, briefly holding her hand over the mouthpiece of the phone. She uncovered it and put on her most businesslike tone.

"Yes, Mr. Rosa. Sorry, I just spilled some coffee on my desk. No sir, she has the Do Not Disturb light on her phone. I can't…a what, sir? A tape?"

Silence.

"Just one moment, sir."

Rudi crawled over to her on both knees, his hands locked in prayer. Gloria looked at him sternly. He was endearing on his knees, she thought. She kind of liked him that way.

"Yes sir—just hold for a moment, Mr. Rosa. I'll see if I can interrupt her."

Rudi heard Rosa's voice through the receiver as Gloria abruptly put him on hold. She stared at him and began to speak, but didn't get out a word before he pulled the automatic from his pocket and fired. There was a barely audible *phutt*. She lurched backward, blood streaming from a small hole in her head. He got up, brushed his pant legs, and walked slowly to the door. He turned the dead bolt to lock and waited. He checked his watch, humming "Baa, Baa, Black Sheep." His mother used to sing it to him when he was a kid. It calmed his nerves. "Three bags full…and three more to go."

Then he tried to remember another calming nursery rhyme from his past. "Three little pigs went to market. Three little pigs came home. Two little pigs had roast beef. One little pig had none." Then it happened.

He watched the brass handle to the enormous cherry wood door move down and then stop. It moved down again and stopped again. He slowly and quietly released the dead bolt, then stepped behind the door as it slowly opened.

Just outside the door, Kirby sensed that something was wrong. It was too quiet. And the DA's suite shouldn't be locked before five p.m. He had his hand on his partly drawn service revolver as he entered, followed by Carmen who was holding Lily's hand. Turning toward Gloria's desk, he had no time to react. He was instantly blown against the rear wall of the office. His overcoat exploded as he flew backward and then fell in a huge heap like a bushwhacked bull elephant.

Rudi stepped toward the girls and took aim.

Carmen was the closest She brought her knee up toward her chest and then with a powerful kick, tore into his groin.

He fell instantly to the floor and rolled, gasping in pain. He felt his pants go wet. "Fuck, you little cunt, I'm gonna…"

"Bastard!" Carmen yelled. "Fucking bastard." She looked desperately for the gun, but it was under Kirby. She couldn't take it.

Lily was frozen. The only thing moving was her small trembling mouth and the tears streaming down her face. Carmen yanked her through the door toward the elevator. "Run, Lily—hurry." The elevator doors were closed, and there was no time to hit the button and wait. It was the stairs or eternity, a split-second decision Carmen was forced to make.

"No, Lily, here," She pointed at the door to the stairs as she frantically hit the down button on the elevator, hoping against hope that it would open. But it did not. No time to wait, she thought. He'd soon be off the floor and out the door. She was sorry she couldn't find Kirby's gun. She pulled her sister hard, down the first flight of stairs. Lily fell, hitting her knees on the concrete. The metal door a floor above screeched open. It was him! Carmen slapped her hand over Lily's mouth. "Don't cry. Shh." She listened for footsteps. There were none. He was listening for them, too. She knew that. She silently backed Lily against the stairwell wall, her hand stifling her sister's sobs, and quickly pulled off her shoes so as not to make a sound on the steps. She had Lily do the same. The little girl shook violently, and then silently let out a stream of vomit, all over Carmen's hand and coat sleeve. Normally Carmen would have shrieked in horror, but this time she gave Lily a hug of encouragement, a hug of *it's OK.*

The girls breathlessly made their way to the next level down, tiptoeing in their stocking feet. Carmen tried the door into the hall. It was locked from the other side. They quickly padded down to the next floor. Locked, too.

Footsteps echoed on the hard stairs. Carmen heard them clearly. They were slow and without rhythm. He was hurting, but he was coming. He frantically smacked the hand railing in rage. Carmen and Lily heard the pounding. It was clear that he was close, and he was mad—enraged in fact. He had been foiled by the little bitches, and he was hurt, and had peed himself. He would make the little cunts suffer before they died. But he didn't know exactly where they were—or if, in fact, they were on the stairs.

Carmen prayed for an open door. *Please, please, dear God, let the next door be open.* They silently ran down one more flight. It was! It was propped open with a wad of paper towels. Lucky for them the ladies room on this floor was out of order and employees had ingeniously rigged the door so that it wouldn't close and automatically lock them out. They could use the stairs to the restroom below instead of having to wait for the elevator.

Carmen shoved the door open. It flew against the wall with a crash, leaving the paper towels behind. Both girls pushed the door closed as quickly as they could. The lock engaged. It was music to their ears. He was locked in the stairwell with ten more flights down before he could make his way outside and regain entrance to the building.

But it was also music to Rudi's ears—now he knew where they were, and a lock was never a problem for him.

Carmen and Lily frantically ran into the first office they saw, Cummins and Bradley, an investment banking firm.

"Call the cops," Carmen barked at the receptionist. "Call 911 now. Right now." She vainly fumbled at the door, looking for a deadbolt, but there wasn't one.

"Wait, young lady. What are you doing.?" The receptionist got up from her seat.

"Please lock the door. Please, he'll find us and kill us," Lily begged, her knees scraped and bloodied, her mouth and chin smeared with vomit. "Please, lady!"

The receptionist recognized the look of absolute terror on the little girl's face and felt the need to calm her down. "Here. Come here and sit down and catch your breath. Let's see what's wrong." She took a tissue and began to wipe Lily's face. "Why aren't you in school?" she asked looking at Carmen.

"We don't have time to wait and answer your questions. We'll all be dead if we do. Lock the goddamned door—now!"

The woman stared in disbelief. "Wait here. Let me call the office manager."

Carmen saw that she was getting nowhere, and it was clear that the woman did not appreciate the danger that they all were in. She grabbed Lily by the coat and began to run, pulling her sister along.

"Help!" she yelled into the open offices as she raced past them. "Help. He's coming in here to kill us." She frantically looked for a believing face—a strong face, someone who could deal with the crisis. But she saw none.

"Get them!" yelled a worker as he came out of his office and chased them down the teal carpeted hall. "Where do you think you're going?" Carmen pulled an empty five-gallon water jug from its holder and flung it at the man. She heard *phutt, phutt, phutt.* Then people screaming. Her heart sank. He was here. On a killing spree again.

Chapter **XLII**

"Get Gates for me again," Mike Rosa barked into the phone at his secretary. "How long does she expect me to wait? I'm tired of her antics. She's avoiding me and I won't have it."

"Yes, Mr. Rosa," an intimidated voice responded.

"And bring that couple in here." He looked down at the note that had come with the video cassette.

"Dear Mr. Rosa," it read. "We purchased the Maglio estate at auction. While we were renovating the library, we came across a security camera hidden behind the paneling. In the camera we found this shocking tape. We decided to bring it to you the day we found it." It was signed "James and Margaret Snyder."

Rosa pressed the PLAY button on the remote he kept on his desk. The monitor came alive, first to an intense blue and then the library in the Maglio home. At the bottom of the screen in small letters was a date and beside it, the hours, minutes and seconds. Rosa hit FAST FORWARD. Christy Maglio swirled by, in and out of the room. He pressed PLAY when the timer showed 11:00 p.m. as Christy was coming into the room, followed by a figure, a dark figure in a uniform—a cop. She seemed to be crying. Then she appeared distracted, almost angry. Her mouth moved but suddenly stopped. Her forehead opened she fell back to the sofa and slid to the floor. The uniformed figure stepped over the body and sat on the sofa, crossing his legs. He calmly looked around the room, obviously pleased with himself. The camera was set so that it was focused on the face and torso. Pennsylvania State Trooper, badge number 4273, name tag Darin Adams. The figure got up and reached for a crystal decanter and poured himself a drink. Then he reached for a book and sat down, making himself quite at home for a minute while he sipped from the half full glass. He then got up, fumbled with a photo which was out of focus but appeared to be two children. He smiled, looking almost lovingly at the picture and then disappeared from the room.

Rosa hit FAST FORWARD and stopped when Joe Maglio appeared. Surprise. A short scuffle, a shot at close range to the temple. Maglio fell. The killer put the gun in Maglio's right hand, smiled, saluted the dead man, and walked out, leaving the hidden camera trained on two bleeding corpses.

Rosa had already called the State Police. They had no Darin Adams and there was no badge number 4273. The frames showing the killer's face had been sent over the Internet to the National Crime Information Center and the Pennsylvania Crime Information Center.

"Mr. Rosa?" James Snyder broke Rosa's concentration. He wore a black jogging outfit with a Polo logo plastered across his chest. "We decided to come directly to you instead of the police. We didn't want to hand the tape over to someone we didn't know." He exhaled, folding his hands in his lap. "Especially since the man in the film was a police officer."

"I'm afraid," said Margaret Snyder, anxiously. She rubbed her forehead with her left hand. Her four-carat princess-cut diamond glinted wildly. It was enough to blind anyone in its direct path. "I'm afraid that *our* lives are in danger, too. I just can't go back to that house while *he's* on the loose."

Rosa sat back and smiled. "Ma'am, I wouldn't go back to that house, or anywhere, as a matter of fact, wearing that boulder on my finger. You're a billboard for muggers, rapists and murderers. You might as well advertise on I-95. Trust me. I know about these things."

Margaret looked at him in dismay, slightly teary-eyed. "I know. But I *want* to wear my jewelry, not hide it away in a safe. Why have it then?"

"Exactly," James agreed, nodding in approval. "We don't want to lock ourselves and our possessions away and live in fear."

"Well then, hire yourself a full-time body guard and check into the Four Seasons," Rosa fired back unsympathetically. He paused and then, taking a softer tone, said, "OK. Let's get back to this film.

You absolutely did the right thing coming to me with it. We've sent the pictures to the Crime Information Centers and we think we have a match, but we're not sure." He paused. I hope you haven't told anyone about this film?"

"No, just you," James said hurriedly, his brow furrowed in concern.

"OK. Don't mention it to anyone. Did any of the workers, carpenters, or any other mechanics know about this hidden camera?"

"No. We found it," Margaret answered.

"OK. Now I mean this. Your lives depend on your being absolutely closemouthed about this film. We are not going to break this to the news. If the media gets wind of this, you can rest assured that you won't see the sunrise. Got it?" He glared sternly at the worried couple.

Wide eyed, both nodded affirmatively at the same time, more frightened than ever.

"And I sure as hell won't be able to help you. Because this killer is a master of disguise. And he's quick—you'll never know what hit you."

Margaret's face paled. "That poor family," she cried. "I wonder what they did to deserve *him*."

"Breathe," Rosa said, standing, signaling that it was time to leave. "I'll give you an escort home."

"No." James put his hand out to shake Rosa's. "You've convinced us. We're going to check into a hotel."

"Good." Rosa took the outstretched hand. "We'll call you on your cell when the coast is clear."

"I hope you catch him soon," Margaret whined. "I don't want to live in a hotel."

"Hotel's better than a grave," Rosa said, ushering the couple out the door. "Susan, get me Nick Ceratto," he commanded his secretary. "I want to talk to him now—right now."

"Mr. Rosa, do you want me to continue to try to reach Ms. Gates?" she asked, looking puzzled.

"Forget her. I want Ceratto now."

Chapter XLIII

Marina Doletov was dwarfed by the heavy mahogany witness stand, which made her look more diminutive than she actually was. Her shoulders barely showed over the top of the heavy wood surround. Her blond hair was tightly pulled back into a neat pony tail tied with a black velvet ribbon. At under five feet, she looked innocent and childlike as she testified—particularly so when her clear, baby-blue eyes brimmed with tears. Although her Russian accent was heavy, her English was good, as were her lies, when she testified about what she had seen when Sean Riley arrived at Metropolitan Mercy Hospital.

"Ms. Doletov, can you tell the jury what Doctor Manning was doing, if you know, when Officer Riley arrived in the ER?" Nick asked in the low, kindly voice, typical of attorneys when soliciting the information they want from their own witnesses.

"Yes." She hesitated. Her mouth quivered slightly, as if she were afraid to say the words. "I'm sorry." She shook her head. "I'm nervous…I'm new to this country…the language. I was never in a court before."

"Take your time, Ms. Doletov." Nick stopped at the railing in front of the stand and looked her in the eye. *I'll just bet you've never done this before. What an actress*, he thought. *What a con. What a bitch. What a cold, murdering bitch. Who would ever think that Alice-in-Wonderland here was a murderer.* "Here." He reached into his breast pocket and pulled out a white silk pocket handkerchief.

"No, no," she said, smiling. "It's OK."

"Here," he insisted. "Please, the jury understands." He looked her squarely in the eye. "It's OK."

"Thank you, sir. Attorney…ah…?"

"Ceratto," he smiled.

"Yes, Attorney Ceratto." She dabbed her eyes and took a deep breath then looked at the jury, seemingly regaining her confidence. "Doctor Manin had just finished a previous surgery. It was repair of an abdominal aneurism, if I recall. He wanted to get out of the operating room as soon as possible. He said that he had to meet his wife for a big dinner, a charity dinner that she had organized."

"How do you know this ?" Nick prodded.

"I had assisted him in the operation." She dabbed her eyes again with the silk handkerchief.

"Go on, Ms. Doletov." Nick leaned toward her, urging her on.

"…and he talked about the dinner and his wife and how he had to wear a tuxedo, and how he was always late for these affairs, and how she was always mad at him for that. This time, he said, he had to be on time because it was *her* dinner. We all left the OR. Doctor Manin went off to change; then he got paged. Then I saw him rushing past me in his shirt and tuxedo pants. Captain Riley was brought into the OR. I was called to assist with the surgery. When I arrived, Captain Riley was already prepped. We waited and then, shortly, Doctor Manin comes in, plops on his cap, and mutters to me, under his breath, that he had to do this operation, too. Nobody else was competent in the hospital. His wife was going to kill him—he…" She paused, struggling to finish, "He whispered, 'Son of a bitch, I can't ever get out of this place on time…'"

"Liar!" Manin yelled, pointing at her. "Lying bitch, you lying…"

John Asher put a hand firmly on Manin's shoulder to restrain him.

Manin went limp, sagging against the back of his chair, aware of another fatal mistake.

"Calm down, Victor. What's wrong with you?" Asher hissed into his client's ear. "You're making things worse."

Judge Barnes smashed his gavel onto its block, twice. The cracking sound was earsplitting, causing every member of the jury to wince. Marina buried her face in the silk handkerchief and cried quietly, her shoulders shaking.

"If I hear any further remarks or outbursts from you, Doctor Manin, I'll have you removed from my courtroom for the duration of this trial. You will respect this court and never do that again." Barnes glared down at Doctor Manin and hunched himself, vulture-like over his mahogany desk. The heavy shoulder pleats of his black robe made him look twice as large as he was, and twice as ominous. He had learned early about the magic of the black robe. And when he put it on, he relished the transition from Jekyll to Hyde.

John Asher stood to make the appropriate excuses. "Your Honor, my client apologizes to you personally, and to this entire court, particularly to the jury." He shifted his weight awkwardly from one foot to the other in a supplicating, "aw shucks" mode. "Doctor Manin has been under an incredible amount of stress…"

"Very well." The judge looked down, pretending to write on his empty yellow legal pad. Actually he was scribbling possible solutions to Sunday's *New York Times* crossword puzzle, which he kept in his desk drawer until they were complete. When finished, he carefully put them in a file, by year, for reference. He could not rest until each week's was filled in—in pen, and 100 percent correct. "Mr. Ceratto, you may continue with your witness."

Marina Doletov was not in the mood. She put her hands over her face, shaking her head and sobbing. "I can't…I can't…hurt him anymore."

Nick pretended to buy into her act. He offered her water, tissues, and then finally stepped away and walked toward the bench. "Your Honor, may we have a short recess?" *What a fucking actress,* he thought. *She deserves an Academy Award for this. Her cut must be big enough to retire on for life. She could probably buy the whole Ukraine and have enough left to buy a string of nail salons.* He looked quickly at the jury, checking their expressions, their body language. The vibes coming from them told him they were buying it, all of it. Except for Alonzo Hodge who wore the same skeptical smirk, sending the same silent message: *You're all full of crap. Now get on with it, jerk-offs.*

Asher jumped to his feet. "Your Honor, may we approach the bench?"

Barnes nodded in reluctant approval, wondering what these two manipulative bastards were going to try to put over on him. Whatever it was, he would resist it, he thought. Because it wouldn't be good for him, for his trial schedule, for his Supreme Court bid. He sat back in his chair, causing the attorneys to strain their heads upwards. He liked that. He never bent down to listen to a lawyer. It was bad for his image.

"Your Honor," John Asher went on in barely audible tones, "I'd like a recess to speak with my client. May we adjourn this trial until tomorrow morning? I want the time to go over the damaging evidence again with him. And now that he's heard it with his own ears, and sees the problems he has, or we have—" correcting himself, looking at Ceratto in acknowledgment of the power of the plaintiff's case—"he may be willing to settle this case. I'm asking you for time." He put his hands together hoping to signal his desperation to the man in control—to no avail.

"If he hasn't seen the light yet, Mr. Asher, I doubt that he ever will. Fifteen minutes for both of you and that's it. I want to move this case along."

Nick nodded. "Your Honor, I'd like to put my expert on now. In the interest of saving time and money. He's costing me two grand an hour. Can I get him on and off? His testimony won't take long. He's here and ready. In the meantime Miss Doletov can take a short break. I'll call her back right after the expert."

Barnes liked economy, especially when it was of his time. He didn't give a flying fart about Ceratto's money. They were all whores: the attorneys, their clients, their expert witnesses. And they could all go to hell in a hand basket, he thought. Their only service was to keep him in his job, and pretty soon he wouldn't have to listen to drivel anymore. Pretty soon he'd be at the top, making law instead of keeping bullies from tearing each other apart and taking over his courtroom.

Asher said, "I'm going to object, Your Honor. To put the plaintiff's expert on out of sequence just bolsters the witness.

Ms. Doletov's evidence just becomes more credible when she resumes. It will be devastating…"

"Too bad, John," Barnes said, smiling and looking toward the back of the courtroom at Doctor Jacob Humphrey. Humphrey was from Johns Hopkins, a renowned vascular surgeon, professor, and researcher. He sat ready in his tweed jacket and brown tie-up shoes. With his lightly tousled hair and horn-rimmed glasses, he couldn't have looked more the expert. "This may help you talk some sense into your client."

"Thank you, Your Honor." Nick wanted to get Marina off the stand as soon as possible.

"Miss Doletov, you may step down briefly. You may leave the courtroom briefly. Please take the time to compose yourself, and Mr. Ceratto will call you back to the stand after the next witness."

"Thank you," she whispered as she stepped down from the witness stand and moved quietly past Silvio and Levin into the back of the shabby, inhospitable room. Only the sound of the squeaking door broke the silence as she disappeared from view.

Nick called Doctor Humphrey, and like a seasoned pro, the doctor recited his background and qualifications: member of the board of Johns Hopkins University, professor emeritus of Johns Hopkins medical school, and board certified in surgery, plastic and reconstructive surgery, and vascular surgery.

The jury sat with open mouths as the expert went on and on, detailing the many articles and texts he had written and the research projects and symposiums he had conducted—all except Alonzo Hodge. He could care less. He knew the game—pay 'em enough and they'd say whatever the fuck you want.

Silvio and Levin sat back, nudging each other when a point was made. They marveled at the good job Ceratto was doing. Too bad the money would never be his. They were going to sue his ass for ripping the client from them. And sue the Rileys for going with Ceratto. That is, before they had him whacked and buried so far underground they wouldn't find his remains for a thousand years.

They could taste the verdict and smell the money. This was going to be a big one.

Nick read all this. It was obvious. The more points he made, the more he twisted the knife into Manin, the happier they looked. What could he do? What the fuck could he do?

"The autopsy report showed that the closing of the wound was inadequate," Doctor Humphrey droned on. "The suturing was far too close to the approximated edges of the severed artery. The quality of the suturing was poor, and as a result the artery opened from the effect of the pressure of the blood reentering the artery as soon as the forceps were removed on the proximal side of the wound. Further, the response time for the code was entirely too long, especially since the patient was bleeding and obviously in trouble. There should have been an immediate response by a qualified surgeon."

"Doctor, how long did it take the defendant to respond?" Nick asked, holding the code sheet from the hospital records in his hand.

"It took twenty minutes." Doctor Humphrey glanced down at his copy of the code sheet, shaking his head.

"How long should a response take in a case like this?"

The Joint Committee on Accreditation of Hospitals Standards calls for five minutes or less. The recovery room nurse—I believe that it was Nurse Doletov—called an immediate code for immediate assistance."

"And how long did it take for Doctor Manin to arrive?"

"Twenty minutes…it was far too late at that point. The heart was pumping, but the blood was being pumped out of the body. The patient exsanguinated."

Nick looked squarely at Doctor Manin. "Doctor Humphrey, in your professional opinion, was that a breach of the standard of care that should have been rendered to Sean Riley? In other words, did Doctor Manin fail to give Sean Riley the kind of care he deserved and available to him?"

"Yes, it was." Doctor Humphrey paused. "An incredible breach of the standard of care."

Nick walked toward Mrs. Riley, who was silently crying at counsel table. Her shoulders shook as Nick put his arm around her and gave her a tissue. Then he walked back to his witness. "Doctor Humphrey, is there any other way that this could have happened? Is there any other way that Sean Riley could have bled to death?"

Humphrey looked at Nick, his eyebrows raised in surprise at the question. He paused to think, cocking his head to the side. "I suppose so…"

"How?" Nick asked strongly, aware that he had just committed professional suicide.

"Well…the sutures would have to be purposely pulled…" He shook his head. "…and then the nurse or person in charge of the recovery unit would have had to purposely ignore the emergency. But I don't see how…based on the chart…"

"Thank you, Doctor. That's all."

Chapter XLIV

There was no way out. No back door and no windows that would open. Besides, they were on the fifth floor—too high to jump even if they could. Carmen kicked the bathroom door open and pulled Lily inside. She locked it. She knew she had only a few seconds more to think of something. She frantically looked around for anything that might save their lives. She could find nothing.

Carmen pushed a stall door open. The stall was wide and had grab bars for the handicapped. It was perfect for the two of them. "Come on, Lily, up here," she whispered, her voice shaking. "Up onto the toilet seat. Hurry up," she commanded.

The little girl obeyed although she was shaking from head to toe. She was speechless. Nothing would come out of her mouth even if she tried. Carmen urged her sister toward the back of the toilet, and Lily slipped.

"Careful, don't fall." Carmen held her hand, helping her sister regain her balance as Lily's feet straddled the seat.

Carmen quickly locked the stall door and stepped up onto the seat. She held one of the grab bars as she carefully turned and faced the door. Now both were up on the toilet, their feet not visible in the opening at the bottom of the door.

But what now? Carmen asked herself. *What to do? Think, think, think fast.*

Then she saw it. She knew what to do. She jumped off the seat, unlocked the stall door, and grabbed Lily's hand.

"Come on, Lily, get down for one minute."

"No, I'm scared."

Now, Lily. Now." She pulled her sister off the seat and lifted the heavy lid off the toilet tank. "Get back up now. Just get up and face the wall," she commanded.

Lily quickly obeyed, steadying herself with a hand against the stall wall. She whimpered pathetically.

"Shh." Carmen balanced the heavy porcelain lid under her arm as she pulled herself onto the seat using her free hand and a grab bar. She balanced and turned herself around to face the door, holding the tank top up with both hands. She heard the outside door knob rattle, then a loud thump that sounded like a kick, then *phutt, phutt,* the dreaded sound of the silencer—the sound she had come to learn and fear during the last ten or so minutes.

Steps echoed on the tile floor as he slowly approached. She heard him open a stall door—the stall next to them. She saw his feet. They were huge in black, shiny shoes. He stopped.

She waited. Carmen could feel Lily's breath and her trembling, little body behind her.

The door opened slowly and then—smash! Without hesitation Carmen swung the tank lid into Rudi's face with a two-handed back swing. Her body crashed into the side of the stall from the momentum. She heard the cracking of bone as his nose and orbital socket shattered under the weight of the heavy porcelain lid. Blood sprayed everywhere as he fell backward, hitting the sink. The mirror was splattered with red, and so was Carmen. She dropped the blood-smeared lid, which shattered into large pieces as it hit the floor, and then wiped the greasy red residue from her face.

"Let's go." Carmen grabbed Lily's hand, and they flew out of the bathroom into the carnage Rudi had left for them. There was blood everywhere, and she was disgusted by its feel and smell. But there was no time. "Come on!" she yelled.

Lily finally let out the scream she had been holding back for the last twenty minutes. It was ear-shattering. But it didn't matter. No one could hear it. No one could respond.

Carmen and Lily skirted two bodies lying on the floor next to empty desks. Two secretaries with their faces shot off. Down the hall there were three more men in jeans, contorted in various positions on the floor, not moving, presumed dead. Carmen didn't look into the offices as she ran through the narrow hall, deftly avoiding the corpses. She picked up the first phone she saw behind an empty work station, its receiver dangling from a vacant desk, and dialed 911. "Don't look," she said as she covered Lily's eyes. The worker who belonged in the now empty work station lay under the desk, her head gaping open at the brow. Brain matter was spattered over her chair and the surface behind it. Red globules dripped thickly down the white surround.

"Hello, is this the police?" Carmen had no patience. She cut through the questions of the 911 operator, which she considered wasteful and time consuming. "Look, just send the cops and an ambulance. No," she paused, "send about five or six ambulances— because they're all dead. And I killed one of them—myself."

"I don't know what you're trying to pull, Mr. Ceratto, but I'm sanctioning you right now. You will pay this court five hundred dollars. And each time you pull a stunt like that, it will be a thousand more. And if you force me into calling a mistrial, I'll have you confined for contempt. And then I'm going to file a complaint with the Disciplinary Board and see to it that you're disbarred in Pennsylvania and every other state you try to set foot in." Barnes, red-faced, drew in a breath and, choking on his own venom, coughed loudly.

"Are you all right, Judge?" Nick asked in a sincere tone while wishing the man in black would strangle on his own saliva.

"No, I'm not."

"Look, Judge. There's no need to be so upset with me. I'm only doing what I'm supposed to do as an attorney."

"Sell your clients down the river?" The judge's eyes bulged with hatred for the young man before him.

"No. Get to the truth."

"Truth, shmuth. You're trying to force a mistrial and your own ruin. I'm telling you, Ceratto. Don't."

"Judge, I'm an officer of the court like you, and my interest is that justice is served, not simply to win a case. And neither you nor any other judge is going to threaten me on or *off the record* like you're doing now." Nick cocked his head to the side, wearing his best street corner smirk. "That doctor is not guilty. He didn't do a fucking thing but try to save that cop's life. I know for a fact that the cop was murdered—to set this case up—and the fucking bitch who did it is the one you let compose herself."

"Mr. Ceratto, you're beyond reprimand. You're beyond sanctioning—you're teetering on the edge of arrest. How dare you insult this court with foul language and slanderous accusations— unfounded accusations, I might add." Barnes's voice shook with anger, especially because Nick appeared so cool. He simply smiled and listened. "Either you have a death wish or you are totally insane. I prefer to think the latter. I prefer to think you are under pressure with a case you inherited that is simply too much for you, and that is the reason for these antics. So, Mr. Ceratto, which will it be, jail, a mental hospital or the courtroom? You choose."

"No, Judge. *You* choose," Nick snapped, still smiling. "You see, the way I look at is if you have me locked up, I'm safe. At least I won't wind up in the morgue. And you'll have to declare a mistrial. Then I'll go to the press and your goose is cooked. The hospital? Those two murdering assholes out there, your buddies, would take care of me the same way they did Sean Riley. But the case still mistries and you lose your perfect record. The press will ask a million questions. They'll eat up what I say, even from the loony bin. But you'll never make the Supreme Court—not if this lunatic can help it! Or—" he took a long breath, cocking his head, squinting defiantly—"you let me try this case, the way I want to. If I win, you win. If I lose, you still win. But that jury out there…" he pointed to the door, "makes the decision, not you."

"Are you threatening *me*, Mr. Ceratto?" The judge's voice dropped two octaves. His expression changed.

"No, Judge, I'm just telling it like it is, that's all. Threats never work. I learned that the hard way. You've got to walk the long walk, and I have good strong legs."

"Then let's talk, Mr. Ceratto and see where you're headed." The judge angrily smacked "0" on the speaker phone and barked at his secretary, "Get Mr. Asher in here."

The second pot of coffee had been brought into the room where the jurors sat—or at least were supposed to sit—in quiet detachment. Juror number three checked her makeup in a compact mirror she always carried, adjusting her curls now and then. Two of the older men played cards—highly unusual and hardly permitted during Barnes's trials, but this one was an exception.

Alonzo Hodge paced like a caged animal, arms folded, purposely not socializing with any other juror.

"Mr. Hodge, I'd appreciate your not walking about. You're making me quite nervous and just making things worse for everyone," Mrs. Carla Fisher, an English teacher at Central High said with her most tolerant, tutorial smile. She looked at him squarely, waiting for a response, the smile still pasted on her jowled face. She got none. She adjusted her tortoiseshell half-glasses, closing her hardback copy of Dickens's *Hard Times*. "Mr. Hodge?"

"Look, teach," snapped Alonzo, quickly pivoting to face her. "I'm not one of your students. I got a family to support and a job I probably lost to worry about. You bein' paid your fifty thousand dollar salary while we wait for these assholes to get on with the case. So, shut the fuck up, OK?"

"Mr. Hodge. There's no need to become vulgar and abusive," she indignantly. "I didn't know…"

A portly truck driver named Domenic DeMeo slowly rose to his feet. He was between thirty-five and forty. The ravioli and all his other favorite dishes had taken their toll, and he strained as he lifted his two hundred and seventy-five pounds from his chair. "Come on, all you people," he interrupted. "We gotta get along here. We got important decisions to make." His outstretched arms summoned peace. "Look, we all wanna get outta here, so let's play nice, and when the game is up we vote guilty, give the widow lady a bunch a money, and get outta here."

Mr. Hirsch puts his cards down and shook his gray head. "Highly irregular, Mr. DeMeo. We're not supposed to discuss the case, let alone make decisions, until the end—until all the evidence is presented and the judge gives us our instructions. Then we deliberate and vote, and *then* and *only then* do we reach a verdict."

"What are you—a lawyer?" mocked DeMeo, his stomach jiggling with laughter.

"No, but my son is. And I know a little bit about the process. And *I,* Mr. DeMeo, have a conscience. *I* don't find people guilty and ruin their lives just because I want to go home."

"Exactly," chimed in Mrs. Fisher. "We've sworn an oath to uphold the law and do our duty as jurors. I will not be part of a biased jury."

"OK, then let's tell the judge and go home." The curly blond pressed her lips together to evenly spread her newly applied lipstick. "I have a date tonight and I would like to pick up a new pair of shoes on the way home, sleep late, and not come back tomorrow. Does that sound like a plan?" she giggled, putting her recently sculpted, inch-long fingernails to her mouth.

"This is bullshit!" Alonzo smacked is hand on the chipped, brown table. "Look, Mr. Justice." He pointed at Hirsh. Then he turned to DeMeo. "And you, Mr. Quick-fix." Then looking at juror number three, "And you, Ms. Bubble-Brain." She giggled, unfazed by the slur. "Teach is right. We swore an oath. I don't like bein' here. I don't like losin' my job. But what's done is done. I don't like this, but I gotta accept this shitty job they forced me to do. So do you. So let's get together and do our job." He paused, looked up at the stained ceiling, and began to pace. "I smell a rat here. Some shit's goin' down here and we better keep our eyes and ears open."

All eleven sat upright and listened attentively as Alonzo Hodge pontificated, doing exactly as they had been admonished not to do.

Chapter XLV

The empty courtroom echoed with the crash of a heavy door forcefully flung open. The old bailiff appeared, holding his chest as he tried to catch his breath. He ran, half limping toward the door of Judge Barnes's chambers.

Grace had been dozing in the hard chair in the back of the room. She was jarred out of her half sleep by the noise and found herself alone. She quickly looked at her watch and saw that Nick had been in the judge's chambers for a half hour. She didn't like it. She also didn't like the action of the bailiff. She knew Louie, or at least had seen him in courtrooms before, and there was no way this old man—this seasoned beneficiary of old time Philadelphia patronage, would attempt to run anywhere—for any reason. Except, maybe to escape a nuclear blast.

Louie had disappeared into the rear sanctum. Grace quickly left the courtroom, hoping to find out whatever the bailiff knew or had seen that had jet propelled to Barnes's chambers. She saw an empty hall. She found it particularly unusual that the newspeople had gone. She knew how they hung around day and night when they smelled blood. The only possible conclusion was that there was fresh meat somewhere else. Then from around a distant corner of the narrow, dingy hall, beyond her sight line, she heard noise— running feet clattering on the vinyl tile floor and muffled shouts. She picked up speed and hurried toward the noise.

A crowd of reporters milled around something, poking cameras and microphones toward the center of the crowd. Grace gathered that whoever or whatever it was, was important. Perhaps more important than what was happening in courtroom number 613.

At the outside of the ring of bodies she recognized Shoes.

"Shoes," Grace called from a distance, her voice barely audible in the racket. "Shoes!"

He turned his head, looking over his shoulder. He was viciously chewing his gum, a sign that this *was* important. He nodded his head to her, signaling her to hurry up. When Grace reached him, he stepped back from the crowd and leaned against the wall.

"What's going on?" she asked. "Is the president visiting this dump?" She pushed back a fallen lock of red hair.

"Nah," he answered standing close to her, close enough so that the smell of spearmint almost knocked her out. "Just the DA"

"The DA? She gets all this attention—all this fuss? What did she do?"

"Nothin'. She just got herself killed," he snickered.

"Oh my God, that's horrible…"

"She deserved it. She was a bitch," he said flatly. Then smiled, nodding his head. "What goes around, comes around. She fried a lotta people…a lotta my friends."

Grace was shocked. She had just seen a news clip on CNN about Muriel Gates that morning while she was dressing. Nick had a habit of turning CNN on each morning and never turning it off until he got home at night. She was cleaning up the crack houses in North Philadelphia with a vengeance…and now she was dead? It was unreal. Grace didn't realize that she had actually been verbalizing her thoughts until she heard Shoes' response.

"Yep. That's what all the fuss is about," he said calmly, picking lint from his black, sharkskin jacket. His pitiless eyes, surrounded by dark hollows, showed no emotion.

"Who's in there—in the middle of that mob? Do you know?" she asked.

"It's your ex-bosses. Two other winners."

"Silvio and Levin?"

"Yep. One of their lawyers, a girl I think, was shot wit' her. Killed, too. Shame about her, but she was probably a lesbo, too. No big loss." He shrugged his shoulders.

"Margo Griffin?" Grace's green eyes widened.

"Don't know her name." He sucked on a toothpick, twisting it in his mouth and being careful not to catch it in his gum.

"She's the only female attorney in the firm."

"Then it must be her. I heard she was a real fox, too. Too bad she wasted herself on the fat dyke." He shook his head.

Grace walked toward the moving circle, pushing her way into the center of the crowd. A middle-aged woman, angling her large frame in for a close camera shot, accidently struck her in the head with a heavy telephoto lens. Grace didn't flinch. Instead she placed the high heel of her shoe on the photographer's instep and ground down on it like a discarded cigarette butt. The woman squealed and fell back, leaving Grace room to make her way into the middle of the fray.

Marty Silvio was flailing around in a vain attempt to get out of the ring. Harry was holding his jacket over his head and face, more to protect himself from all the hard metal being shoved at him than to hide his identity.

"Sir, I understand that the young woman killed along with the district attorney was your employee…and there was a relationship… What about the detective who was shot…Did you know him?"

Silvio glanced at the reporter, shaking his head, still trying to claw his way out of the herd, sorry he had left the courtroom during the break for some stale air and a cigar.

"No—she was not your employee? No relationship?"

"No!" Silvio shouted. "I'm not answering any questions and get that thing out of my face, before I shove it your mouth."

Grace had seen what she needed, and started to step back. Fortunately Little Al was behind her in the middle of the mess, and with his substantial girth he was able to create a hole for her as he backed and elbowed her way out of the ring.

"Margo Griffin." She uttered the name, in shock. "Why would anyone want to kill *her*, and how did anyone get past security to kill the DA? I don't understand."

"I do. It's easy to get into public offices. I done it a hundred times. But it's hard to get out." Little Al brushed himself off, and then bent down to wipe the footprints off his Italian slip-ons. "Fuck, I hate it when my shoes get messed up. I just paid five bucks for a shine. It was a hit, and the fucker who shot them shot up a whole office on another floor to get at two kids. Killed everyone but the kids. The two kids was wit' the detective, but they escaped."

"What about the detective?"

"He's alive, they say. He had Kevlar on, but he had a heart attack and ain't doing too good."

"Did you hear any names?" Grace asked anxiously, hoping that it wasn't who she suspected.

"Nah, I ain't too good wit' names. The detective's... you know...Irish, like Kelly."

"Could it be Kirby?"

"Could be," Al said, shrugging his shoulders. "The two kids are spics—I mean Spanish," he grinned sheepishly, correcting himself. "Let's see." He looked up at the ceiling. "Garcia, Gutierrez. All them names is alike. I can't remember. They was two girls. I know dat."

"Possibly Lopez?" Grace asked.

"Yeah. Could be. Two little girls, dey said. An' one of 'em got the shooter— hit him over the head wit' a toilet tank top. Imagine dat—a kid whackin' a hit wit' a toilet top!" His face became bright red as his shoulders shook with laughter. "How embarrassin'."

"Al!" she shouted. "Listen to me. Try to remember the names. The names, Al," she commanded.

He closed his eyes, scratched his forehead. "Yeah. One's named Lily. I remember hearin' dat name. Reason I know...my mudder's name is Lil. At's how I know... Right."

"Lily!" And with the speed of a gazelle, Grace fled the gray granite building, making her way through the beggars in the courtyard, past the stench of urine and into a cab waiting at the corner of Fifteenth and Market Streets.

Grace had been a paralegal with the DA's office, and she knew investigative procedure like the back of her hand. They would take the kids to Central Detectives, prop them up on a broken-down desk, give them ice cream, teddy bears, french fries, Coke (the brown, liquid kind), and make them feel as though they were at Grandma's.

Grace knew Carmen well. She had spent a lot of time with the young girl, old beyond her years, when her mother brought her in on school holidays. She knew Carmen could use a computer as well as she could, and she also knew that Carmen was curious about the operation of Silvio and Levin—the cases in inventory, the individual stories of clients, and office gossip. And her mother shared everything with her. Carmen and Lily had been in danger. Had almost gotten killed. This was clear. Carmen's savvy and guts had saved them this time. But what about the next time? And until Silvio and Levin were behind bars, there was sure to be a next time.

Within minutes Grace found herself at Central Detectives thanks to the rocket speed of a brown cab driver with one gold tooth, front and center. His name was Shamir something or other, and his dark face, laminated in plastic on the acrylic window dividing him from her, smiled at her as he wildly wove through traffic. She made the sign of the cross and braced herself, then bowed her head in thanks as he screeched to a halt in front of the dirty brick building, blackened by the fumes of too many exhausts over the past decades. The City of Philadelphia was certainly not spending the taxpayers' money on cleaning its facades. Rather the funds went into the bottomless pit of the city agencies and pension funds where administrators could siphon off their cut without detection. Even its crown jewel, City Hall, covered with rust and lichen and trash trees growing through its ornate eaves, gave testament to decades of politics—Philadelphia style. The sight never failed to break Grace's heart, even at this time of urgency and need to focus. It was a flash of depression that she felt, and then it was gone as she made her way to the front desk.

"Grace, what brings you here?" There was instant recognition from the cop who had been assigned to the front desk for the last ten years due to a gunshot wound that had shattered her right knee.

"Hi, Helen. I need to speak to the captain."

"What about?"

"About this morning's murder and two Latino girls you guys are holding. I know them very well. Their mother and I worked together."

"Ain't it a bitch?" The cop shook her oiled and coiled braids, which glistened in the overhead fluorescent lights. "What's the world coming to?" She fixed on Grace's red face and shook her head apologetically. "I don't think I can do that, hon. The captain has orders. This is too high profile. You see, even the newspaper and TV boys and girls are nowhere in sight. Right now they're at the coroner's office and in front of 1421 Arch Street. The captain doesn't want anyone near the kids. Not even me." She rolled her dark eyes and pointed to her ample chest, tightly wrapped in a spotless blue blouse.

"Tell the captain that I can help him. With the kids…" Grace paused and took a deep breath. "Look, Helen, I don't have time to explain, but there's a lot going on now…"

"Tell me about it, girl. DA murdered—a dozen folks gunned down—one of our best detectives hurt—God knows how bad…"

"Who was the dick?" Grace asked, interrupting her litany. She didn't have time to hear, again, what she already knew.

"Ralph Kirby. He was about to retire. Now he may have to retire permanently before he wants to—you know what I mean?" She rolled her eyes again out of habit.

Grace mentally prepared herself for the worst. "Is he going to die?"

"Don't know. They say his vest saved him. The miracle of Kevlar." She paused, examining her manicured tips. "But he has a bad heart and now that's the problem."

"Helen, I need to see the kids. Just ask. Do me a favor, OK? There's one named Carmen, a thirteen-year-old, smart as a whip. In more ways than one."

Helen smiled cynically. "I know about that one. She's a pip— threatening to sue the police department. She wants a lawyer…

'cause she's the one that clobbered the hit man with the toilet tank, and the fucker ain't dead, either."

"She's not being booked, is she?"

"No, ma'am. She deserves a medal. We told her that. But she won't open up. Doesn't trust us. Doesn't trust anybody."

"Can't blame her, can you?" Grace was quick to interrupt. "She's had a tough time, and she doesn't come from a neighborhood where they trust cops."

Just then what had been muted shouting became audible, something that sounded like, "Get me a lawyer or get me the fuck outta here!" It was Carmen all right.

"See what I mean—foul-mouthed little witch," Helen said, shaking her head. "They should put her in the slammer for a few hours to cool her off."

"Tell the captain I need to talk to him, Helen. You can do that for me, can't you?" Grace smiled tensely.

Helen looked squarely at Grace for a second, and then, convinced of the urgency, she nodded her head in the affirmative. "Can't hurt, that's for sure. And if you can shut the little foul-mouthed twit up for a while, my headache might just get a little better." She got up and moved her bottom-heavy frame toward the rear of the dingy reception room, which was in bad need of a paint job—among other things.

Grace paced, looking at her watch. She was anxious to get back to the trial. It had been fifteen minutes since she had gotten into the jet-propelled cab. She wasn't sure where she should be, where she was needed most: with Nick or with the girls. She knew that somehow she had to try to be at both places, as close in time as possible. She knew there was a connection here. She was sure—with all the murders—with the Lopez girls, and with the Riley case. She had to find out what it was. Why were the girls a target? Why had Gates and Griffin been targets? And what was Kirby doing with them? Kirby couldn't talk, and maybe he never would if his heart gave out. She needed to find out more—Carmen was her only hope.

Just then, the captain emerged from his office, if one could dignify his quarters with the word *office*. He was red-faced, which wasn't unusual for him since he was Irish and the Irish are a ruddy lot, but the captain happened to be ruddier than usual today. His blue eyes were bleary with exhaustion as he squinted at Grace. It was a look inspired by Job himself. His patience was wearing thin, and he was having a hard time holding his temper. And what a temper he had. It was a curse peculiar to him, and it took great control to keep it from exploding. His white crew cut, the same haircut he had worn as a Marine drill instructor, stood more on end than ever, and his pink scalp was pinker than ever from all the blood rushing to it. He wiped a bead of sweat from his Catholic brow, more accustomed to being touched with the sign of the cross, which he had made at least a hundred times this morning while praying for the patience—the patience not to strangle the little tan skinned girl with the sinful, foul, disrespectful mouth.

"Gracie," he said, using the name he had called her by since she had been baptized. They had been neighbors for years as she was growing up, living only two doors apart in Port Richmond, a bulwark of Irish Catholicism. That was before she had run off like a common hussy to live with a married man of the Jewish persuasion, who had no intention of making an honest woman of her. She had said she didn't care because he was a good influence on her and besides Jesus was Jewish and Christians including Catholics were originally Jews. Her lover had inspired her to go on to college for her bachelor's degree in criminal justice and then had left her just before graduation to go back with his wife. But Grace had pulled herself up by the old you-know-whats, went to confession, did her penance and was back in the fold of the Catholic Church again. The captain had helped her get her first job as a paralegal in the DA's office. She had always been under his nose, asking questions, looking for evidence, documents she wasn't supposed to see, samples from the crime lab she shouldn't have been tampering with. So one day the captain had told her so in a controlled manner. But she got her Irish up, used a string of unmentionables that only the Jewish man could have taught her, and walked the hell out. Then got a job with that backstabbing, thieving personal injury firm and totally tarnished herself forever. And what in the name of the Holy Family did she want from him now! "What brings you here this lovely morning?"

"Captain, this is not the time to play coy. I need your help and I want to help you." Grace's face almost matched her flaming mop of hair, blown wildly about from the ride in the crazy cab whose windows wouldn't stay closed. Her green eyes flashed in defiance of his authority.

"So you learned some big words in college, did ya? I don't understand 'coy,' Grace, speak to me in English, not in uppity University of Penn lingo," he mocked.

"You understand the name Carmen Lopez, don't you? The little girl you're holding back there."

"Is that the little foul-mouthed brat's name?"

"Sounds like you're torturing her." Grace lifted an eyebrow. "You know there's laws against abusing kids."

"Abusing *her*?" The captain almost choked. "She can take care of herself, that one. Do you know what she did to the guy in the bathroom?"

"Yes, I heard. But don't you mean the killer? The assassin, the fucker who deserved to die at least a dozen times. The one who almost killed her and her sister?" She took a deep breath. Her chest was about to explode. "Look, Captain, I know these girls. I worked with their mother, Celia Lopez."

"Lopez…" He looked quizzically up at the ceiling, as if trying to recall the familiar name, even though it was a common Hispanic surname.

"Come on, Cap, the woman who was murdered last month on Butler Street."

"Look, Grace, there's a lot of murders in this city. I can't remember them all."

"Maybe you should consider a long vacation." She stopped, instantly feeling ashamed of her harsh treatment of the good captain who had been like an uncle to her. "You should remember this one. Ralph Kirby was assigned to the case. Gates pressured someone to close it and then just recently reopened the investigation. It was in the papers."

"Look, Grace. If you want my help, my cooperation, this is not the way to get it." The captain turned to walk away.

"Don't—I'm sorry." Her eyes filled up. She followed close behind him, hoping he would turn around. She touched his arm.

He did.

Chapter XLVI

"Is the plaintiff ready to proceed?" Judge Barnes said, looking down his patrician nose at his notes. The last words scribbled on the yellow legal pad were: *Doletov, eyewitness, credible.*

Nick rose from his chair and looked behind for support. There was none. Grace was noticeably missing, as were Silvio and Levin—even his own bodyguards. Where were they? An uneasy feeling crept into the pit of his stomach, but he had learned to control it. He had honed the act of control to a fine edge at the firm under Joe Maglio. No matter what he felt inside, the master had taught him how not to show it. Spontaneity was a liability in the law business. Particularly in the courtroom.

Nick put two and two together and came to the conclusion that something had happened, something noteworthy. He remembered how the bailiff had practically broken down the closed chambers door to whisper something in Barnes's ear. But Barnes, like Nick was schooled to reveal nothing. For all that Nick knew, the secret could have been that Barnes's Great Dane had just taken a crap on the antique Aubusson carpet in the judge's library. Barnes had simply waved the little gnome away and off he had gone, limping and huffing out the door of the chambers. Neither Nick nor John Asher had heard a word, and Barnes was not about to reveal anything that might provide someone with an excuse to postpone this trial.

"No, Judge. I'm not recalling Nurse Doletov at this time. I'm calling Doctor Manin as of cross."

A look of surprise sprang up on Barnes's face as fast as a trout snapping a fly. It was gone just as quickly. He had been expecting the normal course of events where the plaintiff's attorney called his own witnesses in his case and not the defendant's. It was obvious that Nick wanted to control Manin's testimony, not simply punch holes in it on cross-examination. By calling Manin as of cross, no holds were barred. Nick could ask him questions on just about anything relevant to the case. Nick could even ask him leading questions and maintain control of the witness.

Nick understood that Barnes would be displeased. The deal they had made in chambers was *no shenanigans* on Nick's part in return for Barnes not stripping him of what little money he had left and then throwing him in jail for contempt. Nick would try his case, represent his client to the best of his ability, and let the jury decide the fate of Doctor Manin.

But Nick had decided to chance infuriating His Majesty. His position was that calling Doctor Manin in the plaintiff's case was not a shenanigan. It was a legitimate trial tactic, and recognized under the Rules of Civil Procedure in Pennsylvania. Barnes couldn't stop him. The game was being played within the Rules. If the judge tried to stop him, it would be *his* neck on the block, not Nick's. At any rate, he thought, that it was a plausible theory.

"Very well, proceed, Mr. Ceratto." The judge lowered his head toward the yellow notepad and rested his forehead on his hand in order to conceal his anger. He was now determined to look for any opportunity he could find to strip this little wop of his livelihood. If not that, to teach him a lesson not to fuck with Judge Joseph Barnes, and not to try to take control of *his* courtroom.

Manin hesitantly rose from his seat next to Asher, hoping his attorney would protect him with some sort of objection. He glanced momentarily at Asher as he rose, but Asher was expressionless. There was no signal to sit back down, nothing to indicate that his attorney was going to protect his ass. He slowly walked toward the witness stand, feeling as if he were walking to the guillotine. Manin avoided the eyes of the jury although he could feel their multiple stares like a cold wind at his back. He had been told by Asher to make eye contact with them at every natural opportunity, and this might have been one of those opportunities, but he just couldn't. He was afraid that he might recognize his executioner among them, and he did not wish to see which one it would be.

He stood stiffly as the bible was almost irreverently shoved under his left hand. He was left-handed. It was his strongest hand. But he couldn't stop its shaking, and he wondered whether it was obvious—whether the jury would be convinced that he was indeed an incompetent surgeon because of his tremors, among other things about himself which were of concern to him.

Brown hollows surrounded his eyes, which were now slits from lack of sleep and stress. Nick approached the witness stand slowly and with purpose. Their eyes met, and now both men focused intently on each other. It was clear that the doctor had not slept the night before. He blinked with each footstep taken by his enemy. It was also evident to Nick as he got closer that the good doctor hadn't shaved that morning. Gray and brown stubble speckled his cheeks and chin. He was wrinkled and unkempt, one step away from looking as if he belonged in a box on the streets or in one of the recesses of Suburban Station. Manin looked worse at trial than he had at his deposition. This was a one-eighty for him. Nick recalled seeing his photos in the Philadelphia Inquirer on the society page—always dressed to the nines in a tailored tuxedo with a rose in his lapel—and in the *Philadelphia Magazine*'s "Top Docs" issue in a crisp white lab coat. From riches to rags, from prince to pauper. *Oh, what the law can do to you,* Nick thought, wondering about his own fate—teetering on the edge, as it was.

The last thing on Manin's mind was his clothes. As a matter of fact, he didn't care about anything except getting out of there— off the witness stand, out of the courtroom, and on with his life— whatever was left of it. He was beyond caring about his career. It was ruined anyway. His estranged wife had taken everything that wasn't already repossessed. He had nothing left but his honor—his belief in the truth, that he was a good doctor who cared about his patients and who cared about Sean Rilcy.

Nick could read all this in Manin's face. There was a certain resignation stamped on his tired features. Nick stopped just in front of the witness stand.

"Doctor Manin, my name is Nicholas Ceratto. I represent the Estate of Sean Riley and the interests of his widow, Mrs. Riley, and his family present here in the courtroom."

Victor Manin smiled and nodded. "I know," he said softly, shifting on the cold, hard chair.

Nick went through his notes, methodically asking questions about the doctor's education, his training as a resident, whom he trained under, his hospital affiliations, his degrees, his publications, his lecture circuit, his distinctions—all easy for the doctor to answer—in fact, enjoyable. He hadn't thought about his accomplishments in such a long time. He had almost forgotten that he was Phi Beta Kappa at Harvard, had gone on to Harvard Medical School, done a residency in vascular surgery at Massachusetts General, was triple board certified. He had moved to Philadelphia when he was offered the chairmanship of the vascular surgery department at Metropolitan-Mercy Hospital where he had a research lab of his own, which was funded by the Federal Government and private companies with money to burn. Being reminded of all he had done gave him enough confidence to finally look at the jury, even at Alonzo Hodge, who remained unimpressed. As far as Alonzo was concerned , this was just professional bragging, flaunting titles for the poor folks.

Manin recognized the humanity in most of the jurors. The two older men in the rear looked at him with a certain intelligence. They appeared to be interested in what he had to say. They weren't the demons John Asher had painted them to be—the vultures who would finish off a dying man, and then pick out his brains. His spine relaxed as the young woman, juror number three, gave him a faint smile from the jury box, an admiring one at that.

"Doctor Manin, thank you for giving us your impressive credentials. Now, sir, we must move on to the night Captain Riley arrived at Metropolitan-Mercy for emergency treatment of a severed femoral artery. That date was…"

"June nineteenth, nineteen ninety-five." Manin grabbed the date out of Nick's mouth, halting him in mid-sentence.

"I'm sorry for interrupting," he said softly, apologizing. "It's just that I remember the date so well."

"Good, then your memory of the events should be just as precise," Nick responded, sharply. He hated it when someone stole his thunder.

"I hope so." Manin nodded sincerely. All eyes were on him now. He was about to tell his story—to the twelve gods who would determine his fate. It made him feel queasy, but at the same time, relieved. If he could just make them believe him—at any rate, no matter what, it would all be over soon. This was his only consolation—and he might just be able to rest, to sleep peacefully.

"Can you begin, Doctor, with your first encounter with the decedent…with Captain Sean Riley?" Nick looked back briefly, to check his audience. He saw no one, only the widow clutching a used tissue so tightly the veins in her hands bulged from the pressure. And the Riley boys, both leaning forward at the edge of their seats, ready to react to each and every anticipated lie.

Manin felt the Rileys' stare. He knew they wouldn't believe a word he said. But he also knew that it didn't matter. It was the Alonzo Hodges of the world that mattered. He knew that he had to get past him to get to the others in the jury box. He sat back and took a breath. *Here it goes*, he thought as he heard his heart pounding against his chest wall.

"I was changing out of scrubs to go out to meet my wife at a black tie affair, a charity function for the homeless." He quickly glanced at Alonzo Hodge, who managed a blink at the word *homeless*. "I heard myself being paged to come to the ER. I went immediately, examined Mr. Riley, and ordered him to be taken to the OR where he was given an emergency Betadine splash prep so I could immediately start to repair the femoral artery. I quickly scrubbed while Officer Riley was being anesthetized. Then I began the repair. It was not a complex procedure. I debrided the wound and irrigated it. And then I repaired the severed artery. After the procedure, we removed the clamps and checked that there were no leaks, that the artery was firmly sutured, his blood pressure was normal, his vitals were fine. Then the external wound was irrigated again and closed. I stayed throughout the procedure to make sure the patient was stable. I left and went back to change. I had asked a nurse to phone my wife and tell her that I would be late before I started working on Captain Riley—I forgot to mention that."

"You were concerned about being late, about disappointing your wife?" Nick asked in a sarcastic tone.

"No, she's used to it." Sarcasm returned, which caused a knowing smile to break across the faces of two of the men in the rear of the jury box. How well they could relate.

"I see. Does this, your always being late, bother your wife— even though she's *used to it?*"

"I should put that in the past tense. It *did.* You see, Carla's not with me anymore."

The smiles faded from the men's faces, and the curly blond shook her head in sympathy.

"And on those occasions when it did—did bother Carla—what did she do?"

"Well, *I* wound up on the couch."

Alonzo broke his icy stare, and a smile appeared on his face. No one on the jury could resist a chuckle, not even Alonzo.

Nick continued, "And this was a consistent pattern in your private life? Is that right?"

"Yes, pretty much," Manin sighed, resignedly.

"And didn't this bother you?"

Manin thought for a moment. "At first, yes. But after a while, it didn't. You see I got used to it. It was a price I was willing to pay. My patients came first."

Nick watched the curly blond's eyes. They were glued to the thin figure on the stand. He was handsome, despite his disheveled appearance. He could sense that she was beginning to be turned on. He had seen the look so many times on women's faces, particularly on the faces of lonely, middle-aged women, desperately seeking a mate—preferably a doctor or a lawyer. Married was acceptable, but a single doctor, or lawyer was highly prized among such "barracudas," as they were known among their wary prey. Nick sensed her mentally licking her chops as she examined Manin's good bones and craggy features. She was probably wondering how he looked undressed, without the distraction of those wrinkled, baggy clothes. She was possibly thinking about how she could dress him up and make him look cool, perhaps in tight faded jeans, a leather jacket, maybe a black Harley T-shirt. *Nah*, thought Nick, *definitely not Manin's style.*

"All right, Doctor. Let's go back to the hospital after the surgery on Captain Riley. You went back to change back into your tux. Is that right?"

"Yes."

"Not a rented tux?"

"No, I *owned* a tux."

"A custom tailored tux, I assume—made especially for you?"

"Yes. That was back when I could afford it." Manin watched as a look of approval began to appear on the jurors' faces. He felt a growing acceptance. Even Alonzo Hodge appeared sympathetic. He even grinned as he shook his head. *Doc's not a bad dude*, was the message that Manin got.

John Asher was wondering where the hell Nick was going with this line of questioning. Nick hadn't flinched at Manin's answer. And so many irrelevancies. But who was he to object? His client was looking better by the minute.

Nick went on. "OK. You changed or were in the process, I gather. And did something happen then?"

"Yes. I had taken a quick shower and had almost finished dressing when I heard my name again."

"On the pager?"

"Yes, I was paged. I must say I grumbled to myself, that is…"

"You grumbled?"

"Yes."

"Explain that, please."

"You know…kind of 'what the heck is going on? Why me again?'"

"Did you say this out loud?"

"No. I said it to myself. Because I was late, and now I was going to be later. I went to the phone to answer the page—and then I heard a code being called."

"A code?"

"Yes. A code. An emergency procedure when a patient is in trouble."

"Trouble? Can you explain that?"

"Yes. A code is called when a patient suffers cardiac arrest, or stops breathing, is in need of specialized resuscitative equipment and drugs. I rushed out of the doctor's lounge. When I got to him, he was still in recovery and the code team was working on him, trying to revive him."

"And then what happened?"

"Their efforts failed. Captain Mr. Riley was pronounced dead."

"And did you ask what caused his death?"

"Yes. I actually saw what caused his death."

"What do you mean?"

"He had exsanguinated. He had bled to death. His blood was all over the bedclothes, the floor."

"What was your reaction?"

"I was shocked. I couldn't believe it. I was sure that he was fine when he left the OR. I had seen to it that he was stable before being brought into recovery. The incision was fully closed. There was clearly no leaking from the artery. His blood pressure was perfect, respiration normal, heart rate was normal. The surgery had gone smoothly, as smooth…"

"Did you examine the wound afterward, after Captain Riley had expired?"

"Yes."

"And what was its condition?"

"It was open. There was blood all over the place. I told you."

"How do you think this happened? I mean—you said that you closed yourself, and everything was fine. What…?"

"I don't know how it happened." Manin lowered his head, almost apologetically. "I've never seen or heard of anything like this before. I just don't know.""Doctor, did you ever hear the name Donna Price, before?"

"Yes, she was an OR nurse. She was present at the surgery. She assisted while I closed. I'm sure she could tell you…"

"She can't, Doctor. She can't tell us anything at this time. Would it surprise you if I told you that Ms. Price is dead?"

Manin's gaze shifted, his head still lowered. He took a deep breath. "She disappeared just after the surgery. I've been trying to locate her for almost two years. Now I understand."

"Would it surprise you if I told you she was murdered?"

Manin looked as though he had been kicked in the stomach. He had suspected something had happened to her. Donna was a top-notch nurse and a friend. She had assisted him in many difficult operations. He could always count on her. She would never have voluntarily abandoned him when he needed her the most.

"Mr. Ceratto. I must stop you. Where are you going with this line of questioning?" Barnes's face was glowing red with rage. He wanted to tear Ceratto's throat out to shut him up. He resisted the temptation to leap over the bench in Nick's direction.

"No, it wouldn't," said Manin, completely ignoring Barnes. He was doing well with the jury and was not about to be interrupted.

"Doctor Manin!" shouted Barnes. "I'm speaking to plaintiff's counsel. You are not to proceed."

"Why wouldn't it surprise you?" Nick asked, defying the bench. He was on a roll and he wasn't about to stop either—not for Barnes—not for anyone.

"Because Ms. Price had no reason to hide from me, to run away. She was dependable, efficient, pleasant, happy at her job…"

"Dr. Manin—" Barnes's gavel fell like a thunder clap. "Shut up!"

Asher sprang to his feet. "Your Honor, objection. This…"

"Sustained!" Barnes shouted, interrupting Asher in mid-sentence. "Mr. Ceratto, you're out of order. Sit down."

"No, Your Honor!" Asher shouted. "I want an objection on the record. Dr. Manin should be permitted to answer Mr. Ceratto's question."

"You're objecting to *me?*" Barnes's ears glowed crimson. "You can't do that. Not in *my* courtroom. You're out of line, out of order." His voice cracked. "Mr. Asher, sit down."

The jury's heads turned back and forth, following the volley. They paid close attention, intrigued by the exchange. This was great entertainment—they couldn't get better on TV.

Alonzo Hodge was about to stand up and yell, *Let the man answer the question. We want to hear what the doctor has to say. We want all the information, not just what you want us to hear, you jive, red-faced, honkey motherfucker. Who do you think you are—we make the decisions, not you.*

Seamus Riley couldn't contain himself. He stood, "Hey, Ceratto. Where you goin' with this bullshit? I thought you was *our* lawyer."

"Silence!" Barnes slammed his gavel down and hammered away like a child having a temper tantrum. "I'll not have you make a mockery of this court and turn this trial into a circus. I'm calling a recess. Bailiff, remove the jury. I want both attorneys in my chambers immediately. Dr. Manin, step down."

"I will not!" shouted Manin. The veins bulged in his neck. "Ms. Price disappears and then gets murdered. I want to know why!"

John Asher stood. "Your Honor, you can't silence the defendant. He has a right to know the truth, and so does the jury."

"I'll silence anyone I please, Mr. Asher. You're in contempt. You're all in contempt. Bailiff, take them away. Arrest them—all of them!" Saliva sprayed from his angry mouth.

The old bailiff limped toward the bench, totally at a loss. Two other guards followed, looking just as bewildered. "Who, Your Honor?"

"Them—them!" Barnes yelled, pointing with his gavel, sweeping it from the plaintiff's table to the defense table.

"Everybody?" asked one of the guards, checking to see if there were enough hand cuffs to go around.

"Yes, you idiot!" Barnes screamed.

"Even the woman—Mrs. Riley?" The old bailiff was now more confused than ever.

"No. Not her, you stupid fuck!" Barnes's obscenities echoed across the room. He was out of his senses and he didn't care. Ceratto had gotten what he wanted, he thought. There was no way this case wasn't a mistrial. And there was no way that he, the judge, wouldn't be censured for his behavior—demoted, possibly booted off the bench. He had always been in control, ultimate control. And now, he wasn't. Now he had lost it, the control and the respect. The question now was, how to regain it? He shook uncontrollably as his mind raced for a solution.

The widow Riley sobbed. She pushed her chair back and turned toward her sons. "Help me, Seamus, Patrick." Her knees shook and then gave way, and down she went into Patrick's arms. Seamus leaped from his chair and lunged after Nick, but Nick was too quick. He knew what was coming. Always strike first. *Shoot first, ask questions later. Never be a sucker. It can kill you.* Nick dodged the huge lump of a man, and as Seamus went down, Nick kicked him in the balls to keep him down. A technique that never failed.

The court reporter leaped from her chair, knocking her machine over as she scrambled toward the judge's chambers, toward safety.

"Everyone sit down," commanded Barnes. "Please—" turning to the jury, half of whom were standing ready to flee the mayhem— "ladies and gentlemen, please be seated." He didn't know *what* to do.

The bailiffs descended, still confused as to who was to be taken out of the courtroom. One grabbed Nick, cuffs dangling from his right hand. Three sheriffs' deputies arrived. One grabbed Seamus Riley from behind in a headlock, gun pointing at Seamus's spine. The other tackled Patrick. The paramedics were on their way for Mrs. Riley. Barnes himself was about to flee when the heavy door at the rear of the courtroom swung open with a loud crash. The noise broke the momentum of the melee.

"Nick!" shouted Grace as she looked for him in the tangle of bodies below the now empty bench. "Get the fuck off him!" she screamed at the deputy who held a gun to Nick's head while another attempted to handcuff his arms behind him. "Nick, she's here. She's here!"

Chapter XLVII

The following day was an official day of mourning. Black crepe draped from the arches of City Hall. All over Philadelphia flags flew at half-mast. Newspaper headlines screamed, *DA Murdered!* As usual, the *Daily News* was tasteless in its announcement, *Pearly Gates For Muriel!* Every network featured news items on the DA's life and there were reruns ad nauseam: Muriel being sworn in as an attorney in the early seventies with long stringy hair, wearing a frumpy, flowered dress; Muriel as an aspiring DA in the late seventies, a little heavier but better groomed; Muriel in the late eighties as a successful prosecutor, sporting a black, tailored suit and a severe haircut; Muriel in the late nineties, running for political office, touting her victories over drug lords, child molesters, and killers—killers of the mind as well as the body. Gates had hated smut. She specialized in closing down porn shops and breaking up prostitution rings. Crimes against women were particularly loathsome to her. And she had no mercy with those defendants.

Who would fill her shoes now? The first assistant district attorney, Frank Forester, was more of an administrator than a dedicated prosecutor. He was more interested in increasing appropriations from City Council than he was in fighting crime. His priority was hiring more assistant DAs and renovating and finely appointing his office with antique reproductions and prints of old Philadelphia..

Hardly any newsprint or TV coverage was given to poor Gloria Henley, Gates' loyal secretary, or to Ralph Kirby, who was fighting for his life. But Margo Griffin got a full page. Beautiful, young lawyer cut down in the prime of her life. There were innuendos, buried here and there, about her relationship with the late DA, but nothing scandalous, nothing that would trigger a libel suit.

The killer was featured prominently on the second page of the *Philadelphia Inquirer*, and on the front page of the *Daily News*.

His photo was plastered next to Gates'. Then on the next page was a collage of photos: Rudi as a cop, Rudi as a cab driver, Rudi as an EMT, Rudi as a Montgomery County detective. Rudi's car had been found and his trunk searched. In his bag of tricks were all his fake IDs, copies of which had somehow made their way from Central Detectives Homicide Division to the *Daily News.*

Carmen and Lily had not been identified because of their ages but nevertheless were cast as child heroes in bringing down a vicious assassin. The networks were scurrying around frantically trying to locate a guardian who could OK an interview and later a talk-show spot that would instantly make the little orphans rich and famous.

Federal, state, and local police were everywhere, swarming over 1421 Arch Street. They were particularly visible at Metropolitan Mercy Hospital guarding the entrances to the rooms assigned to Kirby and Rudi, where doctors were working hard to keep both alive—Kirby because he was a good cop and Rudi because they wanted to know more.

Intrigued by the news but not terribly upset by it, ordinary Philadelphians did not change their habits one iota. They rode the trains to work, faces stuck in their newspapers. Once inside their office buildings, the "Did ya hear?" and "Ain't it awful?" lasted about fifteen minutes, and then everybody was back to normal, listening to voice mail and turning on their computers between bites of mustard-smeared soft pretzel and swigs of Pepsi, favorite Philadelphia breakfast foods.

Judges and politicians, relieved that they had not been on Rudi's hit list, went about their usual routines of administrative inadequacies, stupid decisions, and doing anything politically expedient to get ahead. In other words, business as usual.

Except for the headlines and the black bunting, and the incessant prattle on television news, one would never guess that an important political figure, the city's chief law enforcement officer, had been gunned down in cold blood.

Judge Barnes had been relieved of his duties as trial judge in the Riley case. He had been rushed to Hahnemann hospital with severe chest pains after the fray in his courtroom had been broken up by uniformed police in full riot gear. Barnes remained in intensive care through the night and into the next day. He was heavily sedated because of his fits of crying. His doctors suspected he was having a severe psychotic episode and recommenced that he go to Friends' Hospital for a psychiatric evaluation.

But the jury was not dismissed, nor was the case declared a mistrial. Judge Anthony Primavera was assigned as the new trial judge. He had read the transcripts of the trial to date and was prepared to deal with the mess. He was familiar with all the pretrial maneuvers and the motions made by the attorneys, the decisions made by Barnes, and the trial testimony taken thus far.

Judge Primavera was fair. He liked his job and had no designs on the Supreme Court. He drove a ten-year-old Jeep Cherokee, and vacationed each summer in Sea Isle City, New Jersey. He had been law review at Penn Law School in the late fifties. He wore round, tortoiseshell-rimmed glasses, a tartan bow tie, and a comfortable cable-knit cardigan under his robe. Besides the law, all he needed was Maggie, his wife of thirty-four years; his yellow Labrador, Honey-bun; his fly rod; and his collection of original Sherlock Holmes. Primavera was a happy man, a fearless servant of Justice. Best of all, he was in no one's pocket. And today *he* was in control as he took his place on the bench.

"Mr. Ceratto, please call your next witness."

Nick rose slowly. He was clean shaven, but his left cheekbone bore a dark bruise from the day before when Seamus Riley had smashed his face against the counsel table. Nick avoided the first hit but the body slam was quick and accurate and Nick's face hit the mahogany. Both Riley boys were conspicuously absent this morning, having been arrested and confined to the House of Detention for at least the rest of the trial by order of Judge Primavera.

"Thank you, Your Honor. I call Donna Price."

A murmur echoed from the jury. All had a look of puzzlement on their face. Was this a ghost, or perhaps a hoax, some trick being played on them?

Nick looked toward the back of the courtroom, empty except for six armed guards stationed at the door, three on each side.

"Very well, Mr. Ceratto. Officer, please bring in Ms. Donna Price."

One of the guards nodded affirmatively to Judge Primavera and stepped out to the courtroom next door where all witnesses had been ordered to wait until called. Only the attorneys, the judge, the jury, the plaintiff, and defendant were permitted to be together in the courtroom. The press had been ordered stay outside City Hall, no closer than fifty feet to any of the entrances.

All eyes in the jury box shifted toward the door as they waited for her—the woman they had been told was murdered.

They had agreed over their morning coffee that the trial was better than any TV drama or any miniseries. Every man and woman was dressed for the occasion. Today there were jackets, ties and dresses instead of sweaters, blue jeans, and jogging pants. It was a clear sign that the jurors were aware of the importance of this case, and even more so of the importance of their task. Even Alonzo Hodge was noticeably erect. He was dressed in an ivory three-piece suit and a bright yellow-and-orange rep tie with stick-pin. His hands were folded tightly in his lap. It signaled to all that he was ready to do his job.

Donna Price walked self-consciously toward the witness stand, escorted by the limping, gray haired bailiff. The only sound was the click of her heels on the terrazzo floor. She looked down, her porcelain skin flushed from the unwanted attention. She smoothed the back of her navy blue skirt as she sat down and cleared her throat, moving the microphone slightly forward. It had been set too close to her mouth. She knew to do this from having been a reluctant speaker at various nurse's conferences. She moistened her lips and, almost inaudibly, assented to the oath to tell the truth and nothing but the truth.

Nick quickly led her through the preliminaries of name, address, career credentials, her association with Dr. Manin, and the details of the surgery.

The jury listened intently as Donna told her story. She spoke slowly, almost as if she wanted the men and women listening to her to hear and understand each and every word.

"Now, Ms. Price, please tell us what you saw when you entered the recovery room where Captain Riley had been taken."

Donna hesitated, clearly unsettled by the prospect of having to relive the terror of her encounter with Doletov and the assassins. "When I entered the recovery room the first thing I did was to check the op site. I saw blood. He was bleeding badly. I yelled at Doletov who was in the room. I was about to call a code when she came at me, knocked me down, and tried to inject me with something. I pulled her foot out and ran for help. I managed to call a code, but no one responded. Then Doletov yelled something in Russian and they came at me."

Juror number three gasped out loud as if she had been hit in the face with ice water after Donna recounted escape from the hospital and the close call the would-be assassins. Alonzo Hodge squinted, and nodded in affirmation as if to say: *I knew some shit went down there.*

The jurors' eyes were riveted on her as she told them about changing her identity and becoming Jane Welles, and how she started a new life in Pasadena. That is until the arrival of Nick Ceratto and company.

"Ms. Price…" Nick paused momentarily, knowing that at this point he had total command of the courtroom. No matter how he phrased his questions, no one would object, certainly not John Asher. After all, Nick was trying his case for him. Nick was better at defending Manin than Asher was at this point. Nick seemed to know a hell of lot more than Asher did. So he would just let him go on.

Judge Primavera listened intently, but without expression. His interest lay in simply getting to the truth and stopping all the nonsense.

"Tell us how you came to be here, if you will. For instance, tell us how you first encountered me and what I told you."

Donna flushed nervously. She didn't feel any hostility coming from the jury; the vibes were benign. So she let it rip.

"I was forced to come here because of you, Mr. Ceratto—you and your cohorts—a woman and a man who broke into my apartment and intimidated me…"

"What did I say?" Nick leaned cockily against the witness stand and lowered his head as if to concentrate on every word.

"You said that I had to come to court to testify, to tell the truth about what I saw in the surgical recovery room where Mr. Riley was taken. You handed me a subpoena."

"And did you want to come? Voluntarily, that is…"

"No. I told you that I didn't want to testify."

"And…?"

"I told you that I was afraid of returning to Philadelphia—and you told me about incidents at the hospital.

"What incidents was I speaking about?"

"Trumped up cases, Mr. Ceratto. Where lawyers have people killed so they can make millions with lawsuits. I told you that I couldn't go back to Philadelphia, that I'd be killed because I knew too much. I had seen what I wasn't supposed to see."

"And…?" Nick gently prodded.

"And you said that you would help me—that you would protect me. That I was probably a target in Pasadena since you had most likely been followed there." Donna's eyes reddened and brimmed with tears. She wiped the narrow streams, which fell down her face into her lap. She shuddered slightly and took a deep breath, closed her eyes momentarily, and quickly composed herself. "I told you that I'd be on a morning flight, the day before the trial. That I'd testify. I said it to get you—you all out of my apartment—out of my life. I was terrified. And I was not…I mean I intended not to testify. I was going to run again until…" She paused.

"Yes, Ms. Price?"

"Until *she* was killed."

"Who, Ms. Price? Who was killed…tell us."

"My roommate." Donna tilted her back to prevent another cascade of tears and dabbed at her eyes with the back of her right index finger. "My roommate, Carol."

"What happened to Carol?"

"That night, the night of the day you—" she hesitated "— you broke into my apartment, Carol had taken my shift. She left the apartment, maybe around two a.m. I was asleep when I got a call from the hospital police. I guess it was around three a.m. They had found Carol in the hospital parking lot with her throat slit. They thought I was Carol because she looked like me and she had taken my purse from the dining room table by mistake. We coincidentally had bought the same black bag. It had been on sale. We laughed about it."

Donna took a breath, shaking her head. "The police found my ID in my bag and assumed the victim was me. Carol and I looked so much alike. We were the same height, blue eyes, blond. And our driver's license photos were almost identical. Even our hospital picture IDs got confused sometimes if we left them around the apartment. So we used to make sure that we put them in our purses when our shifts were finished, before we came home. Poor Carol." Donna wept. "It was supposed to be me in the morgue—not her. She had a husband. She had just gotten married. He was supposed to come to California in two weeks to start a new job. They were supposed to be together…"

"Ms. Price," Judge Primavera interrupted. "Would you like a brief recess?"

"No. No, Your Honor. I want to get this over with—please."

"Very well." Primavera nodded his head compassionately. "Continue then, Ms. Price."

"The police came that morning to question me and to search the apartment. They found a bug and surveillance camera. I was being watched by the killer. He couldn't tell the difference between Carol and me. So he killed her by mistake.. I decided after that, that my life and the lives of others were in danger if this continued, if *I* allowed this to go on. I told the police everything—about what happened to Captain Riley, what I had seen, my identity change. I told them about you, Mr. Ceratto, and what was happening in Philadelphia with people being murdered. About what you suspected, about what you knew."

"And what did they tell you—the police, that is?"

"They told me that they would give me an escort to Philadelphia so that I would be safe. They said that they would be working with the FBI and the Philadelphia police on this."

"And here you are." Nick turned to the jury.

"Yes."

What can you tell us about Dr. Manin, the defendant?" Nick swept his hand toward the defense table.

"About him in general?"

"Yes. Let's start there. How long have you worked beside Dr. Manin?"

"Oh, at least five years. I've worked with him on at least fifty surgeries."

"And what is the level of service that he gives his patients? In other words, is he a good surgeon. Does he take care of his patients?"

"My goodness, I can't remember a better surgeon. I've never seen a more caring, competent doctor. He takes his time with his patients. He frequently does things himself that many other doctors hand over to a resident. He loves his work and he's good at it."

"What about with Captain Riley?"

"I remember that he wanted to perform that emergency surgery because it was a police officer who was injured. Dr. Manin is a friend of the police. He decided to stay for the surgery instead of leaving for a dinner party. And he was very careful during the operation. The repair went smoothly. He closed the wound after it was irrigated. He checked it and then said he had to leave. Usually he would stay to make sure that the patient was stable and doing well in recovery—but this time he couldn't. He had to leave. He told me to check Captain Riley. He said that his wife would have a fit if he stayed any later. He was never on time for anything other than his patients. Most doctors wouldn't stay to personally check their patients. But Doctor Manin did—except for this time." She swallowed hard and looked over the jury's heads at the wall behind them. "I wish he had. Then I wouldn't have found Captain Riley like that and things would have been different." She paused to dab her eyes. The room was silent for a few seconds. Then there was an audible sigh as the contagious tension was released.

"Mr. Ceratto." Judge Primavera leaned into the microphone, which had been purposely set at a distance from him. He disliked amplification, especially when it picked up unwanted sounds, like body functions and the racing of his pen across the yellow legal pad as he took copious notes. He knew that for most people the courtroom was an inhospitable place, and he didn't want to make it any worse. "I want to recess at this time, and I want to see both attorneys in my chambers. Ms. Price, you may step down now. However, please stay in close proximity to the courtroom until you are called, which will be shortly. You *may* not leave the building. You *may* not speak with anyone."

Donna nodded her head and slowly got up, nervously smoothing her skirt before she stepped down.

Primavera waited until she took a seat in the back of the courtroom close to the door which was guarded by four armed police officers. "Ladies and gentlemen," he went on, looking through his owl-like glasses, "you have heard testimony this morning which is compelling, to say the least." The judge turned and looked at Theresa Riley. He was concerned about her. She was pale and didn't look well. She sat motionless. Her expression was distant and flat. It was obvious that she didn't understand why her lawyer seemed to have turned against her. She wasn't alone. All Mrs. Riley knew was that someone had murdered Sean. If it was the Russian nurse, why wasn't she on trial? Where was she? It looked as if the doctor was going to get off and no one would be responsible. Was the doctor in cahoots with the nurse? With Doletov? With Price? She was confused. And her head hurt. All the lawyer talk, the judge talk, the recesses. What went on behind those closed doors? Were they making plans? Were they all in cahoots? Her lawyer wasn't telling her anything. Her sons had been right. He was selling her down the river. But someone had to pay, big-time for her husband's death. She tried to get up from her seat. Her lips moved, but no sound came from them.

"Mrs. Riley?" Primavera wanted to offer assistance, but it was too late. Her knees buckled and she crumpled like a rag doll onto the floor.

Chapter **XLVIII**

Judge Primavera stepped into his robing room and picked up the ringing telephone.

His secretary, Julia, had been told never to interrupt him during trial unless there was an emergency and the emergency somehow related to the matter before him. Both criteria had been met.

Asher and Ceratto waited nervously in a separate room, if one could dignify the space with the designation *room*. It was closet sized and had one broken metal desk, a leftover from World War II army surplus, and two mismatched chairs, both of which were badly in need of glue. The overhead fluorescent light buzzed and flickered, enhancing the lunar quality of the space. It was referred to by court employees as "the holding pen."

Primavera picked up the first of the two waiting calls. His secretary had told him that Fred Connley was on one and Mike Rosa on two. He didn't discriminate on the basis of rank; he simply pushed the first lit button, which was Connley. Mike Rosa was left on hold, which he wouldn't like one bit.

Connley summarized, as briefly as he could, the messy series of events that would likely have an impact on the Riley case and the decisions the judge could be asked to make from the bench—like postponement or dismissal. As far as Connley was concerned, this case belonged in criminal court, not civil court.

"Your Honor…" He always felt awkward when he addressed Primavera as *Your Honor.* They had attended Bishop Newman high school together, but Primavera had gone on to college while Connley had gone to the police academy. Although Primavera was never stuck on himself or his academic achievements, Connley still felt he had to address his friend formally when he called on him in his professional capacity.

"You don't need to kiss my ring, Fred. You can call me by my real name."

"OK, Tony…"

"That's better."

"Thanks. I feel better, too. OK, let me begin by saying that we arrested Marina Doletov at the airport. She was about to board a plane for St. Petersburg. She had twenty Gs on her in cash and a one-way ticket. The Pasadena police notified us this morning that Doletov was involved in the murder of Sean Riley. They got this information from a Donna Price, whose roommate was mistaken for Price and killed. We knew that Doletov was still under subpoena and was supposed to testify. We tailed her. She was seen getting into a cab bound for the airport. We thought that was a little strange for someone who had been ordered to hang around City Hall. She's at headquarters now. She's got a lawyer and she's prepared to deal."

"So soon?" Tony Primavera's skepticism was clear. He knew that attorneys, especially criminal defense lawyers, loved to delay and obfuscate. This didn't make sense to him.

"Yeah, Tony. This is like a house of cards—like dominoes. Pull one out and the rest fall like an avalanche." Sensing the judge's reluctance to buy the story, Connley pressed for time. "Let me go on and you'll see what I mean."

"Fine, but hurry, I have Mike Rosa on hold."

"Let him hold. He's kept me waiting dozens of times."

"Yes, but I have a trial to conduct and I don't have time. I've got two attorneys and a jury of twelve who want to know what the hell is going on. So make it quick."

"OK, I'll try to make this brief. One of my men named Ralph Kirby was shot along with the DA and the other two women. He's alive but in bad shape. He was able to ID the shooter from a photo. The shooter, Rudolph Hines, aka Rudi, turns out to be a hired gun. He's in the hospital, too, with a fractured skull and a busted face. But he was able to babble about his deal with—guess who?"

"Dammit, Fred, don't play games! This isn't a game show. Who?" Primavera was clearly losing patience.

"The noted Martin Silvio and Harold Levin. Neither has been seen or heard of since yesterday. We have warrants for both of them, there's an APB out on them and stakeouts everywhere, including the airports. And the clincher is that we found out these guys fabricated a lot of their cases. Big cases, cases involving death. We have records, lists of cases involving setups. And the Riley case was one of them. The little girls, Carmen and Lily Lopez, who banged the shit out of the shooter when he came after them—"

"Wait a minute. What do these kids have to do with all this?"

"That's what I'm trying to get at, Tony. The kids' mother, Celia Lopez, another murder victim, kept a list of cases set up by Silvio and Levin. She was their receptionist and she would eavesdrop. She overheard conversations and made lists of cases where the injuries were set up. Some involving murder to create big damages—like turning off monitors in hospitals, particularly in nurseries— overdosing patients with meds, substituting wrong medication. Either leaving the victim dead or brain dead, or crippled for life. These cases brought in the big money, and they were always winners because they fucking created the evidence—sorry for the expletive."

"Fred, this is all hearsay. You know that—this list of cases. The woman is dead. She can't testify."

"No, but the kids can. They would come in with mom on their days off and sometimes after school when Celia stayed late. And wait—this is the real clincher."

Primavera decided he had to listen to the rest of what Connley had to say. Mike Rosa, Nick Ceratto, John Asher, and the jury could wait "Go on," he said.

"Carmen, the older one, the one with iron balls who clobbered the shooter with a toilet lid—she recorded at least ten meetings where plans were hatched. She also gave a case list to Kirby who gave it to Gates. Silvio and Levin found out about the list through Margo Griffin, Gates' girlfriend, and they put out a hit on everybody in the way of that list. Kirby got in the way and so did the kids. The list was destroyed by the shooter. But little Carmen—oh, what a kid!—she had another copy tucked away at home and still had the tapes. Her mother was going to use them as her retirement plan. Silvio and Levin, the cheap bastards, never put her on any pension plan. So she was going to blackmail them for a heap when she was ready to leave. But they got to her first. She was iced by Rudi. We have his statement—well, as much as we could get out of him with a busted face. But he fingered them, Silvio and Levin, as the masterminds behind all this." He paused, sighing deeply. "Tony, there were two hundred and fifty-three cases on this list dating back to 1995. This is how those bastards avoided the slump in the personal injury business. They *manufactured* them, and Joe Maglio brought in the bacon. Only when he found out about the case factory, they knocked him off, too, or Rudi did. He confessed to murdering Maglio's wife and kids, too. We found a tape made by Joe, of himself, in Gates' office. It was a message to Ceratto, his protégée, telling him to get out of the firm—that he might be the next victim. Gates wasn't investigating that. The tape was sent to her by the Montco DA. But she decided it was Rosa's problem, according to a memo we found in her office. I think her girlfriend, Ms. Griffin, had a lot to do with her keeping it under wraps."

There was more, but Primavera didn't need any more. "OK, Fred. You've given me enough information. Thanks."

"Don't you want the rest?"

"No, not now. Let me do my job." With that Primavera gently pressed line two, disconnecting his old classmate and connecting to Mike Rosa.

"Yes, this is Judge Primavera."

"Judge!" Rosa yelled into his speakerphone, his voice echoing around the room. "Let me take you off speaker. I know it's annoying, but I wanted hands free while I waited. Hope you didn't mind."

"No, Mike, but I'm pressed for time. Can you make this brief?"

"As brief as I can, Your Honor." Mike Rosa then told the judge about the surveillance tape in his possession, which showed in grim detail the murders of Christie and Joe Maglio. Mercifully there had been no camera in the children's bedrooms.

He described the killer as having worn a state trooper's uniform. The stills made from the film identified the killer as a person named Rudi, now in the custody of the Philadelphia police. The guy had a string of aliases. The Montco police were charging him with four additional murders. And God knows how many others he might have committed.

Rosa continued that he was in the process of handing over certain secret foreign bank records to the FBI, which had mysteriously showed up at his office. The envelope containing the records was postmarked Tel Aviv, and the records contained information leading to Harry Levin and Marty Silvio. He didn't know who had sent them, but he had a good idea. The account showed transfers from a nested account in the Cayman Islands to an account at Bank Naomi in Israel. The balance in the account exceeded sixty million dollars. He suspected that Marty Silvio and Harry Levin were connected to the Maglio murders and possibly others. Additional warrants were being prepared for their arrest. He could go on, but he was really busy and suspected he was going to be busier dealing with his end of the mess—and he was late for a press conference.

The judge thanked Rosa politely, put down the receiver, and then took three Advil in hopes of quelling the migraine that was starting to blur his vision and was beginning to threaten his ability to think. He slowly drank a full eight ounces of cold water, closed his eyes, and willed the pain away. Then he summoned Julia to escort Mr. Cerrato and Mr. Asher into his chambers.

"Gentlemen, after hearing the testimony of Ms. Price and being informed of various events which have a direct bearing on this case, I'm inclined to entertain appropriate motions at this time. Mr. Asher, I'm assuming that you're prepared to move for a non-suit? And Mr. Cerrato, based on the testimony you yourself are eliciting, which strips your case of any legitimacy, are you in agreement with this? Or would you move to postpone the case until all the criminal matters have been disposed of? In other words, are you convinced of Dr. Manin's innocence in the death of Sean Riley?"

Nick lowered his head, avoiding eye contact with the judge. His dark hair was tousled from running his hands through it at least fifty times while waiting for Primavera. "Your Honor, you obviously know that I believe that Victor Manin had nothing to do with the death of Sean Riley. And you know that the facts I presented demonstrate that Captain Riley was murdered. I'm sorry for Mrs. Riley, I'm sorry for the Sean Riley's sons…"

"I understand fully," Primavera broke in. "But, as you know, your first duty is to this court is to this court, not to the Rileys. You serve justice, not simply clients. And this court thanks you for your adherence to your duty as an officer of the court, despite the fact that you could have won a considerable verdict had you not disclosed this evidence." The judge nodded his head and smiled. "And you could have walked away with a huge fee as a result. Not many lawyers would resist that temptation."

Nick wondered about himself—about his choice of justice over cash—certainly not a choice he would have made before this past Christmas. But these were the cards he's been dealt and the cards he had to play. "Thank you, Your Honor. I have no desire to bring a motion to continue this trial to a later date."

"Mr. Asher?"

"Your Honor, I'm extremely proud to have served in this trial with Mr. Cerrato and I deeply respect him for his convictions and his honesty. Doctor Manin, I'm sure, will be pleased."

Asher stood and offered his hand to Nick. Nick stood and took it warmly.

"Maybe the doctor will get a good night's sleep tonight. I sure need one," Nick said.

"Yes, I'm sure he will."

"Well, gentlemen, we'll adjourn to the courtroom to formally put motions on the record." Primavera rose slowly from his worn leather chair, pushing his horn rims back up the bridge of his nose.

"Your Honor, I'd like a minute with my client," Asher said, sweeping up his briefcase and making a dash for the door before anyone had a change of heart. This didn't happen too often and he wasn't taking any chances.

"Mr. Asher," Primavera called out, "make it short."

"Yes, I will, Your Honor."

Nick followed him out the door. "Asher," he called out.

The natty, pinstriped defense attorney pivoted around on the ball of one foot. "Yes?"

"What do I tell *my* client?" Nick asked sarcastically.

"The truth. She doesn't have a case."

Chapter XLIX

Freezing rain pelted the dirty windows and ran down in rivulets until it hit the pavement four stories below on the sidewalk of Penn Square, where city officials' cars were parked helter-skelter in the paths of the pedestrians. This was one of the privileges of City Council members, judges, and other elite bureaucrats. They got free parking and never a ticket, no matter where they parked or for how long. And some never bothered with the inconvenience of renewing a driver's license. A select few never had one.

John Asher paced back and forth in the grimy City Hall anteroom, four stories up, trying to explain—for the tenth time—the legal maneuver called a motion for a non-suit, which would get his client out of the courtroom scot-free and back into the real world, where he wouldn't have to pay a dime to the Rileys. Neither would Asher's real client, the medical malpractice carrier, except of course to cover his substantial fee for defending a case that had become a no-brainer—a gift from God.

He almost had a heart attack when Victor Manin said *no*. Asher checked his watch. The judge would not be patient much longer. "Why, Victor? Why won't you agree to my making this motion to end this trial and your agony and mine? Have you completely gone 'round the bend?"

Manin sat, stonily staring ahead. He had never expected this turn of events where he would win by default, by a legal maneuver instead of a verdict. "I suppose you would think I have. And in fact, I may have. But you attorneys don't care how you *win* as long as you win. Well, I care. You knew I always cared from the start. I don't want to escape on a technicality. *I* want to win—" his voice rose to a shout, totally atypical of him—"to *really* win based on the belief of those twelve people sitting in that box." He pointed to the door that led into the courtroom. His hand shook as he held it out.

"I want *them* to *find* me innocent. I want *them* to vindicate me. Only *they* can restore my life—not a legal maneuver cooked up between two lawyers." Manin stood up. "Let's go back in there. Do your job. OK? Make them find me innocent. That's what you're being paid for, isn't it?"

"You're a greater fool than I thought, Doctor Manin," Asher said, straightening his tie.

"Why am I a fool? It's a sure-fire winner, isn't it?" Manin grinned weakly for the first time in two years. He wasn't even sure he could do it. His facial muscles were so unused to the expression.

"Nothing is sure-fire with a jury," Asher said coldly. "You're always playing Russian roulette with the folks in the box. Can't you see that? Don't you understand? You *can* lose."

"I'll take that chance." Manin rose slowly from the chipped brown chair and followed as Asher led the way into the courtroom.

Theresa Riley stared at Nick shaking her head in utter disbelief. "You mean you're going to let him go? The man responsible for my husband's death?"

Nick threw up his hands. "Mrs. Riley, for the umpteenth time—there is no case against Doctor Manin. Your husband was murdered, not malpracticed on. And *I'm* not letting him go, the judge out there—" Nick pointed to the adjoining room where Primavera was busily reviewing the ruling he would make on Asher's motion for a non-suit. "—he's going to let him go. I'm just warning you ahead so you won't—" Nick paused. He wanted to say "freak out," but he restrained himself. "So you'll be prepared."

"Prepared? Listen, you bastard!" she yelled. Nick was taken aback by the one hundred and eighty degree turn in her demeanor, from the sweet little Irish widow to a snarling harpy. "My husband's dead and somebody's gonna pay," she growled. "That doctor in there was in charge of my husband's life and he left him to die. He left him in the hands of a murderer to die—while he went to get ready for a party." Her face had reddened to the color of a cooked beet, and the veins bulged in her sagging neck.

"But he didn't know…"

"But he was in charge," she hissed as spittle spewed from her mouth. "If he'd stayed with my husband awhile like he did with the others, Sean would be alive today—and I wouldn't be alone…" She broke down into sobs.

Nick dropped his hands to his sides, reached out, and took her trembling body in his arms. It was no use trying to reason with her. He was of little comfort, he knew, but he tried. "Come on, Mrs. Riley. We'll do the best we can. I won't let you down. Let's go into the courtroom and see what the judge does."

"You won't let him throw the case out, will you?" she sniffed, wiping her eyes with the ever-present tissue, so damp from tears that it had little or no absorbency left.

"Look, I can't make the judge do anything or prevent him from doing anything. I'll just do my best—OK?"

"Promise?" she croaked, cocking her head like an entreating child. Another one hundred eighty degree turn.

Although Nick tried to maintain his objectivity, she had gotten to him. He couldn't help it. Her helplessness reminded him of his own mother, even if it was calculating manipulation.

"Promise." he took her bony hand and led her toward the door.

"You're a good boy," she smiled as she shuffled along. "I know you'll help me. I prayed to the Blessed Mother last night, and she never lets me down. So you won't either. No, you won't, Mr. Ceratto." She smiled as she patted his hand.

"All rise," the court crier's voice boomed across the almost empty courtroom. The attorneys quickly rose to their feet, followed by their reluctant clients. Grace Monahan stood behind Nick.

Primavera glided in and stepped deftly onto the bench. "Be seated." He cleared his throat and looked down at his papers. "Mr. Asher, I believe you have a motion…?"

"Your Honor, my client wishes the trial to proceed to verdict. He doesn't want me to make any motions at this time."

Primavera's mouth fell open. "He doesn't what?"

Asher shrugged his shoulders, turning his hands palm up. "He doesn't want me to make any motions, Your Honor. He wishes to proceed to verdict."

The judge shook his head like someone reacting to a stiff slap in the face. "Very well. That's his privilege," he said reluctantly. He paused, looking skeptically at the doctor through his thick, round glasses, hoping somehow that he could convey to Manin the stupidity of his decision. But even more so, the utter waste of the court's time. But there was no reaction from the defense table.

"Very well, bring in the jury. Mr. Ceratto, call your next witness."

For a moment Nick thought he was dreaming, that he was living his worst nightmare. He willed himself awake, but the nightmare wouldn't go away. He stood, dumbfounded, as the jury filed into their respective seats. The curly blond juror smiled at him as she smoothed her skirt and wriggled into her chair, then quickly checked her manicure.

Mr. Ceratto." Judge Primavera's voice entered the nightmare. "Do you wish to recall Ms. Price?"

Nick, still reeling from the curve ball he'd been thrown, stood mute.

"Mr. Ceratto…"

The judge's voice again reminded him that this wasn't a dream. This was a living nightmare. There would be no motion to end it. And neither the judge nor could do anything about it. And both Dr. Victor Manin and Theresa Riley would have their way. The trial would go on.

"Yes—ah, no. I mean no, Your Honor." He heard his own voice as if it were coming from someone else. "No, I'm finished with Ms. Price."

"Well then, call your next witness." Primavera, although sympathetic, still had a trial to conduct. *Let's see what you can do, Ceratto,* the judge thought. *Let's see how you handle this. Let's see if you learned anything from Joe Maglio. Joe would be smooth as silk. He'd glide right into his next witness as if things were as normal as could be.*

Nick took a breath and turned back to counsel table, smoothing back his hair, a nervous habit he had never been able to break. *Fuck*, he thought. *Why is this idiot doing this to himself— and to me?* His voice rang clear and confidant, despite his churning stomach. "I call Mrs. Sean Riley, Your Honor." He walked slowly up to his client, gently took her by the hand, and led her carefully to the witness stand. She slowly sat. She cleared her throat and touched the gold cross that hung from her neck. She smiled painfully at Nick, her eyes watery but penetrating. He had no choice now. She was on the stand. The judge had said go, and he had a case to try—like it or not. Manin had forced the issue, had put him in this position. His conscience was clear. *Fuck him*, he thought. He picked up the yellow pad, which had no notations on it. He would use it as a prop. He knew he didn't need any preparation for *this* direct examination. She would do a fine job on her own. Just wind her up and let her go.

"Mrs. Riley, tell us about your husband, Captain Riley. Tell us what kind of a husband, what kind of a father he was."

Mrs. Riley took a deep breath and let go. Her husband had been an angel, a good saintly man, a great father and friend to anyone who needed him.

One hour later there wasn't a dry eye among the jurors. Even Hodge had trouble staying cool. He lowered his head and shifted his eyes so as not to make contact with the pitiful soul on the stand. He didn't like cops nor did he place any trust in them, but he knew there were exceptions, and it sounded as if Sean Riley had been one of the exceptions.

Nick had no other witnesses. And the defense was just as brief. Asher put Dr. Manin back on; the doctor testified as expected— that his credentials were impeccable, that he did everything right, and that this was a case of homicide, not medical malpractice. The defense expert, Dr. Leon Schaffer of the University of Pennsylvania Hospital, chief of vascular surgery, and a full professor at Penn Medical School, basically said ditto—and charged Asher's client, Pro-Med Insurance, eight grand for testifying live for forty minutes.

Closing arguments were just as brief. It was no surprise that Asher continually referred to the plaintiff's witnesses' damaging testimony. His closing basically consisted of reiterating Donna Price's version of the facts—actually the only existing account of what happened to Sean Riley after surgery. There was nothing on record to contradict her, no testimony to the contrary; therefore the man was murdered. He had to be, and Asher went on to speculate that the murderer had been present in this very courtroom and then had mysteriously disappeared. Hadn't Marina Doletov been instructed to stay close by, to stay in the building by the Judge? Certainly. Where was she if she had nothing to hide? Asher went on to remind the jurors that they should not let their sympathies rule their reason. That Mrs. Riley's testimony was extremely moving, but it was not evidence of Dr. Manin's guilt. That Nick Ceratto had in fact proven the defendant's case. Asher then turned to Nick and said, "Thank you." He did all but shake Nick's hand before he took his seat at counsel table.

Nick rose and strode to the jury box and turned quickly back to his opponent, pointing at him. "Don't be so quick to thank me, Mr. Asher. This jury hasn't made their decision yet. Please don't insult them. Or me."

The jury was attentive, but Nick couldn't read anything from them—except from Alonzo Hodge, whose arms were folded loosely across his chest. He stared at Nick as if to say, *Whacha gonna do now, man?*

Joe Maglio's words echoed in Nick's head: *Don't try to blow smoke up the jury's ass.* But this time he had no choice. He focused on Alonzo Hodge.

"Remember, folks, when we began this trial—the day I made my opening statement? I promised you that I would level with you. That I would respect you and your intelligence. No lies, no smoke screens, no theatrics—and in return you promised to keep an open mind. Not to jump to conclusions. Not to see everything as black or white, but to recognize the shades of gray that are in every case, in life as a matter of fact? Truth, and respect for each other—that was the deal—remember?"

The jurors were quick to nod their assent. How could they not? But Hodge grimaced as if to say, *Come on man, get on with it. This ain't no kindergarten. We know our job. Now fucking do yours. So I can get outta here.*

"I brought Donna Price to this courtroom, all the way from California, so you could hear the truth—the real story about what happened to Captain Sean Riley. And she told you. And I had to tell my client that she had no case—based on Ms. Price's testimony there was no medical malpractice. And Mrs. Riley"—Nick turned and pointed to Theresa Riley—"was very upset with me. As a matter of fact, she yelled at me and called me a few names I can't repeat here."

Alonzo Hodge leaned back in his chair with a slight smile. *That's what I like to hear. Give it to him, lady. Cut through the bullshit.*

"I have to confess to you that with all our training in the law and years of experience, we attorneys don't know everything. Sometimes we have to learn from our clients, from ordinary folks like yourselves. And I have to tell you I've been humbled by Mrs. Riley's native intelligence and her insight about this case—insight I didn't have. Because when I told her she didn't have a case, she said, 'My husband wouldn't be dead if Dr. Manin had stayed with him like he did with all his other patients. Instead, he got dressed for a party while my husband bled to death.' Folks—you could have knocked me over with a feather—*because she's right. Not only factually, but legally,*"

Nick paused to let his words sink in. Then he started to pace, slowly, as he gathered his thoughts. "The judge will instruct you on the law before you go into that room to decide the fate of the plaintiff and the defendant. He will tell about something called "the standard of care," the rules that a doctor must follow when he treats a patient. Judge Primavera will give you the law on this standard. As a lawyer, I'm not permitted to give you the law. But

I can suggest to you, one thing I can say to you, is that you heard about Dr. Manin's personal standard—one he created himself—one which he *always* followed. And that is that he always stayed with his patients after surgery in the recovery room." Nick stabbed the air with his forefinger to emphasize his words. "He was always available in case something happened. But not this time. Not after Captain Riley's surgery. You see, folks, he was too busy satisfying a social obligation for his wife."

Nick spun around and pointed to Victor Manin. "You see, he was more concerned about Mrs. Manin's feelings than he was about Sean Riley's life." He shook his head sadly. "And, folks, Mrs. Riley was right when she told me, 'If Dr. Manin stayed with my husband, like he did with all the others, he would be alive today.'" Turning to Theresa Riley, he said, "How right you are, Mrs. Riley. Sean *would* be alive today, helping people, doing good deeds, doing his best to serve his community, *if* Dr. Manin had just lived up to his own standard of care."

Nick took a deep breath and turned back to the jury. "Theresa Riley has a greater sense of justice and fairness than I had. And I've learned something from her today. Mr. Asher thanked me today." He turned to the widow again. "Now, I thank you, Mrs. Riley, for showing us all what justice demands."

Chapter L

They ducked into a remote corner of the Striped Bass, attempting to separate themselves from the heavy lunch crowd and the tourists interested in eating in the same place where the anniversary scene in the *Sixth Sense* was shot. It was Joe Maglio's favorite table and it was permanently reserved for him. After his death, Marty Silvio and Harry Levin had dibs. Now it was Nick's, since it was all over town that Silvio had escaped and was running from the FBI and Levin had escaped permanently by putting a bullet into his brain.

Nick stared over Grace's head, past the cooks running about frantically in the open grill. He was oblivious to the clatter of pans and food sizzling on the open flames. He ignored the sounds and smells that had been music to his ears and perfume to his nostrils.

She took his hand, hoping to gain his attention, but he withdrew it coldly, continuing to ignore her. He pulled a Marlboro from the pack he had tucked into his coat pocket. Today he deserved a smoke. He lit it, took a deep drag, and blew the smoke over Grace's head.

"Nick, you're pissing me off. Stop feeling sorry for yourself," she said. "The jury's not even in yet and you're acting as if you lost the case."

"Don't even try to comfort me ," he snapped, finally looking her in the eye. "I don't like losing, and no matter what the verdict is, I've lost. I fucked up. I should have withdrawn from this case a month ago."

"You couldn't have," she said comfortingly, "Barnes wouldn't have let you."

"I should have told him to fuck himself and let him file disciplinary charges. Disbarment would have been better than this." He took another drag, inhaling deeply, realizing that he had never lost his taste for toxins.

The muscle in his right jaw twitched as he snapped his fingers rudely at a passing waiter. Normally he had respect for servers and was overly polite to them, but today was not a normal day.

"A double Sapphire with extra olives," he half shouted as the waiter turned in his direction, "and make it fast. I have to be back in court."

This was not the Nick Ceratto the server had come to know through Joe Maglio. He nodded, but before he could turn his head Grace put up two fingers. She waved the smoke away from her face. "Make it two," she said. *To hell with the baby*, she thought. "Nick you can't help what happened. You tried to help Manin. You tried to clear Joe Maglio's name. The point is, you tried no matter what happens. You did the right thing. Everyone knows that. Why don't you?"

"Yeah, but in this business trying doesn't count. You win or you lose, and that's it."

"The case isn't over yet," she snapped.

"Yeah, and the jury has two choices. Guilty or not guilty. It's a lose-lose situation for me, Gracie. If he's negligent, then I lost because I tried to do the right thing. I worked my ass off to prove this fucker wasn't careless. If he's not negligent, I lost Mrs. Riley's case. She walks away without a penny, and I'm a loser trial lawyer waiting for a malpractice suit. I wanted the judge to take it away from those twelve unpredictable, stupid people charged with dolling out justice when they don't understand shit about the law and don't give a shit about justice." He took a long sip from the flared glass the waiter had just put in front of him, deftly dodging the skewered olives. "Justice isn't about the law. It's a game of chance. It's Russian Roulette, and I just shot myself in the head like Harry Levin."

"Nick, there's causation, too, remember?" Grace said, toying with her glass. "Remember, even if they find Manin negligent, they can still find that his negligence didn't cause Riley's death. And Manin's out. No recovery. No money due. Financially, he's off the hook. And everybody's happy, especially Med Pro Insurance Company."

"You forgot that the asshole wants vindication, not financial relief. He wants a *not guilty*, period. And if he gets that, my ass is in a sling. I'll be taking his place on the stand. I'll be the next victim in the Riley case." He pushed the cigarette down into the ashtray, snuffing it out almost completely, and watched the last puffs of smoke waft across the restaurant toward an annoyed diner who fanned it away with her napkin. "For once in my life I worked against my own sense of greed, my lust for money, my professional ego. I worked for truth, justice, the constitution, the red, white and blue. And what happens, that fucker Manin throws a monkey wrench in the works."

Grace smiled unsympathetically. "So? What's the worst that can happen? You lose and you get what you wanted, but your ass is in a sling. You're sued by the Riley's for legal malpractice. Big deal, you're insured," she paused. "Or do you want vindication, too?" He chuckled, showing her a genuine smile for the first time in a week. She went on, almost yelling, further annoying the nearby diners. "You win, the Rileys are rich and so are you. Manin has no one to blame but himself."

"It's blood money." He took a long sip of the strong martini and winced. "I promised myself when I went to law school I'd go straight. No more hustling, no more bag boy for the bad guys, no more blood money. It's always on your hands. I promised myself, and I promised Joe, too. And so far I've been clean—up till now."

"Stop with the double bind. Stop with the violins." She threw up her hands and pushed her untouched drink across the table. "Give it away then." Her green eyes flashed with anger and then drew up into thin slits of defiance. "Give the fucking money away."

The cell phone in Nick's inside coat pocket vibrated. He pulled it out and flipped it open. "Ceratto," he snapped.

"Mr. Ceratto. This is Judge Primavera's chambers. The jury has a verdict."

CHAPTER LI

It was the moment that every trial lawyer worked toward, sweated blood for, and sometimes laid everything on the table for—emotionally, physically, and in the case of the plaintiff's attorney, financially as well. There would be a winner and a loser, nothing in between. The twelve gods had shuffled into their respective thrones and waited silently for their cue.

"Ladies and gentlemen, have you reached a verdict?" Primavera had asked this question more times than he cared to count. These were the magic words that would unleash the sword that would blindly strike one side down and elevate the other. They would cause agony to one and ecstasy to the other. They would bring tears to one and shouts of joy to the other. Opening Pandora's box was part of Primavera's job. It was the part he liked the least. He preferred listening to testimony, the stuff of everyday life—ruling on objections, deciding what testimony and which documents were in and which were out, what the jury should consider and what it shouldn't. In other words, he liked the academic exercise. He did not care for what it wrought, what laypeople, ordinary citizens, would do with it. People who could not escape their own bias, their own prejudices. People who understood little or nothing about applying the law he so carefully explained, or at least tried to explain, in his charge to them before they retired to the jury room to fight about who was right and who was wrong. In actuality, whom they liked and whom they didn't. Who was a good dresser and who was a slob. Who had to get the hell out to go home, or to go to a job, and who would stay forever just to prove a point. Primavera knew that there was one certainty in a jury trial, and that was that there was no such thing as impartiality—no such thing as fairness. Flesh and blood by its very nature was tainted at birth. Chips were programmed, even his own as he would fully admit, and there was nothing he could do about it but preside over a process which he hoped would result in something resembling fair. He had accepted the fact that the half naked, blindfolded woman with a scale in one hand and a sword in the other was simply a mythical creature.

"Yes we have, Your Honor." It was no surprise that it was Alonzo Hodge who stood as the jury's foreman to announce the decision, which had only taken forty-five minutes to make. He had dressed for the occasion. He wore a navy blue blazer, charcoal gray pants, a white shirt, and a brightly printed red tie. It was his moment, his fifteen minutes of fame, where all eyes were on him, all ears were tuned to him, and lives, important lives, depended on him. Alonzo liked the feeling, the power he had never had. He liked it a lot.

Judge Primavera glanced nonchalantly at the verdict sheet through his thick glasses, pretending to be completely disassociated from the tension that ricocheted off the walls of the courtroom like a racquet ball. He would read the questions both sides had agreed would be presented to the jury, which the twelve had taken to the jury room to be answered one by one. "Question number one: was the defendant Doctor Victor Manin guilty of negligence?" Primavera intoned.

Alonzo Hodge shifted his weight, squared his shoulders, and cocked his head. His eyes went to Manin briefly, and then back to the judge. "Yes," he said in a loud, almost defiant tone.

A low moan came from somewhere, but no one knew exactly who was responsible for it. Manin stood stoically, as he had been told to do by his attorney. "Show no emotion. Say nothing."

Asher took his own advice and willed his shaking knees into a locked position, as well as his jaw.

Primavera appeared unmoved, although he could have been knocked over with a feather. He was a pro at masking his gut feelings. He went on, "Question number two: was that negligence a substantial factor in causing the Plaintiff Sean Riley's death?"

"Yes," Alonzo answered with the same conviction, not hesitating for a second.

Nick's heart leapt. The next question was going to be how much. Every trial lawyer's dream: to get through these first two questions with a *yes*. Emotionally, he was on a roller coaster ride. He wanted to win. After all, he was a courtroom gladiator. But at the same time he wanted to lose—to have the case go away without a verdict. But it didn't and it wouldn't. So he thought he might as well enjoy the ride.

"Question number three: what do you award the plaintiff, Mrs. Riley, under the Wrongful Death Claim?" Primavera asked, following the questions on the verdict sheet. (This was the claim of the widow Riley and her sons for the loss of her husband and their father.)

"Five million dollars." The sum was announced flatly as flatly, as if it were five dollars.

"Question number four: What do you award the estate of Sean Riley under the survivor's claim?" (This was the claim that survived Sean Riley's death to compensate him for his pain and suffering, the legacy to his estate that would be inherited by his widow and sons.) Before the foreman could announce the balance of the verdict, Dr. Manin turned away.

"Five million dollars." Alonzo Hodge's voice drowned the sound of the doctor's chair scraping back as he stood and quickly exited the courtroom. Asher was abandoned to face the pain alone.

Primavera ignored Manin as the heavy door slammed shut behind him. "Thank you, ladies and gentlemen, for your service in this case. You are now excused."

Margaret Riley threw her arms around Nick's neck. Her lined face broke into a tearful smile. "I knew you would win for Sean and me. I knew you wouldn't let us down. You're a good boy and a good lawyer. Thank you." She leaned forward and kissed Nick's cheek.

"You're welcome, Mrs. Riley," Nick whispered still keeping one eye on the judge. He smiled kindly at the woman who could be his mother. "Now let's go talk to the jury," he said, taking her by the hand. "May we approach the jury, Your Honor?"

Judge Primavera always allowed both sides to question the jury to find out what led them to their decision. Usually, he wasn't interested enough to stay to hear what fact, what facial expression, what shift of eye or body, or which witness, had triggered their decision. But this time he stayed put. He needed to know how in the name of God this jury reached this absurd result.

John Asher didn't hang around. He wasn't interested in how or why. He didn't waste a minute. He threw three bulky file boxes onto a cart to be picked up by his law clerk and was out the door, mentally formulating his appeal, in which he would ask Primavera to override the verdict. This was one appeal he felt he could not lose.

Chapter LII

It was a bright, clear winter morning. There wasn't a cloud in the February sky, but the temperature at eighteen degrees nullified the warming effects of the sun. There were only four people at the grave site. Two were in the business and two were genuine mourners, or at least they were there to pay respects because no one else was. But all four were in a hurry to get it over with. It was far too cold to do otherwise.

The undertaker in a frayed black overcoat and a mismatched black suit nodded his head to signal the nondescript clergymen to begin the service. The Reverend Joseph Pick, unshaven and bleary eyed from a bout with the bottle the night before, began the Twenty-first Psalm and finished it in record time.

"What a fucking shame," Nick said under his breath in lieu of a prayer, while staring at the cheap metal box bearing the name of Doctor Victor Manin. Clouds of carbon monoxide billowed from the dented black hearse as it pulled away, leaving Grace and him standing alone in the cold. It was a pauper's funeral for a bankrupt loser—a has-been who had made the fatal decision to believe in the system and trust the jury. He had given them the privilege of pulling the plug, and true to form they had. Nick had gotten the call from Mike Rosa the night of the verdict that Manin had OD'd on heroine. It happened in Montgomery County, at St. Barnabas Hospital, where Manin still maintained a small office, Rosa had gotten the call first. Soon it was out, and the suicide made the major newspapers and small local rags, as well as the local TV stations.

DOCTOR FOUND GUILTY OF WRONGFUL DEATH COMMITS SUICIDE. KILLS SELF OVER PATIENT. TOO MUCH FOR SOCIETY DOC...

Manin had left a short note of apology to Nick and John Asher for the trouble he had caused. Rosa personally delivered a copy to Nick the day after the suicide, telling him that he didn't know whether to congratulate him or console him. He shook Nick's hand and patted him on the back, giving him a little of each. He also broke the news that the FBI had caught up with Silvio in a disco in Tel Aviv. A teller at Bank Naomi had seen through the cheap wig and mustache disguise. It was the way he chewed his cigar that signaled his true identity. The young banker found the habit more disgusting this time than when he'd had the misfortune of having to deal with Silvio in person. And now found it enormously rewarding since there was two hundred thousand dollars on Silvio's head. So the young Israeli didn't pass go. He went straight to the police instead. Extradition documents were prepared and signed, and Silvio would soon be on his way back to Philadelphia. He would face charges from insurance fraud to capital murder.

Nick shook Rosa's hand, accepted the pat on the back, and thanked him for the news. He excused himself and went straight to bed. He wept. And he did not know whether it was from sheer exhaustion or sheer elation that things were finally falling into place, or because he had lost. He had not accomplished what he set out to do. Grace held him closely and he finally fell asleep in her arms. It was the first true sleep he had had in over a month.

It was only fitting that he attend Manin's funeral. Not only had he handed Nick a four million dollar attorney's fee, forty percent of the jury's award, but he also had an irresistible attachment to the man. He didn't know why. He also had an irresistible urge to say good-bye. He knew Manin's wife and family wouldn't be there. He knew that John Asher wouldn't attend the funeral of the man who had lost his firm its major client. Pro-Med fired Asher immediately after the verdict and hired a major competitor to file the appeal. Yes, there was an appeal, but the chances of Pro-Med winning it were somewhere between slim and none. The jury had told Nick after the trial that Dr. Manin had deviated from his own standard of care by not seeing his patient immediately after the surgery— not checking him as Donna Price testified he had done with other patients in recovery. Saying that if he had done this, Sean Riley would be alive. The negligence was in the aftercare, or lack thereof, according to Alonzo Hodge. "He was in a hurry to get with his rich buddies and his bitch of a wife and didn't care what happened to the common man." In other words, they bought Nick's argument, or rather the widow Riley's. No matter that Marina Doletov actually did the job; Manin had made it possible. There was even some speculation among other members that there might have been a conspiracy between Doletov and the doctor—that he would get a cut of whatever she might have been paid. They didn't know if this was reasonable speculation, but they had heard of doctors murdering their own patients, or allowing them to be done in. "What was the name of that doctor in England?" the curly blond asked.

Grace poked Nick as if to wake him from his trance. She pulled her coat protectively around her swelling middle trying to keep herself, as well as her unborn warm. "Let's go, Nick. It's over. Let him rest in peace now." She picked up a half-frozen rose from the lone floral basket tossed on to the brown grass at the foot of the grave. It was from them. Not one of Dr. Manin's friends or relatives had sent any acknowledgment, not even his own children. She gently laid the rose on the casket and turned toward the car.

"Sorry, Doc." Nick pulled his collar up around his freezing ears. "I did the best I could." He took a pack of cigarettes from his coat pocket and tossed it into the open grave. It was the last pack he would ever buy. "Have one. They can't hurt you now. Nothing can hurt you now." He made the sign of the cross and turned away.

The Boxster hummed quietly along Roosevelt Boulevard toward Cottman Avenue and the entrance to Interstate 95. The inside of the car was almost too warm. Nick lowered the heat and down-shifted into second gear as he slowed to enter the Interstate, heading south toward home. He was silent, deep in thought as he watched the white strips on disappearing under the tires of the finely tuned sports car.

Grace was grateful for the sun coming through the windows and the extra warmth it brought. The heat and the humming engine soon lulled her into sleep. She dozed until she felt the car abruptly stop. What seemed to her to have been five minutes had actually been a half hour. She opened her eyes to find that they were in the plaza of the Society Hill Towers, in front of the North Tower. A moving van was parked directly behind them. Nick said nothing to Grace. He opened the car door, got out, and began talking to one of the drivers, giving him directions to the freight elevators used for moving furniture and bulky objects in and out of the building. The driver backed the van up and pulled the huge rig around them, heading in the direction Nick had indicated.

"Moving?" Grace asked jokingly as Nick reentered the driver's seat.

"Yep." He looked straight ahead as he put the Boxster into gear.

"You're kidding," she said with a strained, disbelieving smile. "Aren't you…?"

"Nope. I'm not."

"Wait," she yelled. "Stop the car. I want to talk to you."

He shifted into park and turned the engine off abruptly.

"OK, talk."

"Why didn't you tell me you were doing this? No—wait. First, *why* are you doing this…and…" She hesitated, her eyes filling with tears. "…what about me?"

Nick turned to her and for the first time in twenty-four hours, looked directly at her. "I didn't think I had to tell you—number one. I'm doing this because I'm through with the law, clients, courtrooms, trials, juries, the whole goddamn thing—number two. I want—no, correction, I *need* a new life—that's three. I appreciate what you did for me…"

"Fuck you," she hissed. Her face turned scarlet. "No, you don't. You don't appreciate anything, you selfish bastard. You only appreciate yourself."

"Look, Gracie, I have to do this. I can't stay here any longer."

"OK. Then where are you going?" She folded her arms defiantly over her chest. "Or don't you want to tell me?"

"I'll tell you," he said sharply, reaching in his coat pocket for the pack of Marlboros. But then he quickly remembered he had left them with Victor Manin. He threw up his hands in frustration. "Gracie, remember I told you no attachments, no commitments. Do you remember?"

"Yes, I do." She nodded her head, looking straight ahead. "I just want to know where to send the letter bomb."

Nick couldn't help smiling. *That's my Grace*, he thought. That was the smart Celtic mouth he knew and loved. "OK," he laughed.

"Well?" she prodded.

"Nantucket."

"Nantucket? Where in God's name is that? It sounds like it belongs in a porno movie."

"It's the opposite," he answered defensively. "It's an island thirty miles off the coast of Massachusetts. It's natural. It's clean. It's got dirt roads, no traffic lights, and it's quiet in winter. It's got lighthouses, a windmill, fog, and roses growing on the roofs of houses—and it's got history. It was the whaling capital of America, the Starbucks, the Macys, the Folgers…"

"So what are you going to do? Catch whales?" she interrupted, still not looking at him.

"Anything I can—except people."

"You're going to be a fisherman?" She finally turned to him and burst into laughter.

Nick said nothing. His face reddened. He tapped the steering wheel with his fingertips until she had finished laughing.

"What's wrong with being a fisherman?"

"Nothing. But you're a South Philly punk turned lawyer. You're a slick mouthpiece, not a fisherman."

"I can learn, about boats, about the sea. I always wanted to sail—to be out there on the open ocean. It's clean. It's honest. Look, Grace, I changed careers once and did OK. I went from bag boy to trial lawyer, from one con job to another. I can go from being a con to being a straight guy with a boat. That should be easy."

"My ass," she said scornfully. "It's a dangerous, dirty job. Fishermen get lost at sea all the time. Even experienced ones."

"Yeah, true. But it's no more dangerous than losing your soul like I've done. How many people died for this case, Grace? We were just lucky."

"Nick, tell me one thing. Who's going to teach you to catch these slimy creatures, to pilot a boat?"

"The guy I bought it from."

"What?"

"You heard me. I bought a boat from an old guy who's retiring from commercial fishing. He lives on the island. I saw it advertised in the *New York Times*. He sold me his boat. That's it." He paused for a moment, wondering why he had to explain anything. "What is this, twenty questions?"

She looked away again. "OK, OK, you don't have to tell me the rest. Is there a girlfriend?"

"No, Grace. I'm broke. My condo's for sale. I took out a home equity loan and with the money I'm going to become a fisherman. I bought the goddamn boat and I'm gonna live on it. Does that satisfy you? I'm selling my car, too. Bought a junker, a broken-down jeep with a hundred and twenty thousand miles on it, a rust bucket, perfect for the island."

"But you won't be broke for long. You'll be a rich man when the Superior Court denies Med Pro's appeal."

"Grace, you can't count your chickens before they're hatched. You know that. But I'll still be broke. I took your advice. I pledged my fee to charity. As soon as it comes in, if it ever does, it's going out."

"You're not serious!" she said, eyes wide open in disbelief. "I was only kidding when I said that, Nick."

"But I'm *not* kidding."

"Who's the lucky charity?"

"There are several." Without hesitating, he starting naming them: "Children's Hospital—one million; Saint Vincent's Home for Boys—one million; Safe Haven for Battered Women—one million; James Beasley School of Law Scholarship Fund—five hundred thousand; and the sublime Grace Monahan…" He put his arm around her. "Five hundred thousand."

"What for?" in a disappointed tone.

"For working with me. For being at my side. For endangering your life, and mostly for being a fool like me. I thought you'd be happy."

Grace's eyes filled with tears. She shook her head. "I don't want it," she managed to blurt out.

Nick squeezed her shoulders tightly and drew her close. "Why not? Don't be a fool. Take the money."

She moved away and looked squarely at him. "Because I love you. Because I want *you*—not the money. Can't you see?"

Nick was silent. He did see but hadn't wanted her to know.

"You *are* a bigger fool than I thought," he chuckled, shaking is head.

"No, I'm not. *You* are—if you don't ask me to come with you. I'm the best woman you'll ever find, Nick Ceratto. And you know it."

"You want to be a fisherman, Grace Monahan? You want to live on a smelly, damp boat and be seasick all the time? Huh?"

"I'd love it," she answered defiantly.

"How do you know?"

"The same way you know. You *are* an idiot. How did you ever get a law degree?" She laughed and kissed him on the cheek.

"You want to come with me, lady?" He smiled and tousled her mop of red hair. "You want to be a poor, salty lady?"

"Yeah," she said. "And I'll bet I catch more fish than you. And besides, you need my money."

He thought for a moment. "Are you trying to buy me?

"Yes." She rubbed his hand along her cheek. "I'll do whatever I have to."

"I'm pretty cheap, huh?"

"Yes. You're not worth a penny more than ten thousand, and that's stretching it."

"You sound like a defense attorney."

"Maybe I'll be one, one day."

"Is that so? There aren't any law schools on the sea," he mocked.

"But there are Internet courses, and Harvard's not far, right? An hour away by plane. So, I can afford it. I'll visit on weekends."

"So, you're already quitting the boat and leaving me? You have it all worked out, don't you?"

Grace felt flutters deep inside her. "No, not everything, not just yet." She wondered when she would break the news. Now was not the time.

In the middle of a deep, long kiss, Nick's cell phone rang.

"Ceratto," he answered.

"Mr. Ceratto, this is Henry Pool," said an unctuous voice. "I'm an attorney with Crown Mutual Life Insurance Company."

"Yes?" Nick inquired hesitantly, wondering what other insurance company was in the process of trying to screw him.

"Mr. Ceratto, Joseph Maglio was one of our insureds. He had taken out a two million dollar policy on his life. At first we denied the claim because Mr. Maglio's death was deemed a suicide, which is excluded under the policy. But when we discovered that Mr. Maglio and his wife and two children were victims of foul play, we tried to contact the alternate beneficiary, only to discover that she, too, was deceased."

There was a pause. "Mr. Ceratto, are you still there?"

"Yes, I'm here. Who would this *alternate beneficiary* have been?"

"Let's see. I have it written down here." Nick could hear papers being shuffled. "Ah…here it is. Ms. Maria Elena Maglio. It seems that she was Mr. Maglio's cousin," Pool answered. "She had been trying to prove to my company that Mr. Maglio had not committed suicide. She was in touch with us almost on a daily basis. In fact, she said she was conducting a private investigation and insisted that we not close our files." There was another pause. "Luckily we obliged her and kept the file open. She was quite charming and very persuasive…"

"I know," Nick interrupted. "She was very charming and very persuasive."

"Oh, did you know her?"

"Yes, in fact, I did…" he said, his voice dropping. So much for *Help me clear my cousin's name. Help me restore my family honor.* "But what do I have to do with this, Mr. Pool?"

"A great deal, Mr. Ceratto. You are the second alternate beneficiary under the policy." There was a long silence. "Mr. Ceratto?"

"You said two million dollars?"

"Yes sir. You may claim the check in person at our office in the Public Ledger Building at Sixth and Chestnut Streets, or I can mail it to you. I have it right here in my desk."

"I'll be right there." Nick flipped his phone closed. He turned the ignition key, put the glimmering red sports car into gear, and raced down the hill, turning right onto Spruce Street.

"Nick, where are you going? What the hell's so urgent?" Grace laughed giddily like a schoolchild on an amusement ride.

"Gracie. I'm rich again. Two million dollars rich. But I'm not giving it away this time."

"What the hell happened? Did you hit the lottery or something?"

"Better." He turned north on Fifth Street, passed Independence Hall, and circled around to Sixth to Chestnut.

"What's better?"

"Insurance proceeds. Money I fucking *got* legitimately."

"How?" Grace yelled.

"By staying alive." He pulled into a bus stop in front of the classic marble arched building and leapt out of the car, automatically pulling the keys out of the ignition. He raced around to the passenger side and tapped on the window. "Here," he said, as she opened it, and he handed her the keys, "In case a goddamned Septa bus comes along. And don't take off on me." He leaned down to kiss her.

She would ask no more questions. "I'm never leaving you, babe."

Chapter LIII

The *Eagle* blasted its horn as it rounded Brant Point and glided into Nantucket harbor. She was a big, white, broad-hipped hulk capable of carrying at least fifty automobiles and several tractor trailers. Over the past fifteen years she had carried her share of summer tourists and their over-loaded SUVs with their dogs, cats, bicycles, boogie boards, and beach chairs to the island. In summer she was filled to capacity. Now, in winter, she was mostly empty.

Nick and Grace stood on the passenger deck. They'd left the warmth of the enclosed galley, smelling of coffee and fresh doughnuts, to brave the February chill in order to take in the view as they approached the island which would be their new home.

In the distance, the low, sandy arm of Great Point embraced them, pulling them toward the Gray Lady, as the island is called. It looked magical in the distance, yet snug in its smallness compared to the sunlight sea surrounding it. The ferry slid past magnificent, now empty summer mansions piled atop the low sand cliffs surrounding the harbor.

Grace put her arm around Nick's waist. He responded squeezing her tightly to him. They were silent in their excitement, awestruck at the panorama opening up before them. It was beautiful despite being winter. The towering, white, and gilded tower of the Second Congregational Church was the centerpiece, perched high upon a hill while below were layers of bare trees and gray shingled houses with red brick chimneys. Puffs of woodsmoke rose into the frosty, bright blue sky. Lonely buoys bobbed up and down, waiting for winter's end. Shuttered shops and empty docks came into view as the *Eagle* made her turn with the ease of a ballerina. The sound of her engines stopped briefly and then changed, humming loudly as the captain reversed engines. The screws obeyed, and the Eagle paddled slowly backward until she met the resistance of the tar-blackened pilings and gently thudded against them.

Nick and Grace were awakened from their rapture by the sound of the captain's voice over the loudspeaker, reminding them that they should have been in their car five minutes ago with the engine running.

The metal ramp was already in place when they got to the Boxster below. The five eighteen-wheelers packed with food, booze, building supplies, and other necessities were already off. Nick and Grace were the last to drive through the gaping hole at the back end of the Eagle and onto the empty Steamship Authority parking lot. Nick opened his window. "I like this place, Grace. It smells of freedom."

She stared quietly at the emptiness—the huge, vacant, black macadam parking lot, the lonely piers, closed shops, deserted tennis courts. And she wondered for a moment if she had made a mistake. "Somehow I'm going to have to get used to this," she said skeptically.

"In a few weeks you'll love it. Look," Nick said as he stretched his arms as far as he could, given the confines of the car.

"That's what I mean. Look at this," she motioned with an open hand, "this place is deserted. I have to be honest. I'm a little scared."

"Of what? Of clean air, of natural beauty, of…"

"Of that," she broke in, pointing to the dock and the huge rusted hulk with its enormous outriggers reaching ominously toward them. The boat bobbed up and down in the choppy water. On deck, a white-bearded man in a navy wool pea coat waved to them. On the side of the peeling vessel painted in faded red was the name *Sankaty Lady*.

Nick hesitantly waved back. "Holy shit," he said. "Is that it?"

"What did you think it would be—the *QE II*? This *is* it, Nick. This is your dream boat."

"Let's make the best of it, OK?" he snapped, annoyed at her sarcasm and half scared to death himself. He put the car in gear and drove slowly toward the old sailor and the iron monster.

"You're the new owner, I reckon," the old salt said without cracking a smile, dropping his *r*'s in true Cape Cod fashion.

"I guess," Nick answered, wondering if he had made a huge error while his lawyer's mind searched for ways to escape the deal.

"Don't look like seafaring material to me," he said, eyeing Nick's black cashmere Calvin Klein overcoat. "You'll have to get rid of that," he said, pointing to the gleaming, red Boxster. "Salt air'll turn it into a rusted heap in no time —'less you want to spend all your fishin' money restorin' it."

"OK, what else is wrong?" Nick fired back.

"Got a year?" The old man chuckled, then sighed and shook his head at the city folk wanting to become natives. He had seen this before and was glad that he had been paid ahead, and in cash. "Come aboard," he sighed resignedly. "I'll try to teach ya. Remember, the deal was thirty days. If ya don't learn the boat, the tides, the charts, the fish—too bad. I'm headin' to Florida. Here, grab a line," he said throwing it in their direction.

Grace was the first to catch it and to pull the boat closer. She tied it off, not expertly, but adequately. She had seen clove hitches tied by boaters at the New Jersey shore at the marina bars. She stepped effortlessly aboard, managing to keep her balance as the boat rocked. She shook her red hair and faced the old grump as if to say, *OK, I'm ready, now what?*

Nick was impressed. He followed cautiously as the boat swung out a few feet from the dock again. This was not going to be a piece of cake, getting used to a world that was never still. He fought the urge to be seasick and willed his stomach to behave. He put his arms around Grace and gave her a long kiss on the lips. "Welcome home, honey."

"The missus, I reckon?" the old salt asked, uncomfortable at such an open display of affection.

"No. This is Grace Monahan. She's my partner. She's my first mate. She's proud. She's smart. She's beautiful. And she's Irish."

"Well, that's one thing ya got goin' for ya, sonny." the old man said, focusing on Grace. "Some women are better fisherman than men. They use their instincts instead of just relying on the sonar. Know anything about boats?" he asked her.

"No," she answered, smiling.

"Anything about fish?"

"Just that I like them broiled with fresh lemon," she said, standing her ground.

He cracked a smile for the first time, revealing two missing bottom teeth. "You *will*, missy. You *will* when we're finished. I can tell you're a quick learner, you are."

Grace followed the old man to the companionway and descended to the messy cabin below.

Nick walked to the bow. He took a deep breath of the cold, salt air. It smelled good. He picked up the end of a thick line, coiled on the deck. He looked at it curiously, then gripped it tightly in his hand. Its roughness felt good. It was real. It was honest. *Yes, this can definitely work*, he said to himself. He thoughts turned to Joe Maglio. He smiled—at the sea, at the chattering gulls overhead. "Thank you—wherever you are."

78279845R00201

Made in the USA
Middletown, DE
01 July 2018